the Visions of
RANSOM LAKE

The Visions of Ransom Lake

Marcia Lynn McClure

DISTRACTIONS INCORPORATED

First Edition 2002

Published by DISTRACTIONS INCORPORATED
Copyright © 2002 By M. Meyers

First printing 2002

Library of Congress Control Number: 2001118930

Printed in the United States of America

ISBN 0-9713389-1-4

To Patsy

My angel-friend. . .

For our beloved intrigue with silver queens and old things.

❧

CHAPTER
∽ ONE ∽

"Oh, Vonnie...this is so exciting! Just think...we're out west! Really west like we've only read about. We're actually out here!"

"Hush, Vaden. For pity's sake, hush. My head is pounding from your endless chatter," Yvonne Valmont sighed, placing a weary finger to her even wearier temple.

"But, Vonnie...just look at this land! At the space! Gaze on the beauty of that horizon!" Vaden exclaimed as she marveled at the large, fluffy clouds drifting across the bluest of blue sky. "It's like...like our spirits can breathe out here! And when we get to Aunt Myra's and Uncle Dan's little town...well, they're sure to have quaint little county fairs and pumpkin patches and enormous red barns and town socials and cowboys and..." Vaden rambled as she gazed dreamily out the stagecoach window.

"And gunmen and bank robbers, and wells instead of pumps and plumbing, and bedbugs, and horse manure in the middle of the street," Yvonne added with a prominent tone of sarcasm.

But Vaden Valmont was undaunted. Nothing or no one, not even her prim and proper, ever-apathetic older sister Yvonne, could squelch her enthusiasm about the journey they were taking, the exciting life experience that surely awaited them. So, she smiled and shook her head as her sister frowned irritatedly and closed her eyes.

"Oh, Vonnie...you have no appreciation of nature's beauty. No sense of exploration or adventure. No dreams." And turning her attention once more

I

to the landscape outside the stagecoach, she sighed and added, "How can you enjoy life with such a dreary attitude toward existence?" The stage rattled on and Vaden endeavored to keep her excitement silently to herself.

Oh, it was true that Vaden cherished her sister, Yvonne. Adored, admired and loved her. But Vaden could never quite understand Yvonne's often rather pessimistic attitude toward the simple joys of living. It was Vaden's opinion that Yvonne was far too concerned with propriety and far too incessantly worried about the serious concerns in life. And she felt that Yvonne spent much too much of her time laboring over her own appearance. Though it was true that Yvonne was a profound beauty and that she labored diligently to present herself as such, Vaden thought it a waste of life to agonize as such, endeavoring to look so perfect. She preferred to spend more time in studying other people, not having other people study her. People were interesting to Vaden. And the trip that she and her sister were making west to live new experiences and meet different people seemed far beyond fascinating to her.

The new smells, the freshness of the unfamiliarly dry air of the western United States sent Vaden's mind whirling with imagination. As she watched the passing trees, weeds and wildflowers from the stagecoach window she thought again of how magnificent it was to travel far from home to a different place. How truly romantic the very idea of it was. But as Yvonne squealed and angrily brushed a large black and yellow spider from her sleeve, Vaden sighed, shaking her head disappointedly at her sister's inability to simply enjoy the novelty of their adventure.

"My darlings!" Myra Valmont sighed, putting a hand dramatically to her chest as she watched her two lovely nieces descending from the stagecoach. "My own girls. How...how lovely you've grown to be! I expected to see you two still in braids and stockings."

Yvonne stepped down first, gracefully descending the stagecoach steps and hugging her aunt affectionately. "Vaden should still be dressed in braids and short skirts, Auntie Myra. But I'm quite grown up. Don't you think?" she remarked. Yvonne did not intend to appear greatly conceited. It was simply her naïve, sometimes tactless, manner. She did, at times, have a playful aspect to her nature that was a kith and kin to her sister's, in fact. But in public, she rarely displayed such a thing.

Myra shook her head, delightfully disbelieving as she took Yvonne's lovely face in her hands, marveling at the girl's beauty. Yvonne was tall and slender. Nearly as tall as Myra's own 5 feet 5 inches. Her raven black hair was boosted high and impeccably styled and her hat sat atop her head with just the perfect pitch and angle. Her eyes were the deepest brown and her fair complexion flawlessly free from freckle or blemish of any sort.

"You're an angel!" Myra agreed. "A living angel! I can already see the string of poor broken-hearted boys you'll leave behind you here, Vonnie." Yvonne's cocoa brown eyes sparkled with flattered delight.

"Auntie Myra! Auntie!" Vaden called as she stood perched in the stage-coach doorway.

Myra Valmont released Yvonne and looked up to see her younger niece exit excitedly from the conveyance in a solitary leap from coach to ground. The small, awkward stage steps were completely ignored, replaced by one hurdle of youthful exuberance. Vaden rushed forward throwing her arms tightly around her aunt's neck and Myra laughed. "Dear Vaden. As cheerful and carefree as always. Now *you* haven't changed all that much, have you?"

"I take offense, Auntie," Vaden claimed, though still smiling and obviously elated. Her dark green eyes twinkled brightly as she continued, "You think Vonnie an angel, but in me you see no change?"

Myra shook her head. "Oh, I see that you've grown, niece. I only meant you...your spirit is unchanged. And *that*, my other angel, is a heavenly thing." Myra marveled at how Vaden had, however, changed externally. Her striking nut-brown hair was pulled up as well, but not nearly as perfectly and neatly as her sister's. Vaden's complexion was smooth and faultless, too…but a bit darker than her sister's and Myra had no doubt that Yvonne took greater care to protect her porcelain skin from the sun. Vaden was smaller than Yvonne by several inches and it emphasized her appearing younger and less poised. But Myra could only smile at the girl, for she had always secretly favored Vaden. Vaden's eyes flashed with a deep love of life and merely being in her company, tasting the joy exuded by her spirit, was always completely invigorating to Myra.

"Let's get you two settled in. Your Uncle Danny is out just now, but he'll be glad to see you here safe and sound when he gets back. Oh, I've such plans, girls! And I know you'll like it out here. I know you will," Myra assured them.

The attention of all three women was arrested then by a wet, mucking sound and as Yvonne looked down to see her freshly polished boot ankle deep in a pile of soft, moist, brownish lumps, she sighed, "You see Vaden, horse manure."

Vaden clamped one hand over her mouth to suppress the wild giggle that wanted release and Yvonne glared at her. Aunt Myra made no effort to hide her amusement and laughed quite out loud. The song of Aunt Myra's delightful laughter could cheer even the coldest of hearts. And Yvonne, proper and serious-minded though she tended to be, giggled quickly at the humor of the situation as well.

Myra dabbed at the mirthful moisture in her eyes and sighed, "Oh, Yvonne. You do need to watch your step a bit more carefully hereabout. But you'll love it, you'll see."

Soon after, having changed to more comfortable day dresses, Vaden and Yvonne sipped tall glasses of refreshment sitting at a small table inside the general mercantile. Their Uncle Danny and Aunt Myra owned the mercantile and both girls smiled contentedly as they listened to their Aunt's plans to add a dress shop in one of the back rooms.

"I know we can do it, girls," Aunt Myra was assuring them. "You two are excellent seamstresses. It comes from your mother's diligence, no doubt. And I'm a fair hand myself. There have been so many new people move into the county, and I just know we can tempt the ladyfolk around here. Oh, I've such ideas! And besides, your Uncle Danny's leg is giving him so much trouble these days. We really do need the help in the store. There've been times lately when I can hardly keep up with the customers."

"Mother knew we would be a help to you, Aunt Myra. That's why she let us come," Yvonne reminded.

"I only wish we never had to go back," Vaden sighed. Standing, she strolled dreamily to the open door that looked out onto the street. "I think I should have been born here."

Myra chuckled. "You may not think so for very long, Vaden. It's hard work that's needed out here."

"Hard work is good for people, Auntie. It keeps their bodies strong and their minds busy. It's what God intended. 'Idle hands,' you know," Vaden stated.

"Vaden would not see a gray cloud were she standing in the midst of a hurricane, Auntie," Yvonne offered, smiling at her sister. Yvonne secretly admired Vaden's positive manner. But she worried about it, too, for she feared one day there would be something to blacken her happy heart.

"That's why Vonnie and I love each other so dearly, Auntie. We balance each other out. She helps me to keep my feet on the ground and I help her to have an occasional peek into the clouds," Vaden explained, wrinkling her nose teasingly at Yvonne.

Myra laughed and shook her head. "Oh, I knew you girls would do me good. It's going to be a wonderful year. I know I'll just wither up and die when you leave at the end of next summer."

"Then don't think of it now, Auntie. It's an entire twelve months in the distance and I…" Vaden stopped in the middle of her sentence, her attention arrested suddenly by an approaching buckboard. Or to be more specific, by the person driving the fine looking team that pulled it. "Now there's an intriguing-looking character," she mused aloud. Yvonne and Myra both rose and went to the door following Vaden's gaze down the street.

"Character is exactly it," Myra confirmed. "Well, girls…there you have it. The county hermit," she announced, nodding in the direction of the approaching wagon and its occupant.

"Quit staring, Vaden! I swear you have no manners," Yvonne scolded, trying to pry her own eyes from the vision. But Vaden could not tear her gaze away and continued to stare curiously, as the team drew closer to the store.

The man driving the horses sat tall in his seat. He was dressed in very worn Levi's trousers, a tattered looking white shirt from which the sleeves had been torn completely away at the shoulder seams, and a hat that was well beyond having any resemblance of its original shape. His hair was sable-black, hanging well past his shoulders and a dense black beard with auburn streaks now and again hung nearly to his chest. The deepest of irritated, questioning frowns furrowed his brow, intimidating even the likes of someone like Vaden who found it rare to be unsettled by any human being.

Still, for all the stranger's menacing appearance, as his wagon leveled with the doorway in which they stood, Vaden was further intrigued when Aunt Myra waved a friendly hand and called, "Good afternoon, Mr. Lake." The man reined in his team, rather unwillingly it seemed, and nodded toward Myra. "And what brings you to town today, Ransom? Will you be coming into the mercantile later?" she inquired.

Vaden could not help herself and she continued to stare, mesmerized by the stranger, even though Yvonne's elbow was near to breaking one of her ribs with its continual firm nudging.

In response to Aunt Myra's question, the stranger simply shrugged his shoulders as his gaze fell to Yvonne, lingering only a moment before returning inquisitively to Myra.

"These are my nieces, Ransom. They've come to help us out for the year. This is Yvonne," Aunt Myra explained pointing to her eldest niece who nodded cordially. The man's responding nod was hardly conceivable. "And this is young Vaden."

The stranger's gaze then moved to Vaden and she thought her knees might fail her as the intensity of the odd, light gray tint of his eyes studied her. His fixed attention on her made her feel as if he were reading her mind, knowing every secret she hid within the deepest regions of her heart. It was almost as if the privacy of her mind had been invaded somehow and it was very rattling to her senses.

Yet she managed a smile and stammered, "Hello." The stranger again offered a barely discernible nod in return, then slapped the lines at his team's back, looked to Myra, touching the brim of his hat in a gesture of farewell.

The three women stood silent in the doorway watching the peculiar man until he turned his team at a nearby corner and was out of view.

"I hope he's the only one of those around, Auntie," Yvonne nervously admitted, releasing the breath she'd been holding.

"That he is, darling. A sad, strange man. Keeps completely to himself. Hardly ever utters a word and when he does you can hardly tell what he's saying through all that beard. He lives on a place up in the mountains, but he owns a farm about a mile east, too. Hardly ever works it though. I think he prefers the seclusion that the mountains give him," Aunt Myra explained.

Vaden still stared at the corner around which the stranger had disappeared. "Has he been that way his entire life, Auntie? Or does he have some deep, painful tragedy of recent that keeps him in hiding?"

"Who knows." Sighing, Aunt Myra waved her hand, gesturing ignorance as to the answer. "I've no idea even how old he is. Could be twenty...could be a hundred. Like I said, I don't think anyone's ever seen him clean shaven. He's lived here going on about nine or ten years though. He seems a nice enough man. Always polite and he's one of the first to help during a disaster. I remember after that tornado went through a couple of years back. It tore up a farm house near his and he let the young family that had lost their home live in the house on his land until they were able to rebuild. He did a lot of the work his own self, too, as I recall."

"He gives me the utter willies," Yvonne muttered, returning to the interior of the store.

But Vaden smiled. A *mystery*! Only one hour into arriving for their adventurous year and already a mystery at hand. Something inside of her leapt with anticipation. Her mind began to burn, visualizing potential circumstances. A criminal, perhaps? Hiding out in this small, western town? The possibilities were endless in Vaden's imagination.

"You two girls must be completely tuckered out," Aunt Myra observed, interrupting Vaden's musing. "Why don't you both lay down and rest for awhile before dinner. Your uncle will be home any minute and you'll feel more like visiting after a nap. And besides, there's a social tomorrow night and I don't want my gorgeous girls going with dark circles under their eyes."

"A nap? Auntie, really." Vaden still gazed down the road where the stranger had disappeared around the corner. "We're no longer toddlers." Then, realizing what else her aunt had informed them of, she turned to her excitedly and asked, "A social? Will everyone be there?"

"I expect so." Myra smiled. She loved the look of excited delight in Vaden's eyes.

"How fun! We'll get to meet everyone, Vonnie!" Vaden took Yvonne's hands in her own and tugged at her, spinning them both about in a circle.

"Have mercy on me, Vaden! It's only a social." Yvonne smiled delightedly, however, unable to hide her own enthusiasm.

"How can I possibly nap, Auntie?" Vaden squealed. "How can I possibly sleep with all of this going on?"

"All of what going on?" Myra chuckled, very pleased at Vaden's exuberance.

"All of...all of...all of *this*!" Vaden released her sister's hands, throwing her arms out to her sides and twirling around merrily. "A quaint mercantile.

Townsfolk. Mysterious hermits with no sleeves on their shirts. All of it! It's too exciting!"

"Well, maybe. But stage rides are tiresome all the same, sweet pea. I swear my bones ached for a week after my last visit out to see you and your folks."

Yvonne nodded in agreement. "Well, Vaden may think that the dirt out on the street and the unkempt men in it are the most interesting things in the world...but I for one am weary. I think I will lie down, Aunt Myra. But be sure to wake me when Uncle Danny gets home."

"Of course, sweetie."

Vaden's shoulders drooped, her zest having once again been dampened by the lack of enthusiasm of others. Turning halfheartedly, she followed her sister as she walked to the hallway at the front of the mercantile that led to the house. "I guess it would help me to perk up a bit," she muttered.

"As if you ever need more perking up, baby sister," Yvonne teased.

But as Vaden lay on her bed staring up at the strong wooden beams of the ceiling, she could not keep her mind from returning to contemplation of the odd hermit man who had ridden past the store. His name was Ransom Lake. She knew she would never forget so unusual a name. And there was something about him. Something mysterious and fascinating. His eyes for one thing. They were so unsettling. It had felt to Vaden as if he had looked directly into her soul for a moment when his stormy gray gaze had rested on her. She nearly convinced herself that were she to meet him face to face that she would, indeed, see tiny gray storm clouds floating midst the rain color around his pupils. And she was wildly curious about so many things concerning him. She wondered why a man would intentionally rip the sleeves from his shirt as it appeared he had done. She wondered how a man could tolerate so much hair covering his head and face. She wondered why he was so reclusive. Did he hold some great secret cached away in the depths of his heart? Was he, indeed, a criminal hiding from the law to avoid stretching his neck from a rope?

She hoped desperately that he would visit the store that evening. Then she could get a really good look at him. Oh, she told herself that it would be hard not to stare and that she must be shrewd in her visual investigation of him. It would not do for him to sense any hint of her curiosity about him.

"Vonnie?" Vaden whispered then, rolling over on her side and looking across the room to where Yvonne lay sleeping on her own bed. "Vonnie? Are you awake? I can't sleep."

"For pity's sake, Vaden," Yvonne whined. "Let me rest. I know your mind is a whirlwind of excitement and questions...but I really do want to..."

"Isn't this all just too exciting? I can hardly keep still! Just think of the experiences we're bound to have out here. Experiences that will help shape who we become and how we..."

"Vaden!" Yvonne almost snapped, turning to face her sister, "I am tired. Go for a walk or something if you can't let me rest. Go out into this dusty, spider infested world and see the sights of the town. You're sure to find something to interest you."

"I'm sorry." Vaden knew she could be terribly over-verbal most of the time and she was not angry at Yvonne for being irritated with her. She rose from her bed, smoothing her skirt. "You're right. I'll leave you to rest. Goodness knows you'll need it if you're to remain patient with me for our first few days here."

"What are you doing up, dear?" Aunt Myra asked as Vaden entered the mercantile. "I thought you were resting with Yvonne."

"My body can't rest when my mind is running faster than the wind, Auntie," Vaden expressed with a dramatic, breathy whisper. "I'm just so entirely excited to be here. There's something in the very air, Auntie. My life will change somehow because of this visit. I can feel it in my heart. I can feel it in the depths of my very soul."

Myra smiled at Vaden, amused at her niece's theatrics. "Well, why don't you find something to do. A walk maybe."

"Ah, yes! A walk. Fresh air for the lungs and food for the mind!" Vaden sighed happily, leaving by way of the mercantile's front door. She meandered casually and unhurriedly down the main street of town. She passed a blacksmith's shop, a barber, a feed and seed store, and several other businesses, all very quaint and interesting in their simplicity. But, when she at last came to the corner around which the wagon carrying the mysterious Ransom Lake had disappeared, something impish gained control of her will and she felt her body turn and start down the dusty road. As she walked along the road, the town fell further and further behind her, and she didn't care because the sights to be seen on the roadside were visions of fantasy to Vaden.

First, as she left the last building of town behind her, an enormous pumpkin patch of such vast dimensions that she could not have begun to guess at the number of them, stretched out for nearly as far as she could see on either side of the road. Some of the pumpkins, already a stunning shade of orange, were peeking out from under large green leaves. She bit her lip thinking that a small child could easily become lost among the vines searching for just the perfect pumpkin to carve into a jack-o-lantern on October 31. She would have to ask Aunt Myra who owned the patch and if the owner sold the pumpkins. She would have to own one! She would search for it herself until she found it. It would be such fun wading through the mounds of vine and pumpkin in searching. Vaden felt awash with delight over such a beautiful sight as that simple pumpkin patch and at the thought that harvest would soon be upon Aunt Myra's and Uncle Dan's world. She thrilled at the thought of being witness to it.

Sighing delightedly, she spoke aloud the words of a poem she'd once read, "*And midst the blue of heaven's sky, the orange of sun's set drawing nigh, doves fair and white amid it fly, with plumming purples drifting by...a kiss is born of you and I.*" The verse had simply popped into her mind as verse often did when Vaden felt inspired.

Vaden loved to memorize and recite fragments of descriptive poetry. It was her opinion that particular phrases compounded the beauty of nature and romance, such wordings keeping the resplendence of loveliness fresh in one's mind. Closing her eyes for a moment, she inhaled deeply of the untainted country air savoring its freshness and letting the beauty of Mother Earth lift her spirits to even loftier heights than before.

When at last she reached the final boundary of the immense patch of pumpkin, she recognized the leaves, vines and large ripening ovals of a watermelon patch. Though this parcel of land was not as vast as the pumpkin patch had been, still it was tremendous and, as the rather wicked inclination to taste the ripening fruit without asking rose foremost to her mind, Vaden reminded herself inwardly that her mother would definitely consider it an act of theft were she to snitch one of the lovely melons. She remembered a time when she and Vonnie were children and sat at their Uncle Dan's knee mesmerized by the tales he would tell about *"snitchin' watermelon"* as a boy.

As Vaden walked on, admiring the wild flowers that sprung up in the uncultivated areas along the road, she noticed wagon ruts to her right. It was obviously a well-traveled path, though not enough to have created an actual and easily traversed road. Knowing full well that she could not simply continue following after Ransom Lake (for she might actually meet up with him and have to offer an explanation of her presence), she turned down the wheel-rutted path and walked on.

To her profound delight, perhaps half a mile down the path, she came upon the most enchanting vision of a brook. There before her, winding its way along, perhaps twenty feet in width, and lined on either side by large cottonwoods and maples, was a clear, gurgling creek. A quaint and rickety-looking bridge arched over it nearby and she immediately ran to it, stepping onto its squeaking boards tentatively. The railing of the bridge seemed sturdy enough and she leaned on it peering down into the clear water that traveled beneath it. There were water spiders, minnows, rocks and moss, and in the silence of the secluded area the ramble of the brook sounded like the music of heaven itself.

"This is it," Vaden whispered aloud to herself. All her life, wherever the family had lived, she had needed her own place. A secret, tranquil vicinage of her own where she could escape and think, or mourn, or simply sit. At home she had found such refuge beneath an ancient lilac tree on the family's property. It was a difficult place to reach, for it required crawling on one's hands and knees through the dirt to reach the hiding place behind the tree. Its troublesome accessibility was one of the reasons she loved it so. No one, especially Yvonne, was willing to crawl into it to retrieve or bother her. Certainly this brook was more publicly approachable, but her heart loved it immediately and it was fairly well hidden by the enormous trees that grew along its banks.

She watched a large maple leaf float gently through the air to land quietly on the surface of the water. It traveled away from her as the water ran on and she smiled knowing that autumn was nearly upon this part of the world. Oh, how she loved autumn! To Vaden Valmont there was nothing so beautiful as the earth in autumn. Reds, yellows, oranges, greens and even purples captured the leaves of trees, bushes and vines. The air was crisp and cool and fresh, and apples and pears abounded. She inhaled deeply of the fresh country air and thought of what it must be like to watch harvest erupt in a small western town such as this. Certainly the aroma of baking apples with cinnamon and sugar, or pumpkin laced with nutmeg would sweeten the air nearly every evening as women set their pies to cooling on window sills. No doubt wagons laden heavy with pumpkins would ramble down the road through town whenever whoever owned the monstrous pumpkin patch began to harvest it. She envisioned a wagon overflowing with ripe, refreshing watermelon ambling awkwardly down the road, an ill-placed melon falling from the wagon and breaking open as it hit the ground. She smiled to herself as she thought of small boys dressed in tattered trousers and dusty shirts rushing to the ruined fruit to snatch up sections of it, dirty or not, and devouring it delightedly without any thought to the sticky juice that would drip from their chins and elbows.

Sighing contentedly and glancing at the sun which was hanging low in the sky, Vaden let her feet carry her from the celestial view of the bridge and its brook and back toward town. She hated to leave the brook and the bridge, the watermelons ripe for snitching and the marvelous fields of pumpkin, but as she turned the corner and saw her Uncle Dan standing on the porch of the mercantile looking down the street in her direction, her heart leaped and she waved to him frantically.

"Vaden!" he hollered as he hurried to meet her.

Vaden's smile only widened as she watched him lumber happily toward her, his delightfully bowed legs giving him a funny, awkward appearance. His hair was nearly white where it once was dark, and the wrinkles around his merry eyes were plentiful from many years of smiles and laughter. "Uncle Dan!" she exclaimed as he reached her, taking her in his strong and merciless embrace at once.

He chuckled, his husky voice wonderfully familiar. "Vaden! You've grown up, girl! Just take a look at you!" Uncle Dan held Vaden away from him for a moment as he studied her carefully. "Dang! You can't be that same little girl who used to sneak in on me when I was sleeping at night and stick beans up my nose!"

Vaden laughed and shook her head. "Uncle Dan, you know I was so small then."

"Yeah, I know. But it just weren't too comfortable a way to wake up. Them hard ol' lima beans in my nose." They both laughed.

"It just always seemed to me when I was little that people's nostrils were made for more than breathing in and out of," Vaden explained, giggling at the memory of her Uncle Dan shouting as he sat up from a deep sleep and tried to pry the beans out of his nose.

"Oh, child," Dan Valmont sighed as he cupped her face in his roughened hand. His skin was like tough leather and Vaden liked it that way. "How you've grown. Makes a man feel old, I'll tell you."

"You'll never grow old, Uncle Dan. You're as handsome as you ever were, same as daddy."

Dan chuckled and put his arm around Vaden's shoulder. "Let's get on home. Your Aunt Myra will tan our hides if we're late for dinner. She's got apple pie coolin' on the back porch."

Vaden smiled and sighed contentedly. "I've missed you."

"I've missed you, too, sweet pea."

That night after dinner Vaden and Yvonne sat in the parlor with their aunt and uncle. The day had cooled into a comfortable evening and the early dusk breezes breathed through the kitchen.

"Aaaahhh," Uncle Dan sighed, patting his stomach dramatically. "That was the best pie you ever done baked, Myra."

Aunt Myra smiled and shook her head at the girls. "He says that every time I make a pie."

"Well, I guess you just get better and better at it, honey," he explained.

Vaden looked over at her sister who sat busily working on her needle-point. "It's coming out truly beautiful, Vonnie," she complimented.

"Oh, I don't know. I had to pick a patch out earlier today while you were off wherever you were off to," Vonnie explained, winking teasingly at her sister.

"Well, you're the one who told me to go for a walk, Vonnie," Vaden defended. "And I'm so glad you did! What a pumpkin patch just outside of town, Uncle Dan! Whoever in the world owns that?"

"I figured you might have found that already, Vaden," Uncle Danny chuckled. "That monstrosity belongs to none other than Vaughn Wimber. How he keeps after it, I'll never know. But he's had it out there every year since...well since we been here, ain't that right, Myra?"

"Goodness, yes! It's quite a sight when he starts in to harvesting those fields." Aunt Myra added.

"I can quite imagine," Vaden agreed.

"What else did you find on your travels, Vaden?" Yvonne asked. "Any handsome young man that might do for a beau for your spinsterly sister? You didn't run into that frightening, hairy recluse man did you?"

"No. On both accounts," Vaden sighed, disappointment obvious in her tone.

"What frightening, hairy recluse?" Uncle Dan inquired.

"Oh, Ransom Lake rode through town just after the girls arrived today, Danny," Aunt Myra explained. "He gave Yvonne quite a fright...but I think our little Vaden found him somewhat of an interest."

"He's a good man, that Ransom Lake. I spoke with him just today, in fact. And you'll never believe it, Myra." Uncle Dan dropped his voice at his next utterance, "He's movin' into town for the winter."

"No!" Myra exclaimed in a whisper. Her brow wrinkled and her eyes widened in disbelief.

"True as blue! He's bringin' down his stock and everythin' this year. Says he has his reasons and that he feels like he's neglected the farm here near town for too long."

"Glory be!" Aunt Myra whispered, shaking her head still obviously astounded.

"Where does he usually stay in winter, Uncle Dan?" Yvonne asked. Vaden smiled for she could see that her sister had laid her needlework aside, indicating that her attention was truly arrested by the conversation at hand.

"In the mountains. We usually don't see hide nor hair of the man from October to early May. Not that we can expect to see any more of him when he's here anyway. He's to himself. Likes it that way."

"Why?" Vaden asked simply.

Uncle Dan shrugged his shoulders. "Don't know. Could be he's afraid some little character of a girl will be shovin' lima beans up his nose when he's not lookin'." He laughed heartily then as Vaden rolled her eyes and sighed, pleased by his memories of her.

"Well, now," Aunt Myra began. "You girls keep your mind off ol' Ransom Lake. I got other boys in mind for the two of you."

"Oh, help us all now," Uncle Dan mumbled, shaking his head.

"Quit that," Myra scolded, slapping the man teasingly on one thigh. Turning to the girls then, she said, "I think any number of our young men hereabouts would make wonderful husbands for you two girls."

"Like who?" Uncle Dan asked, unconvinced.

"Like Nathaniel Wimber or Toby Bridges. And that nice Jerome Clayton. Now he's one that'll catch your eye, Yvonne."

"Yvonne and I have pretty high expectations when it comes to beaus, Aunt Myra," Vaden mentioned, grinning lovingly at her aunt.

"Yes. Incredibly high," Yvonne affirmed. "Lofty, in fact."

Aunt Myra chuckled and sat back in her chair, grinning as if she held some great secret. "Believe me, I wouldn't let just anybody come a courtin' my nieces."

"Are there nice girls here as well, Auntie?" Vaden asked.

"Yes. We have some very nice young ladies in town. A couple of real cats, too. But for the most part, they're all darling girls. I'm certain you girls will find some friends hereabouts."

Vaden stared into the fire in the hearth, wondering what kind of friends she would find. All too quickly, however, her thoughts returned to their musing over the oddity of Ransom Lake. He intrigued her so. She had seen him only once, but something about him kept bringing her thoughts back to him.

Even as she lay in bed that night looking out through her bedroom window at the bright shining stars set in the darkened western sky, she thought of him. She wondered again what turned the eccentric Ransom Lake to the life of a hermit. What had squelched the bright star in his soul?

CHAPTER
∞ TWO ∞

After a nourishing breakfast of hot cakes and sausages the next morning, Uncle Dan set out on some errands and Aunt Myra set about teaching Yvonne and Vaden how to tend to the store. There were so many things to be explained…which customers were allowed credit, which weren't, where things were kept, how to work the register that held the money and so forth. So many details. There were numerous people who came into the mercantile that morning and Vaden began to wonder how many of them were in just to gawk at Myra Valmont's nieces, for very few purchased any merchandise.

"Oh, some days I guess folks just want to visit, and others we sell a lot of things. Today I think folks are in the visitin' mood," Aunt Myra explained.

"I'll never remember everyone's names," Yvonne sighed. There had been so many people come into the store in such a very short time that even the ever-positive Vaden felt overwhelmed.

"It'll be easier at the social tonight, Yvonne. Faces and names will come together easier then. They always do at get togethers."

"When will we ever find time to successfully stock a dress shop, Auntie?" Vaden asked, for she was, indeed, quite overcome at all the new faces, new names, and new tasks at hand.

"We'll get to the dress shop eventually." Aunt Myra smiled understandingly at her niece. She knew that Vaden only longed to be out exploring. She understood how madly Vaden pined for the outdoors and its beauty.

"Sable," Myra greeted then as a woman of about her own age accompanied by a handsome young man, approached. "Jerome! How wonderful to see the two of you out today. This is Mrs. Sable Clayton and her son, Jerome, girls."

"How do you do?" Yvonne greeted, taking Mrs. Clayton's offered hand. "I'm Yvonne Valmont and this is my sister, Vaden." Mrs. Clayton smiled and offered her hand then to Vaden, who shook it, smiling pleasantly.

"I'm Jerome Clayton," the young man informed them, grinning first at Vaden and tipping his hat in a friendly manner before turning and repeating the gesture to Yvonne. Vaden smiled at the charming looking young man. His hair was blond and his eyes a deep brown. His grin was rather boyish and delightsome and he was tall and well formed. Obviously he was polite as well. Vaden remembered her aunt mentioning this particular young man the night before and she could see why she had felt inclined to do so.

"Myra has been so excited about your coming," Mrs. Clayton confessed. "We thought she was gonna burst at the seams yesterday morning at the town meeting when she announced you were coming to stay with her and Dan. It's nice to have some lovely new young ladies in town. This should please all the young bucks hereabouts shouldn't it, Jerome?"

Jerome nodded in agreement, winking flirtatiously at Yvonne.

Yvonne blushed appropriately and humbly mumbled, "Thank you, Mrs. Clayton."

But Vaden in her forthright honesty blurted out, "Why? Aren't there any other girls in town? I truly hope you didn't ask us here just to marry us off, Aunt Myra."

"Vaden!" Yvonne snapped scoldingly, turning scarlet with embarrassment.

But Aunt Myra and Mrs. Clayton only chuckled together as Myra admitted, "No. We didn't ask you here to marry you off, Vaden. But...if that's what should come of your visit...I'd only be too happy to have you livin' nearby all the time."

Yvonne rolled her eyes, horrified at her sister's behavior as Myra and Mrs. Clayton continued to look amused.

Jerome, however, seemed to sense the unsettled emotions arising between the two sisters. "Well, on behalf of all us 'young bucks' in town...I'm just plain delighted to have two such lovely ladies to help beauty up the place." Though his eyes were firmly set on Vaden it was Yvonne who responded to his compliment.

"Why, you're too charming, Mr. Clayton. If everyone in town is as nice and complimentary as you and your mother, we'll be spoiled rotten before our first day is done."

Jerome continued to stare at Vaden and she cleared her throat uncomfortably and looked to Mrs. Clayton. "Can we help you with anything in the mercantile today, Mrs. Clayton? We're only just getting our feet wet, but Yvonne and I like to jump right into new responsibilities and challenges."

Mrs. Clayton opened her small handbag and withdrew a piece of paper. "As a matter of fact, Miss...Vaden is it? There are a few things that I've been intending to pick up the next time I was in." She handed the paper to Vaden who smiled, relieved to have a task that might remove her from beneath the unnerving stare of Jerome Clayton, for he was quite handsome and it always made Vaden uncomfortable when a handsome man noticed her.

"Leave it to me, Auntie," Vaden chirped, and she went about the store gathering the items on the list.

Though she busily accumulated the things Mrs. Clayton had listed, her attention was arrested immediately when Mrs. Clayton said to her aunt, "Have you heard that Ransom Lake is moving into town for the winter?"

"Mercy, yes! Danny told me just last night and I thought surely he had misunderstood. Ransom Lake never winters in town. He hides up there in them mountains and I don't know why they don't find him just a sol chunk of ice every year come spring," Myra commented.

"It's true, I tell you. My Raymond saw him just this morning ove blacksmith's. He was telling ol' Manfred Dennis that he'd be needing some new branding irons done up 'cause he planned on bringing his new heifers down with him and he's changin' his brand.'"

Myra shook her head, clicking her tongue in disbelief. "I can't imagine what would've made that man do it. You know how secretive he's always been. Well, this will certainly set tongues to wagging."

Vaden turned and smiled at her sister who also smiled amusedly at the tongues that were already wagging. She was unsettled immediately, however, when her eyes fell to Jerome Clayton to see that he still stared at her, grinning and seeming pleased at watching her. In the next moment Vaden felt a prickling at the back of her neck and shuddered involuntarily. Something in the young man's expression had changed. Hadn't it? She couldn't quite be sure what it was, but for a few moments Vaden felt truly uneasy in his presence. She inwardly told herself that it was her often dramatic imagination and returned her attention to the conversation at hand.

"How I'd like to know what's in that man's mind," Sable Clayton muttered. "What made him take to the hills like he did?"

"My guess is tragedy. Pain of some kind," Myra answered. "A man just don't live like that without something sending him to it."

Vaden set the items she had gathered on the counter and turned to find that a hush had fallen over the room and all eyes, including Jerome's, were turned toward the front entrance to the store. As Vaden herself looked up, her heart began to pound madly with excitement, for there in the doorway stood none other than the mysterious Ransom Lake. He nodded slightly in greeting to the onlookers.

Amazingly, Myra found her composure at once. "Mr. Lake! What can I help you with today?" Vaden could tell by the crimson color that rose to everyone's faces that each and every person in the mercantile was wondering how much of their gossip Ransom Lake had heard before they noticed he had entered the building.

The hermit seemed to sense the discomfort of everyone in the room and simply mumbled, "Boots," in a lowered voice.

Vaden's eyes fell to the well-worn boots that the man wore. And she blushed a deeper hue when she looked up to find him staring defiantly at her.

"Cobbler's out. I need some now. Don't have the time to wait," the man mumbled.

"Well, of course, Ransom," Myra agreed. "I'm certain you've got a busy day ahead, so I'll just bring out a few pair for you to look at." She went to a far corner of the room and began rummaging through a variety of footwear there.

Vaden could not help but stare at the man. He stood no more than six feet from her and his eyes were all the more disturbing. She noticed that his long, black hair was slightly graying at the temples and for some odd reason it appealed to her. It seemed to deepen the mystery that prevailed in the very air around him.

"We hear that you're planning to winter on your farm in town, Ransom," Jerome stated bluntly.

The hermit only nodded.

"It'll be good to have you here," Jerome added. "It's always helpful to have another man around when a hand is needed with wintering cattle and such."

"That's a wonderful piece of property you've got out there, Mr. Lake," Mrs. Clayton remarked.

"Thank you, ma'am," the man mumbled.

"Will any of these do, Ransom?" Aunt Myra asked, holding up a pair of large boots in each hand.

"Do you have any higher up?" the man asked. "To just below my knee maybe?"

Vaden was struck by something about his voice. Something tantalizing. It was quite deep and he seemed to mumble his words more than speak them. It was unusually masculine somehow, even if most folks may have considered it impolite. She could only continue to stare at the man. He was incredibly intriguing. As she had noticed before, the sleeves to his shirt had been torn away at the shoulder seams and his massively muscled and sun-bronzed arms were no less than astoundingly impressive. She had never seen the like! Of course, most men wore sleeves, so their arms weren't publicly displayed as a rule. But she was positive that most men's arms hidden beneath proper sleeving were not of the size and perfect formation that this man's were. Glancing quickly at Jerome Clayton's sleeves she was only more convinced of this fact. Ransom Lake was also taller than she had been able to surmise before and his shoulders were definitely a pair of the broadest she'd ever seen.

"Oh, dear. I'm not sure, Ransom," Aunt Myra mumbled. "Why don't you go ahead and try a pair of these on and I'll have Vaden take a look." Myra handed the pairs of boots she held to the man and he set them down on the floor, removing his own worn ones there in the middle of the store. "Vaden, would you please…" Myra began. "Vaden." Vaden tore her curious gaze from Mr. Lake and looked to her aunt. "Did you see any other boots that might serve Mr. Lake while you were rearranging the boxes this morning?"

"Yes," Vaden offered quickly, excited somehow at the prospect of being able to help the man. "Yes. I think I did. I'll get them at once." She turned and looked up the high rows of shelves that stood nearby.

Mrs. Clayton cleared her throat uncomfortably, gathering her purchases and laying her payment on the counter. "Here you are, Myra. We must be off now, Jerome." She left promptly, taking hold of Jerome's sleeve and pulling on it so that he would follow her, both of them obviously uncomfortable in the presence of Mr. Lake.

Cowards, Vaden thought as she began to stretch up toward the higher shelves. It irritated her that people were such thoughtless cowards when faced with people they didn't know or understand.

"Oh, for pity's sake, Vaden! Use the stool!" Yvonne whined, having turned to see her unconventional sister scaling the tower of shelves in an effort to reach a particular box of boots that sat very high up.

"Be careful, Vaden," Aunt Myra gasped. "You'll fall!"

Vaden secured her right foot on another shelf and reached up further, knowing full well that her feet were anchored on shelving at least three or four feet from the floor. "I've got it now. Don't worry so, Auntie."

"Vaden Valmont! There is a man present. Get down from there at once! I swear. You have no vision whatsoever of propriety," Yvonne scolded in a loud whisper.

Vaden, realizing that she had climbed dangerously high and that Yvonne was founded in some of her scolding, was determined, however, to obtain what she had set out to obtain. Therefore, unaware that both her aunt and Mr. Lake stood directly beneath her staring up expectantly, she stretched her arm high and began tugging on a boot box with her fingers. "I've got it now. You worry too much, Yvonne. I've just about…"

In a last, strenuous effort to clutch a firm hold on the box, Vaden gasped as her other hand, which had anchored her by holding solidly to another shelf, slipped and she felt herself falling down and backward in an instant. Though she landed with great force, the floor did not feel as hard as she had anticipated. This was, she realized in the very next moment, due to the fact that her fall to the floor had, indeed, been cushioned, for she felt strong hands at her waist as Ransom Lake pushed her off his own body to the actual floor beside him. Vaden turned to see that she had fallen from the shelving, knocking Mr. Lake to the floor and landing on him instead. She gasped once more as he sat up in time for the box of heavy boots, tumbling from the high shelf to hit him squarely on the head as it fell a moment after her.

"I'm…I'm so sorry, Mr. Lake," Vaden stammered, horrified as she watched the man put a hand to the top of his head where the box had hit him, then study the appendage as if he expected to find blood there from a head wound. "I was only trying to help and I…I didn't stop to think."

"You rarely do, Vaden," Yvonne muttered. Then, sighing, she added, "You could've been hurt and...oh, are you all right, Mr. Lake?"

Vaden watched as Mr. Lake stood, brushing the dust from the seat of his pants before offering a hand to her. Vaden felt a shudder as the angry, intense gray of the man's eyes bored into her own. Feeling completely undignified, humiliated and juvenile, Vaden took the offered hand. Instantly her senses went whirling for his touch had caused goose bumps to break over her. The man possessed profound physical strength and, as he pulled Vaden to her feet, he either overestimated the weight of the girl or underestimated his own muscle, for his powerful yank on her arm propelled Vaden up and forward with such force that instead of standing gracefully, she stumbled forward, bumping against the man, at the same time stepping mercilessly on one of his stockinged feet with the heel of her shoe. The man let out a short groan and closed his eyes for a moment before the intensity of their tempestuousness glared at her once more.

"Oh, dear," Vaden heard Aunt Myra moan.

Vaden knew Mr. Lake must be in awe of her clumsiness, as well as furious for the damage done him by it. But without a word he simply bent, picked up the boots that had spilled from their box upon hitting the floor and pulled them onto his stockinged feet.

"They'll do," he muttered, looking to Myra.

"Are you sure, Mr. Lake? I mean, I don't want you to feel obligated..." Myra explained.

"They're fine. How much?"

"Well...after what just happened...I don't feel I can accept..."

"Nonsense. How much?"

Vaden dropped her humiliated gaze to the floor when Mr. Lake glanced at her again. Every inch of the surface of her body was crimson. The blush was so thorough that it was almost painful.

Aunt Myra relented and accepted the payment for the boots from the man. Mr. Lake picked up the overly well-worn boots he'd worn into the mercantile and tossed them in the trash barrel near the front door as he started to leave.

"Mr. Lake," Vaden called out. He looked to her again. "I'm truly sorry. It was so terribly clumsy of me and..."

"Yes, Ransom. Accept my apologies as well," Aunt Myra interrupted.

The unnerving gaze of the man lingered for a moment on Vaden. He looked from her feet to her head quickly and Vaden fancied she could almost discern something like a grin beneath his heavy mustache and beard.

"None needed, Mrs. Valmont." With a nod in Yvonne's direction and a finger at the brim of his hat he left the store.

"Good gravy on the taters, girl!" Aunt Myra exclaimed in a lowered voice a moment later. "What on earth possessed you to..."

"Vaden...when will you learn to think before you act so unconventionally?" Yvonne interrupted.

"I was only trying to help," Vaden defended herself. "I'm sorry that you both had to endure the humiliation of yet another of my thoughtless antics." Vaden brushed an embarrassed tear from her cheek as another followed. "I'm not you, Yvonne! I don't have your grace and beauty! And sometimes conventional propriety seems so ridiculous to me that I..."

"Now, girls," Aunt Myra soothed. "What's done is done. And besides...that's the first hint of a grin I've ever seen on the man's face."

Yvonne smiled at her sister and put a reassuring arm about her shoulders. "It *was* terribly funny, Vaden. And I'm sure Mr. Lake will think of it and smile to himself every time he sees you."

Vaden closed her eyes and sighed, further humiliated at the truth of Yvonne's assurance. "Thank you for that, Yvonne. I feel much better," she mumbled, sarcastically.

"It's hard for Vaden to be cooped up, Aunt Myra." Yvonne smiled lovingly at her sister. She admired Vaden's spirit and love of life. "Why don't you take a little walk, Vaden? It always helps you to feel better."

"Yes, sweet pea. You go on ahead. It's almost lunch and then Yvonne can take a little time for herself when you're back." Vaden sniffled, knowing full well that she was simply irritating everyone and they were the ones in need of respite.

Without a word, she walked toward the front door. She paused, however, and, looking back to see Aunt Myra and Yvonne already occupied with something else and not looking her direction, she reached into the barrel near the front door and retrieved the boots Ransom Lake had discarded there. Her daddy had always said that you can tell a lot from a man by studying his boots. Quickly she turned and dashed down the hallway at the front of the store to her room. Bolting the door, she set the boots on the floor, sitting herself down in front of them.

The leather had been good strong leather at one time, she observed. She noticed that the straps at the top of the boots used to help the wearer pull them on were nearly torn away from so many days of being tugged at. She took one boot and turned it over studying the sole intently before turning the other boot over and comparing its sole. "He's left handed," she muttered. The left boot was in much worse shape then the right. The toe was torn away, the sole was nearly worn through, the heel was worn shorter. It had a blackened area at the ball of the foot and Vaden surmised that it was the boot used to kick out coals from a fire. Then, hurriedly, she unlaced her own boots and slipped her tiny feet into the cavities of Ransom Lake's abandoned ones. "Never judge a man 'til you've walked a mile in his shoes," she whispered. Clunking around the room several times, she thought about the boots and their owner. These were boots owned by a driven and hard working man. Boots that had walked, ridden, climbed, waded and run. But the left boot was uncomfortable on one side of her calf. Reaching down, she felt that a sheath had been made inside and she withdrew a large pocketknife. She held the knife up to inspect it better and was intrigued to find that it had an inscription along one side.

"Denver S. Lake," she read aloud. "Leadville, Colorado." She had heard of Leadville, the little town in Colorado that had grown into a rich silver bonanza. "*Silver lines the clouds above. Reflects like rain, is rare as love,*" she recited. She'd never liked that particular badly written line by the poet, Meyers, until that moment. Turning the knife over, she mused aloud, "Denver? Not Ransom." Then she gasped as she realized that no doubt Mr. Lake would remember he had left the knife in his old boots and would return looking for it. What if he already had? What if he had returned to find his old boots gone from the barrel in her aunt's store?

Removing the boots, she shoved them under her bed and put on her own once more. Then, clutching the knife securely in her hand, she dashed out into the mercantile to find it thankfully empty except for Yvonne and her aunt.

"I thought you were out walking," Aunt Myra mumbled with a puzzled expression.

"I...I had to put something away," Vaden answered. "But I'm going now." Without pausing for further conversation, she left the store hurriedly, walking down the street in the direction she had seen Mr. Lake take. As if fate had intended it, Mr. Lake appeared suddenly, having just exited the blacksmith's establishment.

"Mr. Lake!" Vaden called, waving when he turned and looked at her. Immediately she froze as the unnerving color of his eyes settled intently on her. Furthermore, how would she explain the knife being in her possession. She couldn't simply approach him saying, "*I stole your boots from the trash barrel and found this within.*" When she made no move to approach him, Mr. Lake strode determinedly toward her. So entirely determined did he seem that Vaden took two steps backward as he approached, for he was, of course, ever so intimidating.

"I...I..." she stammered as he came to stand before her, his stormy eyes glaring at her from beneath long, dark lashes. "I...I...found this in the barrel after you had gone." Slowly she held out her hand to him and opened it to reveal the pocketknife sitting on her trembling palm. Ransom Lake looked down at the knife, his eyes returning to Vaden's and narrowing as he reached out and snatched it quickly from her hand. Vaden looked to the ground where her foot began to kick at a pebble. "I...I would also like to apologize for...for my fall and for injuring you. I truly am sorry." The man made no audible sound to indicate that he was accepting her apology so she looked up to see him still glaring at her. "I said, I am sorry, Mr. Lake." Still he said nothing, only stood staring at her. Vaden felt the hot blush of humiliation rising to her cheeks. How dare he stare at her so, making not the slightest gesture of offering any forgiveness? "Mr. Lake," Vaden began sternly, "I have apologized to you. A gentleman does not stand silent at such a remark. Even a nod would be more acceptable than your simply standing there glaring at me."

"I'm no gentleman, Miss Valmont," he mumbled. The deep, somehow sultry intonation of his voice as he spoke her name gave Vaden cause to pause as goose bumps enveloped her arms and legs. Vaden struggled to quickly regain her composure.

"Yes you are," she stated. He frowned, obviously surprised at her arguing. "You can hide away in the mountains and grow all the hair you want to try to hide yourself from the world, Mr. Lake. But it doesn't fool me. You were not raised to be a heathen."

Then she gasped, horrified, as the man reached forward taking her chin brutally in one hand. He bent toward her so that she could feel his breath on her face as he growled, "You don't know anything about how I was raised, girl. I am a heathen. A man cursed with afflictions and burdens that a child like you could never even imagine. If you're some overbearing missionary type with wild aspirations of saving my soul...don't waste your time."

Reaching up, Vaden grasped the man's nose tightly between her thumb and index finger. "Let go of my face!" she demanded. Stunned at her own actions, she was determined not to let him know how horribly she was intimidated.

The tumultuous gray eyes that glared at her widened in astonishment, but he did not release her. Pinching his nose tighter, Vaden repeated her demand. "Let go of my face, Mr. Lake."

"Let go of my nose, girl," he barked, but his grasp on her chin did not tighten. The fact that he did not try to hurt her whispered to Vaden that her instincts were right about this man. Her soul sensing this, she felt there was no further reason to provoke him and she released him. An instant later he dropped his hand from her chin.

Vaden cleared her throat, straightened her spine and, smoothing her skirts as she met Ransom Lake's steel glare, she repeated, "Again. I apologize for my clumsiness this afternoon in the store, Mr. Lake."

"Forgiven," he growled.

Vaden nodded, turned and began walking away.

"Thank you," he called out, causing her to stop and turn toward him once more, "for the knife. It...it...it's important to me."

Vaden felt guilty suddenly for treating him so harshly. "You're welcome. I'm glad I could return it to you." Then she watched as Ransom Lake tucked the knife into his new boot before she turned away from him once more.

"That was a quick walk," Aunt Myra greeted as Vaden entered the mercantile only minutes after she had originally left. "But your cheeks are rosy once again so it must have done the trick."

"*Quite* rosy," Yvonne commented somewhat suspiciously as she studied her sister with the curiosity of a cat for a moment.

"Yes. I suppose so. The...um...the breeze was very invigorating." Vaden tucked one fist firmly beneath her chin as she leaned on her elbows over the counter smiling up at her sister and aunt. "Thank you for having us here, Auntie."

"Oh, sweet pea," Myra cooed affectionately, "thank you for coming."

"I'm home, girls! I'm home!" Vaden, Yvonne and Myra turned to see Dan enter the store. "I'm home and I'm ready for the social!" he announced. Vaden giggled as her dear, bowlegged uncle began to perform something akin to a jig on the wood planked floor beneath his feet. "I've been practicin' my dancin' all the day long, girls! Ain't I the perty boy?"

"For pity's sake, Danny! Settle yourself down. What if customers should come in?" Aunt Myra laughed.

"Then I'll show 'em how it's done!" Uncle Dan hollered as he swept Vaden into his arms and started dancing about the room with her. "It reaches my big ol' ugly ears that you've already captured one young man's heart in town, sweet pea!"

Vaden felt her heart leap in her chest. "I have? You mean he…"

"You bet ya! That slick feller, Jerome Clayton, has already got every young man for miles ready to beat down your door! I expect they'll be havin' to go through him first though." Uncle Dan stomped his feet even harder as he danced.

"Oh," Vaden muttered. And then she beat herself mentally for even allowing Ransom Lake's name to jump into her mind when her uncle had said what he did.

"Oh? Every female under the age of 30 and unmarried has been trying to catch that boy for near two years now and all you can say is, 'Oh.'" Dan looked to Myra and shrugged his shoulders.

"Leave it to Vay not to realize a blessing when she sees it," Yvonne sighed, smiling at her sister.

"It's all right, darlin'. I understand. Not every man in the world can be as good lookin' as me!" Vaden smiled again then and her uncle added, "Besides, ya gotta make sure a man's got the right nostrils for bean storage!"

With that Vaden was further amused and joined her uncle wholeheartedly in the happy romp around the room.

Yvonne looked the very model of perfection! As Vaden stepped awkwardly from the wagon, she turned and watched Yvonne alight gracefully from it. Her sister's dark hair was perfectly piled, darling little ringlets cascading everywhere about her face, neck and shoulders. Yvonne walked into the town hall with an air of grace and dignity that only the finest women could master. Her dress of peacock blue was dazzling and Vaden lagged behind her some distance for she felt dowdy and plain in her presence. At the same time she wished she had preceded Yvonne into the town hall so that when she entered, the crowd within gasping in awe, she could straighten her shoulders showing her pride in her sister's beauty.

Vaden's own dress was scarlet and extremely becoming in that it complimented her perfectly curved figure and caused her eyes to look all the more as if tiny diamonds sparkling in the sun had been sprinkled about in them. But Vaden was completely unaware of the fact that she outshone her sister's grace and beauty. Vaden's delight with life blessed her with modesty which shone plainly in her already beautiful countenance, enhancing the loveliness of the young woman beyond description.

"I hate that I look better in scarlet than blue," Vaden mumbled to her aunt as they entered the hall. "See, Auntie. Everyone's staring at me wondering how a beautiful, tropical bird like Yvonne could have such a clumsy, ridiculous-looking sister. See how they stare?"

Myra took Vaden's lovely lace-gloved hand, patting the back of it tenderly and sighing. "Oh, sweet pea. Humility becomes the most beautiful of women all the more."

Almost immediately, Yvonne and Vaden found themselves nearly pounced upon by eight or ten bachelors of rather varied ages. Yvonne immediately flattered and captivated them with her charms, but Vaden almost deplored their attentions, knowing full well that the group of young ladies standing nearby would only resent their attracting such attentions from the men.

As the group of admirers surrounding Yvonne began to introduce themselves to her, the group of young bucks around Vaden did the same.

"Toby Bridges, Miss Valmont," one almost attractive, dark haired young man said, extending his hand to Vaden.

"Vaden Valmont. I'm so glad to meet you," Vaden replied, smiling politely.

"Nathaniel Wimber, Miss Vaden," another dark haired young man offered.

"Mr. Wimber," Vaden acknowledged. She glanced at the group of young women to her right. Yes, they were irritated to say the least. One young, brown-haired girl in particular seemed to be glaring mercilessly at her.

"And you haven't forgotten me, have you, Miss Vaden?"

Vaden looked up to see the flirtatious grin of Jerome Clayton affixed on her. Vaden was immediately unnerved. Somehow this particular young man unsettled her. But being polite was of the utmost importance at social gatherings and Vaden knew that. So she forced a friendly smile and politely offered, "Of course not, Mr. Clayton. How delightful to see you." Then, glancing at the on-looking young ladies again, she added, "Would you excuse me, please. I'd like to meet some of these ladies over here." Mustering every ounce of courage she could find within herself, Vaden walked away from the doting young men and toward the circle of obviously gossiping young ladies. "Hello," she greeted and was at first met by only startled expressions. "I'm Vaden Valmont."

"Belva Tibbits," the brown-haired young woman who had glared at her earlier responded. The girl smiled artificially and offered a gloved hand. Vaden inwardly hoped that her feigned friendly smile to Jerome Clayton had looked more believable than did this girl's. Vaden took the offered hand to find that it was as limp as a dead fish. This girl would be no friend and Vaden knew it at once.

"I'm Selma Wimber," a cute brunette offered with a friendly smile. Her handshake was welcoming and firm and Vaden was hopeful.

"Raylin Wimber," another girl said. The other girls seemed kind as well. Only Belva Tibbits radiated negative feelings. Soon Vaden found herself accepted by nearly all in the group and involved in their conversation, which was characteristic of the type young girls had. They discussed their dresses, all the girls flattering each other endlessly. They discussed their hair and what challenges they had each endured in finding just the right pin points in styling. And, much to Vaden's expectation, it wasn't long before the youthful, feminine conversation turned to another foreseen topic.

"Jerome Clayton walked me home from the mercantile this afternoon!" Selma exclaimed in a hushed and obviously excited voice.

"Oh, Selma! Really?" another young woman with auburn hair exclaimed in a hushed voice.

"That's nothing!" Belva sneered. "I heard that Ransom Lake is wintering in town this year."

"Ransom Lake never winters in town, Belva, and you know it." Raylin was obviously not inclined to believe Belva's announcement.

"I tell you he is. I heard Mr. Clayton talking to Mr. Dennis this morning. He's moving to town for the winter. I saw him riding toward his farm today." Belva beamed with an irritating air of superiority.

"I bet you're just breathing heaven, aren't you Belva?" Selma turned to Vaden and explained, "Belva has had a...an interest in that bizarre hermit that lives in the mountains for years. Personally, I'm scared to death of him."

"Oh, I think he's just not comfortable with people," Vaden blurted out. She regretted voicing her opinion the second after she had for every pair of female eyes around her raised in surprise.

"Is that so?" Belva's eyes narrowed daringly. "And how is it that you can come to town yesterday and presume to know more about one of our citizens than we do?"

"I...I...Mr. Lake came into the mercantile today. He seems nice enough...just wary of people. At...at least that's what it seemed to me." Vaden swallowed hard. Belva already had a way of intimidating her and she didn't like the feeling.

"You mean...you've spoken with him?" Raylin asked, obviously astonished.

"Well...yes. I mean, he came into the mercantile today for some boots and…"

"I hardly think you can accurately judge the man's personality by a single conversation with him, Vaden." Belva was obviously irritated and Vaden decided that the particular moment to confront this girl was not at the first town social she was ever to attend.

"You're right, I'm sure," Vaden surrendered, smiling apologetically. But deep within her heart she knew that her discernment where Ransom Lake was concerned was accurate.

"Would you do me the honor of the first dance, Miss Vaden?"

Vaden looked up to see Jerome Clayton's charming smile affixed to her persona yet again.

"Uh...uh...certainly, Mr. Clayton," she accepted politely, placing her hand in the one he held out to her. She smiled at the group of girls as she left wondering how many more enemies she had made by being the first girl of the evening to dance with the handsome Jerome Clayton. She would much rather have stayed in the company of the girls. Although her mind hesitated uncertainly when he had asked her to dance, Vaden was too polite, too sensitive to the feelings of others and too kind-hearted to refuse him.

"Belva's a pill," was the first thing Jerome said to her as they began to dance. "You don't want to rub her the wrong way. But both the Wimber girls are nice. And Julianna Havens and Laurie Cox are sweet, too. I see you're making friends fast enough."

"Trying," Vaden admitted.

"And apparently you've even softened the likes of Ransom Lake."

Vaden looked up at Jerome astonished. "What do you mean?"

"I saw you speaking with him this afternoon. Actually, you looked pretty put off. But I imagine he can be an exasperating man to deal with."

"He bought a new pair of boots. You remember he came in when you were just leaving. Anyway, he accidentally threw a valuable looking pocketknife away in our trash barrel and I was returning it to him." Vaden wondered why she felt so guilty. Why did she feel that she had to explain her speaking with Mr. Lake to Jerome Clayton?

"That was thoughtful of you." Jerome smiled at her again. His smile was charming. Surely Vaden's discomfort toward the man was caused simply by the fact that he was handsome and attentive toward her.

"Well, it was the least I could do, especially after the incident when I..." Jerome raised his eyebrows waiting for her to continue. "Well, your mother certainly seems like a wonderful woman. My Aunt Myra speaks very highly of her."

"She is a wonderful woman. And I'm sure you'll find that I'm an all right boy...even if you have already labeled me a flirt." Jerome chuckled and winked at Vaden.

Vaden returned his friendly smile, though out of politeness rather than sincerity, and admitted, "Well, it just unnerves me terribly to have people stare at me. I'm sure you can understand that."

"I ask your forgiveness then, Miss Vaden, for staring at you. It's just that you are the most beautiful girl I've ever seen." Jerome continued to smile at her.

Vaden raised an unconvinced eyebrow. Unlike Yvonne, Vaden did not esteem overbearing flattery as a rule, especially when it was handed out on the occasion of only the second meeting between people. She distrusted a man who would say such things so soon. "You really spread the icing on thick, Mr. Clayton."

"I think most women like the icing thick," he whispered.

"Most do." Then, giggling and smiling sincerely at the young man, for she could admit that most women did prefer such flattery, Vaden resigned herself to the fact that perhaps Jerome Clayton wasn't all that different from other young men after all. Perhaps it was just the fact that he was new to her, interested in her, that made her hesitant and suspicious of him. Still, in the back of her mind was the vision of that odd, bearded hermit from the mountain.

Invariably all through the evening Vaden found herself glancing at the entrance to the town hall. She knew somehow that Mr. Lake would not arrive, but still she hoped that he would, if for no other reason then she held a secret wish to simply hear the intriguing tone of his voice once more. But he did not arrive and Vaden spent the evening dancing with every young man in town alternately. Jerome Clayton most often, however. He was quite attentive and charming and Vaden did finally allow herself to admit inwardly that he made the evening a pleasant experience for her. The other young women there, with the exception of Belva Tibbits, were also very friendly. Vaden enjoyed talking with them and was all the more glad that she and Yvonne had been allowed to stay with Aunt Myra and Uncle Dan for a time.

"Isn't it grand to be the belles of the ball, Vaden?" Yvonne sighed contentedly as they lay in their beds late that night. "I simply want to wallow in the prideful knowledge that every young man there this evening was simply mesmerized by our presence."

"'Vonnie!" Vaden couldn't abide her sister's vanity at times. Yet, at the same time she felt that on Yvonne's part it was warranted.

"Oh, I know, Vaden. You'd have rather been off mucking around in a creek or climbing trees to look in birds' nests." Yvonne turned on her side facing Vaden and propped her elbow on her pillow to support her head. "I know that the streak of romantic desire is thicker than pudding in you, too, Vaden. How can you not be profoundly flattered at all the attention we received tonight?"

"Because...because my idea of romance is different than yours, Vonnie." Vaden sat up in her bed and smiled at her sister. Then she looked out the window at the bright, beckoning glimmer of the stars. "You like to have attention. To be flattered and fought over. And I suppose all women are like that. Even me. But I want so much more than that. I want someone to love me. Just me. To be *so* in love with me that I can't even imagine the enormity, the depth of it. And I want to love one man with all my heart. With everything that I am. I want a man that I can laugh with. A man that will hold me in his arms when I need to cry. Someone that needs me as much as I need him. Just me. I want a man whose kiss is so passionate and so perfect that I feel like I might die from the ecstasy of it. I want to marry him and have his children grow inside me...watch them mature into adults that reflect his strength and uniqueness." Vaden looked back to Yvonne who could only stare at her, absorbed entirely in what her sister had whispered in the quiet of the night. "I know it's what you want, too, Yvonne," Vaden added. "The difference is...I guess the difference is...I can't enjoy the attentions of other young men because my heart is always searching for...for him."

"You mean for this love that you dream of?" Yvonne asked. Vaden nodded. "But, Vaden...you expect so much in your dreams. No one is perfect, Vay. I'm afraid you'll be disappointed. I'm afraid you'll let life pass you by. You need to live more for the moment, and not look so much to what you hope the future will bring to you."

"I know, Vonnie. I know. But...but it's me. It's my heart that whispers it to me. There *is* such a man for me, Vonnie. Oh, no one is perfect...I realize that. I'm not saying I want the man to be perfect. I just want him to be perfect for me. And I know he exists. Whether I find him now or in ten years or in twenty. He's there. Somewhere. I know he is."

"You must think me so shallow...so heartless, Vay. But I'm not. Truly."

"I know that," Vaden assured her sister. "Just like you watch me stumble into ridiculous situation after ridiculous situation...put up ever patiently with my spontaneous whims of adventure...and still you know my soul...I know yours. I know that it must be wonderful to be the most beautiful woman in the room and have every man in it at your beck and call. Yet I know that you want the same things I want out of life. A husband who was begotten only for you. Who will father children with you and together they will all bring you boundless joy and fulfillment. I do know that, Vonnie."

Yvonne smiled at Vaden. "How I love you, little sister."

"And I you, elder sister."

Yvonne closed her eyes for a moment and inhaled deeply. "Someone's burning cedar in their hearth tonight. Isn't it a heavenly fragrance?"

Vaden closed her eyes as well and lay down on her bed. "Heavenly." And she imagined a fireplace in a cozy house. She imagined sitting before it watching the fire burn and crackle, wrapped securely in strong, capable, masculine arms. "I wonder why he tears away his sleeves?" she whispered aloud a moment before sleep overtook her.

CHAPTER
∽ THREE ∾

"Well, I have to say it," Uncle Dan began one morning at breakfast. "I just have to say that I don't know what we did for fun before you girls arrived."

"I'll second that," Aunt Myra agreed. "You girls make the days brighter and the nights warmer. And what a swarm of young people we've had around since you two moved in! I swear, I think Jerome Clayton is plum gone on you, Vaden. And every other bachelor in the state must be camping out across the street waiting for Vonnie to come out of the mercantile so that they can catch a glimpse of her!"

Yvonne smiled. "Everyone in town has been very friendly and accepting."

"Everyone except Belva Tibbits," Vaden corrected.

"Belva Tibbits don't count," Uncle Dan chuckled. "Her nose is too long and her eyes are too far apart."

"Now, Daniel," Aunt Myra scolded, trying in vain to suppress her own smile.

"She's only jealous because Jerome Clayton is Vaden's beau," Yvonne stated.

"Jerome Clayton is not my beau, Yvonne. And you know it." Vaden seemed overly defensive, but for the past two weeks she had been teased mercilessly by her Uncle Dan and Yvonne. Jerome Clayton appeared at least once a day in the mercantile, claiming to have just stopped in for a visit with Uncle Dan. He stared at Vaden all through church on Sundays, too,

41

and, though Vaden knew that he was every girls' ambition, she could not wholly commit herself to the idea of having him. His consistent and obvious attentions made her, at times, unbearably uncomfortable. He was too attentive. And often something in his eyes sent a shiver down her spine. Perhaps, she had mused over and over, it was merely because she wasn't used to such intent attention from a particular young man. Everyone adored Jerome Clayton and sang his praises at every turn. Still, Vaden felt differently. And always in the back of her mind lingered the image of Ransom Lake. The profound curiosity and need to know him. Always in Vaden's mind he was there, quiet, alone and tragic. Never did her mind linger on Jerome Clayton that way. Never. At the sound of her Uncle Dan's jolly voice again, Vaden returned her attention to the conversation at hand.

"It seems we've got young folks here and there under foot every free minute of the day. I just can't believe it's been two weeks since you girls got here. How time do fly," Uncle Dan said, his mouth still full as he chewed his toast.

Vaden and Yvonne had made several friends among the girls in town since their arrival. And they did have suitors buzzing around like bees to honey. But it only served to remind Vaden that Ransom Lake hadn't shown his face anywhere near the citizenship since the day he'd been in the store to buy boots. Often, when she had free time or Yvonne and Aunt Myra sent her out on a walk, she would sit in the largest maple tree on the creek bank near the old bridge, or on the bridge itself letting her bare toes skim across the water's top and watch the road that led from town to Ransom Lake's farm, hoping to catch a glimpse of the strange man who kept to himself. But she hadn't seen him and she had almost given up hope of ever seeing him again.

"Vaughn Wimber says he's gonna start his punkin harvest next couple or three weeks, Vaden. I knew you'd be lookin' forward to that." Uncle Dan winked affectionately at his niece as she looked up and smiled. "Maybe you and Yvonne could go out and choose a few of the biggest and best to buy for us to use or sell in the mercantile.

"I'd love it and you know it," Vaden admitted, again returning her attention to the conversation.

"I thought you might."

But as quickly as her attention had been arrested, it was lost and she thought of having finally met, and distinguished, in her mind the two Wimber families in town. One was the Vaughn Wimber family. Vaughn owned the pumpkin patch. He and his wife, Sue Ellen, were Nathaniel's parents. They had two younger daughters as well, who had been into the mercantile several times. Raylin and Selma's parents were Kent Wimber, Vaughn's brother, and his wife, Margaret. This family had three younger children and a new baby as well. Though Vaughn Wimber owned the massive pumpkin patch outside of town and Vaden admired him for it, it was Selma and Raylin's family that Vaden favored.

"Well, I gotta get goin' Myra," Uncle Dan said, folding his napkin and placing it on the table next to his plate. "I told ol' Ransom Lake that today I'd deliver those supplies he ordered."

Everyone startled as Vaden's fork fell from her hand, clanking loudly as it hit the edge of her plate and tumbled to the floor.

"Why don't you take Vaden with you, Uncle Dan. She's been a bit edgy lately and needs to get out," Yvonne suggested, winking at her sister.

"Could you do without her for a couple of hours, Myra?" Uncle Dan grinned at Vaden. He knew how desperately Vaden preferred out of doors to in.

"Of course. I know she'll come back all rosy cheeked and ready to work like the dickens after. Right, sweet pea?" Myra grinned, for she, too, knew how badly Vaden needed the fresh air to motivate her.

"I promise!" Vaden squealed.

Vaden could hardly believe that her Uncle Dan was actually taking her to see Ransom Lake. Of course, he wasn't actually taking her to see the man, but she would see him and that was all that mattered.

"You take after your daddy, Vaden," Uncle Dan commented as they rode in the wagon toward Ransom Lake's farm. "And after me. I hate bein' cooped up in the house all the dern time. Get's me fidgety and irritable. You've been workin' hard since you been here, and I knew you needed to get out."

Vaden reached over and linked her arm through her uncle's as he drove the team. "Look at the beauty of that patch, Uncle Dan." The pumpkin patch was on either side of them now and the beautiful squash seemed to glow orange from beneath the leaves. "Doesn't it just give you all the more reason to appreciate God's creations?"

"That it does, sweet pea. That it does."

They rode in silence then, for they were alike. Both enjoyed the beauty of nature, the autumn scents in the air, the cool crisp breezes. Before Vaden knew it Uncle Dan was reining the team in before a small, white, cozy-looking farm house. A large black dog barked twice and ran to the wagon, wagging its tail and panting happily.

"Hey there, Ragamuffin. How's you doin' today?" Uncle Dan climbed down out of the wagon and scratched the dog's belly abrasively as the dog laid down and rolled over exposing its underside to the man. Vaden climbed down as well and crouched down to pet the dog's face.

"He certainly seems happy," she giggled as the dog licked her hand.

"Mornin', Dan." Vaden looked under the wagon and saw a pair of familiar looking boots approaching from the direction of the house. The sound of his voice uttering a greeting sent a thrill traveling through her bosom.

"I've got your supplies together, Ransom. You sure are stockin' up thorough for winter. It looks about like what you take with you when you winter up in the mountains. You are plannin' to stay out here all winter, aren't ya?" Vaden looked up to her uncle as he spoke, but still crouched down petting the dog. For some reason she suddenly was uncertain as to whether or not she wanted to face Ransom Lake again.

"I am wintering here. Just like to be prepared," Mr. Lake replied. When he walked in front of the team and came to stand before her uncle, Vaden noticed that his eyes narrowed with a frown as he glanced down to see her there. She was startled, for he wore only his boots, trousers and suspenders. He did not wear a shirt! Vaden was unsure if she could keep her composure under such a circumstance. It was obviously no fault of Ransom Lake's that he should appear in such a state of undress, for he would have no reason to think that anyone would deliver his supplies other than her uncle. Still, it was the first time Vaden had ever had such a view of a man's bare anatomy.

"Good morning, Mr. Lake," she managed to choke from her throat at last, standing and offering her hand. The man only continued to frown, making no move to accept and shake her extended hand and simply nodded and looked back to her uncle.

"You missed quite a town social a couple weeks back, Ransom," Uncle Dan said as he walked to the wagon and began lifting out a sack of flour. "Dancin', pies, pretty girls. Just about everything a man could want." Uncle Dan handed the sack of flour to Ransom Lake and he hefted it onto his shoulder, walking to the house and setting it down on the front porch. "'Course, I know you don't go in much for social gatherin's...but still, the pies were good."

Vaden again found herself staring shamelessly at the man as he worked to help her uncle unload the wagon. Actually, her staring had nothing to do with the fact that she had never seen a man in such a state of undress before. Granted, his chest and stomach, his entire torso was a fascinating mass of perfectly sculpted muscles, but Vaden was more intrigued with his manner. He seemed so self-conscious and yet at the same time indifferent.

"Wimber gonna harvest those pumpkins soon?" the man inquired of Vaden's uncle.

"'Bout two or three weeks, so he tells me," Uncle Dan answered. "I hope we'll see you out at the Halloween social, Ransom. It's Halloween night out by the old oak west of town."

Mr. Lake didn't answer. He simply took the sack of sugar that Uncle

Dan had handed him onto his shoulder and carried it to the porch. When he returned he paused and said, "Don't think folks want the likes of me roaming around at the socials."

"They're simply scared of you because you make them feel ignorant." The statement was past Vaden's lips and into the autumn air before she could stop it and she winced as she looked at the man, afraid he might literally bite off her head.

As the turbulent gray of his eyes pierced the softness of Vaden's, Uncle Dan chuckled, "She's got it right there, boy."

"Ignorant?" the man questioned. "Explain that to me, girl."

Vaden clasped her hands together to try to still their trembling as she spoke. "You're obviously a man who wants no one, needs very few services from others to survive. Most people aren't like that, so independent and self-sufficient. They all know you don't need them or want them and they feel less confident in your presence is all. And you do look a bit intimidating. I know that you look as you do intentionally...to disguise yourself from the world for whatever reasons you have. But they probably think you do it on purpose to look frightening and to try to emphasize your superiority."

"Your niece is a very presumptuous girl, Dan. Is the other one this bad?" Ransom Lake scowled deeply as he reached into the wagon and withdrew a bucket of lard.

"The other one is the picture of Missy Proper Polly. This one's honest and says what she thinks. But I'll warn you, Ransom...don't take your eyes off of her or you're liable to find beans up your nose." Uncle Dan looked to Vaden all too aware of her humiliation and chuckled merrily.

Vaden closed her eyes and wished she could melt into the ground so that it could absorb her into oblivion She couldn't believe her uncle had said what he had. It had started out to be a compliment, she knew. But, oh, what an ending!

"Don't know nothing about beans, but I do know something about boots conking you on the head," Ransom Lake added. Vaden opened her eyes to see him staring at her with the possibility of a grin hiding beneath the abundant facial hair he wore. She wanted to feel his hair at that moment, to know whether it was soft or coarse.

Uncle Dan chuckled quietly and placed the back of one hand tenderly against Vaden's scarlet, warmed cheek. Vaden cast her eyes to the ground again, for Ransom Lake continued to stare at her with his unsettling eyes.

"What's the winter gonna bring this year anyhow, Ransom?" Uncle Dan inquired and Vaden almost forgave him for teasing her, for she knew he was taking the attention off her blush.

Ransom Lake paused in unloading his supplies from the wagon, leaning back against it for a moment and folding his muscular arms across his impressive chest. "I'm thinking it's gonna be bad. Birds already leaving, heard some wild geese overhead only this morning." Vaden looked up at him quickly as a pleased grin spread across her face. She, too, had noticed the quiet, barely audible call of the wild geese that morning and had looked up, shading her eyes from the sun, finally catching a glimpse of the flock as they flew high above her and over town. "Skunks and squirrels already digging in and the mountain got snow last night."

Uncle Dan turned and looked to the mountains which sat majestically in the distance. "Shore 'nough," he mumbled.

"It'll wait 'til late November, I'm thinking," Ransom continued. "But then it's gonna bury us in snow and ice this year."

"My bones are achin' already," Uncle Dan sighed.

"I've got some late apples that're ready for picking, Dan. Why don't you go on and fill up a couple of bushel baskets and I'll unload the rest of this stuff."

"If ya don't mind...I think we'll do just that, Ransom. Thank ya kindly." A smile spread like melted butter across Uncle Dan's face and Vaden's smile increased as well, for she well knew her uncle's delight in eating apple dumplings and pies.

"There's a couple of baskets out under the closest tree that I left there last night. Just fill those up and take them." Ransom Lake nodded at Uncle Dan and lifted another sack of flour out of the wagon.

"We'll do it!" Uncle Dan clapped his hands together, rubbing them excitedly back and forth. "Come on, Vaden. You and me ain't picked apples together in years!"

Vaden started to follow her uncle toward the nearby orchards, but paused and looked back to Ransom Lake when he called out, "You be careful, girl. Don't go climbing up higher than you can handle."

Vaden clenched her teeth together tightly and with great indignation turned and walked toward the orchard with her uncle.

A good twenty minutes had passed when Uncle Dan finally said, "I think we 'bout got these full, sweet pea. You come on down from there now and we'll head home."

"Okay, Uncle Dan," Vaden answered from her perch high in the upper branches of an apple tree. "Let me just get this juicy ol' thing on this branch up here. It's just calling to my mouth!" Carefully she began to shinny up a nearby limb, pausing to reach for the large ripe apple that grew at its tip.

"Vaden, your Aunt Myra will skin me alive if you come home all banged up. Now come on down from there." Vaden heard her uncle's instruction, but the apple was just at her fingertips. Just two inches more and it would be hers. Finding a sturdy knot on the limb, she pressed her boot firmly against it and raised herself slightly.

"I've just about...just about...there! Got it!" she squealed triumphantly as she took hold of the apple and pulled hard, snapping it from any lingering attachment to its mother tree. "See there, Uncle Dan?" She held the apple out for him to see and did have a moment of dizziness when she looked down at him and realized that she was much higher up than she thought. "Now there's an apple worth stretching for!"

"Well now...this doesn't surprise me one lick. Nope. Not one." Vaden looked to see Ransom Lake approach and come to stand beside her uncle, both men gawking up at her. "I just knew I'd come out here to find that child stuck up a tree, Dan."

"She ain't stuck. Are ya, darlin'? She just likes the best out of life. Just like her ol' Uncle Dan. Ain't that right, sweet pea?"

"That's right. I am *not* stuck, Mr. Lake," Vaden informed the man. Then, unbuttoning several buttons at the front of her shirtwaist, she placed the apple protectively inside her clothing and began her descent. She was miffed at Mr. Lake's assumption that she had yet again gotten herself into a precarious position. So, when she reached a limb that wasn't quite so far off the ground, but still well above the men's heads, she sat down on it, locked her knees firmly around it, then threw herself backwards and turned one summer sault in the air before landing smartly on her feet and hands in a crouching position before Ransom Lake. Standing with an air of victory, she pulled the apple from its place at her bosom, bit into it fiercely and held it in her teeth as she rebuttoned her blouse, all the while meeting the impressed expression in Mr. Lake's eyes. Then she pulled the apple from her mouth, chewing its sweetness exaggeratedly. "That's a good apple you've grown, Mr. Lake."

"And that's a fine petticoat you're wearing, girl," he mumbled, something of a smile apparent beneath his mustache. Vaden's eyes widened indignantly, but when Uncle Dan's amused chuckle burst from his lungs and into the spicy autumn air, Vaden sighed and smiled. Ransom Lake possessed a good sense of humor. Not that Vaden was surprised, for she had expected as much. But it was delightful to actually see him demonstrate it, no matter how inappropriate his remark.

"Now, we want to see you out at the Halloween gatherin', Ransom," Uncle Dan boomed as he helped Vaden into the wagon after loading the apples into its bed. "There'll be fun and perty girls and pies aboundin'."

"I don't go in much for social gatherings, Dan. You know that." Mr. Lake's stormy eyes met Vaden's for a moment before he looked back to her uncle.

"Nonsense, man! Everyone goes in for pies!"

Ransom Lake looked to Vaden and shook his head as if to acknowledge that it was a losing battle to argue with the man.

"Thank you for the apples, Mr. Lake," Vaden said politely.

He nodded and Uncle Dan slapped the lines at the backs of the horses and the wagon lurched forward. "You come on into the mercantile soon, Ransom. We'll have some pie together," Uncle Dan called over his shoulder. As the wagon pulled away, Uncle Dan commented, "I think ol' Ransom Lake is taken with you, sweet pea."

"I think I cause him to be taken with insanity," Vaden responded. "Oh, why do I act so...so irrationally, Uncle Dan? I can't believe...sitting here with you, still eating this delicious apple...I can't believe I cherry dropped from that tree limb!"

Uncle Dan chuckled. "Well...your pride was at stake, child. You had to defend your honor. And I'll tell you right now that you done a fine job of it. A fine job! We just won't say anything to Aunt Myra or Yvonne 'bout it, now will we?"

Vaden rolled her eyes, imagining what the consequences would be if either of the two females at home found out. "Aunt Myra might never let me out again. And Yvonne...Yvonne would lecture me for six months on propriety and social graces and things unbecoming a young lady."

"I figure that would be the least that you could expect, sweet pea." Uncle Dan chuckled out loud again. Vaden looked over at him and was delighted in the complete mirth obvious in his eyes as they joined his mouth in laughter. "Never seen Ransom's eyes so wide before as they were when you dropped at his feet today."

His eyes *had* widened and he had looked just the slightest bit surprised. That gave Vaden cause to smile. As the wagon approached the turn that led to Vaden's beloved babbling brook and quaint rickety old bridge she asked her uncle if she might walk the rest of the way into town. She hadn't been to the creek in several days and she did long to hear its relaxing murmur and watch the leaves fall to the ground from her perch in the arms of the giant maple.

Uncle Danny agreed, unable ever to deny his Vaden anything, and soon she was where she longed to be, perched in the branches of the maple, not too terribly high above the creek.

Vaden rested her head against a strong limb and closed her eyes. She breathed and listened. Vaden inhaled deeply again, savoring the air and its blessed fragrance. She could smell the bark of the tree against which her head lay and the slight scent of the leaves that fell quietly to the ground. The smells, the scents, the aromas of autumn reached her senses next when the breezes brought the sweet perfume of over-ripened apples and pears, the smell of the grasses in the meadow nearby, the scent of burning cedar and applewood. Scents and smells were cherished by Vaden Valmont for they created divine memories and would often spark sentimental reminiscences at the most unexpected times. Filling her lungs with the heavenly scents of fall once more, she listened intently then. Listened to the trickly, splashing sounds of the creek below. Listened to the breezes as they danced about in the leaves of the maple and the grasses of the meadow, to the comforting lowing of cattle in the distance and to the call of mourning doves somewhere nearby.

"*I long to taste the honeyed breeze and touch the rubied apple's flavor. To speak with soft conversing leaves, the songs of sky's white clouds to savor.*" Vaden whispered the verse quietly to herself, pausing often to ensure its adherence with the softness of her mood and the stillness of the moment.

What reprieve nature gave her! What a lift to the soul did it provide! She opened her eyes and looked about. Off in the distance she could see a herd of cattle grazing, caught the vision of the massive pumpkin patch that was near to being harvested and, for the first time, she realized that it was Ransom Lake's roof and orchards that she could see peeking up from beyond the distant hill. She had often wondered as she had been sitting in her tree if it was, indeed, Ransom Lake's house that was visible. But now she knew it was and she could come and sit in her tree and gaze at his house whenever she could get away.

"Oh, my!" Vaden exclaimed out loud suddenly. She knew she must get home. Aunt Myra would be needing her help and she had dallied long enough. She climbed out of the tree and picked up a large maple leaf that had fallen to the ground. She tenderly rolled each point toward the center of the leaf until it cupped in a manner. Then she removed two of the four apple seeds from the apple she'd been eating. She placed the two seeds tenderly in the leaf's center, then knelt beside the creek, carefully placing the leaf on the water's surface. As she watched it float away downstream and toward Ransom Lake's property she whispered, "Grow another apple for me, Ransom Lake. One as good as I know your soul to be." She watched the leaf for several more seconds before turning and dashing toward the road that led to home.

It was speaking to him again...that vision in his mind...and even though he dreaded the change it might bring, he followed the instructions of his sixth sense and walked to the creek that passed behind his house. Ransom Lake stood at the creek's bank for a moment. It was no more than a few seconds when something in the water captured his attention and he bent down and retrieved a large maple leaf that was floating toward him. Two apple seeds lay on it and he knew they had been of his fruit. He'd known it before he'd even seen the leaf floating in the water.

Vaden smiled and waved to Mr. Wimber as he called out, "Hello there, Miss Vaden," from his pumpkin patch as she passed by.

"Hello, Mr. Wimber!" she replied. "Are they nearly ready?"

"Just about."

Then Vaden smiled somewhat uncertainly as Jerome Clayton approached from the other side of the road. "Hey there, Miss Vaden. Can I walk a ways with you?" he asked politely. Vaden wondered for a moment what his reaction would be were she to tell him truthfully that she would rather walk alone this particular day.

"Why certainly, Mr. Clayton," she answered, sounding delighted, though all delight within her was squelched at that moment. Her thoughts wanted to linger on the mysterious man who hid himself away from the world, not on Jerome Clayton.

"Where you been this morning?" Jerome pried. No doubt he'd been into the mercantile already. Vaden could tell that he was irritated at not knowing for sure where she had been that morning, though she guessed that he had an idea.

"Oh, I went with Uncle Dan to deliver some supplies. I asked him to let me out of the wagon so I could enjoy this heavenly day awhile longer." She smiled at Jerome, hoping he would accept her explanation and not pry further. She was relieved for a moment when he nodded. But her nerves gave a sensitive jump as he spoke again.

"Been out to ol' Ransom Lake's farm, huh? Is he still alive out there?" As she had suspected, he did know where she had been. There was no point in trying to secret it any longer.

"Yes. Quite alive and well. Very well," she added nervously, remembering the vision of him in only trousers and suspenders. "He gave us a couple of bushels of apples and I'm sure Aunt Myra will have Yvonne and me working on them this afternoon."

"Oh," Jerome muttered as a frown puckered his brow. "I was hoping you could go for a walk with me later today."

"Oh, I'd love to, Mr. Clayton...but I promised Aunt Myra I'd help her this afternoon. After all, I've already been out and about while poor Yvonne has been stuck inside." Vaden sighed inwardly, for she didn't feel like enduring a walk with Jerome that day. Actually, she never felt like enduring a walk with Jerome, but he was so persistent that propriety demanded that she be polite in accepting him once in a while.

"You like being outside, don't you, Miss Vaden?" Jerome commented. His smile was understanding and charming and Vaden felt guilty for not wanting to walk with him.

"I do. The outdoors breathes life into me," she confessed.

They talked lightly as they walked toward the mercantile and when they reached it, Jerome tipped his hat to Vaden. She smiled at him before entering the store and thanked him for escorting her home.

"He's plum gone on you, sweet pea!" Aunt Myra exclaimed as Vaden entered the store.

"I think you've got him captured completely," Yvonne affirmed.

"What if I don't want to have him captured completely?" Vaden sighed.

Yvonne laughed. "Don't be ridiculous, Vay! Now, where have you been? Uncle Dan's been home for half an hour!"

"I'm glad you're finally back. Them Wimber children have been waitin' on you near to an hour, Vaden," Aunt Myra scolded lovingly. "Child! You've gotten mud all over your skirt again, dear. You must be more careful. But, then again...you're the one havin' to scrub out the stain."

"I'm sorry, Auntie. I just...I just..." Vaden began to defend herself.

"I know, sweetie. I know." Aunt Myra smiled lovingly at her niece. "Now, what about these little stinkers that have been waitin' on you?"

"But I told them a story only two days ago, Auntie," Vaden reminded delightedly. The Wimber children, and there were so many, being that there were two Wimber families in town, had discovered Vaden's unique talent for storytelling several days after she and Yvonne had arrived. Sue Ellen Wimber had asked Vaden and Yvonne to keep an eye on her young ones and their cousins while she and her sister-in-law, Margaret Wimber, went out to visit old Mrs. Tilits who lived a ways out of town and was ailing and in need of help. It wasn't long before Yvonne's nerves were completely frayed and Vaden was left to tend them alone. So, she had told them a story. The story of Snow White. They had adored it, sitting in silent mesmerization as she dramatically acted out the tale to them. There were five younger Wimber children altogether and the smiling, anxious faces of the two boys and three girls beamed at Vaden as she approached them.

"I just told you a story two days ago," Vaden stated, putting her hands on her hips as she frowned down at the children.

"Oh, please, Miss Vaden! Just a short one. Please!" came their pleading voices in unison.

Immediately Vaden smiled and relented, "Just one short one. Just one." The children squealed delightedly, sitting down where they stood, directly in the center of the mercantile, awaiting their story. "Very well, we begin. Now this," Vaden began, dropping her voice to a near whisper, "is the story of Rapunzel." She rolled the "r" off the tip of her tongue theatrically as she reached up, pulling the pin from her own hair and letting it cascade down her back and around her shoulders.

Uncle Dan and Aunt Myra both smiled to themselves and Yvonne, who stood behind the counter, sighed and rolled her eyes exasperatedly. "It wouldn't be so bad if she charged them a penny apiece," Yvonne murmured.

"Hush, sweet thing. Let the children enjoy the tale," Aunt Myra told her lovingly.

"For you see, Rapunzel had long flaxen hair that shone like gold in the sunlight. She was kept prisoner in a high, high, way up high tower. A tower which had only one window through which the gentle breezes and yellow sunlight could enter. And that one window was Rapunzel's only view of the world. 'Twas a wicked and ugly old crone that kept her locked in the tower so that her profound and glorious beauty could never be seen, for you see, the crone was ever so jealous of the great loveliness possessed by Rrrrr-apunzel."

Some time later, when heavy sighs escaped their lungs and clapping made their hands ache, the delighted children rose, tears apparent in their eyes at hearing the tale of the blinded prince and how his sight was restored by the loving tears of his beloved Rapunzel.

"Thank you so much, Miss Vaden," one of the littlest Wimber girls sighed, taking hold of Vaden's hand tenderly.

"Well, you're welcome, Violet," Vaden giggled. Then, bending to speak into the girl's ear, she whispered, "But wait a few days to return or my auntie will have my hide for not getting my chores done."

Violet smiled, her eyes sparkling with admiration as she looked up at Vaden. "I think you look just like Rrrrapunzel, Miss Vaden," the child sighed.

Vaden smiled, flattered at the child's adoration. "Even though her hair was as gold as the morning sun and mine is as dark as night?"

Violet Wimber nodded. "It reminds me of chocolates on Christmas morning."

Vaden was enchanted and bent, kissing the child sweetly on one cheek. Then she watched affectionately as the children left, waving and calling out their goodbyes to her.

Turning to her sister, she was already prepared for the disapproving expression on Yvonne's face.

"Oh, come now, Vonnie. Let them be children! Remember how wonderful it was to be a child? To believe in princesses and princes, magic and true love?"

"I only remember wanting to grow up so I could dress like a princess, Vaden," Yvonne sighed. "Now, while you've been out wallowing in the mud...I've been telling Jerome Clayton to come back every fifteen minutes for the past hour!" When Vaden sighed disappointedly Yvonne could hold her tongue no longer. "What is wrong with you, Vaden? He's adorable! He's kind and courteous and polite and..."

"And average," Vaden finished.

"He's far from average," Yvonne contradicted. "Any girl in this town would love to have his attentions...which he seems to be directing at you and which you almost rudely choose to ignore!"

"Yvonne...you know how I..."

"Hello, Mr. Clayton. Again," Yvonne interrupted, winking at her sister.

Drawing in a deep breath, Vaden turned to face the handsome young man as he entered the mercantile.

"Hello, ladies. I forgot what time it was you told me to arrive this evening, Mrs. Valmont," Jerome stated to Vaden's aunt. "For dinner I mean." He smiled at Vaden and explained, "I forgot to tell you, Miss Vaden, that your aunt has invited me for dinner this evening and I just wanted to let you know how much I'm looking forward to it."

"Why...how wonderful," Vaden managed to spit out. "I guess we'll have our time to talk after all."

"Yes. One way or the other," Jerome said pointedly.

"We'll expect you at 5:30 sharp," Aunt Myra answered, looking as if she was a child who had just been caught stealing cookies. "Is that all right, Jerome?"

"That's wonderful, ma'am," Jerome nodded. Then he tipped his hat and said his goodbye.

When he'd gone, Vaden turned to Yvonne, disappointment all too blatant on her face.

"I meant to tell you, Vaden. Really. But he just walked in so soon after you finished your story and..." Yvonne began.

"I know. I know. I suppose I should resign myself to him."

"Don't make it sound like an execution, Vaden."

"But he's not...he's not..."

"Him," Yvonne finished for her. "Who is he, Vaden? You act as if you've already unearthed him. And knowing you, that's probably literal."

Vaden wanted to confess to her sister. To shout, *He's Ransom Lake! Can't you understand that?* But she knew she dared not, for Yvonne would not understand. Yvonne did not see Mr. Lake as she did. Her eyes were blurred by his shaggy appearance and lack of social graces.

And so she endured supper with Jerome. Rather, she tried to enjoy it.

He was forever staring at her, flashing his charming smile in her direction, inquiring about aspects of her life and family back east. Yvonne was delighted and Vaden knew it was because she had hopes that this charming, good-looking young man would have a settling effect on her sister's wild-hare ways.

But Vaden knew. She knew herself and she could never settle for Jerome Clayton. And that is what it would be were she to further encourage his attentions. Settling. Settling for far, far less than she wanted, needed, would accept.

"You'll have to take Vaden out to Vaughn's pumpkin patch when he harvests, Jerome. I'm certain she would love to meander through the vines," Aunt Myra suggested. Vaden sighed heavily, though she forced a smile at Jerome.

"It's quite a sight to see, Miss Vaden. Wagons and wagons full of pumpkins. Yep. I'll be sure and take you around when the time comes." Jerome winked at Vaden and continued with his dinner, while Vaden found it nearly impossible to stomach eating her own. Aunt Myra was a wonderful cook, but the company at dinner was affecting Vaden's appetite.

"Ol' Ransom Lake seems to be fairing well," Uncle Dan stated. "I don't wonder if havin' people so close might bother him. He seems to take to Vaden though. I suppose it's because she's so honest in what she says to him."

Every mouth at the table stopped chewing and every fork or spoon paused in midair as all eyes turned to Vaden. Vaden felt her cheeks begin to heat up and, though she loved her Uncle Dan dearly, she could've pinched him hard for bringing up the subject.

"Just exactly what did you say to him today that was so honest, Vay?' Yvonne asked, the snap in her voice all too apparent.

"Nothing. I...I..." Vaden stammered as she looked to Uncle Dan for salvation.

"She plum blurted out why it is that all the townsfolk avoid him so. You know...why nobody seems to feel comfortable around the man," Uncle Dan answered for her.

"And, uh, just what reason is that, Vaden dear?" Aunt Myra asked, though it was obvious she was uncomfortable speaking about another man in front of their guest.

"People are intimidated by him. Frightened at his unconventional ways. That's all," Vaden admitted. She looked to Jerome whose smile had faded and whose eyes were narrow as they studied her intently. Again, the hair at the back of her neck prickled as she looked at the man. Something just didn't set right in her estimation of his character. He grinned at her a moment later, however.

"I figure you got that one square on the head, Miss Vaden," he said in a low voice. "Looks to me like readin' people is another one of your many lovely attributes."

Vaden somewhat resented his syrupy compliment, but she forced a friendly smile and said, "Thank you, Mr. Clayton, but you are far too flattering to me."

"No one could ever be too flattering to you, Miss Vaden," he responded, winking flirtatiously at her. Vaden could not help the blush that rose to her cheeks, for it was embarrassing to have him flirting with her so obviously in front of her family. She knew she'd never hear the end of it, one way or the other, from any of them.

But later that night, as she folded the small square of muslin that secreted two tiny apple seeds and placed it under her bed in one of the large, well-worn boots she hid there, Vaden knew she could not be in love with Jerome. At least, she could not naturally fall in love with Jerome. It would be an actual effort to love him as everyone thought she should or might. And, though love alone was enough for some women, it was not for Vaden Valmont. She needed to be *in* love. She needed to have someone be in love with her. But, as she lay in bed, she wondered if she was doomed to be joined forever to a man that she merely tolerated. She knew that the man she truly wanted was out of reach. Too distant from life and wanting it that way.

Then everything, all the thoughts and emotions that were bursting about in her mind could stay silent no longer and, as she pulled her quilt up around her neck, she whispered, "Vonnie? Promise you won't speak of this to anyone?"

Immediately Yvonne was alert and sitting up in bed. She knew all too well that whenever Vaden spoke that particular phrase the information she was about to divulge was worth listening to. Furthermore, as she swore, "I promise," she knew that Vaden was confident in her sister's loyalties. Yvonne Valmont would never repeat whatever it was her sister was about to confide in her.

"Today," Vaden began in a whisper. "Today when Uncle Dan and I went out to deliver those things to Ransom Lake..."

"Yes? What?" Yvonne prodded anxiously.

Suddenly Vaden sat up and blurted out, "Oh, my goodness, Vonnie! He came out of the house in nothing but his boots and trousers!"

"You mean to tell me he appeared before you with only his undershirt covering his torso?" Yvonne was, indeed, awed.

"No, Vonnie! He wore only his boots and trousers. There was nothing covering his...his...chest!" Vaden confessed. Yvonne gasped in horror and Vaden continued, trying to lessen the shock. "Well, he did have his suspenders on, but they were hanging about his hips and legs so I don't suppose you could actually count them as being worn...because, of course, they weren't being worn. They were just hanging there."

"Vaden! Do you mean to tell me that you've...that you've witnessed..."

"Yes, Vonnie. I have. I've seen a man bare from the waist up. And let me tell you this...it is very unsettling."

"Well, do you mean good unsettling or bad unsettling? Really, Vaden, try to be more specific." Yvonne's eyes were as large as dinner plates and Vaden had a moment of delight in the fact that she had a knowledge that her sister did not.

"Oh, good unsettling definitely. But...I do think that it would depend on whose bare torso one was viewing. The torso of Ransom Lake was rather...sculpted I suppose. So obviously solid and defined. I never quite imagined one to look so. I'm certain that if you were to push at it with your index finger, it would be as hard as rock."

"Vaden!" Yvonne exclaimed in a whisper, covering her ears dramatically with her hands. "Don't speak of such things!"

"And I'm quite certain that were Jerome Clayton to parade around in such a state...well, I'm quite certain...quite certain that the view would not be nearly as...nearly as favorable."

Yvonne sighed and laid back down in her bed, her hand to her forehead. "I'm sure you're completely and utterly corrupted now, Vay. I'm just glad it wasn't me that was forced to witness such an indecent display."

"You, my dear sister, are lying." Vaden blew out her candle, snuggling down into her warm bed.

"One too many sacks of flour, Dan," Ransom Lake announced in his provocative, deep, mumbling voice as he entered the mercantile early the next morning. Vaden's heart immediately began to pound as he carried the sack of flour into the mercantile and set it on the floor up against the counter. This time it was Vaden's elbow jabbing Yvonne's ribs as she noticed her sister staring curiously at Ransom Lake, as if trying to imagine what he would look like bare from the waist up.

"Well, honesty is a lost virtue these days, Ransom," Uncle Dan said, taking Ransom's hand and shaking it firmly. "I thank you, boy."

Ransom glanced quickly to Vaden, but then his eyes went to Yvonne, lingering on her face for a moment before he leaned on the counter and spoke to Dan. "I hear you got young Jerome Clayton paying homage over here near to five times a day."

"It's them nieces of mine," Dan chuckled. Vaden went crimson knowing full well that both men were well aware of the discomfort caused her. "Ain't never seen a man so gone on a filly before as that boy is on my Vaden."

"Well, it may be that you oughta remind the boy of the bean story you mentioned yesterday before he's too far gone." Ransom turned to Vaden, then, an unfamiliar smile taking form on his mouth. "So, what is that whole bean thing about anyhow, Dan?"

"Oh! Uncle Dan," Vaden sighed as she turned, aghast and cranberry, and began frantically dusting the shelves behind the counter.

"You told him about the lima beans, Vay?" Yvonne whispered softly.

"I did no such thing!" Vaden whispered in return, grateful that the men's conversation had turned to other subjects. "Uncle Dan mentioned it."

Vaden tried to look busy as she eavesdropped on her uncle's conversation with Ransom Lake. They talked about boring men type things like the new brand Mr. Lake had registered that morning, and the horses old man Tilits used to raise before he died. Just things men liked to discuss, but Vaden found it interesting if for no other reason than the sound of Ransom Lake's voice was like a soothing breeze across the brook to her senses.

"Well, hey there, Mr. Valmont," Jerome greeted as he entered the mercantile. Vaden sighed heavily and rolled her eyes when she heard his voice and felt Yvonne tug at her sleeve. Slowly she turned around, forcing a smile as Jerome's face immediately lit up at the sight of her. "And to you, too, Mr. Lake. But especially to you two ladies, Miss Yvonne, Miss Vaden."

"Hello, Mr. Clayton," Yvonne greeted gleefully. "And what brings you in so early this morning?"

Vaden wanted to turn and run as Mr. Lake's attention turned to her, his eyebrows raised in obvious mirth at the situation.

"Oh, just thought I'd stop in and thank you all again for the wonderful dinner and company last evening," he answered. Vaden battled the guilt that welled up within her. After all, Jerome was a handsome, charming, polite and perfectly proper young man. But standing there, in the same room with the bearded, rather unkempt looking Ransom Lake, she still preferred the unobtainable to the majority choice.

"You're welcome, Mr. Clayton," Vaden blurted out when Yvonne's elbow met mercilessly with her rib.

"Well, I'll be heading back and let you all visit," Ransom Lake offered as he shook Dan's hand. "Thanks again, Dan." He turned to leave, but paused, turning back to the girls and reaching into his shirt. He drew out a large, golden, perfectly ripened apple and, going to the counter, held it out to Yvonne. "I brought this in for you, Miss Valmont. Your sister got the best one for herself yesterday and I thought you might enjoy one as well, since I'm sure your Aunt Myra has the rest set aside for what she will."

Vaden watched, hot with jealousy, as Yvonne reached out tentatively and took the offered piece of fruit. Vaden also knew that Yvonne was most likely dumbfounded at the fact that Ransom Lake had produced it from within his sleeveless shirt.

"Why...thank you, Mr. Lake," Yvonne said then, and the smile on her face was nothing but sincere delight. Vaden tried to breathe calmly, tried to force into silence the jealous screech that rose in her throat.

Ransom Lake tipped his hat to Yvonne, then started to turn away again. "Oh." He acted as if he'd just remembered something and Vaden's heart beat wildly as his attention turned to her then. "And look here what I found for you, Miss Vaden." He reached into his shirt again and withdrew a perfectly golden, perfectly formed pear. "I thought you might like this, being as how you like to have the best piece of fruit from the highest branch in the tree. I had to climb a ways up to get it, but," he lowered his voice and Vaden fancied that the gray storm in his eyes almost softened as he looked at her, "I'm sure my petticoats weren't nearly as well ironed as yours when I dropped off that pear tree limb." Turning from her, he patted the counter top in front of Dan and said, "Thanks again, Dan. We'll be seeing you, Jerome." He strode out of the store, leaving Vaden's heart pounding madly and Yvonne's eyes as wide as platters as she looked at her sister.

"Petticoats?" Yvonne whispered.

Vaden had no desire to explain the remark to her sister, and, although she was jittery inside to near exploding at the attention received from Ransom Lake, she dove headlong into a conversation with Jerome in order to deter her sister's inquisitiveness.

"We were glad to have you last night, Mr. Clayton," Vaden said, cupping the pear tightly between her hands.

"I...I hope you all will have me over again sometime," Jerome stammered. He seemed uncertain what to think as he stood staring at Vaden.

"Certainly! Auntie loves to show off her good cooking!" Vaden was walking on air. Not even the ever present question of what to do about Jerome Clayton could dampen her mood.

Jerome soon left the store and Uncle Dan went into the back to check some stock. Vaden sighed heavily and bit into the sweet, juicy pear.

"Vaden Valmont!" Yvonne exclaimed instantly. "Aren't you going to wash that piece of fruit off first? After all, think of where it has been!"

"I know," Vaden sighed. "Isn't it just too delightful!"

"Vaden!" Yvonne scolded. "You're...you're..."

"Oh, come on, Yvonne. Go ahead. Bite into that apple that Ransom Lake carried here in his shirt...probably against his bare..."

"Stop it, Vay! You're horrid!" But then a twinkle sparked in Yvonne's eyes and a mischievous smile donned her face. With Vaden enjoying the sweet taste of Ransom Lake's crop, Yvonne bit furiously into her apple.

Late that night, two seeds from a golden pear and its stem joined the contents of the hidden boot under Vaden's bed.

CHAPTER
∽ FOUR ∽

*I*f it hadn't been for the beauty of the season swirling about her, the next several days would've seemed unbearably mundane for Vaden. Fortunately, the autumn flavor in the air, the cool evenings and the majesty of nature's colorful fall wardrobe sustained her delight with life. Oh, how the trees did inspire, their leaves of all colors raining down at each gentle breeze. Vaughn Wimber's pumpkin patch began to fulfill its promise of bounty as the vines began to wither, accentuating the bright orange of the eagerly anticipated squash. And then, on that crisp first day of October, Vaden sensed something rather different in the air. Something rather ominous in character.

Vaden went about her work in the mercantile that day comfortably enough. But all the while an impressive, quiet nagging at the back of her mind gave her thoughts a quantity of distraction. She found herself jittery and startling easily.

Jerome Clayton was in and he spent near to half an hour following Vaden around the store while she busily labored over her chores. Strangely, she was almost glad to have him there for a while that day. He seemed to divert the odd whispering of foreboding in her bosom. And when he'd gone, a strong sense of insecurity began to wash over Vaden as the day further progressed.

Still, there was excitement in the day suddenly when, just after lunch, Vaden turned and looked up from the counter to see Ransom Lake enter the store.

"It's Mr. Male Anatomy himself," Yvonne whispered quietly to Vaden, who jabbed her sister in the ribcage with an elbow.

"Good afternoon, Mr. Lake," Vaden greeted nervously. Every inch of her body was tingling with elation. He simply nodded and continued to stand just inside the doorway, looking about the room as if he himself was wondering why he had stepped into the building.

"Can we help you find something today, Mr. Lake?" Yvonne ventured. Ransom Lake only looked at her frowning, his turbulent gray eyes glaring intently at her.

Vaden was irritated that the man should be staring so at Yvonne. She did not like his attention being quite so settled on her sister. Soon enough, however, the stormy gaze of Ransom Lake moved to Vaden. He turned and looked back directly out the door and then back to Vaden who stood just before the counter and parallel with the open door of the mercantile.

Ransom Lake again looked back briefly and when he finally addressed the two young women there was an air of confusion in his voice. "I...I, uh...only came in to see if your uncle is here. I...I, uh...wanted to speak with him about...some things."

"He's gone down to Mrs. Tilits with Aunt Myra. She's feeling poorly and with the changes in the weather..." Yvonne explained.

"What's the matter, Mr. Lake?" Vaden asked boldly. She looked beyond him for a moment to see a group of small boys playing outside in the street in front of the store. "You seem a bit..."

In that very next instant Ransom Lake glanced back out the mercantile door once more before quickly lunging forward, taking Vaden's shoulders brutally between his powerful hands.

"Move, girl!" he shouted a split second before Yvonne screamed as the repeat of a rifle split the calm quiet. Unable to comprehend immediately what had transpired, Vaden could only watch, dazed and helpless, as she saw the face of Ransom Lake wince before he fell forward, his masculine weight knocking her back against the counter, his head hitting the corner of the same counter with inordinate force before his large body crumpled to the floor.

Instantly a great commotion erupted outside, but Vaden cared nothing for the goings on in the street. Falling to her knees, she gasped when she saw the bright red, moist stain saturating the back of Ransom Lake's shirt at his shoulder. But, even as she struggled to roll the heavy man to his back, she knew that his head hitting the counter could've caused an even worse injury. Every fiber of her own body had ached with pain for him when she had heard the force with which his head had collided with the object. The blood was already matting his hair at his forehead and she tried to brush it aside in order to inspect the wound. A large cut was apparent outwardly, but she wondered if the impact had damaged him worse inside his head where she could not see.

"Don't stand there with your mouth gaping open, Yvonne!" Vaden shouted, looking up to her sister who stood staring down at her in horror. "Run get the doctor!"

"But...but there's gunfire out there, Vaden!" Yvonne was obviously rattled. She stood wringing her hands nervously.

"Go! Look at all the people in the street! Do you think they'd be out there if wasn't safe now? Hurry up!" After only a moment's pause, Yvonne dashed from the store. Vaden felt the tears escape her eyes and begin to travel down her cheeks as she dabbed at Mr. Lake's wounded head with her apron.

"What happened in here?" a man asked as he burst into the store. It was Pete Davis who owned a farm just west of town. His gaze was immediately drawn to the man that lay on the floor. "I saw Miss Valmont in the street and..."

"Someone has shot Mr. Lake!" Vaden cried out. "Help me! I don't know what to do."

Mr. Davis hunkered down beside the girl and looked at Ransom Lake. "Well, he's breathing. Those kids oughta be shot themselves for playin' with guns the like."

"What do you mean?" Vaden asked, sniffling.

"Well, a couple of young boys was playing with a rifle 'cross the street in the alley. It must've gone off before they knowed what hit 'em. Though they're denyin' it like sin."

"It would've hit *me*," Vaden whispered. "I was standing there, against the counter, and suddenly Mr. Lake moved toward me and told me to move. The bullet hit him instead of me."

"Well, child...I don't mean to sound heartless...but a tough old bear like Ransom Lake will survive it a lot easier than you would've."

"Mr. Davis!" Vaden exclaimed, wiping the tears from her face with the back of her hand. "How can you say that?"

"Because it's true. I'm more worried about that cut on his head. Did he hit himself fallin', or what? The bullet wound ain't deep in him. But it ain't a good sign that he's still out cold."

Vaden looked down again to the wounded man who lay before her. She shook her head as the tears increased. "No," she whispered out loud. It couldn't be! Surely it couldn't be her fault that he was so hurt. Taking one of his large hands in her own, she stroked the back of it gently. "He'll be fine. He'll be fine. It was as if...as if he knew it was going to happen," she mumbled to herself as she replayed the incident in her mind. Yes. It was just as if he knew. He had acted so confused and uncertain when he had first entered the store. And he kept looking back out the door like he was expecting to see something there. A cold shiver quickly traveled through Vaden as she stared down at the unconscious man. At the closed, still eyes that hid the stormy gray which mesmerized her so.

"The bullet wound is not my concern, Dan," Doctor Sullivan told Dan Valmont. Vaden stood in the doorway of the spare bedroom in the Valmont home listening intently. "He obviously has a severe head injury, else he'd be conscious by now. I don't want to move him, as I said before. And with everyone in town that is down with illness...I can't be here. You're certain your girls don't mind tending to Mr. Lake until he wakes up or...or..." Dr. Sullivan looked to Vaden's frightened eyes. "Until he wakes up?"

"Of course they don't mind, John. We'll all help the boy. I just can't believe this. Shot and wounded in my own store." Uncle Dan wore an unfamiliar frown across his weathered face. He and Aunt Myra had under-standably been horrified when they had arrived home to find Yvonne and Vaden both in tears and Ransom Lake, shot and unconscious, in their spare bedroom. Uncle Dan looked to Vaden then and, nodding, reaffirmed, "He's a good man to step in front of you like that, sweet pea."

Vaden's voice was lost in her emotions so she only nodded and wiped a tear that had traveled to her chin.

"Come to bed for pity's sake, Vay," Yvonne said quietly from the door-way late that evening. Vaden only continued to sit in the chair at Ransom Lake's bedside, staring down at him.

"It's my fault, Vonnie," Vaden replied softly.

"No. It's not." Yvonne glided quietly into the room, reached down and hugged her sister affectionately. "It's the fault of those silly children that were playing with a weapon. And I'm sure Mr. Lake will be fine. He'll be up and about in no time and you can resume your endless curiosities about him. Now, come along to bed. You need your rest. You don't want him waking up and seeing you all baggy-eyed and pale, now do you?"

Vaden smiled at her sister and shook her head. "Is there never any other concern to you other than your appearance?"

"Never," Yvonne giggled.

And so Vaden did take to her bed. But she awoke every hour or so all through that first night, tiptoeing quietly into the spare room to check on Ransom Lake. To make sure that he did not have fever. To make sure that he was there. That he was there and still alive.

Vaden was fidgety the next morning as she tended the mercantile. She only wanted to be with Ransom Lake, to sit next to him in case he should wake and need something. She was preoccupied when customers entered and needed help, but when Jerome Clayton came in she was somehow so irritated that the emotion replaced her constant concern for a moment. He set a small box on the counter greeting, "How are you fairing today, Miss Vaden?"

"How am I fairing? Didn't you hear? It's my fault," she whispered emotionally, putting a hand to her bosom to stop her heart's ache.

"What? You mean what happened to Ransom Lake?" Jerome took Vaden's shoulders between his hands and looked determinedly into her eyes. She shivered at his touch. Not a pleasant shiver the like she experienced whenever Ransom Lake appeared. Rather a disagreeable one. "It was no fault of yours, Miss Vaden. None of it. Accidents happen and this was just that…an accident." Vaden shook her head in difference. "How is he doing, anyway?" Jerome asked.

"He's still unconscious. The doctor says he can't tell how badly he may be hurt from knocking his head on the counter. I just feel so responsible, Mr. Clayton. The bullet would've hit me…he protected me and if he's terribly wounded…I'll…I'll just…"

Suddenly Jerome pulled Vaden into his arms, embracing her tenderly as tears escaped her eyes. He stroked her hair softly and spoke quietly saying, "Now, this wasn't your fault, Vaden. Not at all. He'll be fine. He's as tough as horse meat." Vaden pushed away immediately, wiping at her tears.

"Look here," Jerome began as he reached for the small box he'd set on the counter top. "Look what I brung you. This oughta cheer you up right nice." Handing her the box, he smiled and waited for her to open it. Vaden didn't feel much like receiving a gift and having to thank anyone graciously for it, but she opened the small box to find it filled with pieces of molasses taffy. "My mama pulled taffy yesterday and I thought you might like to try some. The sweetness will cheer you a bit," Jerome asserted.

Vaden smiled, for it was a thoughtful gift. "Thank you, Mr. Clayton. And thank your mother. I'm certain this will help to take my mind off the fact that Mr. Lake is lying in our spare room near to death. And all because of me." She brushed another tear from her eye.

"Now, you call me Jerome, first of all, Miss Vaden. And quit blaming yourself for..."

"Well, you *should* feel very thankful that he wasn't killed on your behalf," Belva Tibbits snapped as she entered the mercantile, obviously having overheard the last bits of conversation. Raylin was with her and immediately went to Vaden's defense.

"Really, Belva. You know it was no fault of Vaden's." Raylin smiled reassuringly at Vaden. "Besides, Doctor Sullivan said the bullet might have been fatal for Vaden if it had hit her. Mr. Lake will be all right. I'm certain of it." Vaden smiled at Raylin in thanks for her encouragement.

"I certainly hope so. I wouldn't want to be the one to walk around with his death on my head for the rest of my life," Belva mumbled as she glared hatefully at Vaden.

"Belva," Jerome began. Vaden looked to him and could tell that he was angry. The whites of his eyes were reddened and his hands clutched into fists at his sides. "First of all, the bullet wouldn't have killed Vaden. She's...she's too strong a woman for that. And anyway I, for one, think it would be an honor to take a bullet for her. I certainly wouldn't think the same of the likes of you," he growled.

Belva gasped indignantly, glared once more at Vaden and said, "I won't stand here and be insulted! I'll just tell mother that she can come into the mercantile and fill her own list!" She turned to leave, snapping at Raylin, "Come along, Raylin. I've been utterly insulted in this establishment and I won't stay another moment."

"You did the insulting, Belva. Go on home by yourself," Raylin told her.

Belva's bosom rose and fell dramatically with her angry breathing and, shooting another hateful look at Vaden, she did take her leave.

"She twists my patience sometimes, I'll tell you that for sure," Jerome muttered, sighing relievedly himself.

"You two are dear friends to defend me so. But she is right. If he hadn't been trying to…" Vaden began.

"Hello, all," Yvonne greeted upon entering from the back room. She took one look at her younger sister and sighed sympathetically. "Vay, why don't you go on back and sit down for a spell. I'll watch the store now."

Vaden *did* feel the need to escape, so she thanked Yvonne for offering and turned to leave. "Thank you for standing up for me, Raylin. And you too, Mr. Clayton."

"Jerome," he corrected.

Vaden forced a friendly smile. "And do thank your mother for the taffy. I'm sure it'll make me feel all the better," she lied.

Vaden went directly to the room where Ransom Lake slept. She sat down promptly in the chair next to the bed and began wringing her hands. "Oh, please wake up. Open those stormy eyes of yours and comfort me with knowing you're all right," she whispered. She covered her mouth with one hand as she tried to extinguish the sobs that wanted release. After a moment, she drew in a deep breath and tried to calm herself once more. "You'll be fine," she whispered, taking the man's large hand in her own. "You'll be fine." She raised his hand, studying it for a moment. She caressed the calluses formed by hard labor that were on his palms and thought of their picking a certain, and very beloved, golden pear from an upper tree branch. This was his left hand and she knew he had picked the pear for her with it. She lifted his hand to her face, laying her cheek on its back as she thought of the way he had held the lines to his team that first day she had seen him. She studied the small gold band that was on his little finger. It was simple. Just a small band of gold. But, being the curious cat that Vaden was, it piqued her interest suddenly. Ransom Lake, for all other outward appearances, did not seem the type of man for jewelry. A split second of anxiety coursed through her veins as she thought it might be a wedding band! Perhaps he had been or, dreadfully, was married. But that thought quickly eliminated itself, for it would have been on his ring finger were that the case. At least, that seemed the logical assumption to Vaden.

Then, looking about to make certain that no one else had entered the room, she tugged at the ring on Ransom Lake's finger, finding it a difficult task to remove the band. But after a moment of tugging and twisting during which she watched his face closely should he choose that particular moment to awaken, the ring did slip off and Vaden laid the small band in the palm of her hand to study it. It was definitely a woman's ring she determined, for it was small and reminded her of her own mother's wedding band. As she looked inside the small golden loop she could see the remnants of an inscription. But, try as she might, she couldn't make out all of the letters, though she did discern what seemed to be a name.

"D - A - R - L - I - N...Darlin?" she whispered to herself. Could it have been "Darling" she wondered? She looked at the expressionless features of the man lying before her. "Darling?" she whispered again. Could Ransom Lake's hermithood have been sparked by the loss of a wife? It bothered her to think of Ransom Lake having been married to another woman. To think of him loving another woman, holding her in his arms, giving her his heart. But it would be a possible explanation for his cringing from society as he appeared to be doing.

Gently she returned the ring to his finger, then bent until her lips were close to his ear. She could smell the lingering aroma of lye soap on his skin. No doubt Aunt Myra had bathed his neck and arms when the doctor had been attending to him. Quietly she whispered, "Who is the Darling that owned the ring, Ransom Lake?" He remained motionless. "Who is the Darling? Are you married? Were you married? Is the Darling your wife?"

Vaden startled violently when from the lips of the sleeping man broke the word, "No." It was only a breath, but very distinct.

Placing a calming hand to her bosom to try and steady her breathing again, she asked, "Mr. Lake? Are you conscious? Are you awake?" There came no answer and the man remained unmoved. His eyelids did not flinch, his breathing remained as steady as it had been before. Vaden shook her head. Had he heard all she had said to him? Was his mind alert though he remained unconscious outwardly? Vaden sat beside him for a long while, waiting for something, anything. Any sign that he would be well.

When Aunt Myra called for her to come join her in the mercantile, Vaden first went to the wardrobe where her aunt had asked her to hang Mr. Lake's trousers and shirt after they had been laundered. She had noticed a loose button at the collar when he had first been lying on the bed, his blood soaking the cloth of the shirt at the shoulder. How odd that she should notice a loose button at that particular moment. Quickly she pulled the button from the shirt and dropped it into her apron pocket. The least she could do was sew the button back on the shirt properly, she thought. But as the day wore into the night, Vaden found herself finally tucking the button from Ransom Lake's shirt into the boot under her bed.

"I'm a thief, Vonnie," she confessed to her sleeping sister as they lay in their beds in the dark of the night. She wondered on the ring and the woman who had worn it. Who was she? What had she meant to Ransom Lake? Her mind hurt from the wondering, but eventually she was able to sleep until morning.

Vaden wrung the water from the cloth and into the basin, but as she moved to place the cloth on Ransom Lake's forehead she paused, thinking to herself that, although he was not conscious, it might be soothing to his body were she to gently wipe his face and neck with the cloth. But after having done so she realized that it could have done little good for him because so much of his face was covered with his heavy beard.

Yvonne came into the room and asked, "How is he? Still unconscious? It's been two days. How much longer does Doctor Sullivan think it will be?"

Vaden shrugged her shoulders. "I don't know." She studied the man's face for a moment. "I wonder what he looks like under all those whiskers," she whispered to her sister. She'd been wondering the same thing since the day she'd first seen him. But now, with him before her for two days, unmoving and seeming unaware of what was going on around him, Vaden's curiosity was enormous. She'd had hours to stare at him, study him, imagine what he might look like and it was eating at her voraciously.

"Probably worse," Yvonne answered quietly. "I swear, I sit here anticipating his eyes just popping open and that odd color of them stopping my heart cold. His gaze is so...so..."

"Mesmerizing," Vaden stated.

"Terrifying is more like it."

"But...I do wonder, Vonnie. What *does* he really look like? It's impossible to tell through that forest of facial hair." Vaden tried to bury the thought that was springing forcefully to her mind. But it was too intriguing. Too easy to do with Ransom Lake in his present state. Quickly she stood up and went to the dressing table nearby. "Hurry, Vonnie. Boil some water for me and get a couple of extra towels."

"Vaden," Yvonne warned. "You're not actually planning to..."

"How do we ever expect the man to recover unless he's completely comfortable?" Vaden asked as she gathered her uncle's spare shaving soap and mug, brush and razor from the table.

"Vaden! You can't! You can't just..."

"Hurry, Vonnie. Before he wakes up. Aren't you just the least bit curious, too?"

Yvonne drew in a deep breath and released it slowly. "You take the punishment, Vaden. I'll not be on the receiving end of his wrath when he wakes up."

"I will," Vaden promised. "I will. It will be worth anything he throws at me."

Some thirty minutes later the two sister's sat astounded as they stared down at the freshly shaven and astonishingly handsome face of Ransom Lake.

"Oh, my...oh, my!" breathed Yvonne. "You never would've known that he looked so...so...that he looked like that!"

"I knew he would," Vaden admitted as she studied him meticulously. He was far and away more attractive than even she had imagined, however. His jaw was strong and square, a slight cleft in his chin. His cheek bones showed strength and the set of his lips was perfect. He was, without a hint of doubt, the most physically attractive man she had ever imagined. Vaden began to fear him opening his eyes, for she was assured now that the fully revealed magnificence of his face combined with the intensity of his unusually shaded eyes would melt her into oblivion. She reached out, smoothing the hair from his forehead. "All he needs now is a barber's trim."

Yvonne shook her head emphatically. "No, Vaden. He'll probably devour us as it is! No."

Vaden smiled as she twisted a long, ebony strand of his hair about her index finger. "It would be too awkward anyway," she conceded. She released the strand of his hair immediately when a frown suddenly puckered his handsome brow.

"Oh, my gosh!" Yvonne gasped. "He's waking up!"

But Vaden shook her head. "No, he's just...Yvonne. Look."

Vaden watched as a single tear escaped from the corner of his right eye and traveled slowly down his temple.

The crimson of the blood seemed to stain every vision in Ransom Lake's mind. "Not again," the unconscious man's soul pled with his memory.

But it came then. The all too familiar vision, accompanied by the soul wrenching emotional pain, played itself out again in the mind of Ransom Lake as he lay unconscious. The smell was there. The smell of wounded flesh, of blood, of death, of fire and of guilt. He tried to shout in anguish, but no sound could escape his throat.·

"Is...is he in pain do you think?" Yvonne asked.

Something in Vaden's young heart whispered to her then and she answered, "Not from the wound, I don't think." She reached out and caught his tear on her finger placing it gently on her own cheek where her own tears had all too recently been. "Do you think," she asked Yvonne, "do you think he's like Sleeping Beauty, Vonnie? Only a prince instead of a princess? Do you think that he'd wake up and fall in love with me if I kissed him?"

Yvonne moaned and rolled her eyes exasperatedly. "Really, Vaden. You do beat anything else in the world." And, standing up, having tired of her sister's infatuation with the unconscious man before her, she left the room.

Vaden giggled. It was ever so fun to try to provoke a reaction from Yvonne. She enjoyed it immensely. Yvonne did have such difficulty most of the time trying to discern whether or not Vaden was in earnest or jest. But, as another solitary tear escaped Ransom Lakes eye, Vaden's smile faded. She reached out, smoothing the frown from his strong brow gently with her fingertips, and the thought struck her again. Only not as an irritant directed at Yvonne this time.

"Would you, I wonder," she whispered softly. "Would it wake you, Ransom Lake?" Then simply being in the room alone with the man wove a spell of emotional intrigue over her. "*'Tis Heaven's sweet when lips are meet, A nectar most divine,*" she whispered to herself, studying the heaven formed feature of the man who lay before her. "*Two hearts inspire a passion's fire, resplendent kiss...is thine.*" Taking a deep breath in searching for her courage,

Vaden bent and placed a gentle, yet lingering kiss on the quiet lips of Ransom Lake. His lips were unexpectedly soft. She had expected them to be rough somehow. And, though there seemed to be nothing conscious about him, Vaden perceived an enchantingly peculiar warmth permeate her being at having felt of his lips to hers. An excited flutter caused her to shiver suddenly and she broke from him, studying his unflinching features for a moment. He exhibited no reaction of any sort and she sighed, somehow relieved. No doubt the man would be furious when he awoke to find himself shaven. It would've been all the worse were he to have awakened to find himself the unwilling recipient of such a gesture. With a heavy sigh and a warmth in her heart and on her lips that she'd never experienced, Vaden whispered, "*Resplendent kiss...is thine,*" and left the man to his rest.

"Is he still sleeping?" Aunt Myra asked as Vaden entered the mercantile.

"I'm afraid so," Vaden answered, blushing suddenly at the realization of what she had only just done. She scolded herself for taking such a liberty as to kiss an unconscious man. To be so forthright in initiating the kissing of a man at all, for that matter. Yet, she smiled, too, as the feel of his lips lingered in her mind. What a delightful secret she held.

"Well, the Wimber children are here for a story as you can see, sweet pea." Aunt Myra pointed to the group of children sitting quietly in one corner. "You go on ahead and give them a tale. I'm running out to the shed to fetch your uncle, so mind the store while you're at it, all right?"

As the minutes passed and Vaden wove her tale of heroes and princesses, the children were enthralled as always. Vaden loved to see the expressions that crossed their young faces during a storytelling. She'd always held a secreted pride in her uncanny ability to weave a wondrous tale. She smiled, delighted by their now enraptured expressions as she continued with her story.

"'*Try to spin, my dear,*'" she whispered. "'*Try,*' the evil fairy whispered to the princess. '*Spin. Spin the wheel, love.*'" Vaden cackled in an old crone's voice and giggled a moment when the children's eyes all widened in horrified anticipation. "And then...the princess did, ever so lightly, touch the spindle of the spinning wheel, pricking her lovely finger. '*Ouch*' the princess cried. '*Oh, help me, old woman! I've pricked my finger and suddenly...suddenly I feel ...*' The old woman laughed evilly as the princess crumpled to the floor in a sleep so deep as to resemble death." Vaden put her hand to her forehead and swooned gracefully to the floor. "The good fairies came at once to the lovely princess' side and laid her tenderly on a bed of purple velvets and ivory laces." Vaden unpinned her hair, letting it lay about her as she stretched out on the floor before the children. She closed her eyes for dramatic effect, crossing her hands over her bosom. "Then the good fairies flittered hither and yon putting the entire kingdom to sleep so that all would be near, familiar faces who loved the young princess, should a handsome prince ever find her and break the spell she was under. And so she slept. The lovely princess on her bed of purple velvets and ivory laces. She slept as years and years floated past like the sands in an hour glass. Roses bloomed 'round the bed. Beautiful white and fragrant roses and the dust dared not settle on one so lovely as the princess who was sleeping for eternity." Vaden sighed heavily and paused, peering through the slit of one barely opened eye at the emotionally overwrought faces of the children as they waited.

"And...and she slept always?" Violet asked.

"She slept for years and years. Decades and eons until early one autumn day...a day just like this...a dashing prince...the like that had never walked the earth before...handsome and strong was he...she slept until that lovely autumn day when the prince of her dreams was riding by the old castle and curiosity led him into it. He searched each room, seeming driven by some force that only his heart could understand." Vaden's eyes remained closed, her hands motionless at her bosom. "Then, in the very last room to which the prince's heart led him...he saw her. The most beautiful woman he had ever imagined...lying on a delicate bed of purple velvets and ivory laces. '*What magic is this?*' the handsome prince muttered to himself. '*What fairies pure have kept such a creature hidden from the world?*' Then...he went to stand beside her bed and in a moment he dropped to his knees, overcome with sudden and absolute love and passion for the beautiful princess before him."

"What's passion, Miss Vaden?" Violet inquired innocently.

"Um...passion is...well it's like love," Vaden stammered, not wanting to explain the deep meaning of the word. "'*Forgive me, beauty that lies before me,*' the prince whispered softly to the sleeping beauty. '*Forgive my indiscretion...but I must taste of your berry red lips. I must...for my soul has searched for you always and I love you.*'" Vaden smiled slightly when she heard the girls giggle delightedly. "And then," she continued in a near whisper as she lay on the mercantile floor. The children leaned forward on their hands and knees, their eyes wide with anticipation. "And then, he bent and kissed her ever so sweetly as she lay before him, ever lovely on her bed of purple velvets and ivory laces." Vaden placed her own fingertips to her lips kissing them briefly before letting her hand float gracefully into the air. "And as the handsome prince, dark-haired and brave, gazed into the face of his beautiful, nameless love, her eyelashes fluttered a moment before she opened them to see before her her own true beloved as he appeared that very..." Vaden gasped and pulled herself immediately into a sitting position, for as she had opened her own eyes in telling the tale of the sleeping beauty she had found that none other than the handsome, dark-haired and brave Ransom Lake stood looming over her, glaring down furiously.

"Mr. Lake!" Vaden exclaimed in a whisper, for his eyes were as gray and tumultuous as thunder clouds.

"Miss Vaden," he growled. "Would you be able to explain to me how I came to wake up in your aunt's house to find myself completely shaved of my beard?"

Vaden struggled to her feet and stood to face him. But her mouth only gaped open, silent with guilt. He had obviously found his clothes in the wardrobe, for he stood before her dressed in his trousers, his shirt hanging open, and Vaden was glad that he had not chosen to storm out to confront her in only his underthings.

"Let me put it to you another way then," he continued when she did not answer. His chest rose and fell heavily and Vaden knew he was wrathful as he fairly bellowed, "Why in thunderation did you take it on yourself to shave away my whiskers?"

"I...I...thought it might make you feel more comfortable," Vaden stammered.

"Missy, I think I'm a good enough judge of what makes me comfortable and what doesn't!" he informed her, raising the volume of his voice dramatically.

"I'm...I'm sorry, Mr. Lake," Vaden apologized, smiling reassuringly at the children as the entire group suddenly stood and exited the store like the building itself was aflame. "Truly...I was only trying to help you to rest more comfortably. Are you...are you feeling yourself again? You look just as hearty as ever. The color has returned to your face and..."

"Yes. I'm feeling hearty as you put it. But I'm afraid I've seen one too many of your antics, Miss Vaden. You shaved me to see what I looked like under my whiskers. It was your curiosity getting the better of you that finds me this way. Pure and simple. And I'll take a minute to remind you that it was curiosity that killed the kitty, miss."

"I simply wanted to refreshen you, Mr. Lake. A feat of impossibility with such an accumulation of whiskers," Vaden argued in defense of herself. "Therefore, and I've said my apologies...I'm sorry if it has disturbed you. And besides...you are a handsome enough man, Mr. Lake. I can't for the life of me understand why you've been hiding under that mess of a hairy thicket for so long."

"Handsome?" he muttered as if he could not believe what she had said. "You've heard the old saying, Miss Vaden...never to judge a book by its cover." He glared resentfully at her. "I assume it's been Doc Sullivan that's been tending to me. Tell him I'm up and about and fine, and I've gone home." Then he turned, storming furiously out of the store.

Vaden stood where she was for a moment trying to calm her nerves and repinning her hair. Several thoughts battled within the confines of her head. The first being that Ransom Lake was far too attractive! How unkind of the heavens to put such a handsome, astoundingly attractive man on the earth to make beat wildly the hearts of women! Beneath the mass of beard and mustache had been hidden an utter, classic work of art. It just wasn't fair to send a girl's heart racing so.

The second thought that rushed back and forth in her brain was that it was horrid to have him so angry with her. But, after all, what had she expected? She knew he would be furious, but at the time that she and Yvonne had shaved him and found themselves gazing down at perfection in masculinity, that particular concern had not mattered to her in the least. Now, however, she felt differently. She'd vexed Ransom Lake too often already and she knew that this was something he viewed as unforgivable. Third, that she had been lying on the floor, her hair strewn everywhere, her eyes closed and telling a fairy tale to small children was yet another mortifying fact! What he must have thought when he entered the mercantile to find her in such a state.

With a heavy sigh of humiliation and discouragement, Vaden forced herself to finish a few chores in the store.

"He's up? You mean to tell me he just up and walked out of here like nobody's business?" Yvonne squealed, having returned with Aunt Myra and Uncle Dan and heard Vaden's announcement that Ransom Lake was gone.

"I...I think he's had enough of folks being in his business," Vaden answered pointedly to her sister.

Yvonne's eyes widened in understanding and she mouthed, "I told you so."

"Well, I'm sure he was plum irritated to be down in the first place." Uncle Dan just shook his head as if the whole incident was quite trivial.

"Dan. The man is wounded." Myra scolded.

"He wouldn't have left if he didn't have the mind and strength to." All three women looked to Dan in disbelief at his lightheartedness toward the issue at hand. "Girls, all three of you...Ransom Lake's a tough ol' bird. I'm sure he just wanted to get on home."

Aunt Myra's mouth gaped open and she shook her head. "Men," was all she said.

"Was he quite infuriated?" Yvonne asked sometime later when Uncle Dan and Aunt Myra had gone out on an errand.

"Does the wrath of Zeus himself mean anything to you?" Vaden replied. "He was furious! I swear, if I were a man, I think he would've beat me to a pulp!"

"I knew it! I knew it! You should've let him be, Vaden."

"No," Vaden sighed, smiling. The twinkle in her eyes was as bright as the sun itself. "It was worth it. If he never speaks to me again, I think it was worth it. He's heaven embodied, Yvonne. Admit it to me."

Yvonne fought a smile, but her mouth won over her will and the grin spread across her face mischievously. "It was worth it. Anyway, he'll still talk to me."

"Ha, ha," Vaden sneered.

Later that same eventful day Aunt Myra sent Vaden on an errand to deliver a shipment of hair tonic that had arrived at the store. Mr. Polowsky, the barber, had ordered it through Aunt Myra some weeks before and Myra knew he would be in a hurry to receive it.

"Run it over for me, Vaden, please. He's probably simply desperate for it by now," Aunt Myra explained, handing three large bottles of the stuff to her niece.

Still greatly unsettled from being reprimanded so harshly by Ransom Lake, Vaden walked toward the barber's building rather nervously. She felt as if everyone she passed was aware of her vile deed against Ransom Lake, though she knew that no one could possibly know of it.

"Good afternoon, Mr. Polowsky," Vaden greeted as she entered the building. She noticed that a customer sat tilted back in the barber's chair nearest the door, a steaming towel covering his face. Mr. Polowsky was busily snipping away at a young Wimber boy's hair. The boy squirmed almost constantly and Vaden could see the frustration clearly on the barber's face. "Your shipment came in on the stage today and Aunt Myra sent me over."

The man clearly had his hands full, so Vaden began looking about for a place to set the heavy bottles. "Just there, Miss Vaden," Mr. Polowsky directed, motioning to a nearby shelf. "Just set them down and tell your aunt thank you for me."

"There," Vaden sighed, depositing the bottles on the indicated shelf. The small, redheaded boy in the chair began to bounce up and down, annoying Mr. Polowsky further. "You sit still for Mr. Polowsky, Ronald, or I won't finish the story I started today for you next time." The young boy nodded at Vaden and smiled. "You've certainly got your hands full today," Vaden called to Mr. Polowsky as she took several steps backward toward the door, still watching the irate barber battling with the boy. "I wouldn't want to be in your shoes that's for...oh!" Vaden felt her foot catch on something behind her. Before she could even attempt to regain her balance, she was tumbling helplessly backward. She tripped again, this time on the barber's chair closest to the door, and landed solidly in the lap of the man who sat there.

"Ooof!" the man breathed as Vaden's tender seat landed squarely in his lap.

"Oh!" Vaden gasped, reflexively reaching out and taking hold of the man's arm in order to stop herself from toppling completely backward and onto the floor. "Forgive me I..." she apologized. But when the warmed towel fell from the man's face as he sat erect, she gasped as she found herself gazing once again into the tempestuous eyes of Ransom Lake.

The disturbingly attractive man scowled angrily at her, drew in a deep, calming breath, took hold of her arms and pushed her rather roughly from his lap. He was astounding to look at! Vaden could only stand staring at him as he removed himself from the chair and stood before her. "You will be the death of me yet, girl," he growled. Vaden's eyes widened, for she was simply mesmerized by his appearance. His hair had been cut to a neat and smart length and it only served to emphasize his already inconceivably appealing appearance.

"You...you cut your hair," she mumbled.

Ransom Lake's eyebrows rose from a frown to their normal position and he said, "You've taken my beard from me, you little Delilah. I figure I may as well go the whole way as Samson did. And, like I said, you'll be the death of me. I'm starting to believe that. You didn't even have the compassion to take proper care of my face after you stole my whiskers. My face hasn't seen the sun in near to ten years and now it's sore as a mule's behind from razor burn." Then, turning to Mr. Polowsky, he mumbled, "Thank you, Dale." Taking his hat from the hatrack near the door, he looked to Vaden once more, shaking his head disapprovingly before storming off.

After watching Ransom Lake walk a ways down the street, every person he passed understandably gawking at him, Vaden turned to find Mr. Polowsky staring at her with raised eyebrows.

"He needed a shave," she stated. "Don't you agree?"

Mr. Polowsky only shook his head as if he hadn't heard her correctly and returned to his redheaded task at hand. With a heavy sigh, Vaden left Mr. Polowsky's shop and started home. No sooner had she passed the next building, however, when she was bombarded with the attention of Belva, Selma and Raylin.

"Did you see that?" Raylin squealed, taking hold of Vaden's arm. "Did you see that dream of a man that just went walking on by down the road?"

"Yes. I saw him," Vaden answered bluntly, for it only at that moment came to her realization that in having shaved Ransom Lake for her own curious purposes, she had exposed his superb grandeur of physical feature to all the world. Now, every woman for miles around would be pining away after him. She scolded herself inwardly for giving into the temptation and shaving his face. Before she had done it, he had been hers. Yes, Belva, too, had been intrigued by him, but for the most part people had kept their distance from Ransom Lake. Now, it would be different. Painfully different.

"I knew he'd be handsome under all that mess," Belva whispered.

"But did you see that? Sakes alive! He's...he's...unbelievable!" Selma sighed.

"I shaved him," Vaden blurted out. She couldn't stand their not knowing. Her pitiful ego had to divulge the information. It had to let the other girls know that she had been the first to lay eyes on his astounding appearance.

"What do you mean by that?" Belva spat.

"While he was unconscious in my uncle's house. I thought...I thought he might be more comfortable after a shave." Vaden returned Belva's glare, though she could not match the hatred in it.

"What's going on, ladies?" Jerome asked as he and Nathaniel approached.

"You have got to see Ransom Lake, Nate." Raylin squealed. "You won't believe it! He's all shaven, short hair and walking around town like it's nobody's business."

"It is nobody's business," Belva spat. "You all treat him like some freak at a circus. Worst of all you, Vaden Valmont. I've no doubt he thinks you're the biggest nosy rosy busybody in town. Imagine! Taking such familiarities with a man. A convalescing man at that. You had better think twice about this girl, Jerome. Hard telling what she'll try to pull on you."

"What in tarnation are you going on about, Belva?" Jerome asked irritatedly.

"I'm going home," Vaden choked as the tears rose to her eyes. "I'm just going home."

"Miss Vaden?" Jerome reached out and smoothed Vaden's forehead, moving a stray strand of her hair away from her eyes. "What's going on?"

"Let Belva tell you. She thinks she knows everything. I'm certain the story will me much more exciting and degrading to me in her words." With that she turned and fled toward the mercantile.

It did not take long for the gossip to begin about the newly revealed Ransom Lake. By the very next morning townsfolk were coming into the store in droves to quiz Vaden and Yvonne, Uncle Dan and Aunt Myra and whoever else may have seen the shaven hermit.

"They say he's better lookin' than some of them Greek gods were supposed to have been," Sue Ellen Wimber told her sister-in-law as they stood chatting with Myra in the store.

"I've seen him! He's...it's unimaginable why a man that looks like that would hide away like he's been doin'!" another woman said.

"Oh, he's plain as mud," Jerome Clayton argued as he and some other young men entered the store.

"You're just afraid of a little competition, old man," Nathaniel teased his friend.

"Ransom Lake ain't no competition, boys," Jerome assured him. "Miss Vaden, you were the first to see him. Is he as all fired good looking as everyone says he is?"

Vaden cleared her throat. Every set of eyes in the store was intent upon her as the people of the town waited for her answer. Jerome's eyes narrowed and Vaden knew he was irritated about the whole matter.

"He's extraordinarily handsome," she stated. Then as the hot blush began to rise to her cheeks she added, "Excuse me," as she walked through the crowd of people, out the front door and into the street.

Yvonne was quickly at her heels, knowing well the signs of her sister being upset. "Vaden? What's wrong?" she asked.

Vaden paused and turned to face her sister. Yvonne was disturbed when she saw tears brimming in Vaden's eyes. "Nobody cares that he was shot right there in the mercantile only a couple of days ago, Vonnie! All they care about is what he looks like and...and...they're going to hound him and his privacy will be completely destroyed because of me! I'll be surprised if he doesn't grind me into the ground with the heel of his boot."

As understanding enveloped Yvonne she smiled affectionately at her sister. "I'm sure that Mr. Lake will not blame you for that. I had no idea that you were so completely in love with him, Vay. Why didn't you tell me how desperate you were toward him?"

Vaden's indignant expression answered Yvonne's question even before her voice did. "I am not in love with him! And, anyway, I'm entirely certain that you wouldn't have understood why I found myself in this...this...obsessive curiosity where the indecorous town hermit is concerned."

Yvonne cast her eyes guiltily to the ground for a moment before putting a comforting arm about her sister's shoulders. "Forgive me. I've been totally insensitive as of late. Forgive me, darling."

"That was quite a blunt answer you gave in there," Jerome stated, coming out of the store and approaching the girls.

"A forthright answer to a forthright question," Vaden explained rather sharply. She had no desire to deal with Jerome at that particular moment.

"Well, let me just tell you this..." Jerome took hold of Vaden's arm rather roughly as he continued commandingly. "An old goat like Ransom Lake ain't no competition to me."

"How dare you speak to me in such a tone, Jerome Clayton?" Vaden snatched her arm from his grasp, rubbing its sudden soreness and glaring up at him.

"Don't you handle my sister like that!" Yvonne scolded.

Jerome seemed to ignore her and continued to glare at Vaden as his chest rose and fell heavily with withheld anger. "He's probably twice your age. Probably hiding from the law or some woman he done wrong."

"I knew it," Vaden said calmly, looking at him with complete distaste. "You're like everyone else around here. Judge, jury and executioner. I knew you weren't any different from all the other old gossips in town." She despised Jerome Clayton at that moment. How dare he speak so of Ransom Lake? How dare he?

"I'm sorry, Miss Vaden," Jerome apologized, his manner softening instantly. He did seem sincerely remorseful in that moment, but Vaden was wary of him all the same. "It's just that...well, I'm so dang hung up on you and..."

"Then act like a gentleman and prove it to her," Yvonne scolded.

"You're right, Miss Yvonne. Of course, you're right," he conceded. "I'm so sorry, Miss Vaden. I..."

"Let the ladies have their walk, boy." Yvonne and Jerome joined Vaden in looking up to see Ransom Lake approaching from across the street. Though Vaden's heart began to pound fiercely as he nodded in greeting to Yvonne and then to her, she was not so thoroughly shocked at seeing his superb attractiveness as she had been the first time she had seen him unshaven and awake.

"Your daddy's team is for sale I hear," Ransom Lake addressed Jerome. "I'd like to take a look at them if I could. Why don't you come on into the mercantile with me and tell me about them?"

Jerome looked irritatedly to Vaden, but then, nodding, followed Ransom into the mercantile. Yvonne and Vaden both watched in silence as the men entered the mercantile and something in Vaden wondered if Ransom Lake had somehow intentionally coaxed Jerome away from irritating her further.

"I hope those cackling hens in there don't all make complete idiots of the women of the world and swoon right there at his feet," Yvonne whispered as Vaden's hand clutched her own.

Indeed, as Vaden and Yvonne stood outside the mercantile watching what was taking place within, Vaden's heart pounded madly both for the fact that Ransom Lake had nodded a greeting to her and because she now prayed inwardly for the women in the store not to stare rudely at him.

The older women seemed to do fine and, save for the fact that Jerome kept glancing out the window at Vaden, everyone seemed to act rather rationally. Vaden began to heave a sigh of relief, but she felt someone bump her shoulder in passing. She looked to see Belva, Raylin and Selma heading into the store, Nathaniel and Toby Bridges at their heels.

"Well, let's have a good look at Mr. Ransom Lake, shall we?" Belva snipped pointedly as she glared at Vaden.

"Oh, Vonnie," Vaden breathed as she watched in horror. Yvonne's grip on Vaden's hand tightened and Vaden knew that she, too, was watching with great trepidation.

Of course, Yvonne and Vaden couldn't hear what was being said, but it was plain enough what course the conversation in the store was taking when Belva walked up boldly behind Ransom Lake, tapping him on the shoulder to get his attention. Ransom Lake turned and shook the girl's outstretched hand. At the same moment, Jerome seemed to stare with obvious disapproval at Vaden through the window.

"I...I can't watch it!" Vaden cried out as she turned and fled from her sister.

"Vay! Wait! Don't run off!" Yvonne called after her. But Vaden knew all too well what this meant. What the town's sudden acceptance of and interest in Ransom Lake meant. It meant that whatever small amount of his attention she had been able to capture thus far would fall by the wayside in the wake of all the newfound acceptance he would have. Wiping at her tears angrily, Vaden ran down the center street of town, turning off at the road to the pumpkin patch. She didn't even stop to wave to Mr. Wimber when he called out. At last she reached her haven.

Climbing quickly up into the secluding branches of her favorite maple, she sobbed bitterly for some time. He'd made it plain enough the day before. Ransom Lake had told Vaden exactly how he felt about having his face shaved without his consent. And then she'd managed to find herself squarely in his lap at the barber's shop! Vaden buried her face in her hands. She had been nothing but an anvil tied about his neck. An irritating cat that walked between his feet when he was trying to get somewhere. And now... now he would have all the attention, all the help and all the friends he wanted. Even if he didn't want them. Vaden sobbed bitterly. Ransom Lake was completely lost to her now. There would never be another moment when he would walk into the mercantile causing everyone to evacuate in discomfort. More likely they would flock to it like ants to spilt sugar!

An hour passed. A long, excruciating hour during which Vaden accepted the fact that it had all been a silly school girl's dream. Why had she allowed herself to become so enamored of the man? Why hadn't she listened to her sister? To her aunt? Jerome Clayton was a fine young man they all assured her over and over again. A young man of many divine qualities. And it seemed to be true. He seemed safe, she mused. And safe avoided heartache. Oh, Vaden had been one to champion love against all odds, but that day in her maple as she reflected over and over again on the triumphant expression that had been on Belva Tibbits' face, she realized that Jerome Clayton was reality. A nice, safe reality. While Ransom Lake was only a dream. A beautiful, dangerous and unobtainable dream. Dreams were for little girls and Vaden was growing up. It was a harsh, unwanted, unfriendly truth.

Letting the last of many maple leaves that she'd picked float gently down through the air and into the brook, Vaden inhaled deeply and brushed the last tear from her cheek. Her soul had been searched...and in being searched so long and so ardently had lost to the certainty of life. Slowly she climbed down from her perch in the maple and started back toward home.

CHAPTER
☙ FIVE ☙

"You've just been too darn quiet as of late, sweet pea," Uncle Dan explained as he sat beside Vaden on her bed one evening a week or so after Ransom Lake had raised himself from the Valmont's guest chamber and walked out of Vaden's grasp. "Your auntie and I...well, we just worry. Look at them cheeks of yours, girl. Usually all rosy and full of life. They're nearly pale now. And that spark to your eyes is dwindlin' more and more every day."

"I...I've just been a bit downhearted is all, Uncle Dan," Vaden explained. Forcing a smile, she looked at her uncle's concerned face and assured, "I'll be fine soon enough. I promise."

"Well...all right then. I'll let you be for now. I know Jerome will be here any minute to take ya for a ride." Uncle Dan paused and drew in a deep breath as if he'd meant to say something more. But he must have reconsidered for he kissed her affectionately on the cheek and left.

As Vaden looked at her reflection in the mirror, she, too, noticed the pallid complexion that looked back at her. Pinching her cheeks mercilessly, she forced a smile at herself and said, "Jerome Clayton will be here any minute, Vaden Valmont. And each time you agree to go riding with him, or for a walk, or let Aunt Myra invite him for dinner...each time you're coming closer to reality."

Closing her eyes for a moment, she let her mind conjure up an image of Ransom Lake the way he'd looked only that morning when she had seen him coming out of the blacksmith's shop. He'd seemed completely oblivious to everyone looking at him when he passed them by. One by one he'd sauntered past people completely oblivious and completely irresistible. Her heart endured a deep pang of misery, of unhealable sorrow as she thought of him. Several times during the week she had seen him in passing, even once while she had been walking back from her maple near the brook. Each time he'd nodded to her politely, not smiling, however, and not speaking one solitary word to her.

And worst of all, she had willingly allowed Jerome Clayton to begin courting her now. And instead of helping her to move on and try to accept that Ransom Lake would never love her, it only served to drive the dagger of disappointment and heartbreak further into her soul. She had thought that giving herself the opportunity to know Jerome better, to find things to like about him, would help her to accept the inevitability of having to put Ransom Lake out of her mind. But it hadn't helped. It had, instead, made things worse, for every time she forced herself to be pleasant to Jerome, to laugh at his wit, to admit his attractiveness, it was as if someone had driven a needle into some part of her heart. But it seemed the truth of life. Yvonne had told her that Jerome was a wonderful boy. Everyone told her that. And she knew that everyone approved of him. But yet...something in her couldn't accept him. And she was certain that this was because everything in her loved Ransom Lake.

"You don't quite look yourself tonight, Miss Vaden," Jerome remarked as he helped her into the buggy.

"Oh, just a bit tired today, I suppose," she sighed, buttoning the top button of her coat, for it was a rather unusually chilly night. At that moment, as if fate meant to drive the dagger of despair deeper into Vaden's heart, Ransom Lake stepped in front of the mare that was hitched to the buggy.

"How you doing this evening, Jerome? Miss Vaden?" he asked in his delicious mumbling way.

"Just fine, Ransom. And you?" Jerome greeted, standing up, reaching over Vaden and shaking Ransom Lake's outstretched hand as he came to stand next to the buggy on Vaden's side. Vaden didn't look at him at first, afraid that she might burst into tears at the sight of the tantalizing storm color of his eyes. But when he addressed her directly, she knew she must face him.

"You two out for an evening ride then, Miss Vaden?" he mumbled. Vaden's hand had been resting on the rim of the buggy and when she felt the worn leather of Ransom Lake's glove cover her hand she startled, looking directly into his marvelous gaze.

"Yes...yes...it's a nice evening for it. Don't you think, Mr. Lake?" she stammered. Oh, how handsome he was! How enticing!

"I'm just in to talk to your Uncle Dan a minute, so you have fun now," he said, stepping back from the buggy as Jerome slapped the lines at the horse's back.

"Good evenin' to you then, Ransom," Jerome called. Vaden closed her eyes as the buggy lurched forward and away from her heart's one desire. Over an hour later, Jerome pulled in the mare before of the mercantile and offered Vaden his hand to assist her down. As he walked her up the porch and paused with her before the closed doors it was the first time since they'd left Ransom Lake standing there that Vaden fully heard what Jerome was saying. All that night, though Jerome was at her side, ever flattering, ever attentive, her thoughts had been of nothing else but the vision of Ransom Lake standing next to the buggy and so near to her, his eyes intent on hers in somewhat of a disapproving manner.

"I'm sorry, Mr. Clayton. I...I know I haven't been much of good company tonight," Vaden apologized as Jerome took her hand in his, squeezing it tightly. "I've just...just had some things on my mind and..."

"It's all right, Miss Vaden," he accepted. "I think you just need..." and in the next moment before Vaden could've possibly moved to avoid it, she felt the moist warmth of Jerome's kiss on her lips. She wanted to pull away from him, slap his face, but she knew she had led him to this. She had accepted his courting, encouraged him even as of late. What else could she expect? But when his kiss lingered, threatening to become more than a tender affection bidding goodnight, Vaden stepped back from him graciously.

"Goodnight, Mr. Clayton," she whispered. "I do thank you for your company this evening."

Jerome's eyes were narrowed, his expression serious. "I love you, Vaden Valmont. I'm a good man and I'll make a good..." he began.

"You are a good man, Mr. Clayton," Vaden interrupted, though her compliment was not in earnest. She did not want to hear his confession, his assurance that he would be a good companion for her throughout life. "I...just be patient with me, please. Be patient." He seemed satisfied with her response for the moment and smiled, nodding a goodnight as he turned and descended the porch steps.

Vaden watched Jerome disappear down the street and into the night. A heavy sigh escaped her lungs and a horrible sense of guilt and disappointment ate at her stomach. She had allowed him to kiss her goodnight and his kiss had meant nothing to her. It had no effect on her, save that it caused her to want him to leave. She closed her eyes, trying to call up a vision, the sensation of what it might feel like to be in the arms of Ransom Lake had he been the one to have kissed her. She knew with everything that made her Vaden Valmont that had the kiss been from Ransom Lake, however brief, she knew that acute exhilaration and delight would overwhelm her. And she knew that such bliss could never be achieved from kisses forced by Jerome Clayton.

She thought her imagination's invention had come to life for a moment when she heard Ransom Lake's voice near. But when she again heard his voice say, "Miss Vaden," she opened her eyes and turned to find him truly standing at the foot of the porch steps looking angrily up at her.

"Mr. Lake," Vaden exclaimed blushing, for she feared he could read her thoughts somehow.

A frown furrowed his brow as he shook his head slowly. "I thought better of you than that."

"What do you mean?" Vaden asked, folding her arms across her chest.

"He's a worm."

"Who?" she asked, for her most recent thoughts had been of Ransom Lake, not Jerome Clayton.

"Jerome Clayton, girl! Who do you think I mean?" He seemed overly vexed. But not uncharacteristically.

"He's a very nice young man, Mr. Lake. Everyone always speaks well of him. I don't understand why you..."

"He's a worm. Why would you let him kiss you like that?"

Vaden's mouth gaped open slightly as the horrid heat of a guilty blush rose to her cheeks. "What do you mean, Mr. Lake?"

Ransom stomped up the porch steps, standing irritatedly before Vaden. "Why would you let a little worm like that kiss you, girl? He certainly don't know how to do a proper job of it," he growled.

Vaden was completely flustered and speechless. She was horrified in the knowledge that he had witnessed her exchange with Jerome. But Ransom Lake held no great desire for her, so what right did he have to scold her so? She wanted to scream at him. To shout, *You don't want me, so what else is there?* "I don't think this is any of your business!" she barked at him. "He's a very nice young man and I hold him in high esteem." She wondered why she so vehemently defended Jerome when she herself was in doubt of his sincerity of character at times.

"Exactly. So, why are you letting him slobber all over you like a parched camel?" Ransom Lake's eyes narrowed as he glared at her and Vaden felt the heat that preceded stinging tears well up in her throat.

"He hardly slobbered all over me, Mr. Lake," she defended. "And I still don't see what business this is of yours."

"You'd think the boy would at least try to do a proper job of it since you let him kiss you. But he's too wormy to even come close to it. I expected more from you, little girl." He turned and started to leave, but the tone of hurt in Vaden's next utterance seemed to stall him.

"And who do you think you are, Ransom Lake? I suppose you think you could do a *proper* job of it!" Her voice cracked with restrained emotion as she blurted out the words.

Vaden watched as he turned toward her glaring, his broad chest rising and falling with his exasperated breathing. His eyes narrowed once more and he leaned forward until Vaden could feel his breath on her face as he spoke. "You bet them neatly ironed petticoats of yours I could, sweet pea," he growled. Then without any further warning, Ransom Lake took hold of Vaden's mittened hand and pulled her down the steps after him.

"What are you doing? Let go of me!" she protested as she tried to pull her hand free of his grasp. But Ransom led her forcefully to the side of the house and out of the light of the lantern on the porch.

"First thing I'd do is get you out of the light so that every danged neighbor for fifty miles around can't peep at us. Can't kiss you proper with you worried about who might see." Rather roughly Ransom turned Vaden to face him pushing her back against the building. "Then I gotta back you up against a wall so that you can't turn away from me." He took her hands, stripping them of her mittens and tucking the woolen warmers tightly into her coat pockets. He whisked Vaden's cap from her head, tucking it safely into his own trouser pocket. Vaden gasped and tried to grab at his hands as he then unbuttoned her coat quickly.

"What are you…" she gasped.

"Be quiet," he growled. "I gotta get rid of some of this so that you know it's me warming you up and not…"

"What?" Vaden gasped. "I can't believe you would say something like that!"

"Yes, you can. You know me well enough by now, Vaden." And with that, Ransom Lake's utterance of her name so informally, Vaden Valmont was undone. Not that she really wanted to elude him anyway. But now, after hearing and seeing his mouth say her name so familiarly, she was dazed for a moment. She could only stare into those unusual gray eyes as he continued.

"Now," he began in a whisper, and as he moved closer to her she could no longer see the warmth of his breath turning to fog before her as he spoke, "I'll show you the difference between that wormy Jerome Clayton and the likes of Ransom Lake."

Vaden shook her head ever so slightly. She already knew the difference. The profound and obvious difference. She closed her eyes for just a moment as one of his powerful hands caressed her cheek. As his roughened thumb traveled lightly over her soft lips, she looked away from him shyly. He did not force her to look back at him, but as he traced the outline of her lips with his thumb once more he said in a lowered voice, "I'd bet my life that your pretty little mouth tastes sweeter than honey." She looked up to him quickly, unable to believe what her ears had heard him say. He was so handsome, so fatally and lethally attractive. Surely she was simply daydreaming. "Hasn't that wild curiosity of yours ever wondered...haven't you tried to imagine what my kiss tastes like, Vaden?" he whispered.

"No," she tried to state emphatically. "No. Never." Then, her curiosity even at that moment rose to an uncontrollable height and she asked, "But...what do you mean tastes like...I don't..." Vaden stammered, finding it difficult to control her breathing.

Ransom Lake chuckled and a triumphant grin spread across his face. "Well, that right there proves the boy didn't kiss you proper."

"You're just trying to..."

She gasped into silence as she felt Ransom's hand beneath her coat as it rested at her waist for a moment before sliding to her back and pulling her body against his. Again his free hand caressed her cheek and he put his thumb under her chin, pushing her face up and forcing her eyes to find his. His hand moved, his thumb caressing her throat as it encircled her neck. Even for his bulky clothing, his body was warm against hers, the muscles in his chest and arms solid as he held her to him. "He didn't even hold you proper...let his hand feel the softness of your face like he should have before he...you didn't enjoy that kiss at all did you, Vaden?" he mumbled. The deep sound of his voice seemed to echo throughout Vaden's head and she struggled to keep from trembling, from collapsing at his feet.

"Why are you teasing me like this?" she breathed in a frustrated whisper.

"I'm not teasing you. I'm teaching you. Teaching you that you don't go letting every wormy boy in town enjoy your kiss." She looked up and his gaze seized hers.

"What...what makes you different than anybody else?" she managed to ask, though her voice was nearly lost to the bliss of being in his arms.

He grinned somewhat triumphantly then and Vaden's insides began to tremble uncontrollably, for it was definitely her final undoing. "I think you know what makes me different from the likes of Jerome Clayton, now don't you?"

Vaden couldn't speak an answer. She couldn't even nod an acknowledgment to him. She could only close her eyes as his head, his handsome, roughly shaven face and his tempting mouth moved closer to hers. It was too torturous and she was certain he could hear her heart pounding madly. She opened her eyes and tried to look past him to the stars in the skies, the leaves falling softly to the ground from a nearby tree, to anything that might help her not to faint in his arms.

When he spoke next she could feel the warmth of his breath on her lips. It unsettled her so that the wondrous sensation caused excessive moisture to drench her eager mouth.

"There's more to a kiss than my lips on yours, Vaden," he whispered. Her skin prickled with goose bumps as his lips brushed hers teasingly. "There's the feel of my arms around you so that you know it's me holding you here." The tip of his nose brushed her forehead as his lips placed a soft kiss on her own nose. "There's the feel of my whiskers rough on your cheek and around your mouth so that you recognize I'm a man and not some wormy boy."

His hand left her neck and traveled down her right arm to where her own hand brutally clutched the fabric of her skirt in its fist. Tugging at her hand, he coaxed it to release its nervous grip on her clothing, directing it to his face where her open palm rested for an instant before he pushed her hand up, her fingers being lost in the softness of his hair for a time before they came to rest along his masculine and well defined jaw. "If you leave your hand on my face just here, you'll be able to feel it there, too, when I kiss you."

Then, though Vaden was certain she would awaken at any moment to find the dream vanished, Ransom Lake, the man she was beginning to realize she had been born to love, kissed her lips softly and somewhat hesitantly at first, tenderly, teasingly and undemandingly. Brushing her cheek with his own then, he whispered, "Don't hold your breath, girl. You'll faint dead away. There's nothing to be afraid of from me."

"I'm...I'm not a child and I'm not afraid of you, Mr. Lake," Vaden corrected him, barely able to find the breath to do so.

"Oh, I know you're not a child, Vaden. I do know that." The piercing gaze of his gray eyes held hers for a long moment with the miracle of their fascinating storms and then both arms belonging to Ransom Lake embraced Vaden, pulling her securely against his perfectly constructed and powerful body. His mouth took hers at once, moist, demanding, and thorough and she was weakened in his arms, afraid that her knees would give way beneath her. She didn't feel the chilled breeze on her face, and she was unaware of standing in a small mud puddle, the water finding its way into her boots. There was nothing else in the world at that moment. Nothing but Ransom Lake. Nothing but the feel of being in his arms, the taste of his heated mouth as it instructed her responses, leading her instincts in returning the exchange. And he instructed well, led well, kissed fantastically, as if he himself had invented that particular act of physical affection. It was the first thoroughly impassioned kiss Vaden had ever experienced and she knew in that instant that she would never desire such a kiss from any other man. For she was certain that no other man could ever create such a kiss. It could only be from him, this man that held her in his arms at that dreamborn moment. She would never want, never allow another kiss from any man, save it were Ransom Lake.

Abruptly Ransom released her from his embrace, took Vaden's face firmly between his powerful hands and kissed her fiercely one last time before releasing her completely. Vaden leaned back against the wall, afraid she might crumple to the ground in her weakened condition.

"That's how he should've kissed you, Miss Vaden," Ransom stated in a lowered voice. "That's what your first kiss from a man should've felt like. And believe me when I tell you, child...that ain't nothing compared to what would've taken place between us if we were any more familiar with each other. If Jerome Clayton can kiss you like *that*...then I guess I'm wrong about him. But I doubt it." He retrieved her cap from its place in his pocket and plopped it promptly on her head.

Vaden touched her lips with her fingertips, still able to sense the taste and feel of Ransom Lake's kiss there as she watched him walk away through the dark and moonlight. She could do no more than simply stand where she was for several minutes uncertain what to do. She looked about her to see if anyone may have witnessed the kiss. Then she ran her fingers through her hair as she struggled to regain her senses.

She had never imagined! Not in her wildest, most romantic of dreams had she imagined that kissing the mysterious man would be such a completely euphoric experience. "I can't believe it," Vaden whispered out loud to herself. Finally, as the shock and confusion of it all began to wear off she sighed and let her body relax against the building's outer wall. She smiled, completely enraptured by the memory of being held by Ransom Lake, kissed by his capable mouth. Closing her eyes, she let the cool breeze brush lightly across her face, tickling her nose now and again.

Ransom Lake had kissed her! The same Ransom Lake who had occupied her dreams, thoughts and curiosities for weeks now. The same physically gorgeous, flawlessly attractive Ransom Lake that had every female heart in town aflutter. He had kissed *her*! She squealed with delight as she turned and dashed back onto the front porch and to the door. She would simply have to tell Yvonne! That very next instant! But then, pausing before she opened the door and walked into the fire warmth of the house, she remembered what had happened only moments before Ransom Lake had kissed her.

Jerome. The thought of Jerome Clayton dampened Vaden's excitement more than a little. She knew Yvonne approved of Jerome's attentions toward her, seeing him as a suitable beau for her younger sister. He was polite, well mannered and safe. Yes, Vaden thought, that's why Yvonne approved of Jerome. He was safe in her eyes. No doubt he would provide well for his wife, whomever she turned out to be. He would never indulge in liquor or other devastating vices. He would never hide his past or become a hermit. And, Vaden thought determinedly, he would never, rather Jerome could never kiss her like Ransom Lake had. Jerome would never be able to send Vaden's thoughts, feelings and spirit soaring into delicious oblivion with a simple kiss. And Vaden needed to soar.

Maybe Ransom Lake wasn't safe, but he was magnificent, unique, provocative and captivating. And completely out of reach. He would never want her with any kind of permanency. A short, ridiculous girl who was forever causing him discomfort in some form, whether it was boots hitting him on the head, waking to find his beard gone, or finding her in his lap in the barber's establishment. Vaden knew that Ransom Lake could never be hers. But to settle for Jerome? She couldn't do it. She couldn't! Not as long as Ransom Lake breathed the air of the earth! And even if by some unthinkable tragedy his wonderful, his heaven scented breath would stop, even then Jerome would not do for Vaden. She knew it. She had changed a bit suddenly, and she knew that the time had come. Because of that one heavenly kiss from the man of her dreams, she knew that she must tell Jerome. Soon. She must tell him that his pursuance of her was in vain.

"How was your evening, sweet pea?" Aunt Myra asked as Vaden entered the house, her thoughts scattering instantly.

"Um...fine. Fine, disappointing and wonderful all at the same time, Auntie." Myra quirked an eyebrow at Vaden's answer. Vaden simply went to where her aunt sat on the sofa in the parlor and hugged her tightly around the neck. "I know it's not exactly what you wanted to hear, Auntie. But that's the truth of it."

Myra smiled at her niece and kissed her lightly on the cheek. "Well, it's late now. Yvonne's in bed nearly thirty minutes already. You run along." Vaden smiled, giggling as well, as she stood and noticed that Uncle Dan was sound asleep in his rocker, his book open and lying on his chest as he snored quietly.

Vaden entered her room to find it dark. She heard Yvonne's quiet breathing, soft and regular, indicating she slept soundly. Quietly she removed her dress, corset, stockings and such, replacing them with her soft, unrestraining nightdress. She stubbed her toe on her bed leg and gasped trying to stay quiet. But Yvonne lifted her head and sat up.

"You're home then. Was it a nice evening with Jerome?" Yvonne asked in a whisper.

"The evening itself did have one bright spot. The evening with Jerome was barely tolerable," Vaden whispered as she slipped beneath her covers.

Yvonne sighed heavily. "Don't tell me you were rude to him, Vay. How do you ever expect to catch him completely when..."

"I don't *want* to catch him, Vonnie!" Vaden snapped. "I don't want Jerome! Don't you see that? Why is everyone so intent on me capturing Jerome Clayton? I'm sick of it! I'm sick to death of it!"

"He's a good man, Vaden. Why don't you..."

"Yvonne," Vaden began, springing from her bed and going to sit on Yvonne's as she spoke to her in the darkness. "He kissed me tonight. You have no idea what I felt. It was like…"

"Jerome kissed you? Tonight?" Yvonne gasped. Even in the dark Vaden could see the whites of Yvonne's eyes as they widened in astonishment.

"Well Jerome kissed me, too, but…"

"What do you mean, Jerome kissed you, too?" Yvonne was aghast and Vaden knew it.

"Yes, Jerome kissed me. Out there on the front porch. A kiss that I'm certain most girls in this town covet. And yet…and yet I felt like I wanted nothing more in the world but to escape it! To wash my lips off under the pump." Vaden sighed discouragedly.

"What do you mean Jerome kissed you, too, Vay? Are you trying to tell me that someone else…" Yvonne asked, her words trailing off in a whisper and then vanishing in the quiet of the room. It was obvious by the expression on her face that her disapproval battled with insatiable curiosity. Like a cattle rancher and sheep farmer arguing over grazing lands.

"Ransom Lake kissed me tonight, Yvonne. Ransom Lake!" Vaden confessed as the excitement, the all-encompassing, total exhilaration of his kiss returned anew to her memory.

Yvonne gasped as her hand covered her mouth in disbelief. "Vaden! Do you mean to tell me that you have kissed two men in one night?" Yvonne buried her face in her hands and began to mumble. "Where did I go wrong? I've never taught you to…two men…kissing you in one night! Two men alone is bad enough, Vay," she scolded looking up again, "but two in one night?"

"You forget, Yvonne. I didn't want the kiss from…"

"I knew it! I knew that hermit was no good! Imagine! Forcing his…"

"It was Jerome's kiss I didn't want, Yvonne," Vaden interrupted. Then, throwing her head back for a moment, she sighed with heavy frustration. "Yvonne, I don't want Jerome. I want Ransom Lake. I love Ransom Lake. Can't you see that? Can't you see it? I've loved him from the first day we came here! You even told me that you thought I did. And I feel him…"

"Vaden! You feel him? Whatever do you mean by that? What a thing to say to me! I can't believe you, Vaden! You shouldn't be touching him, kissing him, let alone feeling him! Sometimes I can't believe you!" Yvonne was horrified.

Vaden shook her head frustratedly. "I don't mean that, Vonnie. I swear you are the hardest person to talk to. Don't you understand plain speaking? I *feel* him. Here," she whispered, putting a hand to her chest, her voice pleading for understanding from her sister. "I feel him in my heart, in my mind, in my stomach, in my arms! He's become the food for my soul, Yvonne. Can't you at least imagine what it would feel like to love someone like that? Or is it that you're just too aware of propriety, of assured financial stability...of what looks good to the world...are you too worried about those things to understand what I'm feeling?"

Yvonne was silent for a moment. Then she spoke quietly, "It's impossible, Vaden. No one can have exactly what they expect from love, from marriage, from life. You set your dreams, your ambitions, your heart too high. I fear that you'll simply plummet when you realize one morning that Ransom Lake will never love you. He's not capable of it. But Jerome..."

"No. He may not love me, Yvonne. And I know that. But he's capable of loving someone far more thoroughly and honestly than Jerome Clayton is."

Yvonne sighed. "Every unmarried woman in this town, Vay...every one of them...and I suspect there are some married ones that would think of leaving their husbands if the opportunity to possess Ransom Lake came along...every woman is mesmerized by him, Vaden. You can't possibly be certain he favors you."

"He doesn't favor me, Yvonne," Vaden admitted sternly. "I know that, but I love him. I don't love him simply because he's so astoundingly handsome or because he's so mysterious. I love him because I know who he is. I've seen something in him that every other woman in this town is too shallow to see. And obviously, Yvonne...that includes you."

As Vaden stood and returned to her bed Yvonne whispered, "I only love you, Vay. I know that if you have your heart broken...it would break so much harder than anyone else's would. I...I just don't want to watch you..."

"It's already breaking, Yvonne. Just the knowledge that I will never be to Ransom Lake what he is to me...that knowledge in itself, is tearing my heart into bits." Vaden climbed into her own bed and pulled the covers up around her neck.

There was silence for some time and Vaden thought her sister had gone back to sleep. But then Yvonne's voice broke the darkness and Vaden was surprised when she said, "I've never been kissed by a man. Not a man that I consider to be a man, anyway. Oh, there was Charles Rogers on my sixteenth birthday, but he was only eighteen. And then, of course, you know about William Acron. And even though he was nearly twenty-two...he wasn't a man. Do you know what I'm trying to say?"

Vaden was still angry and hurt by her sister's apparently insensitive manner of the previous conversation, but she had no desire to stay so. "I do know," she answered.

"He's a man. Ransom Lake is as much my ideal of a man, as he is yours, Vaden. I will admit that to you. And...and..." Yvonne was stammering, seeming as if she could not find the courage to finish her thinking.

"I will admit to you, Vonnie, that he did treat me somewhat as if he were dealing with a child at first. He began lecturing me on how Jerome's kiss was not a kiss worth wasting time on. You see...Jerome kissed me first on the porch when we were saying goodnight. Then, out of the autumn darkness, Ransom Lake appeared and he scolded me for letting Jerome kiss me. He said Jerome couldn't do a proper job of it. Then Ransom Lake whisked me to the side of the house, removed my mittens and hat and kissed me. I do not exaggerate to you when I say that it was like nothing I could ever have imagined, Vonnie. If I should die tonight, I could not have wished for a more profoundly perfect thing to have experienced in my life."

"Was it wonderful simply because he's older than Jerome do you think?"

Yvonne asked boldly.

"No. It's because he's a man with skills of affection and an unconscious desire to weaken a woman's knees when she's in his arms. He's a man of hard work, of hidden pain. Ransom Lake is a man of passion. I only wish that I were the object of his passion." Yvonne was silent after Vaden's answer. And then Vaden turned in her bed and said, "I can by no means settle for Jerome Clayton, Yvonne. It would be a sinful dishonesty to my soul and to Jerome. I will never be the same again. For, even now as I lay here in the dark, I long to be held by Ransom Lake, held in the power of his arms, and feel his kiss to my lips again. And my heart hurts for I know it is never to be anymore. Goodnight, Vonnie."

"Goodnight, sweet Vaden. You teach me more than you will ever know. And I'm ashamed to be so shallow a woman. When I listen to you, I'm ashamed to be me."

"Be glad you are you, Vonnie, for I would never wish this sort of torturous heartache on even my worst enemy." Wiping soft tears on her pillow, Vaden was silent, knowing that the conversation with her sister was ended. "Well, maybe my worst enemy," she whispered to herself.

CHAPTER
∽ SIX ∽

Vaden tried to breathe calmly as Ransom Lake stood at the far counter several days later. As she watched him studying the merchandise she whispered, "He's so handsome, Vonnie." She paused, mesmerized by watching him. "You know how in summer we used to pass Mrs. Kingston's peach tree over on Delilah Avenue? Do you remember that?" Vaden asked. Yvonne nodded and Vaden continued in a whisper, "Remember how sweet and fresh and moist those peaches were? How we'd look up at that tree and our mouths would just water and water for a taste of just one bite of a sweet, beautiful, delicious peach? That's how I feel now. I watch Ransom Lake while he's just standing there...doing nothing...nothing at all...and I have to swallow constantly because my mouth longs to have him kiss me again. So much worse than it ever longed for those peaches on a hot summer day, Yvonne."

"Shh!" Yvonne scolded in a whisper, hitting her sister squarely in the ribs with her elbow. "He'll hear you! And quit staring. For pity's sake, Vaden."

But, as usual, Vaden could not tear her gaze from the man. She was completely intrigued by him. Every movement of his body, every gesture of his hand, every expression on his dream-born face.

"Are you finding everything all right, Ransom?" Aunt Myra asked as she entered the store from the back room.

"Mmm," he mumbled.

"We've some new books that have just come in. If you'd like to take a look…" Myra began.

"Thanks. But not today," he interrupted shortly. Then, much to the horror of all three women present, he turned on his heel suddenly, his eyes spitting angrily in Vaden's direction. "Confounded, girl," he growled as he strode across the room toward her. "I can feel your eyes burning holes in the back of my head! Isn't it enough that you stripped me of my beard, forced me to have my hair whacked off, trip me up everywhere I go?"

"I…I'm sorry about those things," Vaden apologized, utterly astonished and unprepared for his outburst. "I've already told you that, Mr. Lake. Time and again."

"May be. But every dang time I come in here, you're staring holes in me! Would you like for me to strip down buck naked so you can have a real good, completely thorough look?" he nearly shouted.

"Ransom!" Myra exclaimed reprimandingly.

Vaden dropped her guilty gaze to the floor and blushed bitterly. "I'm sorry," she apologized softly. "It's just that…just that…"

"I know, I know," he sighed. "I'm the town odd man. You're no different than anybody else I suppose."

"Yes, I am!" Vaden spat at him suddenly as tears filled her bright eyes. "I am different! I'm different because I find you positively fascinating. You're a puzzle to me. A soul in torture who…a mystery. I feel as if…as if…everyone else simply…" As his eyes widened, Vaden realized that she'd revealed too much. "I'm sorry," she repeated, wiping a tear from her cheek and fleeing from the counter and toward the other room.

"She's just young, Ransom," she heard Myra remark causing her to feel all the more humiliated. Running to her room and closing the door firmly behind her, she burst into unrestrained sobbing. Going to her nightstand, she removed her most beloved book of poetry from the drawer, opening and removing the long lock of ebony hair she had hidden inside. The lock of Ransom Lake's hair that she'd found clinging to her skirt after she'd returned home from delivering Mr. Polowsky's hair tonic. It must've been on

Ransom Lake's lap when she'd accidentally found herself sitting there. She'd known at once that it was his, for it was at the least eight inches long and the exact color of his hair. At the mere touch of it her fingers began to tingle and she wiped at her tears with her apron. Why was she so fatally drawn to Ransom Lake? It was so much more than the fact that he was so lethally handsome. Her soul craved his company, his approval. Her body was experiencing a strange and aching loneliness that she felt could only be appeased by being held safely in his powerful arms. She ached for his kiss again, to be the cause of a smile spreading across his face, to be able to smooth the perpetual frown from his brow, to ease the pain caused by whatever tormented him. Shaking her head as the tears increased, she whispered, "No! No!" She wouldn't let her mind admit what her heart was telling it. She wouldn't dwell on what she knew she was feeling for the strange and lonely man. The love, the need for his love.

"Vaden?" Aunt Myra's voice called from the other side of her door. "Vaden? Mr. Lake is asking to apologize to you, dear. Do come out."

Looking about the room frantically, her attention was arrested by the window. By the time Myra grew impatient enough to open the door herself, the room was empty, the curtains billowing in the breeze that breathed through the room through the open window.

Vaden let her feet carry her through the alley and out into the street. Because she was trying to hide her tears by hanging her head, she did not see her Aunt Myra and Ransom Lake standing on the front porch of the mercantile. She didn't see her Aunt Myra point to her or hear Mr. Lake apologize to her aunt for upsetting her young niece.

Once she had crossed the street to the road that led to her quiet spot and to Ransom Lake's house, she hiked up her skirt and petticoats and began running down the familiar route, intent on reaching her tall maple and the brook that ran beneath it. The mid-October air was cool and crisp and Vaden wished she had taken a shawl with her for she was not sure she could comfortably endure the chill for very long without it. As she reached the massive pumpkin patch belonging to Vaughn Wimber, her pace slowed to a walk again for there were a number of men picking the large orange orbs and placing them into the backs of several wagons. Vaden's heart landed disappointedly in the pit of her stomach, for even though she had been looking forward to the pumpkin harvest, it seemed sad somehow to know that the patch would soon be empty, the fruit having been severed from the withering vines and only the leaves remaining to fade and die away. Quickly she wiped the tears from her cheeks with her apron as Mr. Wimber approached her.

"Well, hey there, Miss Vaden! You comin' on over to pick out your pumpkins today? Your Uncle Dan said he'd send you over...but I thought he said this evening," the pumpkin farmer called as he came to stand before her.

"I...I thought I'd just come a bit early and look around," Vaden stammered.

"Well, go at it! If you do find a few, just let me know and I'll hold 'em back for you, okay?"

Vaden nodded and smiled. The man was pleasant enough, and Vaden could see the resemblance to his niece, Violet Wimber, in his smile and eyes. As she looked about searching for a starting point he added, "Now right over yonder there's some big ones! Nice and orange...no green left nowhere. But be careful," he cautioned, pointing in an easternly direction. "Somethin' went on over there and there's five or six big ol' boys that went rotten. Mice or somethin' I suspect. It's pretty slick and messy, so watch your step."

"Thank you, Mr. Wimber," Vaden called as she started in the direction he pointed. Maybe it would lift her spirits a bit to wander through the pumpkin patch. Maybe it would take her mind off that man, Ransom Lake. At least, for a little while.

Vaden lingered carefully while inspecting the pumpkins. Even for her damp mood she was delighted, for never had she imagined there would be so many hiding hither and thither beneath the leaves. She rolled several over inspecting their undersides and shapes, but had not yet come upon one that she favored when she heard a voice that startled her.

"Girl, if you ain't the hardest child to track down." Spinning around she saw Ransom Lake approaching, haphazardly stepping over the large orange mounds that were between him and Vaden. Vaden was entirely unnerved and hiked up her petticoats and skirt preparing to bolt again. "Now, hold off there, miss," he instructed, increasing the speed of his approach and shaking a warning index finger at her. "I just run all the way down here to apologize, so don't you go running off again." Vaden dropped her skirt and stood waiting for him to reach her. Her heart was pounding frantically and she doubted whether or not she could stay still to hear him out, for she was all the more humiliated that he should find her wandering through a pumpkin patch after the embarrassing display back at the store.

In another moment he stood before her, his breath somewhat quickened from his pursuit of her. "Now listen here, girl," he began. "I'm sorry I nipped at you like I did. You don't deserve that and well I know it." Again he held an index finger out, pointing at her as if he were scolding a child. "But it's been awful rough on me lately the way people have suddenly started looking at me like I was walking around town stark naked. I'm not used to public attention and it makes me uncomfortable. And to tell you the full truth of it, girl...you're the worst of the lot. Every time I come into the store you gawk at me like you've never seen me before. Not that it's any worse today than it was before we had our moment the other night...but..."

"I do *not* gawk at you, Mr. Lake," Vaden interrupted to defend herself. Her cheeks were vermilion at his mentioning their intimacy.

"Yes, you do," he corrected her. "But that doesn't give me the right to bite your head off like I did. I've come out here to apologize to you and..." As he took another step toward her, his extremely close proximity disturbed Vaden all the more and she took one step back away from him. As she did, however, her foot met with the slick, rotting remains of a large pumpkin that had split open and poured its innards onto the soft ground. Vaden's foot slipped, causing her to begin to topple backward. Naturally she took another step backward to try to keep herself from falling, and instinctively, at the same time, her flailing arms reached forward for support. The support that her hands found was the front of Ransom Lake's shirt. Vaden's tight grasp on the shirt as the weight of her body began to fall backward unbalanced the man and he began to fall forward, unable to get a hold of his own footing due to the slick pumpkin remains beneath him.

Vaden felt herself hit the ground hard, knowing instantly by the cold, moist sensation that soaked her back that she had landed exactly in the space saturated with rotting, orange slime. The incredible weight of Ransom Lake's body coming down solidly on top of her own the next instant knocked the breath out of her completely. Matters worsened when he, instead of raising himself from her immediately, let his body lay on hers as he lifted his hands off the ground at her sides for a moment, inspecting the smelly muck that covered his palms.

"What kind of mess have you pulled me into this time, girl?" he grumbled. His expression and voice only too clearly showed his exasperation and Vaden, still struggling for breath, tried to push him to one side. "Now hold on there," he instructed. "Let's take a minute. I don't want to end up face down in this…"

His words were lost as Vaden managed to squirm from beneath him, his own body landing squarely in the slop that hers had laid in only moments before. Vaden sat up, feeling the back of her head and trying to pull the pumpkin seeds from her hair. Ransom Lake raised himself to his knees and inspected the stringy, seedy mess that covered his entire front side.

When his head slowly turned toward Vaden, she immediately began to defend herself assuming that he was about to scold her much more harshly than he had in the store. "This was not my fault. You frightened me," she began in her own defense.

"I frightened you?" he repeated. "How do you figure that?" His voice was stern, but lacking the intonation of fury that she had expected.

"You...you...I thought you were going to..." she stammered, unsure herself what she had expected.

"Paddle your behind?" he finished. "Wash your mouth out with soap? Well then, you weren't listening to what I was saying, were you? I came out here to apologize to you. Remember?" Vaden looked away from him for a moment, still picking seeds from her hair. "I followed you out here to apologize and you end up pulling me into a...a...a lake of rotten pumpkins!" He sighed, shook his head and raised himself to his feet. Vaden continued to sit amid the muck, feeling it must be her penance for acting so cowardly back at the mercantile. But she glanced up, completely startled, when she heard a very odd, very unfamiliar sound erupt from Ransom Lake's lungs.

Vaden looked to see him standing before her, his shirt and trousers dripping with pumpkin mush, laughing boisterously as if the situation was the first humorous thing he'd seen in his entire life. The pure joy of amusement that was evident in his gray eyes and smile was delightfully wonderful and Vaden could not help but smile with him. He was all the more handsome when a relaxed, amused expression owned his face, even than he was with the nearly perpetual frown he usually wore.

He bent over, laughing so hard that he put his hands on his knees as he sighed to try to stop the laughter. "Look at you!" he gasped. "Just sitting there. Sitting there as if sitting in a mess of rotten squash was the most natural thing in the world. And look at me." He laughed for a moment before he was able to get his breath again and Vaden began to laugh with him, for the sound of his laughter was instantly contagious. Then, drawing in a deep breath and exhaling a long sigh, he wiped the moisture from his eyes and held a slimy orange covered hand out to her. "Come along, girl. We'll run on down to the creek and rinse off a bit before you go home."

Vaden was uncertain how to react. Ransom Lake, standing before her, his hand outstretched in an offering for her to take it? He wiggled his fingers and nodded, indicating that she should take the hand offered her. So, tentatively, Vaden reached up placing her own hand in his and felt herself immediately pulled with such a great strength that she nearly fell headlong into him again before she was stable on her own feet once more.

"Here now," he began, turning from her, but still holding her hand as he led her through the pumpkin patch, "we'll go out the other way here instead of back to the road. The creek is closer that way and, anyhow, we won't have to go tramping through all the pumpkin pickers."

I'm holding hands with Ransom Lake, Vaden thought. And the thought, though perhaps a little dramatic, astounded her. His hand, one of the same that had held her, caressed her so perfectly, was warm and strong and led her with confidence. It was a little disheartening when they reached the edge of the patch and he dropped her hand casually. A chuckle still rose in his throat every now and again as Vaden followed him in silence toward the creek. When they reached the cold, refreshing water, she gasped when he led her to exactly the spot that she favored. She watched as he hunkered down beside the stream beneath her maple and began rubbing his hands together vigorously in the water. Ransom Lake looked up at her smiling and Vaden felt as if she might faint at the pure splendor of his smile.

"Go on," he instructed, nodding his head toward the water. "Rinse that sticky stuff off." Vaden knelt on the creek's bank, not worried about the soil that might stain her skirt, for the backside was already orange forever from the pumpkin.

As she slipped her hands into the water, frigid with autumn, she looked to Ransom Lake when he stood and began unbuttoning his shirt. Quickly she looked back to the water and began rubbing her hands together all the more furiously as out of the corner of her eye she saw his shirt land in a pile on the ground next to her.

Chuckling he offered, "Here's your chance, Miss Vaden Valmont. A few of them curiosities that have been bouncing around in that head of yours are about to be quenched." Then he hunkered down next to her, picked up the shirt and doused it with water. "First of all," he began as he wrung the article of clothing out, "I tear the sleeves off my shirts because they bother me. Always getting caught on something while you're working if you don't roll them up. And if you do roll them up, they're always coming unrolled and giving you irritation." Still Vaden did not look at him, although she inwardly gasped at his knowing that she had considered on the reason for his sleevelessness for some time. "Next," he continued as he took the wet shirt and used it to rinse the pumpkin mess from his chest and stomach, "I don't wear flannels because they itch me. I always hated them and now that I'm grown up, nobody can force me to wear them...so I don't."

"That's very interesting, Mr. Lake," Vaden commented sarcastically. "But I have no idea why you think you need to explain to me the reason for..."

"Next," he interrupted, "and I'm not going to show you my underdrawers, Miss Vaden..'cause a man has to have some privacy..."

Vaden gasped audibly and stood up, staring at him, her mouth gaping open in stunned horror at his impropriety in conversation. But Ransom Lake stood, too, reached out and unexpectedly took her hand, placing it palm down on his stomach.

"Like I was saying...next," and he slid her hand upward over his chest to his shoulder before letting it go, Vaden snatching it away quickly, "*that's* how it feels to touch me." He quirked an eyebrow and lowered his voice. "I mean, it's a different touch than the one the other night. This is how it feels to touch my bare skin." Then, taking hold of her wrist tightly, he pulled her body against his abruptly. Vaden couldn't breathe as he held her firmly against him with one arm. "Kind of interesting, don't you think?" he mumbled, a sly grin spreading across his magnificent features.

Vaden looked away, her breathing rapid both from the embarrassment of his actions to her, and the ecstatic thrill that ran through her at the feel of his skin on her palm. "How dare you!" she scolded as she felt the blush rise to her cheeks.

"Oh, don't go twisting yourself into knots over what's proper and what's not, girl," he told her as he released her and again doused his shirt in the creek. He wrung it tightly and threw it over his shoulder as he grinned at her. "Now, I'd go ahead and walk you back to town, Miss Vaden...but the way I'm dressed...or I guess you might say the way I'm *undressed* on account of you..." He paused to chuckle at Vaden's astonished expression. "I don't think folks would understand. And all I need is more things to get the tongues in town wagging about me."

"You are a completely uncouth...brute!" Vaden exclaimed.

"Well then, talking like that...and I'm not saying you're wrong about it...but I can only guess you've joined the ranks of everyone else in town," he muttered, his amused grin fading.

"You know I interpret that as an insult, Mr. Lake," Vaden scolded. "I just mean that...even though you see me as a child...someone who is forever and always tripping you up in one way or another...it doesn't mean that I don't hold to certain standards. Certain ideas of propriety and respect."

"But you have been wondering about those things. Don't deny it, girl, 'cause I know different." He smiled slightly again, the anger at her accusation gone. "Now, run on home and get that curious little mind of yours thinking of something else that'll give you reason to stare at me with that odd intensity in your eyes next time I'm in the mercantile. Maybe you could set higher goals to speculate about." He dropped his voice and leaned toward her saying, "Maybe now you should start wondering what it feels like to kiss a man when he's only half dressed or what it will feel like when I touch your skin." When Vaden's eyes again widened in horrified astonishment, he chuckled and shook his head as he defended the statement. "I think you took my meaning way too seriously, girl." He laughed again. "I mean to say...that the only skin women ever have showing is from the neck up and the wrist down. And uh..." he lowered his voice again, "seems to me, now you tell me if I'm remembering this wrong...but it does seem to me that I already know what those parts of you feel like."

"Oh!" Vaden gasped. She felt the blush burning on her cheeks. "Oh!"

She was speechless. However could she respond to him when his flirting was of such a profoundly unspeakable caliber.

He grinned at her once more, studying her for a moment from head to toe. Then, nodding at her, he said, "Good day, Miss Vaden, I'll see you at the Halloween social. You've convinced me that it might be fun after all. Especially if there's a pumpkin rotting anywhere in your path." Chuckling, he turned and began walking toward his house.

Walking home, Vaden could not keep herself from smiling spontaneously as she thought back on the conversation she'd had with Ransom Lake on the banks of the creek. Oh, she had acted aghast, and most of her astonishment had been sincere, but his teasing her had sent her heart and mind soaring with delight! For it was obvious, indeed, that she had captured some meager amount of his attentions. How else could he have possibly known all the things she had been wondering about him? How could he have known that she had wondered about the sleeves to his shirts? About the feel of his skin? How could he have known unless he had noticed her, taken some paltry measure of interest in her?

That night, Vaden carefully placed several pumpkin seeds into the boot still hidden under her bed. She had picked them up off the ground at the creek bank, once Ransom Lake had started home following their incident in the pumpkin patch. Just as she slid the boot back into its hiding place, Yvonne entered their room, yawning as she climbed into her own bed.

"Well, Vay," she began. "You were gone for quite awhile this afternoon. Have you anything to confess to me? Any great adventure?"

Yvonne's sarcasm irritated Vaden, so she dramatically went to the bedroom door and closed it tightly. Then she walked to Yvonne, plopped herself down on the foot of Yvonne's bed and announced calmly, "I've touched the bare skin of a man's chest."

Yvonne gasped, her hands flying to her mouth as it dropped open. Then she began swooning from side to side as if she might faint as she continued to struggle to catch her breath. "Don't tease me so, Vay! You nearly stopped my heart!"

"But I'm not teasing, Vonnie. I have done it. I've touched a man's bare…"

"Don't say it again! Vay! What are you talking about? Whenever would you have had the chance to…"

"Today. Ransom Lake sought me out…he truly sought me out, Vonnie," Vaden whispered delightedly. "He found me in the pumpkin patch and was apologizing to me. I fell into a pile of rotten pumpkins, and he fell with me so we both were covered in seeds and stringy squash."

"Are you telling me that…that you and Ransom Lake…Vaden! Most people at least choose hay to roll around in if they're going to act so irrationally…so immorally!" Yvonne was pale and Vaden felt guilty suddenly for worrying her.

"No, no, no, Vonnie. It was purely an accident. I slipped and, trying to avoid the fall, pulled him down with me."

"How then…if this all was so innocent…did you end up touching his…his…"

"Chest," Vaden finished. "He helped me up and we walked to the stream to wash our hands…only his shirt was soaking with pumpkin so he removed it to…"

"He removed his shirt in your presence?" Vaden now feared that Yvonne might truly lose consciousness. She was more pale than ever.

"It was soaked in sticky squash innards, Vonnie. He used the shirt to wash off his chest…"

"Did he not wear his flannels beneath? Are you telling me the man doesn't wear flannels?"

"No, he doesn't. He says they itch him. Anyway, it was amazing, Vonnie. He said he knew I had been wondering how he…felt…so he took my hand

and ran it over his stomach and…"

Yvonne clamped her hands over her ears. "Don't speak it, Vay! Don't speak it!" Vaden did not speak it, for she felt worried at shocking her sister so. Yvonne closed her eyes for a moment, then opened them again and dropped her hands from her ears. Then an odd glow captured the depths of Yvonne's eyes and she took hold of Vaden's shoulders. "How did he feel, Vay? Tell me at once! How did he feel? Was it horrid? Was it…"

Vaden smiled. Yvonne was as curious as she was. She imagined that every woman was and that sisters were blessed to have each other to share their experience and knowledge with. "He felt…well…his skin was soft. As soft as mine. But his stomach…or rather the muscles beneath the skin of his stomach and chest were as solid granite, Yvonne."

"Was he warm or cold?"

"Warm. Very warm."

"Was it a pleasant experience or a horrid one?"

"Well, I suppose it would've been marvelously pleasant had I not been so completely unnerved. But, Vonnie, it unsettled me so. However, something deep within me tells my soul that had any other man appeared so scantily clad before me…the effect on me would have been quite different."

Yvonne nodded emphatically. "Well! I would be worried all the more if it hadn't. But, Vay…you cannot make a habit of touching men! Especially bare ones."

Vaden smiled, amused at her sister. Yvonne was as curious as she was and Vaden knew it. Yet, Yvonne was ever the perfect example of a proper lady. "Oh, but Vonnie," Vaden whispered, "Ransom Lake is no ordinary man. He's more like…Adonis."

"Help us all, Vaden Valmont!" Yvonne scolded. "You've got the likes of Jerome Clayton chasing madly after you and you're obsessed with this…hermit man." Vaden sighed and rolled her eyes exasperatedly. Yvonne sighed as well, then smiled softly. "I will admit, Vay…Ransom Lake puts even a handsome man like Jerome to shame." Taking Vaden's shoulders once more, she added, "But you mustn't be touching him in such a manner again, Vay. Do you understand?"

"I know. I know." Vaden admitted the knowledge because she did know the impropriety of it from her sister's point of view.

Yvonne sighed and smiled, convinced that her sister understood the seriousness of the situation. "Off to sleep with you, baby sister. Though I doubt it will come easy to you now."

Yvonne was right. Vaden could not go to sleep for long hours, for the vision of Ransom Lake smothered in pumpkin and smiling down at her kept itself vivid in her mind until the wee hours of the morning.

CHAPTER
∽ SEVEN ∽

*A*s Yvonne and Vaden sat in the back seat of the buggy on the way to the harvest and Halloween social in town, Vaden found it difficult not to fly from the conveyance and run headlong toward their destination.

"Oh! Why is he going so slow, Vonnie?" she whispered irritatedly to her sister. "Doesn't he know that this mare can go twice this fast and not be winded?"

Yvonne smiled at Vaden and shook her head. "I'm certain that everyone will still be there when we arrive, Vay. It's still a quarter of an hour before the party begins!"

"But we should be there early...to...to help with things," Vaden stammered, though she knew she could not fool Yvonne. Yvonne knew full well why Vaden was so anxious to arrive at the social.

"You're going to break Jerome's heart tonight if you ignore him completely, Vay," Yvonne whispered.

"I won't ignore him completely," Vaden assured her sister. However, the mention of Jerome dampened her spirits enough that she no longer felt the need to complain about Uncle Dan's relaxed attitude toward arriving at the social.

When at long last the Valmont's did arrive at the large oak just west of town, Vaden's heart soared for a moment before sinking as she noticed that Ransom Lake had, indeed, decided to attend. There he stood not far from the large oak's trunk, completely surrounded by the ladies of the town, young and old. To make matters worse, Jerome was upon her instantly, offering a gallant hand to help her down from the buggy.

"You look more divine than the stars in heaven tonight, Miss Vaden," he flattered.

Vaden forced a smile. "Thank you, Mr. Clayton. But you flatter far too dramatically."

Jerome smiled and winked at her, offering her his arm. As Vaden walked with him toward the platform that had been raised for the purpose of dancing, she looked to where Ransom Lake stood surrounded by female admirers. His eyes held hers for a moment and he nodded a greeting. Vaden nodded in return, praying inwardly for him to simply break free of his admirers and approach her. Please, she pled with him inwardly. Please come to *me*, Ransom Lake. But Belva Tibbits tugged on his sleeve then and he looked to her and away from Vaden.

"Well," Jerome sighed and Vaden looked up to him, feeling guilty, for she was certain he had caught her staring at Ransom Lake. "Ol' Ransom Lake has certainly taken the town by storm since he rid himself of his whiskers, hasn't he?" Vaden frowned, slightly disturbed at the barely discernible twinge of resentment in Jerome's voice. She looked at him, but his face showed no sign of what she had felt in his voice. "I know you're just as fascinated by him as the next girl, Miss Vaden. But don't worry." He covered her hand with his own and patted it warmly. "I'm patient. I know it's just the mystery of it all that catches your attention. I can wait until it's passed."

Vaden shook her head, unable to be certain that she had understood him correctly. "I am not infatuated with Ransom Lake, Mr. Clayton." The statement was true enough, for Vaden knew that her love for Ransom Lake went far and away beyond mere infatuation. "And I think you should understand that…"

"Sshhh," Jerome whispered, putting an index finger to his lips. "I know. I know. You're going to say that you're not like the other girls in town. That he doesn't cause you to act as they do. I know. I know you're different.

That's why I've chosen you. And, Vaden...I do think it's time you started calling me by my given name. Don't you?"

Something about the conversation was making Vaden very uncomfortable. Jerome's implications where she and he were concerned were far too serious. Furthermore, she hadn't liked his using her first name and was determined that he understand that she would not use his. "But, Mr. Clayton, I think a formal address between us is more…"

"Let's dance," he interrupted, helping her to step up to the dance platform. He smiled benignly and Vaden felt relieved. She had been reading too much into the conversation. She obviously had a tendency to do this often, for even though she and Ransom Lake had shared at least two intimate conversations or moments, he seemed almost indifferent to her as he assisted Belva Tibbits onto the platform and led her in a dance very near to where Vaden danced with Jerome.

As the night wore on, Vaden was hurt and dismayed when the situation did not change. Not once did Ransom Lake ask her for a dance, though he seemed to dance with nearly every other female on the premises. To make matters worse, Jerome was entirely too attentive to Vaden, almost possessive, and she began to resent him for it. She was all too relieved each time one of the other young men would ask for a dance. It became a chore...the social. A chore in Vaden's eyes instead of a party. A grand and glorious disappointment.

And then, late in the event, nearly at its intended ending time, Vaden broke free of Jerome's attentions long enough to stand before the enormous bonfire alone for a moment. She looked up into the dark night sky, watching the sparking bits of wood that would break free and fly into the blackness above, lighting it for only a moment. The burning wood smelled comforting and warm and Vaden hugged herself, sighing wistfully.

"*And so burns the cedar, warm...with spice. Lending fragrance to the air and,*" she began to recite to herself. She happened to glance to one side and caught sight of Ransom Lake standing nearby, Belva Tibbits attached to his arm. He was looking directly at Vaden, a mischievous glint to his mesmerizing gray eyes. As Belva babbled on about something that Vaden could not discern above the crackling of the fire, Ransom Lake continued to stare at her. Vaden looked away for a moment, unnerved by his intense scrutiny of her, only to look back to find him still staring at her. A sly grin slightly curved the corners of his mouth as he held out a hand toward her, motioned with his fingers for her to move toward him, then proceeded to place his hand at his stomach running it up and over his chest in exactly the manner he had directed her hand to do only a week earlier.

Vaden's mouth dropped open in an indignant gasp and Ransom Lake's smile broadened at her reaction. At that moment Belva tugged on his shirt sleeve once again gaining his attention and Vaden wondered why it was that he even owned a nice shirt with sleeves to wear to such a function, for it had twice taken his attention from her. Vaden looked away from Ransom Lake and through the flames of the fire could see Jerome talking with Nathaniel, Toby, Frank Hodges, and Randy Lange. Though Vaden had been to several gatherings at which Nathaniel and Toby were in attendance and was familiar with them, she was not very familiar with Frank and Randy, though she knew they were about Jerome's age and two of his friends. Jerome paused in his conversation looking about and Vaden could only surmise that he searched the darkness for her.

"I'm going home, Vonnie," Vaden informed her sister after pulling Yvonne aside from the table that was overflowing with good things to eat.

"What?" Yvonne asked, utterly perplexed. "You can't go home now and why would you want to anyway?"

"I'm going, Vonnie. Just tell Uncle Dan and Aunt Myra for me, will you?"

Yvonne frowned, for it was entirely unlike her sister to want to leave any kind of social gathering. And to want to leave one at which Ransom Lake was in attendance was completely unthinkable.

"I'll come with you then, Vay. Are you sure you're feeling all right?"

"Yes. I'm fine. And you stay here. I'm just...just tired. I want to go. Stay here, Vonnie. It would upset me too much if you were to give up your fun for me." Vaden hugged her sister and turned toward home.

It was a beautiful night for walking Vaden noted as she reached the town's main street. The sky was clear, the air crisp, and the stars bright overhead. She smiled as she passed Vaughn Wimber's house, which had a grinning, impressively carved Jack-O-Lantern donning every window. What a harvest he had! She admired him for working so hard at growing pumpkins.

The air was scented thickly with the mingling aromas of apple wood and cedar burning to make houses warm and cozy. The chill nipped at her cheeks and nose delightfully and Vaden managed a somewhat half-hearted smile for the wonder of October.

Then her thoughts turned to less pleasant venues as she thought again of Ransom Lake's nearly ignoring her at the social. Of his instant and irritating popularity there. Of Jerome Clayton and his possessive attentions toward her. Her evening had been a dismal experience and in one way or the other each of the men in her thoughts had contributed to it.

So deep in thought was Vaden Valmont as she walked along the deserted street on Halloween night, that it wasn't until the smothering wool blanket was covering her head, something else binding her arms to her sides, and someone lifting her into a wagon that she even realized there had been anyone else near to her. She tried to scream out, but something was tied around the blanket at her mouth and she could only struggle. She heard laughter. The laughter of Halloween pranksters. But not of children intent on tipping over outhouses. This cruel laughter was the laughter of young men. And her fear rose to immensity as she felt the wagon lurch forward.

"We need to bury someone, Miss Vaden Valmont," a man's voice that was being altered intentionally whispered in her ear. "We got to appease the spirits, you see. Offer up someone. You ever been buried before?" it asked. "Well, sweet thing...there's a first time for everything they say, now don't they?" Again there was the laughter of evil mischief and Vaden struggled with all of her might.

"Where's that little sister of yours, Miss Valmont?"

Yvonne turned to see none other than Ransom Lake standing before her inquiring about Vaden. She thought of how utterly thrilled Vaden would be to know that the man had asked after her.

"She's gone home, Mr. Lake. She said she was tired," Yvonne answered, smiling at the man. Her smile faded, however, when his face immediately puckered into a frown.

"On Halloween night? Doesn't she realize that the tricksters are out in full force about this time?" he asked.

"Tricksters?"

"There isn't a county in this good country in which the boys and young men of the town don't pull pranks all Halloween night long, miss. I'm not sure it's all that safe that she's gone home alone."

"She'll be fine, Mr. Lake," Yvonne assured him, though now she, too, was ill at ease. "It's Vaden after all."

Mr. Lake nodded, still seemingly unconvinced. And, closing his eyes for a moment, he seemed less so. "Well, guess I'll run on home now. You tell your sister I missed her this evening, Miss Valmont. Shoot, I didn't get conked on the head, sat down on, shaved, or covered in squash. I feel pretty unfulfilled."

Yvonne giggled even though Ransom Lake's frown deepened as he gave her a nod of departure.

Ransom Lake closed his eyes and shook his head several times at the pain in his head on his ride home. The feeling was there. The sensation of despair, of ominous evil lurking somewhere. He felt the fear in his heart. At least he thought he did, but there was no picture in his mind. Nothing to guide him. For the first time in his life, Ransom Lake found himself intentionally searching for the visions in his mind, but nothing came to him. Only the frustration of the uncertainty. He shook his head and tried to ignore the tightness in his chest. He tried to convince himself all the way back to his place that all was well.

When he arrived home, Ransom removed his shirt, tossing it onto a nearby chair. He went to the kitchen and got himself a glass of refreshing water. Suddenly he dropped the glass and it shattered as it hit the floor. The mad pounding of his heart increased as the all too familiar feeling of deep anxiety possessed him. Rushing to the door, he pulled on his boots, pausing for a moment to close his eyes and search for a vision. But still none came. No scenic premonition to help him pinpoint the fear he felt. Someone else's fear. Nothing to help him ease his panic. And he remembered again the thing he could never forget. The first time he'd felt the horrid panic rise within him, beckoning his soul in a direction it must go. He'd sworn that never again would he brush it off as he'd done the first time. Though he'd sensed something earlier on his way home, there had been nothing to confirm it, only the beginnings of the sense of panic. But now he felt it wholly.

Rushing out into the cool late of the night, he took only the time needed to bridle his horse. The feeling of panic, of impending doom, caused his hands to tremble violently as he mounted the animal's bare back and dug his heels into the horse's flesh to signal a gallop. He knew what was pushing him out into the night, and he knew where he was being sent. And it frightened him, for thus far he'd only had visions of one person in this town since he'd come. He had no doubt at that moment that it was that same person's need that prompted his soul now.

"Why...Ransom," Myra stammered as she opened the door to find

Ransom Lake standing before her only half dressed. He nodded, not waiting for an invitation to enter, and stepped into the house past Myra, walking directly to where Yvonne sat on the sofa in front of the fire.

"She's not home," he stated rather than inquired.

"No. No," Yvonne sputtered. She didn't know whether to avert her eyes or look at him while answering him. He wore no shirt and no flannels either. He stood before her bare from the waist up, and she realized why Vaden had been so overwhelmed at touching him.

"We're beginning to worry, Ransom," Myra admitted. "In fact, Danny has gone out to look for her. It's cold out and *so* late and I know she didn't take a suitable coat. Ransom? Ransom? What's the matter?"

Ransom Lake stared into the fire as it popped and crackled in the hearth. Closing his eyes, he waited, for he felt it approaching his mind. The insufferable sense of fear, the horror and panic of being closed in, and it was sucking the air from his own lungs. There was more in that instant and he knew where to go then.

"It's bad. I've got to get to her now," he mumbled to Myra as he rushed from the house.

"You mean you know where she is?" the woman called to him from the front porch as she watched him mount his horse.

"I...I have an idea," he answered before riding away at a gallop.

The tears streamed down Vaden's temples as she tried to calm her breathing. She could not sob, for it would surely smother her, her mouth being gagged as it was. The blanket had been removed from her head and body, but now a cloth bound her mouth and ropes held her arms to her sides and her feet together firmly. She had to breathe calmly through her nose. If she continued crying, her nose would stuff up and she would not be able to breathe, she reminded herself again. So, her mind prayed for release, for safety. She tried not to think of the fact that she couldn't move, couldn't speak. She wondered over and over why the young men had chosen her! She wasn't even sure if she knew her tormenters. In the darkness and with all the scuffling she hadn't been able to see their faces. What had she done to provoke such actions from them? She heard them laughing and heard something hit the lid of the coffin.

"We're buryin' ya now, Miss Vaden. Don't mind it too much. You'll just run out of air and go to sleep. It won't hurt none." And then she recognized that it was Frank Hodges' voice speaking to her. She knew him! One of her own peers, a supposed friend was doing this to her? She heard him laugh as another thud sounded on the wood over her.

Then she did begin to panic. She tried to thrash, to loosen the ropes that bound her arms and her feet. She cried, then, unable to stop the tears and sobbing that rose from her because of the fear and panic attacking her mind and body.

"Settle down in there!" Frank shouted. "It'll only make it worse for you." She stopped thrashing when she heard him say, "Who? Who's coming?"

Trying to remain silent, Vaden listened and felt hope rising within her as she heard the drumming of an approaching horse.

"What are you doing here?" one of the other men shouted.

She heard a scuffle, shouting and then a voice that she thought she was dreaming growled, "I oughta tear your throats open for this." She held her breath, unable to believe what she had heard. Whom she had heard! There were more scuffling sounds and shouting and then she began to cry as she heard someone prying the lid off the pine coffin. When the lid lifted and the moon and starlight shown in, breaking the darkness of impending death, Vaden closed her eyes offering a thankful prayer, for there, looking down at her, stood none other than her cherished Ransom Lake.

"What kind of fools would..." he mumbled angrily, profound concern apparent in his fiery eyes as he reached into the coffin and pulled Vaden from it. Embracing her momentarily, he let her feet drop to the ground.

"They should have their hearts torn out for this," he continued to mutter as he removed the piece of linen from her mouth, drew the knife from his boot and cut away the ropes that bound her. As the ropes fell from her body, she collapsed into him. He didn't hesitate, but gathered her into his powerful arms, carrying her toward the wagon that stood nearby.

Vaden glanced about to see that Frank Hodges, Toby Bridges, and Randy Lange were lying about on the ground, each bleeding from their nose and mouth and doubled over clutching at their midsection. Her own supposed friends had done this? It was unthinkable! How could they?

"You get up there and drive that team, boy!" Ransom commanded, looking to Nathaniel Wimber whose face was, indeed, bloodied and bruised, but he still stood. "Now, boy! Unless you want another dose of Ransom Lake when he's mad!"

Laboriously, Nathaniel climbed onto the seat of the buckboard as Ransom lifted Vaden into the wagon bed, climbing in behind her. He whistled to his horse and the animal approached, allowing its master to secure its reins to the wagon. Her rescuer settled himself against the sideboard, pulling Vaden into his arms and against the security of his warm body. "Get a move on, boy!" he shouted. "I think you know where to go, now don't you?"

Nathaniel paused, looking back at his friends. "What about..." he began.

"I don't care if the coyotes tear them to bloodied shreds, boy! And if you don't want to join them in Hell, you get this team moving toward Dan Valmont's place now."

Nathaniel clicked his tongue and the team lurched forward. Vaden had begun to tremble excessively, her nerves and emotions completely out of control. Ransom wrapped her tightly in his arms and spoke soothingly, "It's all right now, girl. It's all right."

His warm breath in her hair and the sympathy in his low voice caused her to tremble all the more and she let her tears flow free. It took her several moments before she realized that her cheek was flush with the bareness of his chest. His skin was soft and warm, but she pushed herself from his embrace all the same. It was all too improper, even for Vaden. The thought went through her mind quickly that Yvonne would've dropped dead on the spot at knowing her sister had allowed a man's body to touch her own so.

But, when the tantalizingly attractive Ransom Lake reached out and wiped the tears from her cheeks with the back of his hand, Vaden Valmont cared nothing for propriety and threw herself into the comfort of his arms once more.

"They meant to...to..." she stuttered.

"They meant to frighten you, is all. But there's nothing funny about a prank like that," he spoke quietly. His voice was so deep, so soothing that in a moment Vaden began to cease her trembling.

"All the same...I thought they meant to..."

"We only meant it as a joke, Miss Vaden," Nathaniel defended. Vaden's arms slid around Ransom's waist for comfort. She pulled herself tighter against him, trying to drown out the sound of Nathaniel's voice. But her anger, anxiety and residual fear only heightened as he added, "Looks to me like you're the one who's needing a lesson or two, Ransom Lake. Forcing that poor girl against yourself like that. You're nothin' but a dirty old man."

"You can shut your mouth or be signing your own death certificate, boy," Ransom growled. Nathaniel spoke not another word, only continued to drive the team.

As the wagon rolled on, the noise of it rumbling along the road to town heightened as the terrain became rougher and rougher. The loud rumble of the wagon wheels on the hard earth, the sideboards rattling...all of it added to Vaden's anxiety. At least, she thought, Nathaniel wouldn't be attempting to speak to her, for the noise was profound. Even if he did attempt it, she was comforted to know that she would not be able to hear him.

Vaden began to feel warmer, within and without. It was an inebriating sensation being held by Ransom Lake. His strong hands stroked her hair comfortingly as he held her and the horrid fears and anxieties she had experienced at the hands of the young men were lessened for a time. She marveled again at the warmth of him. And it testified to her of how the temperature had dropped.

"I'm sorry," she spoke to him. "To drag you out in the cold like this. I…"

"What? Don't you be apologizing for anything," he scolded. "This is none of it your fault, girl."

"I shouldn't have left the social, shouldn't have been so foolish. And then…then…I was so scared. I know it's silly of me. Stupid to let a prank get to me so…" she began, tears still streaming down her face.

"None of this was your fault. And anybody would've been scared near to death at having this done to them." Ransom Lake took her face between his powerful hands and glared into her eyes. Vaden's own eyes widened, for the anger apparent in his gray eyes was almost frightening. "It's over now. You put it out of your mind."

"I can't," she cried. "I can't…I keep thinking about…"

"Then think about something else," he told her calmly.

"I…I couldn't move! I couldn't breathe! All I could smell was that pine box and the dirt and…"

"I know," he comforted. "Sssshh."

Then, because of the state of lingering panic and fear in Vaden's mind, because of the interminable need she felt to receive comfort from him, to feel security somehow, she did stop crying and her attention at that moment was completely arrested by his mouth.

"Ssshhh," he whispered again as he held her face in his hands.

Before Vaden could stop herself, her fevered, tormented mind had instructed her body to act and it did. She reached up, pulling his hands from her face and freeing it from his grasp. Raising her face to his, she kissed him directly on the same enticing mouth that had tried to verbally silence her fears a moment before. She did not kiss him long, nor passionately, but, indeed, longer and betraying more of her own desire than she intended. She had closed her eyes in that moment of the kiss, letting the warmth and strength of him push aside the horrid thoughts of what she had endured before he had come for her. She opened her eyes to see him frowning at her, his expression otherwise was one of surprise. Humiliated suddenly at her brazen act, Vaden fought for an explanation.

"I...I..." she stammered. "Thank you. Thank you for coming for me. I...I...only wanted to thank you."

He continued to frown at her as if he did not believe her reason for kissing him was merely a thank you for his chivalry. He said nothing. Uttered not one word. Only persisted in staring at her in his unnerving manner. As the heated blush of her ever increasing humiliation began to burn throughout her body Vaden attempted to push herself free of him. But each time her palms would push fiercely against his powerful chest, his strong arms would only tighten about her body. Finally, as tears flooded her cheeks once more with her frustration, he abruptly released her and she scooted away from him to the other side of the wagon bed. She looked at him for a moment as he stretched his arms out, resting them on the side of the wagon that he sat against. His eyes still studied her incessantly, the frown still on his brow. Vaden looked away to what lay behind the wagon and when the terror of the incident only renewed itself, for she could still smell the sickly sweet aroma of pine, she turned and looked at the team of horses that pulled the wagon toward home.

The air was more than chilled now, it was cold, and Vaden, without a proper coat, was beginning to shiver. Drawing her knees to her chest, she hugged them against her body tightly and looked once more to where Ransom Lake sat across the way, ever staring with his stormy, disturbing eyes. She looked away from him again and glanced at Nathaniel, who drove the wagon on determinedly. But when she could still feel the heat of Ransom Lake's gaze on her, she looked to him once more and said curtly, "Aren't you cold? Why didn't you wear a coat? A shirt at least?" Her voice was too brusque and she knew it. But he was making her uncomfortable now. The Heaven sent man who had saved her from further anguish and pain was the cause of her irritation now.

"Didn't have time to dress for the weather," he answered loudly yet still in his mumbled, low, almost slurred manner. "And aren't you glad I didn't waste the time on it?" Vaden sighed and looked away, ashamed that she would talk so rudely to him. "And besides," he continued, his voice taking on the provocative intonation that always sent Vaden's innards to taking flight, "it's not like it's anything of me that you haven't seen before, now is it?"

Instinctively Vaden glanced to Nathaniel who only continued to drive the team, seemingly having not heard Ransom Lake's rather personal statement.

"That sounded terrible! The way you put that remark!" Vaden scolded him.

Ransom scowled and tipped his head to her. "What? What did you say, girl?"

Again, Vaden looked to Nathaniel to insure that his attention was straight forward and he was not listening over his shoulder. "I said, that sounded terrible! The way you..."

"What?" Ransom Lake interrupted, cupping a hand to his ear.

Vaden exhaled exasperatedly. Then, moving forward until she was on her hands and knees in the wagon bed and closer once more to the man so that he might hear her, she repeated, "I said, that sounded terrible! What if he had heard you?"

"What? Heard me say that out by the creek the other day, I took off my shirt and you..." Ransom Lake was silenced immediately as Vaden lunged forward and put her hand over his mouth.

"What are you doing back there, Ransom Lake? That's Jerome Clayton's girl you got back there and I don't think he..." Nathaniel began as he started to look over his shoulder.

In one swift movement, Ransom Lake's powerful arms left their resting place on the wagon board, pushed Vaden's hand from his mouth and took hold of her wrist tightly, rendering her unable to move back to the other side of the wagon. "Keep your eyes on home, boy," he growled. "Unless you want me to break your neck and leave you out here to the coyotes."

Nathaniel was silent as Vaden tried to pull her wrist free of Ransom Lake's grasp. But as her other hand attempted to pry his fingers from her body, *his* other hand took hold of her free wrist as well and he held both tightly as he frowned at her. "What are you trying to get away from me for, girl?" he asked in a lowered voice.

Vaden dropped her head as she began to sob once more. Her strength was gone. Her will to defend herself from great harm or simple teasing was gone from her. She felt weak and tired and insecure, so that when Ransom Lake's hands released her wrists, his strong arms encircling her body and pulling her once again onto his lap and against the warmth of him, Vaden simply collapsed. Letting her arms encircle his waist for a moment, she inhaled deeply of the scent of his skin as her tears bathed his chest where her face lay against it. Then her hands slid up the length of his back to his shoulders where they rested as she returned his comforting embrace.

After Vaden had cried out the anguish in her heart for some time, she lifted her head from him, wiping her tears with the backs of her hands and asked, "How did you know where they had taken me? Did you simply guess at it? I've seen no one else out this way since we started for home. How did you know where to look?"

Ransom Lake sighed heavily and let his hands travel to her waist, holding her firmly as he sat her between his legs, drawing his knees up on either side of her and resting his forearms on them. Vaden watched, intrigued, as his jaw visibly clenched and unclenched several times as if he was fighting not to say something.

"I just...I just knew," he mumbled, looking away from her.

"What do you mean? How could you just know?" she asked.

"I guessed at it," he nearly snapped, glaring at her. "I...I just figured it's where boys might go to...to...play pranks." He took Vaden's shoulders and turned her so that her back leaned against his chest, her legs stretched out on the wagon bed before her. She sensed that he didn't want her to look at him. She wondered what he was hiding. "Now, them dragging you out here and acting like they were going to bury you. That's all they did, right?"

"What do you mean is that all they did?" Vaden snapped, wishing she could turn and look at him again. "I think that's a horrid enough thing and I…"

"I mean…your shirtwaist…the collar on this side and shoulder…" he said, and she shivered delightedly as she felt his fingers fumbling with the fabric that was torn away exposing her shoulder and camisole strap. "They didn't try to…"

"No," Vaden interrupted. His meaning was all too clear and justified she knew. But she hadn't wanted him to have to speak of it further. "It was torn when they removed the blanket that they'd put over my head. I tried to run, naturally."

"Naturally," he repeated in agreement and Vaden's body tensed as she felt his warm, strong hand cup her bare shoulder for a lingering moment.

"I…I tried to run and…and my shirtwaist was torn when one of them grabbed it to stop me." Vaden tried to calm her breathing and her emotions. It was too much, too torturous a night! To be terrorized, fear for her life, and in the next moment find herself in the arms of the man she loved. It was too much. As she felt the warmth of Ransom Lake's breath on the skin of her neck where her collar was torn away, her tears moistened her cheeks again. She thought of the moment when they had stood on the banks of the creek and he seemed to have read her mind, knowing full well that she had wondered what he felt like, why he tore the sleeves from his shirts. She remembered him telling her to go home so that her curiosity could get busy on other things of wonderment, "…*how it feels for me to touch your skin*…." he had said. As her body broke into an involuntary shiver, goose bumps covering every inch of her, she realized that he had answered that curiosity himself, for she trembled uncontrollably as his hand brushed her shoulder a moment before his fingers slipped caressively beneath the strap of her camisole for an instant. Then he straightened out one of his legs, turning her body so that her legs lay across it, her back against his other leg which was still bent and supporting his own forearm. This action, whether for reasons of his own discomfort or his concern for hers, placed her shoulder, exposed because of the tear in her clothing, under and against his own arm which was resting on his knee.

"You're cold," he mumbled in that low, sultry voice that was Vaden's undoing every time. His arm left his knee then and encircled her shoulders, pulling her tightly against the warmth of his body. "I guess I should've taken the time to bring a coat," he whispered. "You're shaking like a leaf."

Vaden could only shake her head as he let his other arm embrace her as well. She couldn't speak a word, forced into silence by the magnitude of the realization that she was being held, protected, comforted by Ransom Lake. She adored the sensation of her bare shoulder tucked warmly under his arm. She relished the idea of being restrained in his arms, possessed by his will. For those seemingly brief moments between the time he had found her and the time she would arrive home and have to face the memories of the cruelty to her, she rejoiced in the things, the ways, the hint of affections that were given her of Ransom Lake.

Her head nestled firmly against his chest, she reveled in the low, rhythmic sound of his heart as it beat to give him life. It was a strong, powerful rhythm given to a strong, powerful man and she fancied for a moment that the rhythm therein increased suddenly. Looking up, she found that his puzzled frown had returned and that he once again studied her intently.

Why do you look at me that way, she thought to herself.

As if to have read her mind he whispered, "It would be mighty easy for a man to take advantage of this situation, girl."

"How could a man take advantage of this situation?" she asked, though she knew…she *hoped* she knew…what he had intimated.

"Don't play the fool with me, Vaden. I know your mind. You know full well what I mean," he chuckled.

Vaden was delighted to delirium at his addressing her so personally. "Well then...if it would be so easy," she paused, unable to believe that she was going to say the words she intended. But she did. "Why don't you?"

Immediately his eyebrows rose from their intensity of a frown to that of astonishment. He chuckled shortly and shook his head. "Did they hit you over the head when they drug you off?" he asked.

"No. But I want you to..." Her words were cut short when his fingers pressed against her lips and he hushed her. *I want you to kiss me*, she finished in her thoughts.

"Now, don't be saying things that you'll regret later, Vaden," he mumbled. She smiled slightly when she noticed the way his eyes lingered on her mouth as she pushed his fingers away. "You're just upset over the things that went on and..." His words were lost and Vaden felt her heart soar as, continuing to stare at her mouth, he moistened his own lips with the tip of his tongue.

Ransom Lake had lived a solitary life for no one knew how many years. But Vaden Valmont had guessed long ago that the years had been many. She knew enough of men to know that a man of Ransom Lake's strength, health, age and years of loneliness must own some yearning, some need of a woman's soft affections. The mesmerized expression in his storm-filled eyes told her that she was correct in her estimation of him. So, she placed her own fingers gently to her lips, kissing them softly before she reached out, placing them tenderly on the lips of Ransom Lake. His lips were warm and, as her fingers lingered caressively on them, Vaden began to doubt for a moment that he could be weakened. But an instant before she would've pulled her hand away from him, he took it firmly in his and closed his eyes for a moment as he kissed the delicate tips of her fingers determinedly. Then, guiding her hand under his arm and around to rest on his back, he bent, cradling her securely with both arms and kissing her fiercely.

From the first touch of his lips to hers, Vaden imagined that the bonfire that had burned so ferociously and hot at the Halloween social that evening was holed up within her. This kiss was different than the kiss she'd received from Ransom Lake while standing in a mud puddle some weeks earlier. This kiss revealed his absolute masculinity, his intense virility. It was insistent, demanding reciprocation and Vaden responded willingly, for as she knew how desperately the powerful love she secreted for him needed this physical attention...she knew, too, the needs both emotional and physical that Ransom Lake had been deprived of. Or had deprived himself of.

The short whiskers of his roughly shaven face scratched at the tender flesh around Vaden's mouth as this likeness of perfect masculinity, Ransom Lake, worked a kiss of a magnitude to be entirely thorough and passionate. But she worried not for this discomfort or for the discomfort of nearly having the breath squeezed from her lungs so tightly did he hold her against his powerful body, for in those wholly shared moments of impassioned kisses, Vaden Valmont knew that Ransom Lake was her own. Even as her mind and senses whirled with the bliss of his intimate attentions, she knew that it would end and that he would then again be lost to her. But for those glorious moments in time, for the enraptured duration of their kiss, Ransom Lake was hers. Vaden sensed that, though the chance would be merely an instant, she controlled the powerful, independent man. She alone held the reins to his mind, his desire and his will in that instant. She let her hand rest at his jaw as he had instructed her to do on the previous occasion of his kissing her. The fire that blazed within her burned feverish in her heart as she could, indeed, feel the intensity of his determination to draw from her the essence that would quench his desire. As her hand caressed his jaw her thumb rested for a moment in the slight cleft of his chin and she marveled at his mastery of manipulating her emotions.

Suddenly, however, he broke from her and, as she gasped for breath, for she truly had not realized how much his consummate kiss had deprived her of it, he held her tightly to him, whispering in her ear over and over, "I'm sorry, Vaden. I'm sorry. I'm so sorry." Then he took her chin in his hand and looked remorsefully into her eyes. "I would never do anything to hurt you. You've been my...sweet...loyal...friend." He stumbled over the words as if he were trying to find them as he went. Vaden's heart, which only moments before had been soaring in the heavens of love, began to fracture once again. With his admission to her that he valued her as his friend only, all the pain she felt at knowing he could never love her as she did him, all the pain inflicted her by the cruel men that night, all of this pain fused together and Vaden Valmont knew she would never thereafter be the identical person she had been. In an instant, the naivety of youth was stripped from her soul and she knew true, painful heartache and disappointment. True fear. Vaden Valmont had changed.

As the wagon stopped before her uncle's house, Aunt Myra and Yvonne dashed out of the door and into the street. Ransom Lake lifted Vaden, whose heart was now heavy with hurt, cruel treatment and loss, down from the wagon. As Aunt Myra took her lovingly into her arms, Vaden felt nothing. Nothing but the lack of her own caring.

"Land's sake, child! What happened?" Aunt Myra gasped at viewing her niece in such an obviously traumatized state.

"We only meant it as a prank, Mrs. Valmont. I swear it," Nathaniel began to explain. But his efforts in defending himself were in vain when Ransom Lake reached up with one powerful hand, took hold of the young man's shirt and pulled him from the buckboard, throwing him to the ground.

Ransom Lake moved quickly to Vaden, took her face in his hands and spoke to her directly as his stormy colored eyes pierced her own. "Let this go, Miss Vaden. All of it. Don't linger on it. It will only destroy your spirit if you do." Then he untied his horse from the wagon and walked to where Nathaniel still lay on the ground, having had the breath knocked from him in his fall.

"You tell your folks about this, boy. You do it...'cause if I have to come to your house to tell them...I don't know if I'll be able to keep from beating you into your own grave! Do you hear me?" Nathaniel only glared at Ransom Lake. Yvonne and Aunt Myra gasped as Ransom Lake's boot met Nathaniel's midsection with brutal force. "You hear me now, don't you, boy?" he asked. Nathaniel doubled over, clutching his stomach and nodded.

"What happened, Ransom?" Aunt Myra asked the man that stood before her angry still and yet ready to take his leave.

"They had her nailed up in a coffin out by the grove of elms east of town, ma'am," he explained bluntly. "They had her mouth gagged, her arms bound to her sides and her feet tied…all the while she was lying in a pine box with them telling her that they were gonna bury her alive."

Myra gasped and shook her head as horror at the thought pierced her heart. "Vaden! Honey! Are you all right?"

"They threw a blanket over my head when I was walking home. Then they took me out there…tied me up," Vaden stated bluntly, her voice void of emotion.

"They should be whipped near to death, Myra. Jailed up in the least. But I suppose all they'll get is a good talking to," Ransom Lake mumbled. He swallowed hard and dropped his head for a moment before straightening his shoulders and looking directly at Myra. "There's…there's something else I think you should know, Myra. Where I'm concerned, I mean. Concerning my own behavior tonight. I suppose that really I don't have any right to be beating this boy around after what I myself have done where your niece is concerned."

Vaden looked to her aunt who's frown deepened. "What are you trying to say, Ransom?" she asked. She was tentative in her question as if she feared the answer.

"Well, I…ma'am, I…" he stammered.

"It's obvious, Auntie!" Yvonne interrupted. "He's feeling badly about not being properly dressed, can't you see?" Vaden glanced at her sister. "Isn't that it, Vaden?" Yvonne prodded. Vaden wondered why Yvonne would defend Ransom Lake so.

"Yes. He did have his arms around me on the way home, Auntie," Vaden confirmed. "It was so terribly cold. He only meant to keep me warm."

Ransom Lake looked at her, a frown of disbelief puckering his brow. "But, Myra, I…" he stammered, unable to find his words, for the emotion of surprise seemingly stifled his thoughts.

"For pity's sake, Ransom Lake!" Myra exclaimed, throwing her arms around the man and hugging him gratefully. "Do you honestly think that would worry us at a time like this?"

"Myra, I…" he began, but Vaden stepped between him and her aunt and met his confused gaze.

"Thank you, Mr. Lake, for….for coming for me this evening." And, having thanked Ransom Lake for the last time that she intended, she turned and entered the house, a worried Yvonne following closely at her heels.

"Thank you, Ransom," Myra whispered. "Thank you so much. How did you know? When you came here…how did you know?" Vaden paused just inside the house and listened, for she, too, still wondered at how the man knew where to look for her.

"I…I guessed who might be up to no good tonight and where they might be at it," he mumbled as he mounted his horse.

For one instant, Vaden nearly turned to rush to him, to plead with him to stay with her, to hold her safely in his arms again. But now even the zealous Vaden Valmont wouldn't dare to do that, for she had changed in that one late hour. She had changed. Vaden Valmont would never see the world as sweetly rosy and wonderful again. Tragedy, violence, cruelty, and severe, unhealable heartache had wounded her irreversibly tonight.

CHAPTER
∾ EIGHT ∾

*V*aden stood at her bedroom window, staring out but looking at nothing. She didn't think on the beauty of the white, frosty flakes of snow floating through the air during the soft flurry that was occurring outside. She didn't evoke a line of lovely poetry from her memory to recite in their honor. She didn't think on their beauty because she didn't see their beauty. She didn't see anything as she stared silently out. She didn't see the Wimber children run past on their way into the mercantile to ask if their beloved Miss Vaden could tell a story. She didn't hear their disappointed groans as Aunt Myra sent them away with a, "She's not herself today, children." She didn't care if the trees had lost their leaves, their branches flocked in glistening frost. She didn't care whether or not Aunt Myra had made a heavenly apple pie for dessert. She didn't care if Yvonne thought her ignorant, didn't care if Uncle Dan wore a perpetual frown of worry on his face on her behalf. She didn't care that Jerome Clayton dropped into the mercantile four different times that day to ask Yvonne how Vaden was fairing. And, although she heard Ransom Lake's voice drifting down the hall from her aunt's parlor as even he inquired about her well being, she was too stunned, still too unbelieving of what had happened three nights before, too filled with heartbreak to sneak into the hall and have a peek at him who was such a wondrous attraction.

For there was an inner struggle to face a new day, to breathe, to find the radiant love of life again, battling within Vaden Valmont. The horrors that could be in the world had touched her. Damaged her emotions and mind. That people could think to be so cruel to another person, and then to find humor...amusement in someone's terror was beyond comprehension to Vaden. Vaden, who had always seen the shiny side of the coin, who had always seen the beauty in the world and the good in people, now found herself struggling to find any beauty, any good. Vaden, who had believed that true and destined love could be hers, had been shown that it could not. She hadn't spoken a word to anyone for three days. She'd said 'yes' and 'no' when it was absolutely necessary, but no other verbal indications. Her smile had faded and the sparkle of delight in life had dulled and was gone from her beautiful eyes.

"Ransom Lake is here to inquire about you, Vay," Yvonne whispered as she entered the room. "Surely you'll come out for him."

Vaden only continued to stare out the window, for not only was she facing heartbreak where Ransom Lake was concerned, but it seemed that the only emotion left to her, felt by her, was humiliation. And she felt it deeply each time she thought on her attempt at capturing the man for her own that night in the wagon bed. How could she ever face him again? What he must think of her!

Yvonne sighed and began wringing her hands mercilessly. She worried desperately for her sister. She even blamed herself, feeling that somehow her constant nagging at Vaden to see reality in the world had caused this to happen to her precious sister...to squelch that delighted joy in life that Vaden possessed and spread to everyone who knew her. "Come on, Vay. We could hurry and get you dressed. I mean...he did rescue you from...oh, Vay, won't you even come out to see Mr. Lake?"

The single spark of happiness, of joy in Vaden's heart did glimmer at the thought of him. In fact, it began to burn with a renewed brightness, but as Vaden reminisced again of the humiliation she now felt at having been found by Ransom Lake in such a state as she had been, having acted as she had, she buried the glow and only spoke softly to Yvonne. "Tell him...tell him I thank him. I thank him more than he can ever know." She was silent again as she unlatched the window and opened it. Perhaps the cold, crisp air of November, of approaching winter, would clear her mind of the horrid memories and the battle raging within her.

"Oh, Vay," Yvonne sighed. But she knew it was futile to try further, so she left the room.

Vaden closed her eyes and inhaled deeply of the cool air that entered her room through the open window. She felt the snowflakes alight on her cheeks, nose, lips and eyelashes and tried to enjoy the feel of their moisture as they melted against the warmth of her skin. She inhaled deeply again, struggling with everything she was to find a scent of loveliness on the air. Something to fill her lungs and chase away the smell of pine and dirt, to drive from her mind the feel of a dirty handkerchief at her mouth, of the ropes that bound her arms and feet rendering her helpless. Something to gladden her broken heart.

And then, as if by magic, a tear escaped her softly closed eyes as a faint scent of a thing beloved and familiar did tickle her senses. It was the scent of shaving soap, of leather gloves, of horsehair and saddles, mingled with the fragrance of freshly baked bread. Aunt Myra had been baking bread and Vaden had been breathing the comforting aroma for some time. But now it seemed stronger, closer somehow and she opened her eyes to behold the enchanting vision of Ransom Lake standing before her. He stood just outside her window looking in at her, his expression plain and indiscernible, a loaf of Aunt Myra's freshly baked bread wrapped securely in a cloth and tucked beneath his arm.

He put a fist to his mouth as he coughed several times before he frowned and barked firmly, "Snap out of it, girl."

Vaden parted her lips to try to say something, but no sound could be forced from her throat, for she did not know what to say to him. He coughed again, reached through the window and took her chin determinedly in his gloved hand.

"Don't let it beat you down. Don't let one bad thing in life beat the warmth of your heart into the dirt. You'll lose it forever if you don't buck up now. I know the fact of that." Ransom Lake tugged at Vaden's chin in his hand and she leaned out the window toward him. The house's foundation being only a foot or less from the ground put her gaze nearly level with his and the warmth of his breath on her face caused Vaden's heart to begin racing with excitement once more. His face was so near to hers as he stared intently into her eyes that were she to move less than one more inch forward she might have accidentally been blessed with a taste of his lips, and it thrilled her. She scolded herself inwardly for even thinking on it, for she knew now the consequences of acting so boldly.

"Rein in, girl. Don't let it get the better of you. Next time I'm out this way I want that spark for life back in your eyes. You hear me?" Then he released her, coughed twice more, and as quickly as he had appeared before her, was walking away down the alley.

Vaden watched him walk away through the flurry of snowflakes and the glow of love left in her did not fade away, but rather stayed, warming her bosom some. She knew it was the feeling of love for the man, Ransom Lake, that had kept her from completely losing herself. Even if he would never love her, she did love him and she had been his friend at least. He had said so himself. And that was something. She put her hand out the window then and caught several flakes of snow on her palm. "They are charming bits of loveliness," she mumbled to herself. Her attention was arrested by a small boy running down the street. He twisted and turned as he went, his face turned upward, his mouth open wide and tongue hanging out as he tried to catch the frozen particles of moisture in his mouth. At watching the child's carefree joy, the corners of Vaden's mouth turned up slightly for the first time in days.

Aunt Myra radiated her joy from every pore as Vaden, fully dressed and feature of face relaxed from frowning, sat down to supper with the rest of the family that evening. "Are you...are you feeling better, sweet pea?" she asked.

Vaden smiled and said, "I will. I know I will, Auntie." Myra sighed relievedly.

There was no reference made to anything too important during supper and Vaden knew the family was being sensitive to her tender emotions. Uncle Dan discussed trivial things about the stock and neighbors, and Aunt Myra complained about the condition of her bread, its imperfections caused from having the oven too hot or too cool.

Then, just after dinner as the family was retiring to the parlor, there came a loud knock at the door. Yvonne responded to it and returned momentarily with a small wooden box in hand.

"This was on the front porch," Yvonne announced as she entered the parlor. "It's got a paper here with your name printed on it, Vaden. Rather sloppily if I do say so. Perhaps one of your little fairy tale lovers has left it."

Vaden reached out, taking the small box from Yvonne. Removing the envelope from its place on top of the box, she set it on her lap and opened the envelope that simply had '*Miss Vaden Valmont*' written on it.

"To Vaden," she read from the small piece of paper within. "That's all it says," she added, looking at the back of the paper just in case.

"What is it?" Aunt Myra asked, now curious as well and coming to stand beside her niece.

Vaden opened the box and there beneath a layer of white linen lay several tan colored objects that resembled some sort of cookie.

"Pralines!" Aunt Myra exclaimed! "Oh! They are soooo delicious! And I know of only one person in town that makes those. Sable Clayton!"

Vaden felt her heart immediately sink slightly. "You mean you think...you think...Jerome Clayton left these for me?" she asked disappointedly.

"Well," Aunt Myra explained sensing her niece's rather odd disappointment, "Sable sells them, too. I suppose someone could've purchased them and left them for you."

"My, my, little sister," Yvonne teased lovingly. "Your first secret admirer."

Vaden did smile then, for whether or not she desired attention from Jerome, it was a romantic gesture. Picking up a piece of confection, she tasted for the first time the brown sugary, pecan blended flavor of the praline. "MMMMmmmm!" she sighed. "That is the best thing I've ever in my life eaten! Try this, Vonnie."

Yvonne sighed and nodded. Carefully she broke off a small piece of the candy and placed it daintily on her tongue. "I've not tasted anything like that!" she admitted quite sincerely.

Vaden passed the small box around until Uncle Dan had taken two and Aunt Myra, scolding her husband for being greedy, had taken one. Then, when Myra had given the box back to Vaden, Vaden scowled as she noticed a piece of straw protruding from beneath the linen on which the candy sat. Carefully, so as not to damage the confection, she pulled back the linen and saw that nestled in a handful of straw was a rock.

"That's odd," she murmured as she looked at it. "Why would the box be weighted with a rock?"

"Perhaps he, whoever he is, feared that a wind would come up and blow the thing off the porch," Yvonne offered.

But as Vaden lifted the linen and candy completely out of the box she saw another note lying next to the rock. Carefully she drew out the second piece of paper and opened it, reading to herself.

"For pity's sake, Vay, what does it say?" Yvonne whined.

"It says, '*Hard, cold and unfeeling to look at. But look inside. I'd like to see the smile that this will bring to your pretty face, for nothing on earth can match the beauty of your smile.*'" Vaden, still too traumatized to be over flattered, frowned, though Aunt Myra and Yvonne both giggled delightedly. "How can you look inside a rock?"

Aunt Myra shrugged, as did Yvonne. But Uncle Dan's eyes seemed to twinkle and he said, "Turn it over, sweet pea. Look inside." Vaden smiled at him, for it occurred to her that this secret admirer could very well be her sweet, dear Uncle Dan. Quickly she took the rock from its nest of straw and immediately an odd thrill ran through her body as she touched it. Then, turning it over, she drew in a quick breath as her eyes beheld the inside of the rock which was hollow some, yet with inner walls covered in beautiful amethyst crystal.

"Would you look at that?" Aunt Myra exclaimed in a whisper.

"I've never seen such a thing before," Yvonne added.

"It's a geode," Uncle Dan stated, holding out his hand. Vaden smiled and placed the lovely thing of nature in his palm. "Them crystals form inside some kinds of rocks. It's deceiving, ain't it?"

Vaden smiled knowingly at Uncle Dan and whispered, "Thank you, Uncle Dan."

But Uncle Dan shook his head as he handed the stone back to Vaden. "I didn't have nothin' whatsoever to do with this, darlin'. No matter what you're thinkin'." Vaden smiled all the same and the love she felt for her uncle helped further in healing her heart somewhat. It was good and wonderful to be loved by family and friends. Especially certain friends, she thought.

Within three or four more days, Vaden was something akin to what she once had been. She could laugh again, though not as heartily. She could see beauty in life, though not as much of it. Little by little, a much more grown up Vaden was finding fragments of herself again.

Jerome, who had been excessively concerned about her well-being, came to see her often. The fact was that Vaden's emotions were not as passionate as they once were, thus allowing her to be more tolerant of his still undesired attentions. She found the patience to pity him in seeing his side of the situation finally.

"Will you come for a walk with me this evening, Miss Vaden?" Jerome inquired of Vaden on that particular afternoon. "It would do you good to get some fresh air."

"Oh, I think I've had enough fresh air for a while. But I thank you for asking, Mr. Clayton. And I appreciate your concern." Vaden reached out, squeezing Jerome's hand reassuringly when his features dropped disappointedly. "I'm sure I'll feel like a walk very soon."

Jerome smiled, encouraged. "Well, soon then. Soon. I've been miserable without you, Miss Vaden. After what happened and you were so...so...not yourself. I found myself dreaming of that beautiful smile of yours."

Vaden looked to him quickly, but she could not discern whether or not there was hidden meaning in his remark about her smile.

Then he lowered his voice and spoke, "Forgive me, Miss Vaden. But, I've been so angry, so enraged, about what those men...my supposed friends did to you."

Vaden shook her head and turned from him, not wanting to be further reminded of the experience. "It's in the past. The near past perhaps, but the past all the same, Mr. Clayton. Let's not speak of it."

"Please. Let me finish. Let me say my peace, Miss Vaden." He was so stern and blunt that she did, indeed, nod and wait for him to speak. "I was so angry with them that it took me until yesterday to think on what happened afterward. What happened when Ransom Lake found you. I...I've heard that he wasn't even hardly dressed. And that he was forcing you to..."

"Nathaniel Wimber abducted me from the street, Mr. Clayton!" Vaden exclaimed, suddenly very vexed. "Nathaniel, Toby, Frank and Randy! People I thought were my friends...tore my shirtwaist handling me so brutally, tied me up and forced me into a pine box and nailed it shut! And you stand before me questioning Ransom Lake's behavior? Ransom Lake stopped it! He stopped their cruelty to me and brought me safely home. Do you think it matters a whit to me, my aunt and uncle or anyone else who could imagine what I had gone through...do you think it matters to anyone else that he didn't pause to dress for the occasion?" Vaden calmed herself as another thought struck her. "What else did Nathaniel tell you, Mr. Clayton? What other slanderous things did that miscreant tell you? My clothing was torn away at the shoulder, Mr. Clayton. I was without a proper coat for protection from the cold that night. Ransom Lake did nothing more than keep me warm. Nothing more than protect me from the people that had hurt me!"

"You're very protective of him, Vaden," Jerome stated. Vaden was irritated at his use of her given name. "Nathaniel said that you and he were…"

"Were what?" Vaden exclaimed. "What? I may be very protective of Ransom Lake…protective of the man who delivered me from those idiots you call friends…but you're unusually protective of Nathaniel. Do you agree with what he involved himself in? Do you think what they did to me was amusing? Do you wish they would've invited you along so that you, too, could've enjoyed my terror?"

Jerome sighed and his face softened somewhat. Shaking his head, he said, "No. No, of course not. They were wrong. And you're right. There's no reason to accuse Ransom Lake of any misconduct."

Vaden untied her apron and slammed it down on the counter top. "You're right, Mr. Clayton. I do need some fresh air. A walk would be very nice. A walk by myself!" After going to the back room, snatching up a wrap and telling Yvonne that she was going out, Vaden left by way of the mercantile front door, leaving Jerome looking guilty and discouraged.

It was thus that Vaden found herself perched high in the branches of her favorite maple. The dear tree was nearly half barren of leaves now and it made for a broader view of the landscape. The late afternoon air hinted of the frigid evening to come. Perhaps snow. Vaden sighed heavily as she gazed out across the land at Ransom Lake's rooftop. It was some time before she realized that no smoke rose from the chimney. Odd, she thought, for it was very chilly out and, no doubt, he would've built his evening fire by now. Something cold touched Vaden's spine as the realization penetrated her mind and an oppressive feeling of uneasiness washed over her. Climbing down from the tree, she started toward the road and was relieved to see Vaughn Wimber driving his wagon in the direction of Ransom Lake's home.

"Mr. Wimber!" she called out, walking to him when the wagon stopped and he nodded in greeting. "Good evening, Mr. Wimber. Would you per chance be going to visit Mr. Lake?"

"Miss Vaden, I want you to know that we're so sorry about Nathaniel's behavior the other night," the man apologized very sincerely. "We just can't believe that our boy would do such a thing and..."

"It's forgotten," Vaden lied. She had no time to accept apologies. She felt in her soul that something was not right where Ransom Lake was concerned. "Are you, indeed, going to visit Mr. Lake?" she asked again.

"Well, yes." Vaughn Wimber looked puzzled. "I'm going out there this minute with my own apologies for his trouble as well. Would you like to come along? I'll only be a minute and then I'll drop you back home."

"That would be fine. Just fine. Thank you, Mr. Wimber," she sighed, climbing onto the buckboard beside him. Glancing back to the bed of the wagon, she let her mind linger only an instant on those wonderful moments she'd spent at that very spot in Ransom Lake's arms. Then she looked ahead, no more looking back, and tried to sit still as they rode slowly toward his house.

Vaden's heart began to pound wildly as it always did whenever she was anticipating a meeting with Ransom Lake. As the house came into view and the wagon approached it she feared Vaughn Wimber might actually hear the mad beating of her heart because of its fierceness.

Vaughn Wimber pulled the team to a halt just before the house and helped Vaden down from the wagon. Then he followed her as she rushed to the front door and knocked firmly.

As they stood together before the door to Ransom Lake's house, Vaughn muttered, "It sure is dark in there. And where's his dog?"

Vaden began to panic and kicked the door three times with her foot. They waited and Vaughn sighed saying, "There. Here he comes," as they heard a scuffling from the other side. The door opened slowly and Vaughn Wimber greeted, "Afternoon, Ransom. I've come to offer our family's apologies." But as Ransom Lake stood before them wrapped in a blanket and coughing violently, his cheeks blazing red and his eyes only open narrow slits, Vaughn Wimber stepped in front of Vaden, pushing his way past Ransom Lake and into the house. "How long you been sick like this, Ransom?" he asked.

Vaden was horrified to find Ransom Lake in such a weakened condition. She followed Vaughn into the house and looked around noting the cold, dark and cluttered state of the room.

"Just got me a bit of the under the weather," Ransom Lake forced out, his voice raspy and fevered.

"You got more than a bit of it." Vaughn put a rough hand to the man's face. "Yer plum burnin' up! How long's this been goin' on?"

"It'll pass," Ransom Lake stated. Again he coughed and Vaden could hear that it came from deep within his chest.

"It was the bitter cold on Halloween that found you this way," Vaden remarked as a familiar pang of guilt dug at her heart.

"Just a bitty cough, girl. Nothing to take too serious," Ransom Lake argued.

But Vaden knew better. Immediately she practically pounced on the man, holding one palm to his forehead while the other hand fumbled with his grasp on the blanket at his chest. "Let this go!" she demanded, and more out of surprise than anything else, Ransom Lake relaxed his grip on the blanket. Vaden put an ear to the man's sculpted and overly warm chest and listened intently. "Go for my Aunt Myra, Mr. Wimber. Doctor Sullivan is gone to visit his daughter for the holiday and Mr. Lake's lungs are rattling something terrible. Have her bring some broth and...well, she'll know what else. Tell her he's got fever, rattling lungs, chills...she'll know what to do."

"Well, I...I can't just leave you here alone with the man, Miss Vaden." Vaughn Wimber was obviously unconvinced that he should leave.

"I've been in far worse predicaments, Mr. Wimber," Vaden reminded him, though not cruelly. "It's plain he's worsening and not getting any better. It could be pneumonia! My Aunt Myra will know what to do. Hurry!"

With a nod of determination and something of guilt, he left quickly. Vaden stripped off her wrap and let it fall to a heap on the floor. Quickly she built a fire in the hearth. The room needed warming.

"Let's get some water boiling." She went to the stove in the next room and began stoking a fire there, as well. "The steam will help you breathe better. I can't believe you haven't been into town for help. Actually, I can. Men. They think they're impervious to disease and illness and..." but she stopped talking when she heard his weakened body fall to the floor in a heap not far from where she had dropped her wrap.

"I think I'm sick, Natalie," Ransom Lake moaned.

"Natalie?" Vaden repeated curiously in a whisper as she tried to pull him to his feet. His heavy body was terribly weak and awkward and it was with great difficulty that she helped him toward a chair near the fireplace and replaced the blanket around his shoulders. Instead of sitting, however, he laid down on the floor.

"I'm hot," he breathed, throwing the blanket aside. "It's so hot in here."

"You're feverish," Vaden explained, going to the pump and wetting a cloth beneath its cold running water. She returned to the ailing man and, folding the cloth, placed it on his forehead. "This will help cool your body," she explained soothingly. She sat down near his head and was surprised when he raised himself long enough to scoot his body up, depositing his head in her lap.

"I guess I should've taken a moment to grab a coat that night," he said, his speech more mumbly than usual. "At least you're not taken ill."

Realizing that he was, indeed, coherent enough to know who she was and that his calling her by another name must have been purely an accident, she asked, "Who's Natalie?" She felt at that moment, serious as his illness was, that she must know about the woman in his past. The woman that perhaps sent him into seclusion. The woman who may once have worn the ring that Ransom Lake now wore on his smallest finger.

"Natalie?" he repeated, seemingly startled.

"Natalie. You called me Natalie before." Vaden watched him and he seemed unsettled by her question.

At once his body was wracked with the violence of his coughing. He inhaled deeply and continued to let his head rest on Vaden's lap.

"So," Vaden prodded, undaunted, yet feeling fairly guilty for pushing him to answer when he was clearly so ill.

"So, what?" Ransom Lake mumbled irritatedly. "I don't feel like talking right now, girl. Can't you see that?"

"Just tell me who Natalie is and I'll let you be." Ransom Lake glared up at Vaden and Vaden glared back. What was he hiding? What had he been hiding for so long? She had to know. She had to know about this Natalie.

After glaring at her for several more moments he finally said, "Natalie was...was Natalie. And that's all of it."

"But that's no..." Vaden began.

"That's all of it, girl," he growled angrily at her. "Now, close that curious mouth of yours and help me heal...or leave me in peace."

"Is Natalie the reason you..." she began. But when his glare intensified she knew she was wrong to push him. Ransom Lake held his secrets cached deeply in his soul. He would not share them and she was a fool, an idiot to suppose that if he did, he would choose an imbecilic young girl like her. So, she was silent. She picked up the cloth from his forehead and turned it over, placing the other side to his skin. Then, as he closed his eyes and seemed to rest for a moment, she stared into the blaze in the hearth.

It seemed hours to Vaden, the minutes of sitting there waiting for help. Sitting there with the ill, stricken, silent man. And in those moments of silence and intense worry, Vaden stared into the flames and thought of the tragedy of not being able to win over the man she loved so desperately. It was sad, grievously lamentable, that she would love him so completely as she did and yet know that he would never be hers. She thought again, however, that though he was unattainable, she had owned at least a part of him for a moment, for she still knew that during those intimate kisses they shared in the wagon bed, he had been hers. His manner, his soul, or something surreal had spoken to her mind in those moments assuring her that he knew it was Vaden Valmont he held in his arms. Vaden Valmont that had caused him to lose his senses for a brief time. It was Vaden he meant to kiss, not some long ago lost love that he still pined for. Vaden knew that it was her and her alone that he meant to administer his affections to in those beloved, dream-like moments. And if nothing else, if Ransom Lake should wake in the morning healed and decide he never again wanted to lay eyes on the bothersome being, Vaden Valmont, still she would always have that memory of the moments that he had been hers.

Half an hour passed and still Mr. Wimber had not returned with Aunt Myra. Vaden tried to move her legs a bit as they still supported the weight of the man's head and were beginning to tingle with lack of blood circulating through them. She removed the cloth from Ransom Lake's forehead, knowing that it would do no good to him now, being that it was nearly as hot as his body.

As she gazed down at him, listening to his raspy breath, the breath he seemed to struggle for, she thought of Jerome Clayton. Was she doomed to belong to him? Everyone knew he cared for her. Everyone, including Vaden, knew that he appeared the ideal young man. Tall, handsome, charming, courteous, proper. Certainly Jerome Clayton would never remove his shirt in front of a young woman. And Vaden, though she had never spoken it aloud, thought and wondered on how a woman could find attraction to a man when there was no excitement, no surprise, no delight, in one who did not enjoy to some extent teasing a girl.

Still, Ransom Lake could not be hers, and Jerome Clayton already was.

According even to his own admission. With Jerome there would be stability, a home, a husband and, she guessed, a kind father to their children. At the thought of having Jerome Clayton father her children Vaden's face actually grimaced. Just one mere kiss from Jerome had sent her body into repulsed shivers. She could not imagine having to endure more physical attention from him. Still, her own mother, though deeply in love with her father, had told Vaden that it was not always perfect between a man and a woman. That often other factors outweighed the lack of physical attraction. Was this to be her lot in life? No. Certainly the heavens intended a better companion for her, for no matter what his appearances, no matter how admired he was by everyone else, Vaden did not feel comfortable in Jerome's presence. It wasn't so much that she didn't like him. After all, he was pushy and rather possessive, but likable enough. It was something else. Something she just couldn't quite identify. She felt almost, well, unsafe when she was with him. Surely no one could expect her to settle for him when she felt so averse to him. She couldn't expect herself to settle for him.

Looking down into the perpetual frown on Ransom Lake's face, Vaden tried to smooth the wrinkles from his forehead with her fingertips. At just touching him thus, the flesh on Vaden's arms rippled with goose bumps, and she doubted more fully that she could endure a relationship with a man who did not affect her so. She caressed one of Ransom Lake's fevered cheeks with the back of her hand, letting the fingers of her other hand slip into the softness of his hair. She let her thumb trace the outline of his lips gently, and he stirred for a moment, turning himself on his side so that his face was nearly flush with her stomach. This position was not as comfortable for Vaden, for it occurred to her then that this might not look quite decent when her aunt walked into the room. So, placing one palm against his chest and the other on his forehead, she attempted to gently squirm from beneath him. But the fevered man groaned in protest, a scowl returning to his features, and one powerful hand pushed Vaden's hand from his chest.

"Mr. Lake, I...I have to move. My legs have fallen asleep under your weight. I'll...here," she said, reaching for the blanket that he had discarded earlier. "Here." Lifting his head from her lap, she bunched up the blanket and tucked it beneath his head as she moved herself from under him and stood up. Almost immediately, however, the man began to shiver uncontrollably, his visible flesh prickling with tiny bumps. Going to the sofa nearby, Vaden retrieved another blanket and placed it over his fevered body just as the front door opened and her aunt, Mr. Wimber and Yvonne stepped into the house.

"He's very ill, Auntie," Vaden blurted out, relieved that she had removed herself from the man soon enough.

Aunt Myra dropped to her knees beside the man and placed a tender, maternal hand on his forehead. "He's burning up," Myra mumbled. "Vaughn, run get that kettle on the stove and fetch a bucket of water from the pump. Hurry." Vaughn Wimber wasted no time in doing as Myra instructed. "Help me get him onto his back, girls."

Yvonne's eyes widened when, as the three women worked together to turn the man, the blanket covering his body slipped away. Had the situation not been so dire, Vaden might have laughed at the expression on her sister's face. Aunt Myra picked up the cloth that Vaden had used to cool Ransom's head and when Mr. Wimber returned with the water, Aunt Myra combined enough of the boiling water from the kettle with the cold water in the bucket to create just the right tepid temperature necessary.

"Vaughn, go out and get some more firewood. We need to keep it warm in here." As Mr. Wimber left by way of a door that led out through the kitchen, Myra continued, "Yvonne, soak this cloth in the water and bathe his head, arms, neck and chest. It will help to calm the fever." Yvonne's eyes widened in horror, but she did as her aunt instructed. "He's pale, Vaden. Find something to put under his feet."

Vaden looked about frantically, but saw that her aunt had removed the blanket from beneath Ransom Lake's head and quickly snatched it up, bunching it into a bundle and placing it under his feet. She looked to him when she heard him groan once more and begin coughing.

"That cough is deep in him," Aunt Myra mumbled as she pressed a hand firmly on his chest to feel his heartbeat and lungs. "He's worse off than I hoped to find him."

Vaden felt the fear begin to increase in her bosom. *What if*, she began to think, but the sound of Ransom Lake's voice interrupted her unthinkable question to herself.

"What are you doing?" he nearly shouted. "I'm fine. Let me be!"

"You're very ill, Ransom," Aunt Myra told him firmly. "Lay still and..."

"There you are," he mumbled, his voice softening as he looked up at Yvonne who was so startled that she dropped the cloth she'd been using to bathe his fevered skin. "Help me up," he ordered as he reached out, wrapping one arm about Yvonne's waist and taking hold of her arm to try to pull himself up. Yvonne's eyes widened and her mouth dropped open in astonishment. "Help me up! How do you ever expect to find yourself helpless in my arms if I can't even get up there to kiss you, precious?"

It was Vaden who gasped next as Ransom Lake managed to pull himself to his knees, his fevered gaze intent on her sister.

"He's out of his head, Yvonne. Ignore what he's saying to you. Ransom's a good man and don't you go thinking badly of him," Aunt Myra instructed her niece as she put her own arms around Ransom Lake's chest and pulled him away from Yvonne. "Help me get him to the sofa, Vaden. He needs to be sitting up." Vaden paused for only a moment, preoccupied by her sister's all too pleased blush, delighted expression and unfaltering stare at Ransom Lake. "Vaden!" Aunt Myra commanded. Vaden quickly took one of Ransom Lake's heavy arms and placed it about her own shoulders helping him to stand.

"Where'd she go," Ransom Lake mumbled. "That girl sets my mouth to watering." Even in the seriousness of such a situation, Vaden knew the sharp sting of jealousy as it erupted in her stomach.

By the time Vaughn Wimber had returned, Ransom Lake was resting peacefully on the sofa in a sitting position. As she helped her aunt, Yvonne and Vaughn endeavor to help the man heal, the thought struck her that perhaps Ransom Lake was no different than any other man on earth. Perhaps the only reason Vaden had captured any of his attention at all was because he felt Yvonne was too out of his reach. "No. No," she whispered to herself aloud. He was feverish. After all, hadn't he called her by the wrong name only a short time before? Vaden tried to dispel her anxiety by comforting herself with this knowledge.

It was a long and fearful night for Vaden. Aunt Myra had sent Vaughn Wimber home hours before and now Yvonne rested peacefully in a nearby chair and Aunt Myra rested on the sofa next to Ransom Lake. His fever had broken about an hour earlier and Aunt Myra had assured Vaden that he would be fine, but she still wanted to wait until morning after he awakened to leave him alone. Vaden had learned a great deal during those long hours when her aunt had tended Ransom Lake. She knew that the knowledge she had gained that night pertaining to helping someone overcome illness would serve her well in years to come. She thought to herself that maybe the experience would help her in tending her own children one day. The children she would never have with Ransom Lake. Would they be the children that she might share with Jerome Clayton? Her stomach churned at the very thought of Jerome Clayton and a sort of anxious fear engulfed her fatigued mind. Again she wondered what it was that pushed her away from accepting Jerome as the nice, well-mannered, desirable man everyone else thought him to be.

"I feel like a pile of horse manure that's been run over by every wagon wheel in the county." The low, raspy mumble caused Vaden to turn around from where she sat at Ransom Lake's feet, overjoyed to hear his low, mumbly voice again. He pulled himself into a sitting position on the sofa, leaning on his knees with his elbows as he buried his scowling face in his hands for a moment. He frowned, his eyes opening to only narrow slits as he looked inquisitively and rather grouchily at Vaden. "What did you do to me this time, girl?" he asked.

"Nothing!" Vaden spat irritatedly, turning away from him. How horrid that he would assume that, because he felt so badly, she had once again been the cause of it. But his low chuckle stopped the tears from escaping her eyes not a moment too soon. And when she felt the warmth of his capable hand slip beneath her hair and clutch the back of her neck she turned to look at him again. "I'm gonna swallow my pride and thank you for coming with Vaughn last night. I felt pretty badly."

"Well, I'm relieved to see you feeling better, Ransom," Aunt Myra chirped, stretching and standing up from the sofa.

"Much better. I thank you, Myra," the man responded, dropping his hand from Vaden's neck and looking up to her aunt. "And you, too, Miss Valmont," he added, nodding a 'thank you' at Yvonne who could not meet his gaze, for her blush was crimson.

"Well, there's no doubt in my mind that you caught that nasty sickness the night you brought Vaden home, Ransom. And I want to remind you how grateful we are to you for that," Aunt Myra told him, smiling appreciatively.

"My pleasure, Myra. I'm indebted to you for this." He offered a hand and firmly shook the one Myra returned.

"We've left you some muffins for breakfast. If you get to feeling badly again, you drive over to the house, you hear me?" Myra instructed.

"Yes, ma'am," he chuckled.

"Come along now, girls. We've done our nursing well and we need to be getting on home. I don't think you ever dropped off for a rest, Vaden child. You must be done in."

"I'm fine, Auntie." Vaden stood and reached for her wrap, which her aunt had hung on a nearby coat rack. She didn't think she could turn and look at Ransom Lake and still leave him. His pale coloring, weakened state, and still raspy breathing frightened her, coupled with the fact that for some reason she felt a need to run to him and prove that she was as good and desirable a woman as Yvonne.

"Thank you, dear ladies," he mumbled as the women began to walk toward the front door.

"Now you stay sitting, boy," Vaden heard Aunt Myra scolding. "There's no need to see us out." Still Vaden didn't turn to look at Ransom Lake, but only continued to follow behind Yvonne and Myra as they walked to the door. "Let us know if you need anything, Ransom," Myra added. "Bye now. And you take care."

"You're welcome to take the wagon home, Myra. I don't feel right letting you three walk and…" Ransom began.

"The fresh air will do us good. Now, you put yourself to bed. Do you hear?" With that, Myra left the house.

"You have a nice day, Miss Valmont," Ransom called after Yvonne, who turned, blushed, smiled and nodded.

Vaden couldn't wait to escape Ransom Lake's house. She felt panic, sorrow, fear, and heartbreak all over again. But as she started out the door after Yvonne, she was stopped as she felt the back of her skirt catch on something. Turning to see what was stopping her so that she might free herself, she saw at once that one fold of her skirt was, indeed, caught. Caught tightly in Ransom Lake's grasp. Knowing it was unavoidable now, she raised her eyes from her skirt to find him looking at her.

There was no smile to his feature and no frown, as he said, "I guess we're even now, huh? An eye for an eye so to speak."

"I think your deed was much more that of deliverer than ours, Mr. Lake," she managed to say bluntly. Quickly he released his hold on her skirts and took her hand. Vaden glanced out the door to see that her aunt and Yvonne were already to the road and had turned toward home.

"It depends on your point of view, I suppose," Ransom Lake mumbled, and Vaden looked back at him. He smiled slightly and added, "Natalie is my older sister's name, Vaden."

"Oh," Vaden said nonchalantly, though she sighed relievedly within. "Well, that's interesting to know, Mr. Lake." Ransom Lake's smile broadened and Vaden's heart warmed, knowing that, whatever the reason, she was the cause of the smile across his divinely featured face.

"Thank you again," he added with a friendly wink.

"Thank *you* again," Vaden answered, pulling her hand from his nerve stirring grasp. As Vaden hurried to catch up with her aunt and sister, Yvonne turned and flashed one of her dazzling smiles in her direction.

"You were right to send for Auntie, Vay. She knew just what to do." Vaden was disturbed by her sister's beauty at that particular moment. Never before had she been truly envious of it. Vaden had always, though perhaps feeling it a greater challenge to use her less obvious feminine wiles to attract attention, been confident in herself. Never before had she let Yvonne's beauty intimidate her. Until now. For with what had transpired between Yvonne and Ransom Lake while he had been feverish, Vaden was beginning to wonder more and more if perhaps Ransom Lake's serious interest had always been directed toward her sister.

"I knew she would," Vaden answered finally.

"That Ransom Lake," Aunt Myra sighed. "I don't know how he's avoided death this long as solitary as he keeps himself. I'll be honest, and not just to pat myself on the back for knowing what to do, but if we hadn't have helped him through the night...well things may have been much, much worse." Aunt Myra put a comforting arm about Vaden's shoulders. "What's that scowl cutting your brow for, sweet pea?"

Vaden rubbed at her temples for a moment and then said, "Oh, I'm just very tired, Auntie. Truly."

"Well, I think the poor soul should be invited for Thanksgiving dinner." Yvonne looked completely guiltless in her reasoning when Vaden looked up at her quickly. "After all, he's so...so alone. Don't you think so, Vaden?" Yvonne winked and Vaden felt guilty for having thought badly of her sister for a moment, for it was obvious that Yvonne knew it would please

Vaden to have Ransom Lake in for Thanksgiving.

"It's a wonderful idea!" Aunt Myra exclaimed. "I'll come over with your Uncle Dan tomorrow to check on Ransom and we'll invite him then." Aunt Myra frowned for a moment and mused, "Oh, dear. What if someone has already asked him?"

"Then we'll invite him for Christmas!" Yvonne chirped.

Vaden nodded her agreement and her eyes wandered to her left as the road they trod upon passed by the turnoff to her favorite tree by the creek.

"Vaden," Yvonne began that night after the sisters had turned down the lamp and snuggled comfortably beneath their covers. "Vaden, I couldn't bring myself to confess this before...because I was astounded about it on Halloween night when he brought you home...and everything was so trau-matic that I didn't say anything. But, now I have to say it, Vaden. I had no idea!"

"No idea about what?" Vaden asked, though she already knew to what her sister referred.

"Well, I mean...when you told me that you'd...you know...that you'd seen Ransom Lake...improperly attired...well, I just had no idea that he looked so...so..."

"Indescribable?" Vaden offered irritatedly.

Yvonne giggled slightly. "Yes! Yes, that's it exactly!"

"Did you think I made the story up then, Vonnie?" Vaden snapped.

"Oh, no! No! Of course not, Vay! I believed you. It's just that...well, I always thought somehow I'd be horrified to retching the first time I saw such a thing. But...but I wasn't. In fact, I would say the experience went beyond interesting. He's marvelously sculpted, Vay."

"I know."

"And soft skinned. You know, I expected him to feel more like...I don't know...a fish maybe. All slimy and scaly."

"Now that's utterly ridiculous, Yvonne! You're only being dramatic now and I refuse to listen to it!" Turning from her sister, Vaden held the blanket tightly around her shoulders.

"What's wrong, Vay?" Yvonne asked, genuinely concerned. "You've been testy all day. Is it simply fatigue? Or is something else bothering you?"

"Nothing is bothering me, Yvonne. I'm simply too tired to talk." Vaden felt guilty lying to her sister because she knew Yvonne would understand if she were to explain her concerns. But instead she simply mumbled, "Goodnight."

"And to think, Vay...he risked his health to rescue you from the clutches of evil that night. It's terribly tender, isn't it?" Yvonne sighed.

Vaden feigned sleep then. It didn't even occur to her that somehow the tables had turned. Vaden Valmont had begun to loose her ability to dream, to have her heart take flight over fanciful thoughts. While her sister, ever straight-laced and proper before, was talking in the language of fairy tales.

CHAPTER
∞ NINE ∞

*R*ansom Lake recovered. He'd accepted Myra's invitation for Thanksgiving dinner, too, and the time of the dinner was moving closer and closer. But Vaden still battled her emotions. Her uncertainties. Her prospects. Or rather, prospect. Jerome, as always, was overly attentive and charming. In the now three weeks following the incident of Halloween night, he had been more the perfect gentleman and friend than ever. And because he was so, coupled with the fact that Ransom Lake had not shown his face in town since that time, Vaden had neglected to tell Jerome that she could never settle for him. Inwardly her dreams battled with reality, and reality, for once, was getting the better of her. Jerome was an attractive, attentive, well-mannered man. He would, no doubt, work hard to make Vaden happy, to build a family with her and make a decent life for them all. The truth of it was that Jerome was reality.

Jerome came into the store every day, often bearing some small gift as a token of his affections for Vaden. Vaden had taken several evening walks with him as well. She'd even relented to his continuing request, and begun calling him by his given name. Never, however, did she allow him to kiss her again in any fashion.

It began to seem to Vaden that she would need to accept that Jerome was her lot in life. That Ransom Lake had only been allowed to touch her young existence so that she could learn that along with joy and wonderful things, heartache and sorrow were also part of living. She still struggled with the humiliation, the terror, and the tormenting memory of that devastating Halloween night. Struggled with the horrid residual memories of panic. With the blissful memories of Ransom Lake's kiss savored in the back of a wagon. All of these things created a great and unsettled turmoil within Vaden and she often felt as if her thoughts, her actions would never be wholly her own again.

It was two days before Thanksgiving, a cool, autumn Monday morning when Ransom Lake did at last enter the mercantile. Yvonne and Vaden were working straightening the store and Aunt Myra was at the counter when he entered.

"Well, good morning, ladies. Florence Nightingales of the county," he greeted with a smile and in his low mumbly manner.

Vaden felt her heart leap into her throat instantly, but tried to turn slowly to greet him.

"Good morning, Mr. Lake," Yvonne welcomed exuberantly.

"Miss Valmont. Miss Vaden," Ransom greeted, nodding his head at first one girl and then the other.

"You about ready for my world famous pumpkin pies, Ransom?" Aunt Myra asked.

Ransom Lake smiled, nodding his head. "I sure am, Myra. I just hope I can get here on Thursday is all."

"What do you mean?" Vaden erupted, for it alarmed her that he would even imply that he wouldn't be with them for Thanksgiving when she'd looked forward to it so.

"There's a storm coming," he answered, still looking to Myra. "A heavy one. I think we'll all be pretty snowed in nice and tight by Thursday morning."

"But you'll still come won't you?" Yvonne asked. "You can't miss Thanksgiving, Mr. Lake."

"Oh, I suppose I'll make it somehow," he teased, winking at Yvonne.

Vaden was so upset by his attention to her sister that she turned from him and began stacking boxes rather violently.

"Oh, dear. Vaden, maybe you should tell Mrs. Wimber that you can't watch the children while she goes visiting dear Mrs. Tilits. I don't want you getting stranded out there and not getting home to…" Aunt Myra began. Vaden had assured Mrs. Wimber that she would tend the children while she went visiting the day before Thanksgiving.

"I'll be fine, Auntie. Mrs. Wimber never stays too late," Vaden defended, turning to look at her aunt and Ransom Lake. "You know that." Then, unable to tolerate the three pairs of eyes that bored down inquisitively on her for the brusqueness of her remark, Vaden walked toward the front door announcing, "I'm to meet Jerome at nine, Auntie. I'll be back soon."

Without waiting for a reply or permission she left, walked down the street and turned onto the pumpkin patch road. Tears were immediately on her cheeks and she brushed at them angrily as she walked. Why? she wondered. Why were her emotions so close to the surface all the time? Why did she read sarcasm and unfriendliness into everything everyone said to her? Why couldn't she just accept Jerome Clayton for what he was and forget Ransom Lake for what he was? Ransom Lake would never belong to her, it was obvious. In fact, it wouldn't surprise anyone if he ended up belonging to her beautiful and accomplished sister.

She thought that maybe she should send a telegram to her father and mother asking for the money to buy a stage ticket home. She felt unable to sort out and deal with everything that was bottled up inside her. She wanted to scream, to sob more bitterly than ever she had. What was happening to her? What was happening to her life? The events of the past few months, especially these past few weeks, had scared Vaden. Changed her. She now had trouble assuring herself of what she wanted, needed in life. Of what she loved and lived for. Things were hard now. Thinking was hard. Going about her daily tasks was hard. A different kind of hard than before. For now, instead of wanting to leave her chores to go out into the fresh air hoping to bump into her cherished Ransom Lake, she only wanted to leave

her chores to hide in her room away from questions and away from a de-
cision where Jerome Clayton was concerned. She did not love Jerome. She
knew it. Yet, would she ever love anyone again? Ransom Lake had captured
her love, her heart and spirit. Vaden considered Jerome only because she was
unsure that her heart would ever again be completely free. Oh, she knew
well enough that she would continue to live. That some things in life would
bring her joy. But she doubted that her joy could ever be any semblance of
what it would've been with Ransom Lake in her life.

"You don't ever run off to meet Jerome, girl. He always comes looking
for you."

Vaden startled at the sound of Ransom Lake's voice, and she quickly
brushed the tears from her cheeks before turning to face him.

"Mr. Lake," she greeted awkwardly. It was obvious he had followed her,
but the knowledge made her uncomfortable somehow instead of elated. "I
thought you had business in the store."

"I do. But your sister said you must be upset and sent me to fetch you,"
he stated, grinning slightly.

"Why would she send you?" Vaden asked, though she immediately
wished she hadn't, for she feared he might actually know the answer. Ransom Lake shrugged his shoulders. "And how would you know whether I
meet Jerome or not?" she asked, irritated that he would be so assuming.

"I do know. I know that you never seek him out. He always finds you.
Am I wrong?" He was certain, as if he could read her mind.

His eyes were beautiful, too captivating, and she answered, "No."

"Then why did you say you were going to meet him?" he asked. The
mischievous expression on his face revealed that he already suspected she
had done it for his benefit.

"Because...because I knew my aunt wouldn't stop me if she thought
that's where I was bound. They...they think he's a nice young man. A gentleman. A perfect catch."

"You're not yourself anymore, Miss Vaden," he stated then, his face gone serious. "You've lost your way. Is it because of Halloween or is it something else?"

Vaden looked at him. He knew her so well. She knew there was no trying to weasel out of telling him the truth. "I...I'm not sure. Maybe I'm just growing up." She folded her arms discouragedly across her chest.

"Don't try feeding me that. You're plenty grown up." She looked at him as he looked away for a minute rubbing at his whiskery chin with a roughened hand before mumbling, "And I suppose I had more to do with that than was proper." He turned quickly to her, however, and, shaking an index finger in her direction, lectured, "But don't you go doing anything stupid, girl. Who you choose to spend your life with is important. It's not something you go jumping into just because a nice boy comes along and everyone else thinks he's good for you. I don't think he's good for you. If my opinion means anything."

Vaden was angry with him suddenly. "Who are you to tell me what or who is good for me? You act as if you know me so well. As if you...what am I supposed to do Ransom Lake? Wait until your long lost brother shows up? Am I? Do you think you're so much better than every other man that..." Vaden stopped her scolding, for the color had completely drained from Ransom Lake's perfect face. It was visible by the his expression that his jaw was tightly clenched and his eyes even seemed to cloud over for a moment.

"What do you mean by that, girl? My long lost brother?!" he growled.

"I...I mean...you seem to think that you're the only worthy male in this town. And I meant to say that...I know you're unavailable so what do you expect us young women to do? Wait until you find an interest in one of us? Which we know won't happen, so I was simply..."

"Mocking me?"

"Yes, sir." Vaden felt horrible inside. Obviously she'd touched on something very sensitive with Ransom Lake. He looked at her for a moment as if he didn't know what to say or do.

"I...I...I have to get some things from your aunt. You're right. It's none of my business. Forgive me, Miss Vaden." He turned from her and began walking away.

"Mr. Lake!" she called to him, hitching up her skirts and taking out after him. His stride was long and quick paced and she nearly had to run to keep up with him. "I'm sorry, Mr. Lake. I'm sorry. You came out here to try to cheer me and I only upset you in return."

"I'm not upset," he spat.

"Please. I can't stand for you to be angry with me. I'm sorry. Please. I was only upset and..."

He stopped abruptly, turned and took hold of her shoulders tightly as he glared down at her.

"You and I are thrown into each other's paths far too often. Until one or the other of us gets control of who we are again, neither one of us will be content. Isn't that right?" He frightened her at that moment. He had far too great an insight into what she felt, but she wondered at his estimation of himself.

"I don't see how that applies to you, sir," she ventured.

"I belong alone, girl. I was happy that way. Life was easier. I've lost sight of that and I'm trying to find the middle ground of the two."

"And...and I trip you up. Is that what you mean?" Vaden offered as the tears filled her eyes once more.

"Yes. But not the way you're thinking."

Hanging her head then, for the humiliation was heavy in her heart and mind, she whispered her apology. "I'm sorry, Mr. Lake. For my behavior in the wagon that night. I...I'm truly sorry. I know how unbecoming...how completely improper it was and I want you to know that I scold myself inwardly for it every day."

"What?" he asked. "What are you talking about? I swear, you could send a man to drinking trying to understand you sometimes."

"I acted so terribly. I...I tried to..."

"Seduce me?" he finished and Vaden winced at the truth of his words.

"You're trying to apologize for tempting me?" With that, the color returned to his face along with the smile. Unexpectedly he took her in his arms then, embracing her firmly against his body as he chuckled. "You're a funny kid, Vaden Valmont. Has that been what's worried you all this time?" Not wanting him to know that it was only a small part of her worries, she nodded, letting her arms go around his waist. "Well, I'll tell you what, little friend…I'll try to seduce you sometime and then we'll be even. Okay?" Vaden looked up at him, shocked that he would tease about such a thing and hurt once more at him deeming her merely his friend. "For pity's sake, girl. Don't let a little thing like that bother you. Besides, that…that moment between you and me was my fault, not yours." When she did not answer he released her and mumbled, "If it bothers you that much…I'll swear never to do anything like that again. Cross my heart and hope to…"

Vaden reached up, clamping a hand over his mouth to stop the words of such a vow. "Don't even speak something like that!" she scolded, for it unnerved her to have him mention death.

"Something like what? Something like hope to die? Or something like I'll never again do to you what I did in the wagon?" A friendly grin spread across his face once more and she realized he was only teasing her. "Come on. Your Aunt Myra will think I'm up to no good out here with you."

Taking her hand, he began to pull her back toward the mercantile. How Vaden wished her aunt had reason to think Ransom Lake was up to no good with her niece. But it was not to be. Vaden was certain that it never would be again.

As the wind howled outside the Wimber home, Vaden tried to calm her rising anxiety at Mrs. Wimber's not having returned. The hour was later than Vaden had expected to have stayed tending the children and it gave her cause for concern, for the storm was turning violent out of doors. She had visions of not only having to tend the children through the night, but also of missing Thanksgiving Day and the most coveted guest that was to join her family for dinner.

"Violet! Put your brother down, honey. You can't be dragging him around like that," Vaden scolded softly. Violet had been carrying the baby back and forth across the room for nearly half an hour and Vaden was worried that the small girl might be getting more tired and weak than she realized. How she wished that Selma and Raylin had not gone to their uncle's house for the night. Then they could've tended to their young brothers and sister.

"Tell us a story then, Miss Vaden. Please."

Vaden had not felt like telling stories for some time. But Violet's sweet, delighted voice convinced her at last and she nodded her head amidst the pleadings of the children. "Very well."

Vaden glanced at the clock that sat on the mantle and noted that Mrs. Wimber was nearly two hours late returning. Through the window she could see the snow falling and hear the wind and was even more worried that perhaps the children's mother would not be able to get home. Ransom Lake had obviously been correct in predicting the storm and it was becoming a severe one. Vaden did not want to be snowed in with the Wimber children for days and days on end. So, with the anxiety over the storm building within her, yet the hope that she would be able to get home, Vaden began to bewitch the children with her talent for storytelling.

"This is the story of Cinderella. Cinderella was a beautiful young woman. She had been loved so dearly by her cherished parents. Tragically, her mother died when Cinderella was very young and her father, feeling that his treasured daughter needed a feminine heart to care for her, married a widow with two young daughters of her own."

Vaden wove her tale, dramatically as always, to try to keep the children's minds and her own from the howling wind and blowing snow. As the tale wore on, so did the night.

"And Cinderella, in fleeing so quickly as to not be set upon by the castle guards, tripped, and one of her beautiful dancing slippers...princesses *always* wear slippers instead of shoes...one of her beautiful dancing slippers fell from her foot and was abandoned on the castle steps." Vaden dramatically kicked off one of her boots, watching it land with a thud in the middle of the floor. "And there it lay as Cinderella fled, for the guards were so close behind her that she had not one extra moment to spare in trying to reach back and retrieve her lovely slipper."

Vaden continued the tale, telling of the anguished prince who searched and searched in vain for the fair maiden whose dainty foot would fit the slipper, thus revealing his one true love.

"But...why didn't the prince just look for her face, Miss Vaden?" Violet inquired finally. "Why didn't he just know who she was when he saw her?"

Vaden smiled and went to the fire where she carefully dirtied her fingertips with soot from the hearth. "Because, you see, Violet, " she began as she dabbed at her face with her soiled fingertips, "Cinderella's beauty was hidden beneath the ashes and soot that gathered on her face while she was cleaning the fireplaces in the house. So, when the prince came to her stepmother's house to try the slipper on every maiden there, he did not recognize her. And her stepmother told the prince that their servant girl had not attended the ball."

Just then the door to the Wimber home was forced open and in stumbled Mrs. Wimber covered with snow from head to toe. Her face was red and chapped from the wind.

"Mama!" went up the general cheering among the children.

"It's the fury of perdition out there, Vaden! I don't know how Mr. Lake will ever get you home in this! I've told him that the two of you should shelter here, but he says your Aunt Myra was very adamant that you be home tonight safe and sound," Mrs. Wimber explained between gasps and kissing the warm cheeks of her happy children.

"What do you mean, Mr. Lake getting me home?" Vaden asked, confused.

"I thought Uncle Dan would..." But at that very moment Ransom Lake stepped from the furious storm without into the warm room within, closing the door firmly behind him.

"Your uncle's bad leg is acting up, Miss Vaden, and he asked me to see Mrs. Wimber back and you safely home." He was so handsome! His presence so dominating.

"But...but she can't go yet, Mr. Lake," Violet argued, going to stand before him and tugging on his pant leg. "She hasn't finished Cinderella."

Vaden stepped forward, intent on explaining to the child why she must go at once, but she paused when she saw Mr. Lake smile and hunker down so that he was more at the child's level. "Well, then, miss...I guess I'll just have to have a glass of water in the kitchen before I drag Miss Vaden away from you." He smiled and gently squeezed the girl's cheek between his thumb and forefinger.

"Quickly though, girl," he ordered then, standing and scowling at Vaden. "This storm is coming in quick." Then, as Mrs. Wimber smiled at her children and motioned for Mr. Lake to follow her into the kitchen, Vaden thought she might die of humiliation when he tripped over her boot that lay in the middle of the room. "Just a moment, Mrs. Wimber," he said, stooping and picking up her boot.

"Oh, no! It's just part of the..." Vaden stopped when he raised his gloved palm in her direction indicating that she should be silent.

"Cinderella is it, Miss Wimber?" he asked Violet.

"Yes! Cinderella. And the prince has only just this minute tried the slipper on the awful stepsisters and is making ready to leave!" the child offered excitedly. "You see...he can't recognize his beloved Cinderella because she has soot all over her lovely face. See?"

Vaden wanted to shrink down and slip through the cracks in the floor, for at that moment as Ransom Lake looked at her, raised his eyebrows and chuckled, she remembered the soot with which she had dusted her face.

"I *do* see, Miss Violet," he mumbled. Vaden was angry with Mrs. Wimber instantly, for she was unable to suppress a giggle. "But *this* prince was smart, you see Miss Wimber," the man continued and Vaden's eyes widened as he approached her, holding her boot tightly in one hand. "You see, *this* prince could recognize Cinderella with his heart. He didn't need to see her face. And so he paused in taking his leave." Vaden's heart began to beat frantically as he drew closer to her and she shook her head slightly, unable to believe that he was involving himself in her tale. "The prince looked at the small girl in the corner, covered in soot and ashes. And his heart spoke to him, telling him that this was she. The one who had stolen his heart at the dance."

"Ball. It was a ball, Mr. Lake," Violet corrected in a whisper before giggling delightedly at what was transpiring.

"Forgive me. Stolen his heart at the *ball*. The prince approached the lovely Cinderella extending his hand to her, hoping that she would reveal herself in placing her own hand in his." Vaden was instantly mesmerized, for he was astoundingly good at telling the tale.

"Take his hand, Miss Vaden," Violet prodded. "It's in the story." Vaden only then realized that Ransom Lake did, indeed, hold out his hand in her direction. Tentatively she took his hand and immediately his touch, even for the glove covering his hand, sent her body tingling.

Ransom Lake continued, "The prince gazed into the beautiful emerald of Cinderella's eyes and said, '*Pray, try the shoe….*'"

"It's called a slipper, Mr. Lake," Violet interrupted. "Princesses always wear slippers. Not shoes."

"Thank you, Miss Violet," Ransom Lake whispered aside to the small girl. Vaden couldn't help but smile so charmed was she by Mr. Lake's thoughtful attention to the children. "The prince gazed into the beautiful emerald of Cinderella's eyes and said, '*Pray try the slipper, fair maiden. If not for your own ambitions…pray, try it for love of your prince.*'" Then, much to Vaden's horror, Ransom Lake knelt on one knee at her feet, reached beneath her petticoats and drew from beneath them her stockinged foot. "As the prince slipped the shoe…excuse me, slipper…easily onto Cinderella's tiny foot, she said..." he prodded, nodding with raised eyebrows.

"Oh! Um..." Vaden stammered, completely undone by his holding her foot and directing it into her boot. "Um...Cinderella said...she said...'*Thank you, Your Highness*'...um..."

"Yes." Ransom Lake chuckled and stood, taking Vaden's hand in his own again. "Cinderella said, '*Thank you, Your Highness....*'" Ransom Lake paused for a moment and his eyes narrowed, his smile fading as he mumbled, "'*Thank you for seeing beneath soot on my face and loving my soul.*'"

His words seemed pointed, but Vaden was certain she imagined his inferences toward her own willingness to look past the outward appearances of the hermit from the mountains to find the wonderful spirit of Ransom Lake beneath. Yes. She must've imagined it.

"What next?" Freddy Wimber asked curiously. "What next?"

Ransom Lake smiled at Vaden then, dropped her hand, turned to the coat rack and retrieved her coat from it. He helped her to put it on and buttoned the collar button of it.

"What next, you ask, boy?" the man chuckled. "Well, next, the prince bid everyone in the room a good day, swept Cinderella into his arms and carried her off to his castle where they lived happily ever after."

Vaden smiled and giggled delightedly as Ransom Lake actually lifted her into his own powerful arms effortlessly as if she were no more than a child.

"And he kissed her, too. Didn't he kiss her, Mr. Lake?" Violet's wide eyes sparkled with the anticipated answer to her question.

"Now you let Mr. Lake take Miss Vaden on home, Violet. It's bad weather we're having out there and they need to be off," Mrs. Wimber explained to her disappointed daughter. "Thank you again, Vaden. I'm so sorry about this. You tell your Aunt Myra that we'll watch the weather better next time."

"I will, Mrs. Wimber, and it was my pleasure to stay with the children."

Vaden tried to struggle free from Ransom Lake's arms, but he only chuckled and secured her more firmly in them.

"I'll get the door, Mr. Lake," Freddy offered, opening the door wide. Vaden could see the horse and cutter waiting outside. Ransom Lake carried her down the steps, setting her gently on the cutter's blanket-covered seat.

"Bye, Miss Vaden!" Violet called from the door. "Thank you for bringing my mama home, Mr. Lake!"

The child waved delightedly to the man who tipped his hat to her. It was only Violet who stood at the door now and before Vaden could know what Ransom Lake meant to do, he leaned forward, whispering something in the girl's ear that made her giggle delightedly and nod emphatically.

"What did you say to her, Mr. Lake?" Vaden asked as he turned back to her and stood unmoving for a moment on her side of the cutter.

"I just told her that the prince did kiss Cinderella." His hand was at her chin in an instant and his lips pressing to hers before she even realized he had moved. The kiss was sweet and quick, far from the kiss Vaden would've most chosen to receive from him, but obviously enough to satisfy the yearnings of Miss Violet Wimber to see the story ended properly. Then Ransom Lake tipped his hat once more to Violet before climbing over Vaden and sitting himself down next to her on the seat. Vaden waved to Violet, whose mother appeared at the door, waving quickly before closing it to the violent elements of nature.

"I had no idea you were so skilled with children," Vaden commented, raising her voice a bit to be heard over the wind.

Ransom Lake smiled and chuckled a moment. "Oh, I used to be able to weave quite a yarn myself, girl."

"Thank you for bringing Mrs. Wimber home so that I wasn't left there all night with the children. She still must feed the baby most of the time and I was becoming worried." She turned to him, concerned. "Is Uncle Dan all right?"

"The cold has caused his leg and back to pain him. I was over telling your aunt that I wasn't sure I'd make it over tomorrow with all this coming in...and...I knew she didn't want you stuck out here all night." He frowned, however, and added, "But I'm not sure we shouldn't have stayed back there ourselves. It's nasty out here."

Vaden wrapped her scarf securely about her head, tucking it into her coat below her chin. "You're quite a good actor as well, Mr. Lake. What other talents do you secret?"

"None. Doesn't take talent to tell a tale or kiss a girl." Vaden raised her eyebrows, dubbing him vastly mistaken on both counts.

Ransom pulled up for a moment just as an enormous, frigid gust of wind cut through Vaden's coat. He shaded his eyes from the snow and, standing up in the cutter, looked back. "I truly think we should've stayed back there. This is becoming dangerous."

"But we can't be more than three miles from home." Vaden then noticed that she couldn't see a thing through the snow. No trees, nor the road ahead. No visible landmarks.

"Less. But this is bad. We could get lost out here and..." he began. Then, sitting back down, he slapped the lines at the horse's back, turning her off the well defined road they had been on.

"What are you doing?" Vaden asked. "Why don't you just turn around if you're uncertain?"

"Because...I think we'd get lost. Look at the road. In a matter of minutes we won't be able to see it with the snow drifting so badly in the wind. And at this very minute...this place...I still know where we are." Taking Vaden's arm he directed her to sit on the floor of the cutter at his feet. "Get down here. It'll keep that wind off of you and you'll be warmer."

She did as instructed and sat on the floor of the cutter, huddling up against one of his legs for warmth. She was astounded at how fast the temperature was dropping. How the moonlight seemed to have disappeared completely from the sky. The powerful man struggled with guiding the horse and she could feel the taut muscles in the thigh and calf of his leg as he drove. But she knew she would be safe. No one would perish while under Ransom Lake's care. That she knew.

At last, Vaden heard his voice soothe the horse as he pulled her up before a large, dark structure that loomed before them in the night.

"Come on," he said, taking her arm once more and pulling her to her feet, which until that moment Vaden had not realized were numb with the cold. Quickly he walked with Vaden to the lightless building before them, kicked open a door and pushed her inside.

"Wait here," he commanded, then turned and ventured back out into the storm.

"Where would I go?" she muttered to herself as she tried to see through the darkness further into the building in which she was standing.

Ransom Lake returned almost immediately, however, much to Vaden's relief, leading the mare into the building behind him. "There you go, girl," he said soothingly, patting the animal on the neck as he led her back into the darkness. Vaden waited again for him to return, completely uncertain as to what action she should take. He returned again momentarily, took her hand in his, leading her deeper into the darkness of their shelter.

"This old house is on my property," he stated as he led her into a room and stopped before a large fireplace. Vaden was silent, the only noise escaping her body was the violent chattering of her teeth as she watched him laboring to build a fire with a set of flints that he pulled from a box on the mantle. In a very short time, considering his method, smoke began to rise from a tiny bundle of sticks in the hearth and Vaden watched as he blew on the small bit of smoke carefully. Next an orange spark erupted among the kindling and Ransom Lake added some larger bits of wood as the room began to be illuminated by the light and warmth of the fire. He stood up looking about the room and finally picked up a dusty chair nearby and broke it into pieces over his knee, adding it to the small fire. Vaden watched as it blazed brighter and warmer.

"I've got to go out back and root up some better wood." He walked away toward the back of the house and Vaden stepped closer to the warmth of the fire, removing her mittens and rubbing her hands together vigorously to help drive away the stinging numbness in her fingers.

"This wood should certainly burn hot and fast. It's all dried out from sitting out there for so long," he informed her as he returned, his arms laden with large logs. He dropped the wood carelessly to one side of the hearth and added some of the old, dry logs to the fire. They did, indeed, burn quickly and warm. Vaden removed her scarf and coat, tossing them onto another nearby chair.

"Well, I guess you're telling me that we'll be here for awhile," Vaden ventured as Ransom Lake came to stand next to her, removing his own gloves, hat and coat.

"At least the night," he answered, putting a fist to his mouth and blowing warm air through it.

"*All* night?" Vaden inquired. Certainly he could not possibly mean for her to spend the entire night alone with him!

The handsome man looked at her, an expression of puzzlement on his brow. "Yes, *all* night. Would you rather get lost in that blizzard and freeze to death?" He looked back to the fire, then around the room. "It's holding up surprisingly well," he mumbled.

"The house?" Vaden asked to assure herself of his subject of comment.

"Yes. It hasn't been lived in for so long, but it doesn't look any worse for the wear, except for the dust and creatures that have moved in." At his mention of living things perhaps lurking about, Vaden unconsciously took a step sideways and closer to him. He chuckled, "Nothing dangerous has taken up residence in here, I'm sure." But Vaden's legs began to prickle and itch all the same as she then noticed various large cobwebs donning every corner of everything. "You warming up all right, girl?" he asked in his delightfully mumbly manner.

"Yes. Fine," she assured him. She glanced to him then and her eyes could not tear themselves from his fine good looks, and tousled hair. He was truly magnificent and she smiled slightly at the thought that struck her.

"What?" he asked, noticing her smile.

"Nothing," she lied, looking away.

"No, what? Tell me."

"I...I was just thinking what Yvonne would say about this situation," she admitted to him.

Ransom Lake smiled, too, then. "Your sister is a strict one when it comes to etiquette and manners, isn't she?"

"Yes. It's a good quality in her." Vaden's smile faded as another thought entered her mind and, as was often the case, her mouth blurted out her thoughts before she could stop it. "You fancy her, don't you, Mr. Lake? Yvonne, I mean."

"What do you mean, fancy?" He still continued to gaze into the fire and blow into his fists periodically.

"I mean...you favor Yvonne. It's all right to admit it to me. You're always telling me we're friends after all and I've seen the way you look at her."

"We are friends," he confirmed looking to her, eyebrows raised in perplexion. "And, yes, your sister is a fine woman to look at." Vaden's teeth immediately began to clench. "But...I don't favor her over anyone else. I don't intend to pursue her, if that's what you're getting at, little Miss Vaden, the curious cat." Since she still stared into the fire, unwilling to look at him, he put a hand to her shoulder, arresting her attention and causing her to finally look over at him. "Whatever would put such a thought into that conniving little mind of yours?"

"My mind is not conniving. Just...observant is all," she told him.

"No. Tell me. Something had to spark such a thought. Tell me," he prodded, turning to confront her face to face.

"The night you were ill. You...you, on two occasions, did or said something to indicate that you..." she stammered.

"For the love of Pete, girl. You're holding something against me that I said when my head was hotter than that fire before you? Chances are I didn't know my foot from my hind end. And besides," he continued, "would there be something wrong about me taking an interest in your sister?"

"So you do favor her."

"No," he chuckled, smiling and shaking his head. "No. I just want you to tell me why you even brought the thing up?"

Vaden scolded herself violently for slipping up and letting him have an insight into her worry over where he might choose to next place his affections. But, trying to stay calm and dispassionate in appearance, she said, "Oh, I was just wondering about it."

"Why? Are you afraid I'll end up with Belva Tibbits?" He chuckled and turned from her, looking back into the fire.

Vaden just shook her head and sighed, irritated with herself. "Are you...are you planning on ending up with someone?"

Vaden wanted to leave the house, to run from him because all the feelings she had tried to secret away in herself over the past few weeks, every dream and hope she held where he was concerned was burning brighter than ever in her heart. Ransom Lake smiled and turned to her with an inquisitive glint to his stormy eyes.

"Why? Are you interested in applying for the job?"

Vaden gasped, looked at him and shook her head vigorously. "Oh! No, no, no!" she assured him dishonestly. "I...I...it's just a natural question, considering the stir you've caused in town among the young women and all."

"What stir?" he asked.

"Don't play the dumb bunny with me, Mr. Lake. You know full well what I mean." She shook her head, irritated that he would take her for such a fool. "I'll admit to you now that it's the reason I left the Halloween social early that night. I was sick to death of being badgered and taunted by the other girls because..." She broke off, thinking it might be far worse to confess that particular example.

"What? Finish what you were saying," he demanded, his voice going low and more mumbly.

"Nothing. It was a bad example. I'll think of another one. I..."

"No. Tell me what you were going to say, Vaden." She looked at him, shocked at his use of her given name and the commanding tone in his voice.

"I mean...it was silly of me to feel slighted anyway. So, it was a bad example. It was no fault of yours. It was petty of me to react so..."Vaden's mind was trying to sort out an escape from the conversation.

"What are you talking about?" he interrupted her unexpectedly.

"You know,"Vaden stammered. "About my feeling slighted because you chose not to dance with me at the social. Actually you chose to nearly completely ignore me altogether. That's why I decided to walk home early. Because I was feeling sorry for myself...as a result of the other girls taunting me about it...not that you intentionally slighted me."

"You mean to tell me that you left the social because I didn't ask you for a dance?" Ransom Lake asked. His expression was that of disbelief and then extreme guilt.

"Well, no." She had to find a way out of the muddy mess she'd slipped into. Something within her told her that he would be very upset to know that she had left because of him. "I know you already think me silly, clumsy and juvenile, no matter how you persist in saying otherwise...and I don't blame you a bit for it, for my own actions that very horrid night paint a pretty clear picture of me. But, it was just too irritating to take the taunting of the other girls for any longer and I was tired of it. So, I left. There you have it. Enough said. I'm so thankful you are handy with a set of flints, Mr. Lake. The fire is so warming."

Ransom Lake only stood staring at her, looking dumbfounded as if a startling revelation had just plunged a dagger into his mind.

"I'm sorry, Vaden," he mumbled and a sort of pain glazed the gray of his eyes.

"For what, Mr. Lake? It was none of it your fault." She felt the need to tie up the other loose end to the story. So, she babbled on as every nerve began to twitch frantically within her body. "And...and I've already admitted to what you said. I...in the wagon...I did want you to...I tried to...my goal was to...that is what you mean isn't it, Mr. Lake? The fact that you knew it would upset me to be slighted by you? And my completely barbaric behavior in the wagon on the way home. How I wish you could just forget it. And those are the reasons that...what other reasons could you possibly have for apologizing to me?" Still he was silent. Vaden knew how her confession could be misunderstood by him. Quickly she tried to correct her meaning. "You're not at all responsible for what happened to cause me to fall into the hands of those men, you know. It was entirely my own fault! My own ignorance and carelessness that found me in that horrid position. I suppose one could view the reason I left the social...one could aptly refer to it as pouting. Yvonne would surely call it that. She is ever and always accusing me of it. And I do admit to being guilty of something like it at times. Mr. Lake? Are you hearing me?"

Vaden was uncomfortable as his gray eyes met hers intensely. "Why would they be teasing you about *me* not asking you for a dance?" he asked plainly.

Vaden began to fiddle with the long lock of hair at her temple. "Whatever do you mean by asking that?" Then she looked at him, studying his eyes and general countenance. Could it truly be that he was unaware of his effect on the general female population? "Are you seriously ignorant as to the reason?" she asked plainly in return.

"Yes," he stated.

"They all are desperately attracted to you." Vaden looked from him and into the flames in the hearth. She would be honest with him. She would simply tell him bluntly, for it did, indeed, seem as if he was still completely unaware of the infatuation that every female in town held for him. "You were the buck of the ball, so to speak, Mr. Lake. All the girls in town were simply swooning as you passed because each and every one was holding her breath in hopes that the mysterious *Ransom Lake* would beg a dance of her."

He chuckled quietly. "You are quite the prankster yourself, aren't you, girl?"

Vaden looked to him again, but he smiled and turned from her. "You are truly innocent of it all, aren't you?" she questioned. "I thought...especially after your antics that first evening you kissed me...I thought you were all too clearly aware of the effect you've had on all the women in this town."

He chuckled again, but when he looked at her then his smile faded and she could only guess that he had seen the sincerity on her face at last. "My *antics*, as you call them, have nothing to do with the women in this town. Antics?"

Avoiding the issue of the previous affectionate liaisons between herself and Ransom Lake, Vaden rushed boldly ahead in her explanation of the events of Halloween. "Belva Tibbits was the worst! I swear she had aspirations of being the first you chose to ki..." She stopped for she knew she had already said too much.

"You're telling me the truth, aren't you?" he whispered as a deep frown furrowed his brow. Vaden nodded, dropping her guilty gaze to the floor. "You say they were teasing you. How? What were they saying?"

Vaden smiled, shook her head and waved one hand in front of her face in a gesture of trivial subject matter. "Oh, nothing really. Certainly nothing to justify my stomping off like a coward."

"What did they say?" he demanded sternly. "Tell me."

Vaden looked about for a means of escape, but their isolation provided none whatsoever. There was no reason she should not answer his question. "Just things. Mean things females say to irritate other females. Women are more catty than you imagine, Mr. Lake."

"What? Give me an example," he urged harshly.

"I don't remember," Vaden stalled. "Things like...Belva said that a man like you wouldn't be caught dead dancing with me because...because..."

"Because?" he prodded.

"Because I'm the kind of girl that men want to go fishing with. Not sit out under a tree and spark with," she mumbled. "I'm unconventional, you see," she rambled on quickly. "I do like to run through the meadow rather than sit quietly under a parasol. And, yes," she stated firmly, "I'd rather go fishing and wading in the brook as opposed to waiting perfectly docile beneath a tree, my feet tucked properly beneath my skirts as I read on for hours and hours without flinching!" Vaden continued to stare into the fire even though she felt the piercing gaze of Ransom Lake drilling into her. "I suppose that's why those horrid, intoxicated men chose me to torment. Because I'm a good sport most of the time."

Ransom Lake massaged his temples for a moment and Vaden finally looked up to him again as he spoke. "You're telling me that because I supposedly snubbed you at the dance, every female there started in badgering you about it and so you left? Then on your way home you were taken by those idiots and because I didn't heed my...so, basically you're saying that the whole affair was my fault, including what I did to you on the way home."

"Oh, no!" Vaden exclaimed, taking hold of one of his arms. She looked up at him, her soul pleading silently with him as she explained, "It was my own pouty, weak fault that I found myself in that situation. Yvonne's always telling me that I don't think before I act, and she's right. And you did nothing to me on the way home. It was me. I acted so...so..." Vaden shook her head and put a hand to her forehead that was beginning to throb. "Oh...how did we get to this point? I only wanted to explain why I thought you...to apologize to you for my behavior in the wagon...to thank you for coming for me that night. For coming for me this night. How did it all come to this?"

The man at Vaden's side shook his head and returned his gaze to the fire. "Well, I can't make heads or tails of half of what you're telling me, girl. I do think you're exaggerating a bit about my popularity, and, if it helps your ego any, I think I oughta tell you that the reason I didn't ask you for a dance is because...every time I had a chance you were out dancing with Jerome Clayton."

Vaden's heart landed with a dramatic thud in the pit of her stomach. He would've asked her, if only she had been able to keep Jerome at bay long enough. She could've had the chance to be held in his arms just as every other girl had that night. But she felt the triumph rise within her at the knowledge that she had been held by Ransom Lake. Held by him and kissed by him in a manner that the other girls in town were still dreaming of.

"And now I'll say it again," he continued, "and I want you to take this to heart. I'm sorry. I'm truly sorry for what happened. All of it. And I see now that it was more my fault than I even thought." Vaden was disturbed by the look of deep guilt and remorse on his face. Somehow he felt responsible and he wasn't.

"You're not responsible, Mr. Lake. Do you see it now? Not for what happened on Halloween. Not for any of what happened on Halloween. The other girls are only too right where I'm concerned. My pointless babble has left you feeling guilty somehow and I'm sorry. It would be better maybe if I were to just stop talking all together," she mumbled, turning to let the conversation die before the fire.

"You're wrong. You're wrong and I'm tired." He continued to face the fire and sighed heavily.

"I'm never wrong about anything!" Vaden nearly shouted. "Everything I told you was true! They did tease me! It did make me angry! I did try to...wanted you to...I caused what happened on the way home Halloween night. All of it. Every bit of it was my fault. You've only gotten to where you blame yourself for anything bad that happens because...because I don't know why. But you do it. And it's inane."

He sighed and whispered, "You seem to think you know me quite well."

"I do," she said, turning to face him again. "I know you better than anyone else in town. And that's a fact."

He chuckled and shook his head, amused at her assurance of herself. Vaden felt hope begin to burn within her. Perhaps the same feeling someone might feel rising within their bosom in anticipation of witnessing a miracle. As he turned his gray eyes upon her, she knew. She knew that something profound was about to happen to her at the hand of Ransom Lake.

"You make a man feel almost...forgiven," he mumbled.

"Forgiven for what, Mr. Lake?" Vaden asked. She could no longer keep silent the question that had been plaguing her mind since the moment she had first seen him. She sensed that he meant to confess something to her, to confide his great secret to her. Immediately his face turned ashen and he looked away as moisture brimmed in his storm colored eyes. "Tell me! Tell me what it is that causes such a tumultuous guilt in you. Please."

He tipped his head back for a moment, gazing up at the shadows from the fire dancing oddly on the ceiling. Vaden waited. Her heart pounded madly, for she sensed that the moment had arrived. Ransom Lake was about to reveal his terrible secret to her. She would know. No one else. No one had cared to ask him before.

"Well, I suppose if there's anybody in the world that I think deserves to know the truth about me...it's you, Vaden. You tried to befriend me long before you saw what I looked like underneath all that mess of hair." He picked up the poker that lay on the floor near the hearth and, hunkering down before the fire, began using it to kick around a log inside. Vaden's body still quivered from the sound of his voice uttering her name. "It's been driving you plum out of your mind not knowing why I took to the hills like I did, hasn't it?" He glanced at Vaden and she looked away guiltily. "You've been wondering since that first day you saw me in the street. Wondering what it was that made me so...solitary." He sat down solidly on the floor, still gazing into the fire. "Well, I think I'm inclined to tell you on this cold winter's evening when there aren't any ears around but yours. You were the first to see my face, Vaden. You may as well be the first to see the black sludge of my soul."

Vaden held her breath for a moment and tried to settle the frantic palpitating of her heart. She'd waited so long! Wondered so many things! But she was silent, too afraid to speak for fear he would change his mind.

"I was sixteen when my daddy decided to move the family out west. He had a sister, my aunt Shandra, who lived out here with her husband. They had built themselves a nice little house on some land that my daddy had bought for them as a wedding gift. Anyway, I was sixteen that summer when we started out here. There was me and my mamma and daddy, my older sister by a year, Natalie, my younger brothers, Scott and Gavin, they were about twelve and ten, and my baby sister, Serena. Aunt Shandra and Uncle Garth, her husband, had traveled out to Georgia to help us on the way. They had their little baby girl, Sally, with them, too. My older brother, Denver, was already grown up and living out in Leadville. So he wasn't with us.

"The trip went all right. We hooked up with a wagon train going our way right outside of Georgia and there was this girl that belonged to one of the families. Her name was Caroline and she was maybe fifteen. She took a liking to me for some reason and about drove me insane chasing after me and flirting all the time. I didn't have a breath of peace from that moment on. Anyway, like I said, everything went real well on the trip. No disasters with weather or the teams taking sick. Everyone was healthy and strong.

"Then early one morning we were breaking camp about two days by wagon from this very town. Caroline was already stealing my hat and running off, trying to get me to chase her and such. I was pretty near to turning her over my knee and whacking her fanny and it wasn't even seven in the morning." He paused and seemed to be reflecting. Vaden was silent, intent on his story.

"You know, it all seems like a whole lot of nothing now to be irritated at her about, looking back. Anyhow, Daddy told me to help hitch up the team and I didn't want to do it because Caroline was sticking to me like flies to a horse. So, I argued with him and asked him to give me another job, something away from camp that would get her out of my hair. He told me again to hitch up the team and I was mad. 'No,' I told him. 'I'm not gonna do it.' And with him yelling at me to get back to my chores, I stormed off, leaving my daddy mad at me and Caroline feeling put off. But I'd been hitching up the team every morning for weeks and my disposition was bent outta joint over trying to avoid that poor Caroline twenty-four hours a day. So, I stomped off, telling myself that I was a *man!* I wasn't a boy to be bossed around and I didn't need to put up with someone that I didn't want to. Off I went, just walking further and further away. At least a mile as I figure now.

"Then, I heard a deafening noise...an explosion. I turned to see this big black cloud of smoke rising in the air from the direction I had come. I *felt* it at the same moment. Even before I reached the camp, I knew what had happened. It was like a vision in my mind. I turned and I ran as fast as I could back to the wagon train camp. When I got there, whoever had done it was already gone. It wasn't Indians. I found out soon after that a group of outlaws that had escaped from prison had been robbing and killing in the area. I'm sure that's who did it, though I don't have proof to show anyone." He paused again and Vaden could see the fire reflecting in the moisture in his eyes.

"Everyone there was dead. Everyone. Not one living soul was left. Believe me, I know, because I checked every one of them over good before I buried them. I buried twenty-nine bodies that day and the next. Twenty-nine people who had been killed. Some of them had been shot through the head or heart. Some of them had their throats slashed open and some had been beaten to death. A couple of the children...some had been hung from a nearby tree." Vaden winced and covered her mouth to try to stop the wrenching in her stomach. "I won't go into more detail than that. I'll just tell you that I buried my whole family except for one brother that day. And I've spent the last ten years wishing I'd died along with them. Knowing that if I'd hitched up the team like my father told me to, we might a been out of there before..." Ransom Lake looked at her, his eyes narrowing. "I think that's the quietest you've ever been at one stretch in all the time I've known you, girl."

"They would've tracked you. Whoever it was would've tracked the wagon train," Vaden told him firmly, breaking her unusually long silence. "And it would've been unnecessary...wasteful and unbearable for you to have been killed, too. That would've left your brother, Denver, all alone in the world."

Ransom Lake looked back to the fire and he winced painfully. "He is all alone in the world. He...he doesn't know that I wasn't killed."

"What?" Vaden exclaimed in horror. She couldn't believe what she was hearing. "You mean you never told him that you..."

Ransom Lake shook his head. "No. I'm a coward and I call myself one. Because I couldn't face him. I couldn't face him, tell him that the family was gone, wiped out because of me. I...I sent him a telegram when I finally reached town and pretended I was someone else who had happened upon the massacre."

"But...but it had nothing whatsoever to do with you! You were a boy! There's nothing you could've done to...your family would've wanted you to be saved. Your brother...you have to let him know..."

"No!" he shouted angrily, rising to his feet. "No. Let him think I'm dead. It's less painful to him than the truth would be."

Vaden clenched her teeth to keep from arguing with him. Now was not the time and she knew that. "How...how did you survive? I mean how did you come to own your land? Buy your food and pay for your shelter?"

Ransom Lake shrugged his shoulders. "I...I knew where my father had hidden his money and deeds to the land. Under a board in the wagon. He had put all his money and deeds in a strong box and hidden them there. My mother's wedding ring was in there as well." He paused and glanced at the gold band on his smallest finger. "I had possession of the rights to this land, and my daddy was very wealthy. He had thousands and thousands and thousands of dollars hidden in that box in the wagon. The thieves didn't find it. I did. I say this land because I own the land this very house sits on. It's only a mile and a half out from my farm. This was my Uncle Garth and Aunt Shandra's house. It's just as they left it ten years ago. I came to town with the deeds and since I looked like a full-grown man even though I was only sixteen...nobody knew the difference. They just all assumed that my Uncle Garth had sold me the property."

Vaden hugged herself tightly and a chill traveled through her body as she looked around her. But still the horror of what the man standing before her had endured was the focus of her attention. "How horrible for you," Vaden whispered, wiping a tear from her cheek. What pain he must have endured. What horrible visions must there be in his memory.

Ransom Lake turned on her again, raising his voice as he spoke. "What do you mean? I'm the one still alive! Still breathing! I wasn't tortured and mutilated!"

"It's not your fault." Vaden was not offended by his outburst. She knew that for the past ten years Ransom Lake had blamed himself for the atrocities that had befallen his family and friends. "If you had been there...you would've been killed, too, and what would that have accomplished?"

"I should've died, too! If for no other reason than I was disobedient!"

"Why? So your family could've watched you suffer as well? So your name...your bloodline would be forever extinguished from the face of the earth? So the people who murdered your family would have yet one more murder on their heads come judgment day? Or is it for purely selfish reasons? Because, since you did live, you've had guilt." Vaden was on her feet facing him now as her mouth poured out her heart's feelings. "Oh, I don't mean guilt over the fact that you were disobedient to your father, or because you weren't there when it happened. I mean the guilt you're feeling because you know you have so much to offer other people...to offer the world. And instead of helping others, instead of bringing joy to others, you've chosen to hide away for years, selfishly keeping to yourself!"

"I've helped people plenty, Vaden! Whenever tragedy hits I..."

"Yes! Tragedy! You do help then! More than most men would and I'll not deny that it's wonderful deeds you do! But what about daily? What about the other hearts that are secretly aching like yours is? What do you do then? I mean...it's selfish that you kept yourself hidden behind that pelt of hair for so many years! Just imagine the women who would've had their day brightened, their hearts filled with delight at simply laying eyes on a man as handsome as you!"

Ransom grinned a bit, the anger seeming to rinse off him immediately as he then chuckled quietly. "Oh, Vaden. Leave it to you to come up with something like that as a method of doing good in the world." The gloom and oppression that seemed to hang heavy in the room a moment before lifted and, smiling, he walked to her, taking her shoulders between his hands and saying, "I know there's reason to what you say, girl. But...it's worn on me for ten long years. It's not just gonna go away because I told you about it. But I know you mean well. You're a good kid, you know that?"

Vaden closed her eyes and wrenched herself from his grasp, turning to look into the flames of the fire. Her heart still ached from the pain of his story and now that was added upon by his condescending compliment. "I am a woman, Mr. Lake. Not an infant goat!" She was hurt. It hurt her deeply every time he brought to light that he saw her as a child.

"Now come on. I didn't mean it like that," he explained.

"Why is it that Yvonne being nineteen, only one year my senior...why is it that because she's beautiful, elegant, soft spoken...why is it that she's considered a mature woman to be sought after by every eligible bachelor in the state? But because I'm short, plain, speak my mind...why is it then that I'm viewed as a child? Yvonne knows how to portray something that she isn't entirely made of. I'm truly myself. At all times and in all places. Why is it that everyone still treats me as a child? Everyone except Jerome Clayton."

Ransom Lake said nothing for a moment and she assumed that he was still thinking of his painful memories. But then he did speak. "It's the spark in you. That light that shines in your eyes like the brightness of the sun. It's why I was so mad when I realized what those boys had done to you on Halloween. A life can be robbed of that spark. Of that love for living. If anybody knows that, it's me. I was afraid that they'd stolen your innocence that night. That you'd never be that sweet thing always getting yourself into a fix and putting her foot directly into her mouth. But you pulled through it." Vaden turned to see his eyes narrow as he approached her and once again took her by the shoulders. "You bucked up. Kept your wits and your love of life about you. I'm not blind. I know it scarred you. That it made you recognize ugly things you hadn't before. And I suppose you'll never be quite the same now. But you were the one talking about making people feel happy. Putting joy in their souls. Well, I figure that's how folks feel when you're around. Comfortable. Not like they've gotta treat you different. But like they're your friend. And speaking of Jerome Clayton, it's why I got so mad at you for sparking with the boy that night. He's not worthy of you. He doesn't appreciate you or know how to make a life for a girl like you. I was mad at you for even considering on him. I'm irritated that you still do."

"Is that why you chose to be so cruel to me that night? That first night you...in the alley? Are you trying to tell me that the reason you...you..."

"Kissed you?"

"Yes. Thank you." Vaden was uncomfortable. The thoughts of Ransom Lake's tragic life were pushed aside for a moment as his intense gaze made her uneasy. "Are you trying to tell me that the reason you...did that is because you..." She was uncharacteristically tongue-tied for a moment. The hypnotic quality of his stormy eyes as they gazed at her in the firelight caused her to stumble in her words. "It was cruel," she finished.

"Cruel? How?" he asked in a whisper.

She couldn't possibly tell him the truth. That because of his kiss she knew she would never be able to kiss another man and not pine away for Ransom Lake. That his kiss had only served to seal her love more deeply. "Because...because..." she stammered, "because you knew...you knew when you did it that I could never...that I could never be content with a man like Jerome Clayton."

"A boy like Jerome Clayton," he corrected. He smiled at her, dropped his hands from her shoulders and said, "We're too tired to be discussing such things, girl. You look tired. I think I've taxed your mind and emotions enough this wicked night. Why don't you just lay down on that old sofa over there? It's dusty, I know. But it'll do."

Vaden turned from him and closed her eyes, squeezing a tear from each one and letting the droplets of emotion sit on her cheeks as she opened her eyes again and looked into the fire.

"I'll warm up here for a minute more, thank you," she mumbled.

"One more thing," he added then. "What I've confided in you tonight...it can't go beyond this room. Do you understand?"

Vaden shook her head and wiped at the tears. "Why don't you just give me a good paddling and send me to bed without my dinner, Mr. Lake?" The sarcasm and hurt in her voice were heavy.

"You're one to be pointing the finger at self pity!" he nearly shouted, unexpectedly. "There isn't one man in town that thinks you're a baby, Vaden." Vaden turned to face him, surprised at his outburst. "So, quit trying to coax me into giving way to my weaknesses where you're concerned and kissing you again." He cleared his throat and looked back toward the fire. "Now, settle your little fanny down on that sofa."

Vaden stood aghast at his remark. "I...what do you mean by...coax you into...I can't believe you would even say such a thing! I've apologized for that! And you should forget about it! I can't believe you would say..."

"Oh, yes, you can. You know me better than anyone. Or so you professed to me just a minute ago. It doesn't shock you one bit." He moved to her again, taking her forcefully into his arms and pulling her body against the strength of his own. "Why don't you just tell me the truth about it all. Rid your conscience of what you've been trying to say to me tonight in the lonely seclusion of this house."

She was helpless in his arms. So surprised had she been to find herself there that she was unable to react at first. And now, now it was such ecstasy to be there, bound tightly in his powerful arms, the warmth of his body heating her own and the smell of his skin, his hair, and his breath filling her lungs and taunting her senses, that she was stunned into silence. Paralyzed with delight.

"Scold me for it if you must, but spit it out, girl. You're angry with me for going about it the way I did that first night I kissed you. That's it, isn't it?" he whispered, as he dusted the long forgotten soot from her cheeks with the back of his hand. "Maybe angry at me, too, for being weak that night Nathaniel was driving us home. But you...you provoked me." He paused for a moment, his eyes narrowing. "More than that, girl, of your own admission you willfully tempted me into taking advantage of you like I did."

"I...I..." she stammered, unable to defend herself, for he spoke no more than the absolute truth and she knew it.

"I'm not blaming you, Vaden. I'm not even telling you that you did anything wrong. You were frightened, sorrowful, and I was there, probably seeming to you the knight in shining armor. But I was weak...in an uncertain state of mind myself." Vaden closed her eyes, humiliated and unable to look at him as he continued. "And...and I want you to understand that I am sorry. I'm sorry that I failed you that night. That I let myself..."

"Stop it. Just stop it," Vaden pled in a whisper, shaking her head. "None of it was your fault. None of it. I...I was angry with you in a manner. Hurt because you slighted me so obviously at the social that night." But he wasn't listening. He seemed lost in his own thoughts. His own guilt. And, when he spoke, his words puzzled Vaden.

"The night I caught Jerome Clayton slobbering all over you, maybe I wasn't so tender and patient with you. But remember, I'm way out of practice. And in the wagon...well, I *am* a man, Vaden. How did you expect I would react?"

"I have no idea what you mean," Vaden forced out in a whisper. She had to get away from him. It was too much, too wonderful to be in his arms, the fire warming them, the scent of the wood burning.

He lowered his voice when he spoke next and the provocative intonation of it was Vaden's undoing. In Ransom Lake's arms, nothing else mattered in the world.

"You want to be treated like a woman, is that it? And you don't think I treat you like one, do you?" Still holding her tightly against his body with one arm, he raised a hand to her face, cupping her cheek against his palm while his thumb traced the soft outline of her lips. "Well, maybe you're right. And I'll confess that there's a reason for that. But there isn't anybody here now, is there? Nobody to gossip, nobody to get jealous, nobody to scold me."

Vaden closed her eyes for a moment, trying to believe what was happening. But she opened them again almost immediately to find his storm-filled eyes intent upon her.

"Do you want me to kiss you, Vaden? I mean, kiss you the way I didn't on those other occasions? There are so many different ways to kiss a woman. The way I kissed you the first time, that was a teaching kiss. A kiss to prove something. The way I kissed you the second time. Now that...and I'll say it to you plain...was a kiss from a man who had been tempted physically by a girl he..."

Vaden opened her mouth to speak, to try to deter him, but no sound escaped her lips.

"Those other occasions were different. Forced somehow, I guess. I couldn't possibly have done a good job of it either time before, but look at me now. The fire burning warm, nobody around for miles. So...you just give me the chance, Vaden Valmont, and I'll kiss you like I didn't have time to before."

Vaden closed her eyes once more, digging deep within herself for something to cling to. Something to anchor her to reality. She had to refuse him. To save herself, her heart, she must refuse him, remove herself from his embrace. But there was nothing. Only Ransom Lake standing before her. The vision and feel of her love for him permeating her heart, mind and soul. The desire was too strong. She wanted nothing else in that moment but to feel his lips on hers again. To taste his divinely perfect kiss.

"You can trust me, you know, sweet thing. I'm no rounder."

Then, before she could stop herself, she heard a barely audible, "I know it," escape her lips. She prayed that he hadn't been teasing her. Hadn't been tormenting her just to make a fool of her. To prove her a child. But this was Ransom Lake and he was not capable of rendering such a cruel gesture to her. As he pulled her even tighter against his body, her hands rested gently on his solid, muscular chest and she could only stare into the warm storm in his eyes as he grinned triumphantly for a moment before his face went solemn as it moved down toward hers. But an instant before his lips would've touched hers, Vaden turned her face from him and tried to push herself away.

"Vaden?" he asked quietly.

"I'm...I'm not good at it," she confessed, ashamed somehow of her innocence and inexperience.

He took her chin in his hand and turned her face to his once more, an amused grin warming his features. "Vaden...you're good at everything. I wouldn't be trying this on you again if you hadn't a boiled my blood the very first time."

"But you're...you're *Ransom Lake*," Vaden told him as if he wasn't aware of the information.

"Yes, I am," was all he whispered before he took her lips to his suddenly before she could shy away again. His first kisses were like honeyed confection, sweet and tender, but after a few moments she felt his hand caress the back of her bodice as it traveled from her waist, over her back, finally entangling itself in the softness of her hair. He tugged ever so gently on her hair and she tipped her head back slightly, gasping as she felt his kiss leave her lips and travel to her neck. He placed several long, soft kisses on her throat. The impassioned turbulence in his eyes captured her bliss-filled ones a moment before his kiss to her mouth was hers again, full, demanding and enrapturing every fiber of her being.

Vaden understood in that moment that there was nothing to be gained from experience when it came to returning a man's kiss. She knew that either a woman loved a man and for that reason her soul and body knew how to kiss him, or she didn't and her soul, mind and body had no cause to want to kiss him. However, Vaden knew with everything she was, with all her femininity that Ransom Lake was a man whose kiss went far beyond that of the average man. Ransom Lake was unusually proficient at it. The way his arms held her, the way his chest rose and fell with his breathing, the way he toyed with her mouth one moment and exhausted it with overwhelming and demanding passion the next. Vaden perceived that she was made to fit his kiss perfectly. To return it the way he would most enjoy and relish.

Suddenly, however, he pushed her away gently, taking several steps backward as he ran his fingers through his hair, an expression of confusion on his face.

"What am I doing?" he mumbled, a look of something akin to panic controlling his handsome features. Vaden felt self-conscious and somehow ashamed. "Your Uncle Dan would kill me. What am I doing?" Then he lunged forward, taking her face between his hands as he nearly shouted, "What are you doing to me?"

"Nothing!" Vaden forced the defense from her lungs as tears escaped her eyes. "I...I...haven't done anything."

His fingers went to her lips, caressing them with unusual softness as his hands shook anxiously. Taking her chin firmly in one trembling hand, he pulled her face to his once more, ravaging her mouth with a final, moist, intensely passionate kiss. When he ended it, slowly, tenderly, his trembling had ceased and he smiled at Vaden understandingly.

"I've never tasted anything as satisfyingly delicious as you, Vaden. Not in my whole life. I think you're my favorite flavor." Then he turned from her, retrieved another log from the nearby pile and tossed it into the hearth. "Now, you go on over there and cuddle up on that sofa...alone. We'll get you home first thing in the morning. And...uh...this...this business between me and you...I...I know you'll understand when I say that...it's just the moment here. The situation nearly demanded that I...the loneliness of the night and atmosphere."

She wanted to scream, *No! I don't understand! I love you and you must at least care for me, else you wouldn't have told me your secrets! Why can't it happen every day, every minute?* But she nodded and muttered, "Yes."

She sat for long minutes that turned into an hour, simply staring into the flames of the fire as the wind moaned outside, causing anxiety to settle into her mind. Ransom Lake continued to sit on the floor before the hearth toying with the poker every now and again, causing sparks to rise and crackle from the burning logs.

"I've learned a lot tonight, haven't I, Mr. Lake?" Vaden said softly as she finally stretched out on the sofa, pulling to her shoulders a dusty, heavy quilt that had been folded in half long ago and laid on the back of it. He sat down on the floor before her, resting his back against the sofa. "I've grown up quickly tonight. I've learned that the elements of heaven and earth can endanger a person's life. I've learned that there are things people have witnessed, have experienced...things that only nightmares are made of. Things that eat their hearts away and leave their minds scarred and tormented. Things that can never be forgotten or put aside."

"It's a lot to realize in such a short time. But that's usually how such things go. They blind-side you. You don't expect them or see them coming," Ransom Lake added. He put down the poker he still had in hand, turned and looked at her. "And what else have you learned, Vaden?" His gray eyes narrowed, his features soft, his chest rising and falling slowly with his calm breathing.

She smiled at him, though she was beginning to feel sleepy. "I've learned that I was right about you, Mr. Lake."

"You were?"

"You are an angel in disguises. Disguises both physical and of character."

He smiled and shook his head. "You think you're pretty smart, don't you?"

"I am. I am very smart, Mr. Lake" she answered, returning the warmth of his smile in her own. She would not call him by his given name, for she sensed it would be her complete undoing. She sensed she would lose her ability to resist throwing herself at his feet and begging for his love. She smiled mischievously at him then and whispered, "I'm so smart I've figured out that you're twenty-six years old. I think you look twenty-six."

He chuckled and shook his head, amused at her again. "Is that good or bad?"

"You figure it out," she giggled softly. Her eyelids were feeling heavy and hard to keep open. Even though the dream-born vision of Ransom Lake was only inches away from her, an apparition of reality before her very tired eyes, she was giving into the warmth of the room and the need for rest. Her anxiety about the storm was gone, for the security that he radiated was strong and reassuring. Just before her eyes closed completely, and she drifted off to sleep, Ransom Lake pressed his thumb to his lips, placing the same thumb on her own for a moment.

"Goodnight, Sleeping Beauty," he whispered.

"Cinderella," she corrected and she heard him chuckling as she drifted into a light, uncomfortable sleep.

She dreamt of visions, horrid visions that might have tainted the memory of Ransom Lake. She could smell the death at the wagon train when the young man had returned to find his family slaughtered. She could smell the dirt as the young man dug shallow graves. Hear the sound of the shovel cutting the earth as he worked. She could feel the grief, the over-whelming, unendurable grief piercing his heart every minute for days, weeks and years to come. And the pain of the grief was suffocating. It burned in her throat as she watched the visions in her mind. It hurt her limbs and body.

Vaden awoke with a start, her muscles aching from the tension in her body. She couldn't move for a moment, paralyzed with the grief and horror of her dreams. When finally she could move, she looked to see Ransom Lake standing before the hearth once more. Her intuition told her that he hadn't slept as she had. Hadn't dozed for even a moment. He stood staring into the fire, which blazed warm and red. His feet were planted firmly apart and his massive, muscular arms were folded across his chest. He had removed his shirt and it lay haphazardly over the arm of a nearby chair. Vaden was quiet for long moments just watching the man who watched the fire. His frown was intense and furrowed his brow deeply. He was lost in his thoughts and she knew they were grim, for his jaw was clearly tensed. The room was still only lit by the fire, which burned almost too violently, heating the room beyond comfortable. No light streamed in through the dusty windows and Vaden surmised that it was still very early morning. So deep in thought was Ransom Lake, in fact, that he didn't see Vaden rise quietly from the sofa and he did not turn to look at her when she quietly walked to stand behind the man.

Vaden's heart was heavy in her bosom with the sympathy she felt for the man she loved. What tragic horror he had endured. It was no wonder to her that he had withdrawn from the world, hidden himself away from any chance of being hurt again. Then her love for him, her profound and endless love for him, coupled with the anguish in her heart for his pain, overtook her prudence and she moved forward, pressing her cheek to his back as her arms encircled his waist in a loving embrace. Immediately she felt his body stiffen and his hands covered her own that were linked one with the other at his waist.

"I'm so sorry, for you, Mr. Lake. For your pain. I'm sorry that everything was taken from you so violently. I'm sorry for the scars that it left in your heart and soul," she whispered to him. Vaden scolded herself inwardly for she felt the fool then. Ransom Lake had confided his deepest secrets to her and as she looked back on the conversation now, she was angry with herself, for her experience on Halloween paled so greatly to his. Further, he had blamed himself for her pain of that night. He had only placed further burdens on his already guilt-ridden mind. As her tears moistened the flesh of his back, she whispered once more, "I'm sorry."

"Thank you," he mumbled as he removed her hands from his waist and walked forward and out of her embrace. "Only, I'm not certain if I did the right thing in telling you."

"Of course you did," she assured him, a bit embarrassed that she would've acted so familiar with him. "A burden is not meant to be borne alone."

"But...now I've taxed your mind with the horror of it. You'll never be free of the knowledge again." He paused, clearing his throat, yet he still mumbled when he continued. "It was wrong of me to deprive you of your innocence in yet another area of life." He turned to face her, his eyes narrowed, his voice low and angry as he spoke. "I've corrupted you in a manner. Before I interfered you knew no difference between the touch of one man compared to another. You knew nothing about the weakness of a man when his physical desires were taunted. You knew nothing about such horrors as murder, mutilation and guilt."

"You make me sound like quite the complete idiot, Mr. Lake," Vaden snapped at him. "Aren't all those things part of human existence? Just because I experienced them at your hand doesn't mean I am corrupted! I think what you really mean to say is that in your eyes I'm marred somehow. Weak because I succumbed to your...to your..."

"To me," he prodded.

"Yes. Thank you."

"I meant no such ridiculous thing, and you know it," he argued then. "I only meant to say that...you've changed in the past weeks and don't deny that it is mostly on my head."

Vaden's voice softened. "You've taught me much these past weeks. I've told you already what I've learned just this very night. And in the weeks past there have been many things of life that I have learned at your hand. None of them, whether good or bad, pleasant or unpleasant, would I trade. For they are things that will help me in life, one way or the other, in my considerations, my decisions." Swallowing hard and straightening her back, she looked at him determinedly and added, "And now I will be bold and forthright in telling you that...that you're wrong not to tell your brother that you are alive. Consider on his pain and loss for a moment." She stopped talking when he raised his hand in a gesture indicating that she silence herself and shook his head.

"Don't make me regret confiding in you any more than I already do, Vaden," he growled. He looked at the ceiling for a moment as if to gain control of his thoughts, then looked back to her saying, "The storm stopped almost an hour ago. I figure the sun will be up in a few more hours. We'll leave for home at the first sign of it."

At his mention of their leaving the secluded place, the place where he had opened his heart to her, Vaden felt immense sorrow and fear. Never again would she have him wholly to herself, completely hold him so near to her...so solitarily near to her.

"Now, why don't you try to rest some more," he mumbled, turning from her and back toward the fire.

"Quit treating me like a child!" she cried out, causing him to turn, surprise dominating his expression. "I don't want to rest anymore! Don't you see that? In a short time we'll leave here and...and this won't ever happen again! You won't ever again confide in me as you have this night! You won't ever share such intimate conversation with me like you have tonight! We'll be back in town with every woman in the world groveling for your attentions and I'll go back to being the irritating little girl at the mercantile who is forever and always an inconvenience to you. I'll go back to being your little friend instead of someone you confide in. Someone you choose to..."

His eyes narrowed in puzzlement and, after inhaling deeply to try to calm herself, Vaden added, "I don't want to rest anymore. So, please...please quit ordering me to do it as if I were..."

"I have not once treated you like a child tonight, Vaden," he protested calmly. "You're hung up on thinking I have because you think everyone else treats you like one. But it's not true. People who care for you are protective of you. They like to handle you with kid gloves, protect you from agony and harm. That doesn't mean they consider you a child. I think my personal treatment of you proves that I for one do not look upon you as a child, Vaden." He moved toward her, reaching out and taking her shoulders between his powerful hands. His eyes narrowed and his voice lowered. "But if more...convincing is necessary...then I for one am willing."

"Why do you tease me so?" she asked, knowing full well that he did, indeed, only tease her with his implications.

"It's in my nature to tease people I like," he answered grinning. Then he lowered his voice as if he expected someone to enter the room and eavesdrop on their conversation. "You said it yourself. In a short time we'll go back to town and everything will return to normal. No more bearing our souls to each other, no more finding comfort in each other's arms. And definitely no more tasty kisses." Vaden looked away shyly for a moment. "Things will be different than they are at this moment. No doubt I'll look back at this night and beat my brain to death for allowing this to happen. No doubt you'll look back on me as the man who taught you too much about life. And you'll be relieved to be rid of me because of it." His hands encircled her neck, his thumbs caressing her throat lightly. "But," he whispered, "I suppose we can both live with our guilt and whatever method it chooses to torture us. Can't we? We can each live with it for one more taste of each other?"

Vaden's mouth began to water for want of his kiss and a tear ran slowly down her face as she nodded, knowing that this memory must live with her forever, for it would be the last.

"And I'll tell you something, Vaden Valmont," he mumbled in the familiar provocative tone that was his. "Let go of your inhibitions toward me. Be the girl that fears nothing, cares nothing for what anyone else thinks. Be yourself, Vaden, and I promise you..." He leaned forward, placing his cheek against her own as he whispered, "Ransom Lake is yours 'til sunrise. No matter what happens in the future. No matter who you decide to live your life with...no matter who ends up in mine...right now I'm yours. Just as I was that night in the wagon...and well you knew it, for you're too smart not to have known it. And you know that my word is sincere now." He kissed her neck just below her earlobe tenderly and a thrill erupted within her entire being. "You kiss me first, Vaden. Kiss me first. Prove to me that the girl who found my soul, the one who drew me out of hiding from beneath my whiskers, is still there inside you...and I'm yours until daybreak...if you want me to be." He dropped his hands to his sides, stood erect and stared at her with the gray intensity of his eyes.

Vaden found it almost impossible to breathe. Her breath, in fact, was unregulated as she looked at him standing before her. Weeks ago she would've been able to draw the courage to kiss him quickly. She would not have even paused perhaps in the same situation. But self doubt and uncertainty, as well as heartache, had scarred her deeply and now. With what she wanted and loved most in the world standing before her, hers if only she would reach out and take it into her arms, she paused, frightened and unsure of herself. She was unsure of his sincerity in his promise. What if he only laughed at her? What if he drew away from her, having only been teasing her? But deep within her soul she knew better. Ransom Lake would never behave so. "You...you won't laugh at me?" she whispered all the same. Her confidence was still lacking, the demon of doubt still causing her mind to question.

Ransom Lake closed his eyes for a moment and sighed. "Vaden," he whispered scoldingly and began to turn from her. Instantly, her hand shot out and clasped his. He paused, looking at her hand, then to her face questioningly. With the few shreds of courage left in her heart she reached out and took his arm with her other hand, stepping closer to him. She focused her gaze on his hand that she held as she tried to muster the bravery of her soul. In a moment, she released it, letting her palms caress the power in his arms and shoulders as her hands traveled up the muscular appendages to settle finally at the back of his neck.

She felt his hands clasp her waist between them and it gave her the courage to look up at him then. His eyes were narrow, calm and expectant as he gazed at her. She raised herself slightly on her toes and placed a lingering kiss on the cleft of his chin. Then she took his face gently between her small, trembling hands and tipped his head toward her, kissing him sweetly on the mouth. She was further encouraged of his sincerity when he involved himself in that first tender kiss as well as the more earnest one she administered next.

Instantly, she was in his arms, held firmly against his body as the now familiar, powerfully passionate kisses he could manipulate burned between them. His strength and pain, his need and sincerity at being her own, for that time, were all evident as the magical hours passed. Hours that found Vaden in awe of what was happening. Hours of shared affections that were now tender and soft, and now demanding and passionate. Often he would separate their mouths and hold her to him tightly, whispering her name with something like regret evident in his voice. Once he lifted her swiftly into his arms, going to the small sofa and sitting down with her on his lap where they sat in continuance of their affections, he always the gentleman in every respect, for he never attempted anything beyond impassioned kisses. Kisses moist with flavor and barely restrained desire, perhaps. But he was ever the gentleman. Vaden was comfortable, for she knew that he would not force any improper attention or affection.

All too soon light broke through the dusty west window of the old house, flooding the room with sunlight, further enhanced by the brightness of the snow outside. With the illumination that lit the room, the fire dying in the hearth, the spell that Ransom Lake had twined about Vaden and himself began to fade.

Taking her face in his hands and kissing her deeply as if trying to quench an unquenchable thirst one last time, he let his thumb trace her fragile lips that were then scarlet from his attentions and whispered, "Our moment is lost with the sunrise, Vaden. Time to leave the fairy tale and return you to your uncle. Who," he added as he gently pushed her from his lap, "would strike me down dead if he knew what I'd done to you while you were in my care." Standing, he walked to the chair that sat across the room and retrieved his shirt, buttoning it quickly, and ran his fingers through his tousled hair before putting on his hat and coat and pulling on his boots.

What have you done to me, Ransom Lake? Vaden thought. *In these few hours you've fulfilled my dreams of you and yet broken my heart.*

Picking up a bucket that sat near the front door, he exited the house through that very door, returning in a moment with the bucket full of snow. Vaden watched, relacing her own boots slowly as he doused the fire in the hearth with the bucket of snow, causing steam and an odd odor of wet wood to rise in the room. Taking Vaden's coat from the chair over which it lay, Ransom Lake held it for her as she slipped her arms through the sleeves. Then, turning her to face him, he grinned almost lamentably as he buttoned the coat's top button for her and pulled her hood up over her head.

"It's freezing out there...but at least the wind isn't blowing. I put the horse back outside when the storm stopped and she doesn't seem any worse for the weather." He opened the front door to the house and motioned for Vaden to precede him out of it.

Vaden's eyes narrowed to a squint as the brightness of the sun's reflection on the new fallen snow met her eyes, which had been so long adjusted to the dark. All was perfectly quiet. No rustling of wind through tree branches, no snow birds' songs or calls of wild geese. Not a sound. Vaden looked about for a moment marveling at the endless horizon of undisturbed white powder and frost that covered the earth. Her mesmerized wonderment was lost as Ransom Lake held his hand out to her to assist her into the cutter.

As the cutter slipped away toward home, Vaden gazed back at the lonely house that stood midst the quiet of winter. It was a house whose beauty was in its quaintness of design and she smiled sadly, thinking it would forever be a fixed vision in her memory.

Not one word was spoken between Ransom Lake and Vaden Valmont as the mare struggled to return them to town. Vaden found that her silence was induced by sorrow and shyness at the memories of her intimate moments shared with Ransom Lake in the house.

"Entwine thine arms about me, love. Protect me from the cold. Release me not for need of breath...nor fear of growing old. Keep safe our love with thine embrace. Keep warm my lips with thine. Let no one interfere this space, that Heaven deemed is mine."

It was the first time since that dreadful Halloween night that Vaden's mind drew forth a favored verse from her memory. And, though it was somewhat bittersweet, it seemed fitting. Vaden glanced at Ransom Lake several times and concluded that his silence must be derived of the regret of letting what happened happen, for he wore a perpetual frown and did not once look at her.

CHAPTER
∽ TEN ∽

At long last, the cutter pulled to a stop before the mercantile and Vaden and Ransom Lake were immediately set upon by Aunt Myra, Yvonne and Uncle Dan as all three came bounding out of the house and into the snow beside the cutter.

"Oh! My darling!" Myra cried out, taking Vaden in a tight embrace the second she had stepped down from the conveyance. "We were so worried for you! Oh, my dearest!"

Yvonne was next and Vaden did not notice her pause and puzzled frown as she hugged her sister, quickly looking to Ransom Lake curiously, then back to Vaden. "We feared the worst, Vay," she said. Her relief at seeing her sister safely home was obvious and sincere. "The storm was so violent and there was no way to find out if Mr. Lake had even made it to the Wimbers'."

"Thank you, Ransom," Uncle Dan greeted Ransom Lake, putting a grateful hand to the man's shoulder. "I'd have been beside myself if it had been anyone else but you that had gone for her. Did you weather it out at the Wimbers' then?"

"No, sir," the rescuer stated plainly. Vaden watched the color drain from Ransom Lake's face as he removed his hat and looked her uncle squarely in the eyes to continue. "I...the storm moved in much faster than I had antici- pated and the dark overcame us. So...we weathered the night at an old house that is out east on my property."

"Oh, how terrible for you!" Aunt Myra exclaimed. "And just look at your face, sweet pea!" Aunt Myra reached out and gently touched the reddened, chapped looking area around Vaden's mouth. "Look how chapped your face is from the wind and such! Poor dear."

Vaden noticed Ransom Lake close his eyes for a moment at her aunt's referring to her damaged lips and draw in a deep breath before he began to confess to her uncle. She knew he meant to confess to him, for she felt his guilt radiating from him like the brutal flames of a brush fire.

"Sir," he began. "I want you to know...that, although the elements demanded my stopping with Miss Vaden to weather the storm...that I did not act..."

"He saved our lives, Uncle Dan!" Vaden interrupted immediately. "For we would surely have been lost and frozen in the blizzard had Mr. Lake not had the foresight to stop in time." Vaden's eyes met Yvonne's, whose expression was suspicious and delighted at the same time.

"Of course! Of course, my boy!" Uncle Dan assured the man. "Like I told you before, I would not have sent anyone else for her, for I knew she would be safe in your hands." Uncle Dan smiled at the man who glanced guiltily at Vaden once more. "Now, let's get in the house and warm you two up."

"Oh, no, Dan. I really should check on the stock and..." Ransom Lake began.

"Nonsense, Ransom! It's Thanksgiving Day! You've accepted an invitation to dinner and there's no sense in going home when you're already here, now is there!" Uncle Dan was smiling and jolly as usual.

"Really, Dan. My stock. I'm bound to have cattle that didn't weather too well and..." Ransom Lake began and Vaden sensed that he wanted only escape from the situation. From her.

"Uncle Dan sent Marcus Donaldson out to your place this morning," Yvonne assured him. "Marcus offered last night to check on everyone out of town when morning came. He'll let us know if there has been any problem at your place."

"I'm...I'm not dressed for..." Ransom Lake began.

"Oh, now, Ransom Lake!" Aunt Myra scolded. "A body would think you were trying to weasel your way out of spending the day with us. Is it my cooking that scares you away?" she teased.

"Now, Myra. You know there's not truth to that at all," Ransom Lake chuckled, finally grinning a bit.

"Good! Then go on in before you all freeze out here. I'll take care of the horse." Uncle Dan took hold of the mare's reins and led her out behind the mercantile where the barn was. Ransom Lake glanced quickly at Vaden, shrugging his shoulders in defeat.

Aunt Myra took the man's arm and led him into the house, babbling unceasingly about the baking she'd been about while her mind was plagued with worry during the night. Yvonne took Vaden's arm and stayed her so that Myra and Ransom Lake could not hear their conversation. Lowering her voice to a whisper, Yvonne asked, "Well? Are you going to tell me what happened, or not?"

"Nothing happened," Vaden lied.

"You're lying, Vay, and I'm not as stupid as you think I am! I know you and I know how you feel about that man in there. So tell me...did you seduce him into kissing you?"

Vaden gasped and looked at her sister, eyes wide with indignation. "What a thing to say to me, Vonnie! I can't believe you would..."

"And I suppose your lips are berry red and chapped from the windless drive home this morning." Yvonne giggled and Vaden knew she was not being unkind, only playful.

"This is not the time nor the place to discuss the matter, Yvonne. To-night. Tonight when things are quiet and Mr. Lake has gone home. Then I will talk with you about this. Perhaps."

They entered the house, Yvonne giggling and Vaden smiling, though somewhat sadly, for it was at an end now. Her romantic adventure with Ransom Lake, the stuff of daydreams, the fairy tale...was over.

Thanksgiving Day had dawned bright and sunny, but as the morning wore on the sun was hidden behind dark clouds and the snow began to fall heavily. Ransom Lake was nervous, pacing this way and that the entire morning as Uncle Dan conversed with him in the parlor. Finally, some time after the noon hour, Marcus Donaldson arrived and reported that all was well with Mr. Lake's stock. The windbreaks had sheltered the cattle and the remaining stock were safe in the barn, fed and watered.

Vaden watched as Ransom Lake reached into his front pocket, offering the man a handful of paper money in exchange for his time. Marcus nodded and told Ransom that he needed to learn what neighbors were for and that he could return the favor at some later date.

"Everything will be fine over to your place 'til morning, Ransom. You go on ahead and enjoy your Thanksgiving with these fine folks," Marcus said, tipping his hat to the ladies as he left.

"You see, my boy!" Uncle Dan exclaimed, slapping Ransom Lake heartily on the back. "Nothing at all to worry about."

"Still, this weather is turning severe again," the worried man mumbled. "I should get back before I get snowed in another night away from home."

Uncle Dan chuckled and lowered his voice, but Vaden's ears were cocked and tightly tuned in and she heard his teasing remark to Ransom Lake. "Oh, I'm certain another night in the company of my niece won't do you a bit of harm."

Vaden glanced up at Ransom Lake whose face had gone as white as the snow outside.

"I, uh...I, uh, want to be sure that you understand that I meant no..." Ransom Lake began in a lowered voice.

But Uncle Dan's chuckling interrupted him. "Now, I understand perfectly, my boy. Don't you worry no more about it. I know that she was safer with you than any other man on this green earth probably. A bit of sparkin' now and then never hurt nobody."

Vaden felt her face flush red and decided that she must break her horrid habit of eavesdropping. As soon as Ransom Lake was no longer under the same roof as she, that was.

The turkey was splendid, the pie supreme! The conversation friendly and jolly. And the storm was monstrous. Just after dinner, Vaden heard Ransom Lake ask her uncle for a lantern and extra coat to borrow in order that he may make his way home. It occurred to her only then that the two of them had barely spoken a word to each other throughout the entire day. She chose that very moment to break her silence toward him.

"You can't go out in this!" she exclaimed, horrified at the thought of him out in the snow. All eyes, including Ransom Lake's were on her immediately.

"She's right, Ransom," her Aunt Myra agreed strongly. "You can't possibly be thinking of going out in this storm. You'll be lost and frozen for certain. Listen to that wind!"

"You're staying the night right here with us, Ransom. I'd be a crazy man to let you go out in this weather," Uncle Dan boomed.

"You all are very generous...but I've stayed my welcome way past what I should've and it's time for me to leave," Ransom Lake informed them.

"Nonsense," Aunt Myra sighed. She walked up to him and promptly removed his coat from where it had been slung over his arm. "You're staying right here. We've plenty of room and I'll not have you catching another cold...maybe the death of you this time."

Ransom Lake's eyes met Vaden's for a moment and she read their emotions immediately. He wanted escape. Escape from her. He'd been her own for one night and she knew he had no wish to be in her company any longer. Indeed, she had played out her welcome in his presence.

"We've the spare bedroom, Mr. Lake," she offered quickly. "My aunt and uncle would be more than overjoyed to have holiday company. And don't worry. You won't be disturbed." His eyes narrowed as he looked at her and Vaden was aware of Yvonne studying both her sister and Ransom Lake carefully. "In fact, I feel more than completely done in. It's been a very long day. I think I'll go to bed myself now."

"But...but it's only just seven o'clock, sweet pea," Aunt Myra reminded her niece. "Are you certain you want to..."

Vaden nodded. "I'm tired. Very tired. I think I'll just go on to bed. Thank you again, Mr. Lake. For everything." Turning to her aunt, she added, "And thank you for the wonderful meal, Auntie. You've been so wonderful to us since we've come. I bid you all goodnight then." Leaving everyone astounded at her early retirement, everyone except Ransom Lake, she went quietly to her room, readied for bed and slipped beneath her covers as her tears moistened her pillowcase.

She'd had to leave him. In order for him to remain safely under her uncle's roof, she knew that she could be no more bother to him. She thought of the boots hidden beneath her bed, but she would not look at them tonight. She would not touch them. For tonight the pain in her heart was too great and she could not endure the sight of anything belonging to him.

Vaden was quite startled when she awoke some hours later to the darkness in her bedroom. Yvonne was in bed breathing quietly and rhythmically. The clock in the hall struck a quarter past some hour of the night. Had he stayed she wondered? Had he been so tired of her that he had decided that another night anywhere near her was unendurable and ventured out into the storm? She wanted to wake Yvonne and ask her, but she knew that all that would ensue would be question after question fired at her by her sister until she had heard of the previous night's antics and her curiosity had been quenched.

So, quietly she stepped from her bed and tiptoed out into the hall. Even in the hall she could hear the wind howling outside and knew that the orange light emanating from the parlor was the fire in the hearth that Uncle Dan had left burning to try to heat the house. It was terribly cold and she wished she had taken the time to wrap herself in a blanket. The door to the spare room was closed. For fear that Ransom Lake may, indeed, be asleep in the room beyond, she dared not open it, for it would more than likely squeak open like every other door in the house. So, she placed her ear to the cold wood and listened, hearing nothing beyond. With a heavy, disappointed sigh she made her way into the parlor to stand before the embers of the dying fire. She closed her eyes for a moment, remembering the fire, the hearth and the many warmths of the night before. The warm, provocative tone of his voice echoed through her mind. His arms had been so strong, so capable and warming when he had held her. His face so handsome, his eyes so hypnotic. His kiss...his kiss had been euphoria perfectly embodied.

She startled, jumping nervously, as she heard a voice behind her ask in a whisper, "What are you doing up at all hours of the night?" Turning, Vaden found herself face to face with the very subject of her thoughts, who stood dressed in only his trousers, holding a glass of water in one hand.

"I...I...couldn't sleep and I...I thought I might sit by the fire a moment," she stammered.

"You need your rest. You've been greatly deprived of it lately, I think," he muttered. Instead of returning to his room, however, he came to stand beside her.

"I suppose," she admitted. She looked about nervously, trying to find something other than the man on which to focus her attention, for it was greatly unsettling to see him again only half clothed as he was. "I mean...do you have everything you need? Are you comfortable in your room, Mr. Lake?"

He grinned and held up the glass of water before saying, "Already got what I needed. And I'm snug as a bug in that room. But thank you just the same, Miss Vaden." His eyes were stormy and mirthful and she knew that he knew she was uncomfortable.

She nodded agitatedly as her fingers fumbled with the bow at the throat of her nightdress. "I...ah...I...I need to say another thank you."

"For what?" he asked, taking a drink from the glass.

"For...for coming to get me last evening. I know it was no small task and I wanted you to know that I have an immense appreciation of your deed."

His grin broadened as his eyes traveled the length of her, resting at her bare feet. Vaden turned from him, immediately going to stand nearer to the fire.

"I'm sincere in my thanks, Mr. Lake. I wish you wouldn't look at me with that amused look of doubt each time I find myself thanking you or apologizing to you."

"What amused look of doubt?" he asked nearly in a whisper.

"*That* look. The one that is on your face just now," she said, turning toward him and pointing to his fine feature of face.

"Well, it does seem that you're always apologizing to me for some sort of something, now doesn't it? Would you like it better if I were grouching at you every time? I swear, I'd spend most of my time in town grouching if that were the case. And besides, maybe I'm the one who needs to be thanking you for that warm evening last night."

Vaden blushed furiously, but she made no effort to defend herself, for she knew that she would only succeed in making herself all the more uncomfortable. He remained standing beside her before the fire and they were both silent for a moment. Then, an instant before Vaden would've turned and left him for fear of verbally spilling her heartfelt love for him should she linger longer, Ransom Lake spoke two words that astounded her as they ever did when he spoke them.

"I'm sorry," he muttered quietly.

"What?" she asked, unable to believe what he'd said or to understand why he had said it.

"Now," he continued, "I see Jerome and Belva have stepped out of the room. So what say we have us a dance?"

"The proverbial water under the bridge, Mr. Lake," Vaden whispered, relieved that he was only teasing her once more.

"Not to me." He looked at her, the firelight reflecting mischievously in his eyes. "I feel the need to make amends. And I promise that I never make the same mistake twice." He set his glass of water down out of the way and put a hand at her waist, gesturing for her to place her hand in his outstretched one.

Vaden smiled at him and blushed slightly as he began to waltz with her. He kept his steps small and she fancied he held her too closely, but she was entranced by him as he danced with her, the only music for them being the warm crackling of the fire. His steps weren't as smooth and fluid as Jerome's had been and she was glad of it. He was heavier on his feet and she knew Jerome would never contemplate holding her so closely. In fact, a few moments after they had begun, she cast her gaze downward and began to tremble slightly when she realized that he held her close enough to his body that every few steps she could feel the firm muscles of his upper chest brush against her chin or cheek. That every other turn she would feel the solid power of his thigh against her leg as he led her.

"You're cold," he muttered, misinterpreting her shivering. "You should get back to bed." He stopped their waltz and released her. Then, as she stood gazing rather dazedly up at him, he whispered, "And for Belva's benefit…" and he stooped, kissing her warmly on the forehead.

Vaden smiled even though she sensed tears wanting to rise to her eyes. How desperately she wished to relive the night before when he'd held and kissed her and whispered her name almost lovingly.

"But you see, Mr. Lake," she told him quietly, "you've only just proven the other girls' point. I'm the kind of girl you want to take fishing. The kind you kiss on the forehead sweetly as you would a child. The kind you toy with in private once, when no one can see...but not the kind you make a habit of..."

Before she could finish her sentence, Ransom Lake cupped Vaden's chin in his powerful hand and kissed her soft lips plainly and not so very quickly. Vaden felt the now familiar and instantaneous fire ignite within her as his mouth began to work a spell over her as it had the night before. She marveled at how instantly wonderful the feel of being in his arms was. How instantly familiar the warmth and taste of his kiss was to her. But almost as quickly as he had begun to kiss her he stopped, holding her away from him.

"I'm a guest in your uncle's house, Vaden. I'll not take advantage of that by..." he explained.

Vaden was suddenly humiliated, feeling as if she had again provoked him into faltering somehow. She felt a panicked desperation. He would leave her once more and truly never be close to her again, for she knew that these past two days were never to be repeated. Never.

"But I...I..." she stammered, fighting to stop her mouth from saying what it had begun to confess to him.

"Don't say it, Vaden," he demanded, closing his eyes tightly as if to block out her words. "I'm not what you need. I can't be what you want. You only think that you...it's because I was such a mystery to you for so long. You have the curiosity of a fairy, Vaden. You'll find now that it's quenched...I won't seem as..."

"What on earth do you think I was going to say to you, Mr. Lake?" she exclaimed, though she knew full well that she would have confessed her love for him that very moment had he not interrupted her.

"I know more surely than you can imagine exactly what you were about to say, Vaden. But it's only youth and admiration causing you to think...I've rescued you twice now. I'm a man in your eyes...older than that flimsy Jerome Clayton. It's all just your...imagination. I'm not what you think I am," he nearly growled.

"You may think you know what I was going to say to you, Mr. Lake," Vaden spat then, "but don't flatter yourself. I was only going to say that you were not taking advantage of me, therefore, you were not taking advantage of my uncle's hospitality. I was not being lured blindly into your arms, Mr. Lake. I am not the idiot you continue to take me for."

She could tell by the narrowing of his eyes and the way he studied her face that he doubted...no he knew she was lying. So, she turned indignantly and began to walk away from him. She gasped aloud when next she felt him come from behind her and pick her up swiftly in his arms.

"Leave it to you to be wandering around in the middle of the night and completely ruin a man's chances of getting a good night's sleep. This is the second night in a row you've been the cause of my tired eyes and body, girl," he grumbled as he carried her toward the bedrooms. He paused before the door to the guest room in which he was staying the night. "You think you're too smart to be taken advantage of, do you now?" he whispered. "Well, Miss Know-It-All Valmont...what if old man Ransom Lake was to take you on into this room instead of on to your own? What would you do then?"

Vaden set her jaw squarely and even though her body trembled with rapture at being held by him she said firmly, "Scream for deliverance at the top of my lungs."

The awesomely handsome man glared at her. "You couldn't. My mouth would be exhausting yours and you wouldn't be able to scream." Then he lowered his voice even more and as the beguiling gray storm in his eyes fixed on hers he added, "And you wouldn't want to anyway."

Vaden's mouth gaped open in astonishment at his lewd remarks. "And you pride yourself as holding to high morals. As a gentleman."

"I do, Miss Valmont." Then he turned and headed in the direction of Vaden's own room.

As he started to push the door open with his foot she protested in a whisper, "No! Don't! You'll wake Yvonne and she'll think..."

Ransom Lake looked at her for a moment. "Not if you keep that hon-eyed mouth shut for once, girl," he whispered as the door to Vaden's bed-room slowly swung open. Quietly Ransom Lake carried Vaden to her empty bed as Vaden watched to be sure Yvonne did not stir. He laid her gently on it, then whispered, "You're lucky this night, Miss Vaden, that I chose not to stop at my own room."

Vaden sat up and spat in a whisper, "You would never have seriously considered it." She knew he was a gentleman and also a great friend of her Uncle Dan's. He was only teasing her and she knew it well.

"So sure are you?"

"Perfectly. Don't pretend to be the villain, Mr. Lake. I know better."

"Don't be so sure, girl," he whispered. As he leaned forward, his arms on either side of her body as his hands supported his weight, Vaden melted against him once more as he kissed her with a deep ferocity that nearly caused her to faint from the rapturous intensity of it. His mouth was hot and demanding and left hers too soon. He exited the room quietly, but with haste and anger and Vaden wondered if she would ever sleep before morn-ing.

"Am I dreaming, Vaden," Yvonne whispered quietly from the other side of the room. "I could have sworn I just saw…"

"Yes, you must be dreaming, Vonnie. And so must I be."

Vaden was uncomfortable at breakfast the next morning. She could feel the blush rise to her face every time she looked at Ransom Lake and he caught her looking at him. He seemed to wear an eternal expression of knowing amusement and it unnerved her greatly.

"You might as well stay through lunch, Ransom," Uncle Dan stated.

"No. I've got to get back. Hard telling what kind of shape I'll find things in," he explained.

"It'll take you two hours to get home in this weather, boy! You better stay on." Uncle Dan shoveled another bite of eggs into his mouth.

"Nope. Can't. Found myself away from home long enough already, Dan. But I thank you for your generosity. You, too, Myra."

Ransom Lake smiled at Myra and she nodded and smiled back. "Any time Ransom. You're a joy to have around, not to mention being Vaden's deliverer from tragedy."

Vaden looked to him and his eyes captured hers, his tongue moistened his lips slowly as he stared at her mouth and Vaden's eyes widened indignantly. When she next looked to Yvonne, it was to see her sister's eyes practically bulging from her skull, for Yvonne had witnessed Ransom Lake's implicative gesture. It delighted Vaden to know that she had, for now Yvonne had seen Ransom Lake's flirtatious nature firsthand.

As Vaden stood at the window watching Ransom Lake's mare struggling to carry him through the knee deep snow, her depression, her heartache continued. For nearly two days she had been in his company. Definitely two nights, and her body ached for his arms about her. Her mind ached to hear his mumbly, low pitched voice whisper something, anything, in her ear. She wanted only to stare at him every moment of the day. To have him talk to her. Just one of their silly argumentative conversations would've sufficed. She longed for his smile, his frown, the way he rubbed at the whiskers on his chin. Little things were what she longed for as well as the more obvious, such as his marvelous kiss.

But as she watched him disappear around the corner toward his home, she knew that her tale of companionship with the phenomenal man, Ransom Lake, was at an end. He would have all the more reason to avoid her now. She knew that for certain. It was mere common sense that testified to her that once someone had confided some deep felt secret to another person, the person who had chosen in a weak moment to reveal himself often felt uncomfortable around his confidant, wanting only to avoid them at all cost. And there was so much more reason for Ransom Lake to avoid her.

Coupled with the fact that she held knowledge of his pain, she was forever and always tripping him up somehow, and now he professed that she tempted him physically. This final fact she could admit to herself, for he had told her as much. She also knew it to be true, for she knew a man could not feign such passion. Even the best of actors would've slipped up somehow. It was only another reason for him to want to avoid her as much as possible.

She loved him and she would not let him suffer more than he already had. More than necessary. And it was not necessary. Perhaps he didn't want her. Perhaps she couldn't heal his pain or fill his lonely heart. But there was someone who could. She had promised not to repeat his secrets, she had promised and she would keep her promise. But there was someone whom Ransom Lake needed. Someone who needed Ransom Lake. And she would not let the man she loved suffer needlessly any further.

CHAPTER
⮑ ELEVEN ⮐

$\mathcal{V}$aden had sent the telegram to Denver Lake only two days after Thanksgiving. It was a mere one week later that she and Yvonne were tending to the store when a tall, handsome stranger entered. Vaden's heart began to pound furiously, for his resemblance to Ransom Lake was undeniably obvious. He was perhaps even taller, and his own black hair was completely grayed at the temples. He wore the clothes of a man who had great wealth and his eyes were the deepest of blues. He was not as striking to look at as was Ransom Lake, but very handsome all the same.

"He's here," Vaden whispered under her breath as she felt it difficult to stay conscious for a moment.

"He looks remarkably like…" Yvonne began, but the man removed his hat and approached the counter and her words were lost.

"Pardon me, ladies," he began. His manner of speech was confident and well enunciated. "I've come to town in answer to a…excuse me, but my explanation is rather complicated. I'm looking…rather, I'm told that there may be living nearby a man whom I believe to be my brother."

Vaden held her breath, barely able to retain her balance and composure under the realization that this was, indeed, Ransom Lake's brother. His only remnant of family. So, it was Yvonne who answered.

"Well, pardon me for being so bold, sir," she began. "But I must tell you that you bear striking resemblance to our own Ransom Lake."

Vaden watched as the man's face immediately drained of all trace of color as he stared at Yvonne.

"Then...it's true...what the telegram said? My brother is living? Living here?"

Yvonne frowned, puzzled, and looked to Vaden questioningly. Vaden only took a step back from her, shaking her head, unable to believe what she had done and the result.

"Yes, sir. If your brother's name is Ransom Lake, I would have to be sure, considering your resemblance to him, that it is one and the same man." Yvonne looked to the man concerned immediately about his reaction as well as Vaden's. "Sir, do you need to sit down? You look quite unwell suddenly."

Vaden held her breath as the man's eyes concentrated on her. His eyes narrowed and he held out a piece of paper to her, not to Yvonne, even though Yvonne had been the one to answer his questions. When Vaden shook her head and took another step backward, Yvonne reached out and took the paper, reading it aloud.

"To Denver Lake, Leadville, Colorado. Sir, I believe it would be in your best interest, as well as that of another, to know that a man believed to be your relation is living near our township. His last name is Lake and he carries with him a pocketknife engraved with your name. Sincerely..." Yvonne looked up to Denver Lake. "It was anonymous?" Vaden could feel that Yvonne wanted to turn and look at her, but she also knew that Yvonne would instantly understand why she mustn't.

"Can you tell me where I might find Ransom Lake?" the man asked.

He glanced again at Vaden who stood paralyzed, unable to inwardly admit what her actions had caused to happen. Here he stood before her, the brother of the man she loved. The brother whom Ransom Lake wanted to believe was alone in the world. And she had betrayed the man she loved in bringing him here. She told herself that, from the depth of the pain and guilt in her heart, the organ must be ripping itself in two within her bosom.

"Certainly, Mr. Lake...he, um..." Yvonne looked again to the telegram and Vaden knew that the situation was almost as shocking to her sister as it was to herself. "He lives not but a mile north of town. And…" Yvonne's voice broke off and Vaden followed her sister's gaze to the front entrance as the color then faded from Yvonne's face.

"Morning, ladies," Ransom Lake greeted as he entered the store for the first time since he'd left them the day after Thanksgiving. "Is your Uncle Dan around?" He approached the counter and stood directly next to his brother, completely unaware of the fact because his attention was directed to Vaden and Yvonne. "Are you feeling all right, Miss Vaden?" he asked as his gaze fell to her. "You don't look yourself. For that matter, neither do you, Miss Valmont. Is everything all right here?"

Vaden felt as if someone had plunged a knife into her chest as she watched Denver Lake lay a hand on his brother's shoulder. "Ransom? Ransom…it can't really be you," Denver muttered.

Someone twisted the invisible knife that pierced Vaden's heart, Ransom Lake's eyes narrowing as he glared at her before turning to see standing next to him for the first time in a decade his elder brother.

"Denver," Ransom Lake mumbled as he looked back to Vaden hatefully for a moment. Yvonne looked to Ransom Lake then to Vaden and back, a frown of being unable to comprehend the situation furrowing her lovely brow.

"Ransom. Where have you been? I was told you had died with everyone else. Why didn't you contact me?" Denver asked, still deeply awed by his brother's existence. The man was obviously battling to control the conflicting emotions of joy, pain and anger, which attacked his soul simultaneously. But Ransom Lake's attention was still on Vaden and she could no longer endure his abhorrent gaze. So, quickly she walked to the end of the counter and out from behind it, meaning to flee past him and out through the front door, but he lunged forward, catching her arm and pulling her to him.

"How could you do this to me, Vaden?" he growled. The storm in his eyes was seething! Raging and violent. She had hurt him deeply she knew. She could only stand before him shaking her head. "How could you betray me like this?" he shouted.

"Ransom," Denver scolded from behind him. But Ransom Lake's eyes continued to glare at Vaden.

"How could you tell him? After you promised me…" Ransom Lake growled at the girl whose arm was held painfully tight in his grip.

"I told him nothing," Vaden managed to force from her lips in a whisper. "I told him nothing. I only…it was wrong of you and you know it. You were wrong. It was selfish. I only…"

Ransom Lake's chest rose and fell heavily with his angered breathing. "I trusted you," he mumbled.

"Ransom," Denver began, taking a step toward his brother, "remember, Ransom. Remember what Dad taught us. 'When a woman provokes you to anger and you're in doubt as to whether to strike her or kiss her…'"

Vaden tried to pull her arm free as Ransom Lake clenched his teeth together and closed his eyes tightly shut for a moment, but his hold was too powerful. Then he opened his eyes to her once more and mumbled, "Dad told us, '*There is no consideration to be made, for the latter releases the frustration faster and more valiantly than the prior.*'" He paused for a moment and, still glaring at Vaden whose tears were profuse on her cheeks, said to his brother, though he still did not look at him, "I would never think to strike this girl, Denver."

Suddenly he released her arm and cupped her chin firmly. "Quit meddling with my life, girl!" he whispered angrily a moment before the hot moisture of his mouth captured hers roughly, forcing a strong, deep and very insistent kiss. The fierceness of the kiss softened almost immediately, but not the sheer magnificent power of it and Vaden's body was weakened from it. Had it not been for his body before her and his powerful arms around her to catch her when her knees failed her, she would've fallen to the floor. All the splendid sensations that had enveloped her the first time he kissed her, and every blissful time thereafter, did so again. In a mere moment she was returning his kiss and they were both lost in its passion for an instant.

"Oh, my! Vaden! Slap him for Pete's sake!" Yvonne insisted, rushing from behind the counter to stand behind her sister. "Vaden! What if Auntie comes in here?" Yvonne hurried to stand between Ransom Lake and his brother, tapping Ransom Lake lightly on the shoulder. "Mr. Lake! Please! Have some decorum!"

Vaden heard Denver Lake chuckle, and heard Yvonne protesting as he took hold of her arm, pulling her back from the embracing couple before her.

"If my brother kisses a woman anywhere nearly as perfectly as I do...then I think we must have something in common other than just our resemblance to our father, Miss Valmont."

Yvonne's voice echoed through Vaden's mind and she did, indeed, raise her hand to Ransom Lake's face. But his kiss was overpowering and, instead of delivering a firm slap, she felt her hand caress his face tenderly for a moment.

His kiss intensified and the passion of it frightened Vaden. She knew that it was a passionate anger and frustration that he must feel, yet to her it seemed somehow to be something quite different. Her own passion for him frightened her, for she wanted nothing else in the world except to stay in that exact situation forever. Suddenly, he broke their kiss and Vaden drew in a deep breath, unaware until that moment that the force of his kiss had made it hard for her to breathe easily.

"Were you sent on this earth solely to torment me, girl?" he barked, taking her by the shoulders and holding her away from his body. "My life is in shambles since you came here! I've no privacy, no self control and no hair either for that matter!"

"More likely she was sent here to save your soul, Ransom Lake! How dare you take such familiarities with my sister!" Yvonne scolded, wrenching her arm free of the strong grip that had held her securely. Vaden knew that Denver had willingly released her sister, for Vaden knew Ransom Lake's strength and expected his brother's to be no less. Yvonne rushed to her sister. She raised her hand to slap Ransom Lake, but he caught her wrist easily.

"I would never harm your sister and you know it. And besides, it's not the first time we've exchanged that kind of affection, Miss Valmont." Ransom Lake released Yvonne's wrist rather violently and turned to look at his brother.

"There's time enough to scold your little pet, Ransom," Denver Lake spoke. "This moment is for you and me. We've far too many things to discuss."

"I'm not his pet!" Vaden was horrified that the man would refer to her so, as if she was no more than a common and ordinary, uninteresting kitten.

"You melt in his arms easily enough, Vaden," Yvonne whispered scoldingly and Vaden felt the stinging tears of humiliation rise to her eyes.

Ransom and Denver Lake still stood facing each other gravely.

"Why, Ransom?" Denver asked in a lowered voice that was filled with pain in its intonation. "Why didn't you tell me?"

Ransom Lake looked to Vaden again, this time his eyes were sad and guilty. Defeated. "Vaden," he mumbled, "why did you do this?"

"I couldn't stand it," she whispered as the tears streamed down her face. "I couldn't stand by and watch you endure such misery and loneliness needlessly for the rest of your life. I couldn't watch you waste your life. It was wrong of you never to tell him that you were alive, to sit feeling sorry for yourself all these years. You can hate me forever if you want, but I did it because I…"

His eyes narrowed as he stared at her waiting for her to finish her sentence.

"Because you what?" he asked.

"Because…because…because somebody needed to and I'm the only one who knew how," she finished. She scolded herself harshly for nearly letting the words of confessing love slip from her lips. "I didn't tell him...I only sent a telegram and told him that there was a man named Lake living here. That's all. I swear it. I would never betray you. You know that."

"Go easy on the girl, Ransom. She did no more than to do right by you," Denver offered calmly.

Ransom Lake hung his head defeatedly for a moment before turning from Vaden to look at his brother. "There's so much you need to know, Denver. Maybe when you've heard it all, you'll wish she hadn't sent you that telegram after all."

"I've never been more grateful to receive a simple piece of paper in my life." Denver approached Vaden then. He brushed at the tears on her cheeks with one of his large, strong hands. "I think you and I should have a reunion of our own one day, miss." His smile was sympathetic and grateful. Then, turning to Yvonne, he offered a hand, which she took, and he shook hers firmly. "Then you, too, Miss...Miss..."

"Yvonne Valmont," Yvonne told him. Vaden was surprised to hear her sister introduce herself so, for she never introduced herself as anything other than *Miss* Yvonne Valmont.

The gray eyes of Ransom Lake narrowed as he looked at Vaden one final time before leaving the mercantile with his brother. Vaden watched them disappear around the corner down the street. She accepted her fate where Ransom Lake was concerned. She had lost him finally now. Had she sensed a finality to his kiss? She was sure she had. Ransom Lake was lost to her, but he was found to what he needed most. Found to his brother and found to the beginnings of healing his heart.

"Never! Never in my life have I witnessed such a display, Vaden!" Yvonne scolded as she returned to her place behind the counter. "What do you mean letting that man maul you like that? For pity's sake, girl! How could you even breathe?"

"I...I couldn't care less if I ever drew another breath, Yvonne. And I'd appreciate it if you'd hold such jealousy in check." Vaden was irritated at her sister's sudden lack of sympathy.

"Jealousy? Jealousy?" Yvonne exclaimed. "What do you mean? I wouldn't want to be in your shoes for anything in the world, Vaden Valmont!"

"Yes, you would!" Vaden turned to face her sister, who was about to endure the brunt of Vaden's aching heart and need to scream. "You've never been kissed like that, Yvonne! Admit it! You're jealous!" Vaden spat, for the consequence of what she had done, that she had signed the death certificate on any chance she had at having Ransom Lake's heart was making itself all the more painfully known.

"Ha! I meant that I wouldn't be in your shoes for the mere fact that you've just assured yourself of losing Ransom Lake for good! He told you in confidence, didn't he? He confided in you at some point...no doubt on that interesting night which you've kept silent about, that night you spent with him before Thanksgiving, that he had a brother. Ransom Lake didn't want his brother to know he was here and you told him."

Yvonne's tongue could be so sharp when she wanted it to be. Vaden brushed the tears from her face. "I broke no confidence, Yvonne. I told nothing that was Ransom's secret. I only...I only let Denver Lake know that a man in town shared his name. Ransom never made me promise not to contact Denver. And you don't have to tell me that I've lost him, Yvonne. I love him too much to let him live without his brother, whom I know he loves desperately. It's...it's much more important that he..."

"I am jealous, Vaden," Yvonne interrupted harshly. "I am jealous. Because you love him so completely, so unconditionally. Because you love him so much that nothing frightens you into not helping him, even the knowledge of losing what relationship you do have with him. You still love him enough to take the chance to make him happy. I'm afraid to love anyone like that. I...I'm afraid to love someone like that and then have to endure life without them. I'm a coward, Vaden, and I admit it to you now. It's why I'm so proper and perfect in my manner. It keeps me hardened. It keeps me safe,

Vaden." Yvonne wiped her own tears as she continued. "You're right, I've never been kissed like Ransom Lake kissed you. I know you're hurting, Vay. I know that guilt is eating at you now as well. But the way he kissed you, Vay!" Yvonne paused, shaking her head in wonder at what she had seen pass between her sister and the man. "He...he wasn't just kissing you, Vay. The man was making love to you."

Vaden put her hands over her ears, shaking her head violently. "No! Don't say that, Vonnie! It's not true! He just...he just..."

"Even if I would've found a man that I would've desired affections from, I would not have allowed it because I would've been too afraid to give into a love like the one you have for that unsettling Ransom Lake." Yvonne hugged her sister tightly. "Do you see now? Do you see what a coward I am? How selfish? Do you see how brave and selfless you are, Vay?"

"I'm as much a coward as you, Vonnie," Vaden sobbed, "for I know that you would at least have the courage to confess your feelings for such a man. But I've never...I've never been able to tell him what I feel, for I could not endure the rejection in his eyes."

"I'm sorry I pushed you toward Jerome Clayton, so, Vay," Yvonne whispered as the sisters separated, dabbing at their cheeks with their aprons. "It was wrong. I just didn't want to see you hurt. But now I know. I know that the saying is true. I know that it is better to have loved and lost..."

"Than never to have loved at all," Vaden finished as she straightened her back, picked up a feather duster and began sweeping the shelves behind the counter with it. She did not doubt the truth of it.

It was merely minutes later when Jerome Clayton entered the mercantile. Vaden's heart, which had been so overly taxed that day already, knew that she must tell him. Truthfully, finally and so that he would understand. She'd tried feeding him clues, little hints here and there, but he was ever persistent.

"Good morning, ladies!" Jerome greeted cheerily. "Can you get away for a walk today, Vaden?" he asked forthrightly. Vaden looked to Yvonne who nodded encouragingly.

"Yes, Jerome. I...I believe it's time we had a talk." Vaden laid the feather duster down on the counter once more and, after putting on her coat, left the mercantile with Jerome. She ignored him when he offered his arm to her. She knew that he was not as unwitting as he pretended, for there was something in his eyes, the way he looked at her with a hint of suspicion. But she shook off her uneasy feeling. It was her own guilt that read the suspicion in him. Her own guilt over having let him hope for so long.

"We're almost a week into December and you still haven't given me any hints as to what you might want for Christmas, Vaden," Jerome stated. His voice was low and irritated. Vaden looked to him and felt that he knew what she wanted to talk about.

"Jerome..." she began.

"He's poisoned your mind against me, Vaden," he interrupted. There was anger apparent in his voice. "He's a violent man and women are often intrigued by his kind. I understand your infatuation with him, but he won't have you, Vaden. He'll use you, corrupt you with his physical dominance, but he won't have you and this infatuation you have will pass."

Vaden could only stand in the street next to him, staring up at him in disbelief. "What are you talking about, Jerome?" she asked. She could not believe what he had said. Couldn't believe that she had heard him correctly. It was completely uncharacteristic of the man to be so vehement and accusing.

Jerome's eyes narrowed and he sneered repulsively for a moment. "Ransom Lake. Do you think I'm blind? Do you think his threats to Nathaniel on Halloween kept Nathaniel from telling me, his best friend, what happened to you at the hand of Ransom Lake that night?"

"Ransom Lake came for me when I was being tormented beyond your understanding, Jerome," Vaden stated firmly. "Your best friend, as you refer to him, was the cause of my torment! How dare you side with him?"

"I can wait. I want you to know that I am a mature man. An

understanding man. I can wait. This infatuation with Ransom Lake will pass soon enough and I'll be here to pick up the pieces when he breaks your heart."

Vaden shook her head, frowning at what was being communicated to her. He wouldn't listen to her if she tried to explain that she could never be his. He had created a reason in his mind as to why she hadn't been his already. And as to why she would eventually belong to him.

"I know he won't ever have me, Jerome. That he'd never want me. But you must understand that it makes no difference. You and I...we're too dissimilar. It won't work. You need someone who'll..." she began.

"I'll wait, Vaden. I'll wait until you grow up enough to see what's before you." Then he simply tipped his hat to her and walked away.

Vaden stood in the snow and mud of the street simply staring after him in disbelief. He always seemed so secure, so sound and well balanced. But to completely deny, to be unwilling to accept what she was trying to tell him, it was not healthy and it worried her somehow.

That day seemed longer than any other of her life. Vaden could not tear her mind and thoughts away from wondering over Ransom Lake and his brother. Would Denver be so angry, so hurt over Ransom not telling him that he was still alive that he would not want to see his brother again? Perhaps it would be worse for Ransom now, especially if Denver did not have compassion for his brother's reasoning. But Vaden shook her head, knowing that Denver seemed a good man. He was, after all, Ransom Lake's brother and it only stood to reason that he would have similar traits of his personality, understanding being one.

Vaden's mind was also greatly taxed over the reaction Jerome had earlier in the day when she tried to confront him with the truth of her lack of feelings for him. It was so oddly calm, his denial. It unsettled her nerves somehow.

So, Vaden tried to endure that day of wondering. And as that night turned into another day, she busied herself with working frantically in the store, dusting and straightening, helping customers and running errands for Aunt Myra and Uncle Dan.

She found herself very fatigued that evening when the family retired from dinner to the parlor. They sat before the cozy fire listening to Aunt Myra and Uncle Dan talk about the townsfolk, their aching bones, or stories of when the girls were young. Vaden knew that her aunt and uncle suspected that something was bothering her, but she was all the more grateful that they didn't ask her about it. Didn't press her for explanations.

The frantic knock on the front door startled them all and Uncle Dan went to see who could possibly be bothering them on such a cold night. When he returned, he held a small wooden box and smiled broadly.

"It's for you again, sweet pea," his deep voice announced as he handed the box to Vaden. "Seems like your secret admirer don't mind braving the elements." His eyes twinkled merrily and Vaden grinned at him, suspicion foremost in her mind.

"Let's see," she began, winking at her uncle. "Who could possibly know that I've been having a rough couple of days?"

"It's a mystery," Uncle Dan chuckled, his eyes brighter than ever with delight.

Carefully, Vaden removed the lid from the small box and looked inside. There was a note, scrawled in somewhat illegible script, and she retrieved it, unfolding it gently and read aloud, "*Remember, the hardened shell protects what's inside. I'm sorry.*" Frowning, for it seemed an odd thing for Uncle Dan to write were he playing the part of secret admirer, Vaden then brushed aside the straw that lay beneath the note concealing something deeper in the box. She was not surprised this time when she retrieved from the straw padding another rock. This rock was much larger than the one she had received previously and the crystal formations inside it that were revealed when she turned it over were white and clear with tiny bits of something that sparkled radiantly when the firelight caught them.

"It's beautiful!" Yvonne exclaimed. "Do you think Jerome is coming to his senses finally, Vay? Is it perhaps an apology for acting so inanely?"

"Oh, Vonnie!" Vaden exclaimed irritatedly. "It's Uncle Dan that's doing this for me! It's as plain as the nose on his face." Vaden stood, went to her uncle and kissed him sweetly on the cheek.

"I tell you again, sweet pea...it's not me that's done this."

Uncle Dan seemed in earnest. But, it took the beauty of the gift away from Vaden if she were to believe that it was Jerome Clayton who had left it. And it was completely inconceivable to try to believe that Ransom Lake would do such a thing. So, Vaden determined that it must be her uncle's way of trying to cheer her.

Still, as Vaden studied the beautiful marvel of nature by candlelight just before she crawled into bed, her mind began to tax itself again wondering on what was transpiring in Ransom Lake's life. She had trouble sleeping that night, and when slumber did finally find her, her dreams were odd and tormenting.

Vaden's heart leapt in her bosom as Denver and Ransom Lake entered the mercantile very early the next morning. They were dressed in heavy clothing and Vaden immediately noticed the expression of peace and joy obvious on both their faces. Her eyes brimmed with tears, for she sensed that they had made their peace and were happy in each other. Aunt Myra and Uncle Dan had left at first light to go out to check on Mrs. Tilits and so Vaden and Yvonne tended the store alone.

"Good morning to you, lovely ladies," Denver Lake greeted loudly.

Vaden looked away at once as Ransom Lake's intense gaze found her.

"Good morning, Mr. Lake," Yvonne replied. "What can we do for you this fine winter's morning?"

Vaden, nervous as she was under Ransom Lake's gaze, looked to her sister quickly, for her voice was all too pleasant sounding. All too delighted.

And she found that Yvonne's face blushed crimson as she looked at Denver Lake.

"Well...I don't know about Ransom here," Denver Lake said, lowering his voice and leaning on the counter in front of Yvonne, "but the best thing you could do for me today, Miss Valmont, would be to hop in the wagon and run down to the preacher's house with me." Vaden grinned as Yvonne's eyes widened delightedly. Denver sighed heavily, as if a great disappointment was washing over him. "I suppose it's always the same story. All the girls around here, including the beautiful Miss Valmont, are probably so in love with ol' Handsome Ransom, as the girls back home used to call him...that you'll never see past him to my ugly mug. Is that right, Miss Valmont?"

Vaden's smile broadened, for it was delightful to see her perfectly proper, always-in-control sister completely undone by the man. Yvonne began to fiddle with the brooch at her collar looking about herself as if something would need doing and save her.

"I...I...no, sir...I," Yvonne stammered.

"So...you don't think I'm good looking then, Miss Valmont?" Ransom Lake inquired teasingly, still looking at Vaden. Vaden's eyes went to him once more and his gaze mesmerized her. Had her sister and his brother not been standing just next to them, she could not have stopped herself from running to him and throwing herself into the power of his embrace.

"Oh! No! I think you're very handsome, Mr. Lake," Yvonne defended herself to the younger Mr. Lake.

"You see, brother. You've turned this one's head and I'll never have a chance," Denver chuckled.

Immediately Yvonne looked back at him. "Oh, no, Mr. Lake! I didn't mean that at all! You've all the chance in the world!" Vaden and Ransom both looked to Yvonne, shocked beyond speaking at her unwitting confession.

Denver raised an eyebrow, and reached out, taking Yvonne's hand in his gloved one. "Well, that's very, very encouraging, Miss Valmont. Very encouraging."

"I mean," Yvonne stammered, pulling her hand from his grasp. "That is to say, that I'm sure that when you find a woman that you desire to…"

"Oh, but I've found her, Miss Valmont. I'm looking at her."

Vaden was delighted. Yvonne was completely undone! It was obvious her thoughts were muddled and her heart aflutter.

"Leave the poor girl alone, Denver," Ransom chuckled. "We need to be heading out."

"Heading out?" Vaden finally spoke, for his words frightened her. Was he leaving? Would he be returning to Leadville with his brother?

"We're…we're going out to visit our family's graves, Miss Vaden," he explained. "We'll be gone two or three days and I was wondering if you'd ask your Uncle Dan to check on my stock for me."

"You'll be back?" Vaden's question sounded more desperate than she meant to reveal.

"Of course we'll be back!" Denver answered, trying to capture Yvonne's hand once more. "We live here!"

"We?" Yvonne whispered.

"Yes. Denver's agreed to move out here with me. He says the silver's all gone in Leadville anyway." Ransom Lake took several steps toward Vaden and her heart began to beat ferociously as he approached. "You and I need to have a few words when I return," he told her in a lowered voice.

"I'm sorry, Mr. Lake. I'm…I thought it would be best for you and I only meant to help." Vaden's defense of herself caused Ransom Lake to close his eyes for a moment and inhale deeply.

"I know it, Vaden." He reached out, brushing a strand of hair from her cheek with his gloved hand. His hand grasped her arm firmly and his strength pulled her against his heavily coated body. "I'm sorry that I reacted so badly at first," he mumbled into her hair.

"Mr. Lake!" Yvonne exclaimed, taking several steps toward them. "I cannot believe your boldness in taking liberties with my…" Her words were silenced and Vaden heard Denver's amused chuckle.

"You've been a good and true friend to me, Vaden Valmont. I'll never forget that."

Vaden pushed herself from his arms and looked up at him indignantly. She meant to lash out at him, to tell him that once again he had hurt her deeply by telling her she was only his friend. But when she glanced over and saw Yvonne held tightly against Denver, her back flush with his chest, one of his powerful arms securing her waist and the other hand covering her mouth, she was so astounded that she could not speak.

"So, if you'd have your uncle do that for me, Vaden...I'd appreciate it greatly," Ransom Lake finished. "We'd best be off, Denver...before you decide to drag that girl off to matrimony before you have a chance to court her."

With a deep, amused chuckle escaping his lungs, Denver released Yvonne who only turned and stood staring at him in some state of shock.

"You'll be careful?" Vaden called to Ransom Lake as he turned to leave. "You'll be back?"

"If the weather gets bad...we'll just find an old house to shelter in," the man answered, winking at her as he left the store.

"Miss Vaden," Denver said, tipping his hat to Vaden. "Mrs. Lake...er...I mean, Miss Valmont," he chuckled, tipping his hat to Yvonne who gasped in astonishment.

Vaden felt a sense of panic and tragedy rising within her and she dashed out the door after her heart's desire who was fiddling with the horse rigging.

"You'll come back, Ransom, won't you?" she called to him.

His head turned slowly toward her and as his intense gray eyes looked at her she saw him mouth, "Ransom?"

Realizing with horror that she had, indeed, called him by his first name for the very first time, Vaden began to correct herself.

"I'm sorry. I meant to say Mr...."

But Ransom Lake was back up the stairs and on the porch before her, having taken her shoulders between his powerful hands before she could finish her apology.

"Ransom," he whispered as his eyes wove their bewitching spell about her. Vaden's body began to tremble from both the cold air in which she stood, and from his touch. When he released her, violently removing his right glove an instant before his hand was at her throat, she thought she might not be able to stop herself from throwing her trembling body into his arms. "Ransom," he repeated again in a whisper as his now bare and very warm hand, caressed her throat, his fingers dipping beneath the collar of her blouse now and again. "Ransom," he whispered a moment before his hand slipped around to the back of her neck, pulling her toward him as his mouth was suddenly hot, moist and demanding on her own. Vaden's body melted against his as his deepening, seemingly hunger driven kiss commanded her to meet it. Though it was brief compared to the kisses they'd shared on previous occasions, it was powerful. It left Vaden breathless, weakened and astonished. Almost as quickly as he had been upon her, he had climbed into the wagon next to Denver and slapped the lines at the backs of the team of horses.

"What did you say?" Yvonne asked, amazed at the display.

"I...I don't know. I only called him by his given name instead of..." Vaden began.

"Remind me to try that on Mr. *Denver* Lake when they return." Vaden looked to Yvonne, unable to believe what she had heard her sister say. "He's dashingly good looking, isn't he, Vay? I noticed the first time he came into the mercantile that he was far and away more of a man than anyone I've ever met," Yvonne confessed with a sigh. Vaden still could only stare at her sister, stunned at what she was hearing pass from her lips. "I wanted to kiss him, Vay. To reach out, take hold of his coat lapels, one in each hand, and kiss him soundly on the mouth!" She looked to Vaden, her eyes sparkling, her smile resplendent. "I've lost my senses in that man, Vaden! Completely lost my senses!" Then, with a heavy sigh and continued radiance bursting from her countenance, Yvonne turned and went back into the mercantile.

Vaden watched the wagon carry Ransom Lake away from her until it was far in the distance. Something told her he would be back. She knew that this was a trip of healing for both men and that such a trip would be watched over by heaven.

"You let him paw at you like an animal."

Vaden startled at the voice and looked to see Jerome appear from the alley. "Jerome," she greeted him as a feeling of impending doom began to creep into her bones. "I tried to explain to you the other day that..."

Jerome mounted the stairs to stand before her. The hatred, the seething hatred was frighteningly apparent in his eyes as he stood glaring down at her. "I don't want anyone else touching what's mine, Vaden," he growled.

Instantly, Vaden's hand stung from the hard slap that she delivered to his face. "I don't want you," she spat at him. She was unnerved when he only smiled at her.

"Yes, you do. He's left you now. He'll not be back. I can assure you of that. You belong to me, Vaden, and I'll wait. I'll wait until you finally come to your senses."

"I don't think you should come to the mercantile anymore, Jerome. You're not welcome here," Vaden warned him. Her voice was unstable and she was truly frightened at that moment.

Jerome looked up at the overhang of the porch and then looked casually back to Vaden. Suddenly his arms embraced her brutally and his repulsive mouth was attacking hers ferociously. Vaden pushed at him, but he was too strong. Her struggling seemed in vain for a moment as his hands worked to restrain her until with all her strength she kicked him soundly in the shin and it was enough to cause him to release her.

"Don't you ever touch me again, Jerome Clayton. My uncle will hear of this and believe me, you are no longer welcome in his home from this day forward!" Tears of frustration and disgust flooded Vaden's cheeks as she turned and fled into the mercantile.

"I'll wait, Vaden. I'm a patient man," Jerome called after her before descending the porch steps casually and walking away down the street while whistling a bright tune.

"What's the matter, Ransom?" Denver asked, having noticed the sudden frown that owned his brother's brow.

Ransom paused. The feeling in his chest, the vision in his mind had only been a flash and now it was gone. Should they go back, he wondered. But the premonition had vanished and so must his concern he decided.

"Nothing. Just...nothing," he answered, though his frown lessened only slightly.

"He's not to be let into this house or my business!" Uncle Dan shouted that night after Vaden told him of Jerome's behavior. "If he tries to set foot in the store...call the sheriff, Yvonne. Do you understand that, Myra?" Aunt Myra nodded and squeezed Vaden's hand reassuringly. "It's one thing to spend some time sparking with a gentleman like Ransom Lake and another to have an idiot like Jerome Clayton forcing things on you, sweet pea." Vaden's mouth dropped open at her uncle's reference to sparking with Ransom Lake. However did he know, she wondered. "This worries me, Myra. This worries me something awful. He seemed like such a nice boy all these years. How could he take us all in like that?"

Aunt Myra shook her head. "I don't know. I just can't believe we didn't see this before. You avoid him like the plague, Vaden. Like the plague!"

"You...you don't think he'd do her harm? Do you Uncle Dan?" Yvonne asked.

"I'm not gonna lie to you, girls. The thought has crossed my mind."

Vaden lay in bed that night praying for Ransom Lake's return. He would protect her from Jerome's vile intentions. She knew he would. He did not love her perhaps...but he valued her friendship and she knew he would keep Jerome from her somehow. Her anxiety was great that night, her fears founded, and so, to soothe her nerves and enable her body to rest, she repeated his name over and over and over, "Ransom. Ransom. Ransom," until finally she was comforted and able to sleep.

Her dreams that night were vivid, emotionally charged and intimate. She dreamt of Ransom. Her love. She dreamt of his smile, his mumbling manner of speech. She dreamt of him standing before the fire in the abandoned house, shirtless and thoughtful. She dreamt the memory of his arms around her, his kiss heated on her mouth, the scent of shaving soap that had lingered on his face. And she woke missing him. Missing him desperately.

"I've spoken with the Clayton's," Uncle Dan announced at lunch the following day. "They deny that their son could behave like he done. Of course. But ain't it just a real big coincidence that he's gone up north to visit some extended family?" Uncle Dan shook his head and chuckled oddly. "Little weasel. We oughta just lump him in with them other boys that pulled that Halloween nonsense. He ain't no better...maybe worse."

CHAPTER
∞ TWELVE ∞

*I*t was in the late hours of the night on the third day since Ransom and Denver had left that Vaden awoke with a feeling of panic and her body awash with perspiration. It seemed in the days since he'd gone that the sense of impending doom had increased in Vaden's soul by the hour. And now, something woke her. It was a feeling. A sensation of great bodily pain and suffering. Of mental anguish. He should've been back by now, something told her. Ransom and Denver should've returned to town by that evening. She leapt from her bed, jumping to her feet as she seemed to hear him calling her name. The sound of his beloved voice seemed to echo through her mind. She pushed against her ears with her hands, but it did not stop and then, as if something was whispering to her, she knew. She knew that he was hurt, dying perhaps, and that she must go to him.

Quickly and quietly, though tears streaked her face and panic wracked her trembling body, Vaden dressed.

"Yvonne," she spoke quietly, waking her sister. Yvonne rubbed at her eyes and frowned at Vaden, incoherent from sleep. "Wake Uncle Dan, Yvonne. Something is wrong. I'm going out to look for Ransom."

"What!" Yvonne whined, sitting up in her bed suddenly.

"Something has happened to him, Vonnie. Just go wake up Uncle Dan and tell him to drive out to Ransom's place and check it. Something is terribly wrong." Yvonne argued not a word, but quickly leaped from her own bed as Vaden left the room.

The snow that had fallen earlier in the evening lay quiet, its frosted icing sparkling in the moonlight. Even for her woolen mittens, scarf, hat and coat, Vaden was cold. The temperature was low in the middle of the night and the lantern burned warm near her face as she made her way down the snow covered road of town.

It seemed an eternity before the familiar grove of elms loomed up before her. Vaden's feet were cold, but it mattered not to her, for the closer she got to the grove of elms, the very grove that had held such terror for her weeks before, the more desperate she became to reach it.

The moonlight was blocked for a time as she entered the grove, but in a moment it appeared again and the sight that it illuminated almost took the life's breath from Vaden's body. There before her was a large elm. And strapped tightly to its trunk, the ropes used to bind him causing his flesh to bleed, was Ransom Lake.

"Ransom!" she screamed as she ran to him. His head hung forward, his eyes closed and she feared at first that he was dead. "Ransom!" she screamed again as tears clouded her vision. His chest rose and fell with his breath, however not powerfully. She wiped at her tears irritatedly as she tugged on the ropes, trying to loosen them. "Oh, Ransom!" she cried as she lifted his head and saw the damage done his beautiful face. His right eye was swollen completely shut. The color about it was so purple it was nearly black. His mouth bled from both corners and a large wound split his bottom lip brutally. Dried blood was caked beneath his nose and his hair was matted at his forehead with blood that emanated from a wound there.

Furthermore, he wore only his boots and trousers and Vaden had no way of telling how long he had been thus exposed to the elements. Even with the mere illumination of the lantern and moon as her only light, she could see the terrible bruising at his ribs. His arms, which were bound against the tree at his sides were bruised as well, and his knuckles were so raw and bloodied that it looked like some animal had chewed at them. The ropes that bound him to the tree were so tightly cinched that they were causing further bleeding wounds to other parts of his body.

Vaden dropped to her knees, hoping that whoever had done this to the man that she loved above all else had not found Denver's knife in his boot. She prayed quietly with relief when she, indeed, felt the bulge in the calf of the boot. It was not easy to retrieve, however, and she cried out in anguish several times before she was able pull it from its hiding place. Frantically she sawed at the ropes with the knife, sobbing madly with frustration and fear. When she'd cut the last length of rope, Ransom's beaten, tortured body fell forward into the snow, seemingly lifeless.

"Ransom? Ransom!" Vaden sobbed. It seemed his blood was everywhere and he did not move as she knelt in the snow beside him and turned him on his back into her lap. "Ransom!" she cried as she hurriedly removed her mittens and placed a warm hand on his cheek. Quickly she unbuttoned her own coat and covered him with it as she rocked back and forth sobbing bitterly. However would she bring him to safety? He was far too large and heavy for her to carry and dragging him would no doubt kill him if he wasn't already fatally wounded. She had to get him out of the snow first of all. Looking around as she sobbed, she noticed a patch beneath a large elm nearby that was free from snow. With every ounce of her strength she dragged his limp body that had always been so strong, to the nearby elm, setting him up against it. She retrieved her lantern, intent on using its flame to build a fire to warm him, but she paused as she noticed that a ways out from the grove stood a lone elm. It had died years before of some cause and would burn hot and bright. Taking her lantern, she ran through the snow to the old tree and endeavored to set it afire. The recent snow made it difficult to catch the flame to the tree. But the wood was dried out and brittle and in awhile it did, indeed, take the flame upon itself. Vaden rushed back to where Ransom sat beneath the elm. Carefully she pulled him away from the tree and laid him in the warmth of her lap as the fire engulfed the dead elm quickly.

"Hang on, my love. Use your great strength and hang on," she whispered soothingly to the unconscious man. She again placed a soft, warm hand to his cold cheek, humming quietly to herself a tune that she couldn't even recognize through her panic. The old elm burned fiercely, cracking and spitting like the fires of Hades. It seemed an eternity before Vaden finally heard shouting and the approach of a wagon.

Relief flooded her body as she saw her Uncle Dan rein in his team in the clearing. "Uncle Dan! Help me! Help me!" she cried. The man looked from the great blazing fire to his niece.

"Vaden!" he shouted as he ran to her. "Vaden! What's going on? I..." He paused, looking at the maimed and broken man that lay in her lap. "Oh!" he groaned. "What happened, Vaden? Who's done this to them?"

"Them?" Vaden asked.

"Denver's back at the house. He came dragging himself up the porch calling for help just as I was leaving, but passed out when we got him in. He's in a bad way...but nothing the likes of this."

"He'll die if we don't hurry, Uncle Dan! Please! Help me!" Vaden cried.

As Uncle Dan hollered at the team, driving them on at a wild speed, Vaden cradled Ransom's head against her breast, letting her tears fall on his bruised face. She knew who had done this to him. Somehow Jerome had been able to overpower her mighty champion and do him brutal harm. There was no other reason that she should find him where she did. She sobbed then, her body wracked with pain from the knowledge that his condition was on her head. She'd brought this on him.

Vaden was grateful that Uncle Dan had possessed the foresight to toss several blankets into the bed of the wagon before he left home. She pulled them tightly around Ransom's shoulders and stroked his hair as she looked down into his face, so bruised and swollen. In that moment the memory came to her of the time so many weeks and months before when he'd lain in her uncle's guest room, unconscious because of her. She thought of the thrill that had rushed through her body when she'd kissed him and hoped for a moment that he would awaken. Carefully, as her tears fell excessively onto his battered cheeks, she kissed him lightly on his wounded mouth. As she looked at his face longingly she heard a groan rise within his throat and in the next moment the gray of his undamaged eye seemed to outshine the moonlight as it opened and looked at her.

"Vaden," he mumbled, and her sobbing wracked her body violently. "I...I'm not up to sparking you just now, girl."

"Don't waste your energy teasing me," she whispered to him, relieved that he was still able to speak at all. "We're almost home. We're almost home."

"They...they took Denver, too," he choked anxiously. "I...I..." She could tell by the frown that furrowed his brow that he was worried for Denver.

"He's fine. He's already at our house. He's fine, Ransom." She tried to keep her voice calm and soothing though she felt she might die of worry for his life.

"Ransom," he mumbled and he was unconscious again.

Aunt Myra fairly flew off the porch as the wagon pulled up to the house. "Vaden!" she cried out. "My goodness child! You gave us such a fright and..." Her affectionate scolding ceased immediately upon glancing from Vaden's tear stained face to the man that lay so maimed in her lap. "Ransom!" she exclaimed in a whisper. "Oh, Dan!" Aunt Myra looked to her husband as he jumped down from the buckboard. "Oh! He looks far worse than his brother."

"Hurry! Let's get him inside. He's beat to a pulp and its hard telling how long he's been out in this cold."

Carefully and as tenderly as was possible, Vaden helped her aunt and uncle carry the massive form of Ransom Lake into the warmth of the house.

"Let's just lay him right before the fire in the parlor," Uncle Dan ordered.

Tears fell profusely from Vaden's eyes as a deep and pain stricken moan vibrated within Ransom as they laid him on the rug before the warm blaze.

"Oh! Gracious providence!" Aunt Myra whispered as the light from the fire further illuminated Ransom's injuries. "I've sent Yvonne for Doctor Sullivan already because Denver was in such a bad way. But I can't believe...quickly, Dan...hot water, cloths, towels!" Aunt Myra snapped her fingers at her husband and pointed to the kitchen and Uncle Dan went immediately to fetch the things she'd told him to.

"Jerome Clayton has done this, Auntie," Vaden whispered.

Myra paused for a moment, frowning at her niece. "Oh, don't be ridiculous, Vaden! Jerome may be an idiot, but surely he isn't capable of causing damage to another man the like of this!" Myra ran her fingers over the terrible bruising on Ransom's ribcage. "These bruises are brutal. There must be broken ribs here and there. But..." Myra pressed on the man's chest, stomach and abdomen. "There's no swelling elsewhere, so hopefully he's not bleeding inside himself." Myra next inspected his hands and arms. "He gave a good accounting of himself from the looks of these ragged knuckles. Same with Denver." She tried to lift the eyelid of the eye that was so blackened and swollen. Vaden held her breath for a moment as she saw the brilliant gray of his eye against the white of it which was no longer white, but completely blood red. "Poor man. Poor, poor man," Myra mumbled. Uncle Dan returned with the water and cloths. "Help me to sponge this blood away, Vaden, so that we can see the true damage."

"I'm telling you, Uncle Dan...someone we know has done this. If you won't believe that it's Jerome Clayton...you must admit that there is a reason I found him tied to a tree in that old elm grove." Vaden's eyes pled with her uncle for understanding.

Uncle Dan nodded and placed an arm about her shoulders. "Well, as bloodied as the knuckles are on these two boys, somebody will have a couple of black eyes and split lips and that won't be easy to hide. I 'spect the light of morning will tell us a bit."

"This is my fault," Vaden cried, burying her face in her hands. "Somehow, I'm not certain yet how, but somehow I've caused this to happen. I refused Jerome's attentions and now he...he . . ."

"That's nonsense child!" Aunt Myra corrected, wringing the blood saturated cloth into the bowl of water. "Nonsense."

Vaden could only sit beside the battered, mutilated body of Ransom Lake and cry her tears of pain and guilt. She knew that somehow Jerome had a hand in this beating. A hand in the near murder of Ransom Lake and his brother. And she knew it was her fault. The guilt she bore was unendurable and she thought for a moment of the pain of the guilt that Ransom had borne for so many years. But that had been quite different. He had not been responsible for the brutal murders of his family. He had been blameless. But she was the cause of this. She knew it. Jerome had done this to Ransom and all for the sake of mad jealousy.

Doctor Sullivan arrived soon and tended to Ransom's wounds. "He's in a bad way," he said. "But, there doesn't seem to be any internal bleeding. He'll recover, though I don't doubt he'll be fairly sore and stiff for a while." After checking on Denver as well, the doctor left and Myra forced the girls to bed.

"I've caused this, Yvonne," Vaden whispered as they lay in their beds. "Jerome did this. I'm telling you he's mad. He's so completely different from what he appears."

"I...I'm afraid for them, Vay," Yvonne began. "They were nearly killed. What if whoever did this tries again? What if..."

Vaden could hear the fear in her sister's voice. Until that moment Vaden had never considered that perhaps Ransom and Denver would again find themselves in danger. The horror of that evening had been too prominent, too vivid for her to think beyond it. But as she realized the truth in Yvonne's words, fear gripped her in its frigid vice's press and she spent the remaining hours of that early morning shaking with fear for Ransom's life.

The scene that met Vaden the next morning as she entered the kitchen caused her knees to give way beneath her and she only escaped fainting to the ground by holding herself up with a firm grip on the counter's edge. Denver and Ransom both sat at the table bandaged, bruised and beaten beyond belief. Denver sipped broth from a cup and Ransom endeavored to do the same, though it was obvious that the pain and stiffness in his mashed knuckles made it hard for him to hold the mug to his lips which were purple from bruising and injury.

"I've uh...I've uh...just been forcing something into these two boys, Vaden," Aunt Myra offered as a greeting. Yvonne was already there sitting beside Denver, a look of grief and concern puckering her dainty brow dramatically.

Vaden looked to Ransom and when his one unswollen eye met hers she felt the tears escape their restraint and flood her cheeks.

"Tell them who did this to you, Ransom," she whispered.

"Can't," he mumbled. "They were wearing masks."

"You know who did this! *I* know who did this! Tell someone! They have to be punished! They can't get away with trying to murder you!" she cried.

"We'll take care of this on our own, girl," Ransom growled.

"You can't! You can't possibly mean..."

"The wagon's hitched, boys," Uncle Dan announced as he entered through the kitchen door. "We'll go whenever you're ready."

"You're leaving?" Vaden fairly shrieked. "You can't go! You...neither of you is in any condition to..."

Ransom slammed a no doubt very sore fist on the table. Then, rising to his feet slowly and awkwardly, for he was obviously still in pain, he pointed a damaged index finger at Vaden and mumbled, "I don't have the energy to argue with you, Vaden. I'm going home to my own house and my own bed. I need some rest and I don't think I can rest here. I couldn't possibly rest when I know..."

"But…" she began to argue.

He tipped his head, however, closed his eyes, trying to draw patience from within himself, and said flatly, "Not now, Vaden."

"We'll be fine at the house, Miss Vaden," Denver assured her as he stood and placed a reassuring hand on her shoulder.

"I'm sending the girls along with you, Dan," Aunt Myra announced. Ransom started to protest, but Aunt Myra hurried on. "I want them to stay just long enough to see you two boys into bed and put something to warm on the stove for you."

"I haven't got the fight left in me," Ransom mumbled as he took the blanket she offered to him and wrapped it about his shoulders before leaving the house.

When they arrived at Ransom's house, Vaden was frightened once more as Uncle Dan insisted that he go into the house first, armed with his rifle. How could she possibly leave him? Knowing the danger he was in! Knowing that he was too weak to defend himself if someone were to attack him in such a state.

"I'll be in my bed if you need me," Ransom mumbled. "Not that I'd be any good for anything anyhow," he chuckled.

"I'll put this pot of broth on, Mr. Lake," Yvonne said, lugging the large pot of chicken broth her aunt had sent with them into the kitchen.

"I feel like somebody chewed me up and spit me out," Denver groaned as he laid himself awkwardly on the sofa in the front room. "But, it was obvious that it was Ransom that they intended to…" He broke off his words glancing quickly and apologetically to Vaden.

"I'm going to have the sheriff look into this," Uncle Dan stated. "Ain't nobody that should get away with something like this."

Vaden stood wringing her hands frantically. She'd removed her coat and mittens and now stood feeling helpless and panicked.

"Run on in there and check on him, will you, Miss Vaden?" Denver asked. "Make sure he went into bed. You know what a hard head he is. He probably snuck out the back door to check on the stock."

Vaden nodded, more than willing to check on Ransom. She entered the hallway and made her way past one room with a locked door to another room to her left. There on his bed, already sound asleep, lay Ransom Lake. He looked peaceful enough. Vaden watched him breathing for several moments to assure herself that he did so. Then, as she was turning to leave him to his much needed rest, a flash caught the corner of her eye and she turned to look at the wall that was across from the foot of Ransom's bed.

What she saw there in the morning sunlight that beamed in through the window amazed her. There were shelves on the wall starting from just a foot or so above the floor and rising every foot or so to the ceiling. And these shelves were laden heavily with all varieties of color and sizes of beautiful geodes! There were perhaps in excess of one hundred and fifty sets of them. A large one standing some two feet tall and bursting with amethyst crystals sat in one corner. In awe Vaden walked to the shelving and looked up and around at the many beautiful stones. On the shelf directly before her sat two stones, each singular, with no matching mates like the other stones owned. Reaching out, she took in her hands the two stones that were the twins of the ones that had been left for her. The ones that she thought her Uncle Dan had given her. And all the time it had been her one true love that had tried to cheer her heart, give her back her hope by bestowing Mother Nature's wonders upon her. Never had she seen, had she imagined such a collection of anything, let alone something so beautiful, unique and marvelous as these rare stones.

Replacing the twins to her stones, she turned and looked at Ransom once more. Going to his bed, she knelt beside it and placed a hand on his head, letting her fingers bury themselves in the softness of his hair.

"In my dreams...I knew it was you," she whispered. He did not wake or move at all. She stared at him for some time before finally kissing him tenderly on the forehead and leaving the room.

"He's got quite a collection in there, hasn't he?" Denver mumbled from his place on the sofa as Vaden reentered the front room.

"Yes," Vaden agreed. "I've never imagined the like."

"Collection?" Yvonne asked, her brows meeting in a puzzled expression.

"Yes. The finest collection of geodes I've ever seen. He must have hundreds of rocks in that room of his," Denver added. His voice was becoming lower and somewhat slurred, making it obvious that he, too, was near to a deep slumber. Yvonne's eyes twinkled and her bright smile comforted Vaden as she looked at her warmly and with understanding.

"I guess he's got to have something beautiful in his room...since he's kept himself from marrying a pretty girl all this time." Yvonne and Vaden both looked quickly to Denver, surprised at his inference. He smiled at them wearily. "But he's got me here now...maybe finding each other again will heal both our hearts, eh?" Denver winked at Yvonne with one of his bruised eyes, and she blushed.

"Let's get on home, girls," Uncle Dan said then. "These boys need their rest and we got a lot to do."

Leaving Ransom Lake at that moment was the hardest thing Vaden had to do. He was so weakened and vulnerable physically and she feared that another attack on him would be fatal.

As it went, Jerome had been out of town visiting an aunt and uncle up north when the incident with Ransom and Denver had occurred. Apparently he was innocent, Uncle Dan had said. But the look in her uncle's eyes and Vaden's own instinct told her different.

After a week or so, Denver and Ransom entered the store one morning looking quite healthy and robust. Their bruises were fading to a yellowish green tinge and both of Ransom's heavenly eyes were visible again. Vaden's heart swelled to near bursting when they entered, for she felt certain that Ransom would be different toward her. More willing to show deeper feeling for her in his manner. But her elation was quickly squelched, for he simply smiled and nodded at her casually as he and Denver approached the counter.

"We've come to thank your family for delivering us from certain death," Denver told Yvonne who immediately began blushing and smoothing her skirt. "We're quite strong and healthy once more and we owe you all a great debt."

"Oh! Oh, that's a ridiculous thing to say, Mr. Lake," Yvonne stammered. It was the first time Vaden had heard her sister veer from propriety and argue a compliment or gratuitous remark. "And may I say that you do look very...quite healthy."

Vaden's eyes widened at her sister's awkwardness. As of yet, Yvonne had confided nothing of tremendous confession as to her feelings for Denver. But it was all too obvious and it delighted Vaden, at the same time breaking her heart, for Denver was completely attentive to Yvonne. He held nothing back. His regard for her, his admiration of her and his profound interest in her were obvious. Vaden glanced to Ransom regretfully, but his eyes only narrowed intensely as he looked at her. For a moment her gaze fell to his mouth, to his perfectly formed, delicious mouth, and she thought of his kiss, longing for it acutely. She'd tried to fight off her dreams of him. Her dreams of being his completely. Of his marrying her, raising their children with her, holding her in his arms every night of their lives. But it was impossible and excruciatingly painful and she winced at that very moment at the pain that struck at her heart.

"It was Jerome Clayton," she blurted out suddenly. Denver and Yvonne both looked to her and Ransom continued to almost glare at her.

"They were masked and it was dark," Ransom mumbled. "There was no way to identify them. Besides, there were five. Not one."

"You may as well know, Vay," Yvonne began, "Uncle Dan questioned Nathaniel and Toby and the others. They truly know nothing, though they do admit to avoiding association with Jerome as of late."

Vaden looked from one person to the other indignantly, finally settling on Ransom. "Why are you so set on denying it? I think you know full well, just as I do who tried to…"

"I think you want it to be Jerome, Vay," Yvonne accused. "But...he's too weak, too sneaky...a coward. Offending you alone is one thing, but two grown men who are much larger than he and..."

"He's a weasel," Denver finished. "At least...from what I hear. He's too big a coward to attempt something like this. And those men that attacked us were strong! It wasn't a group of lilac-perfumed boys that beat us."

"Let's just drop this," Ransom mumbled, going to look at some boxes of work gloves that lay at the end of the counter. "What's done is done. And it won't happen again."

Vaden wanted to scream. Why were they all so set on denying what her heart told her was the truth? Why didn't they want to confront the Claytons? Why did they all just want to go about their business and pretend the horror never happened?

At that moment, every drop of energy, every bit of the love of life that was in Vaden seemed to drain from her and she sat down promptly on a chair. She looked up for a moment to where Ransom and Denver were looking through the boxes of gloves.

"Don't be angry with me, Vay," Yvonne said quietly as she came to stand beside her sister. "I...I just think that maybe you're not thinking things through well enough."

"Were you robbed?" Vaden asked suddenly. Denver and Ransom both looked to her inquisitively. "Was anything stolen from you?"

"No," Denver answered plainly.

"Then...explain to me the reason that these men chose to ambush you and beat you...and tie Ransom to a tree in the very grove of elms where..." Vaden's voice faltered as Ransom's glare intensified.

"I think maybe we should come back for the things we need later, Denver," Ransom mumbled to his brother.

Vaden shook her head and fought to hold back her tears as she stood saying, "No. No. You go ahead and get the things you need. I'll leave." She walked to the front door and took her coat from the coat rack, wrapping her scarf snugly about her neck. "I'll be back later, Yvonne," she announced as she pulled on her mittens. "A walk will do me good."

The moment she left the store her tears burst through her resolve and flooded her cheeks. As quickly as she could, she ran through the muddied street and turned down the road that led to Ransom's house. Wiping irritatedly at her tear saturated cheeks, she slowed her pace to a brisk walk as she looked off in the direction of her tree. Of her creek. Of her solace. But she doubted their power to calm her this day, for she did not understand. She did not understand everyone's need to deny what she knew to be true. She did not understand Ransom leaving her a tender note one moment, taking her passionately in his arms the next and nearly ignoring her even the next.

Perhaps, she thought as she hurried along, perhaps it was time for her to return home. She'd fallen in love and her love did not return the feeling it appeared. But when she felt his hand catch hold of her arm, she sighed relievedly. He'd come for her. She paused before turning around and said, "Why are you so cold and indifferent sometimes?"

"I'm never cold and indifferent to you, Vaden." The sound of Jerome Clayton's voice answering her question instead of Ransom Lake's caused her to whirl about as horror and panic gripped her.

"Jerome?" she exclaimed. He smiled at her pleasantly and innocently enough.

"Glad to see me?" he asked. "I have been gone for some time. I had a nice visit, but...it's always best to be home, isn't it?"

Vaden wrenched her arm free of his grasp and stood staring at him in disbelief at his casual manner.

"And what have you been up to in my absence, Vaden?" he asked.

"I'm no idiot, Jerome." Vaden drew in a deep breath, trying to muster her courage. "I'm not as easily fooled as everyone else in this town seems to be."

"I know you're no fool, Vaden. At least, most of the time you seem to have your wits about you. But...lately I've noticed..."

"Leave me alone, Jerome. You know I don't want to talk to you and my uncle..."

Suddenly, he reached out and gripped her chin firmly in one hand taking hold of her shoulder tightly with the other. "Damn your uncle!" he growled as his face lowered to hers, his seething anger instantaneous.

"I know it was you, Jerome. Maybe you've got everyone else fooled, but not me. I've seen the true color of your soul and it's blacker than night!" Vaden tried to glare bravely back at him. Her only chance was to outwit him, for she knew that he was physically stronger than she.

"You have such a way of muffing things up, Vaden. Actually...I suppose it's Ransom Lake that muffs it all...but you..."

"Get your hands off her, boy!"

Vaden felt relief flood her body at the sound of Ransom's voice from behind Jerome. Jerome sighed heavily and rolled his eyes in a gesture of extreme irritation. He shoved Vaden back as he released her and turned to face Ransom. Vaden saw then that Denver stood beside his brother, both men furious.

"Ransom Lake, you are so the proverbial thorn in my side." Jerome simply shook his head as if he was too uninterested to deal with the men. "What is the problem after all?" he asked. "I'm certain your hands have ventured on much more familiar areas of the girl than mine have."

Ransom Lake's deadly fist was halted a moment before it would've met with Jerome's jaw by the force of Denver's arms pulling back on Ransom's arm.

Jerome chuckled. "You be careful there, old man. I heard that you're in no shape to be defending a woman's honor."

"You dirty..." Ransom began.

"Get on home, boy!" Denver ordered. "You get yourself on home, unless you want to take on trouble all alone this time." He nodded at Ransom who stood, eyes red with his seething. "You go on home or I'll let him have at you."

Jerome clenched his jaw angrily and looked at Vaden for a moment. Then, glaring at Ransom Lake, he threatened, "This ain't over, old man. This is far from over."

Denver had to hold Ransom tightly about the waist to restrain him as Jerome turned and walked away.

"Let the fool go, Ransom," Denver growled and, after a moment, Ransom quit trying to escape his brother's hold and inhaled deeply to calm himself. "Weasely as he is, you're not yourself yet."

"You do know it was him, don't you?" Vaden stared at Ransom, hurt that he would have denied it so avidly.

"You keep out of his way until I'm better. Do you understand me?" Ransom was angry and worried. Vaden could see the concern in his eyes.

"I didn't put myself in his way!" Vaden cried, her tears flowing once more. "And what do you care anyway? Who put you in charge of my well being?"

Ransom inhaled a deep breath and closed his eyes for a moment. "I'm sorry. It's just that you've done so much for me. You've returned my brother to me. You've helped me find hope. You've nursed me back to health twice now and..."

"I've been the cause of your ill health both times."

Ransom sighed heavily. "I just...I just...I just feel responsible for you, Vaden. You've been such a kind and loyal friend and I..."

"I think I'll head on back to the mercantile," Denver interrupted. "Hash it out with him, Miss Vaden. Hash it out. It's the only way you'll ever have your peace of mind."

Both Ransom and Vaden watched Denver walk away, then the pain, the rising heartache, every emotion that battled within Vaden broke the surface simultaneously.

"You just don't understand, do you?" she stated. She couldn't hide her feelings any longer or keep silent about them. Her strength was gone to resist confessing. "You really don't know what you've done to me." Ransom turned slowly to face her. The air was frigid and Vaden felt the cold begin to engulf her body and heart as the words poured from her lips. "I think of you every moment of every day. You dominate my dreams when I'm asleep. Every time I turn around I'm devastated not to see you standing near me."

"Vaden," he began, holding up a hand to stop her.

"No," she said, closing her eyes and shaking her head. "I have to say this to you. If I say it all out loud, then at least it's been said and I won't have to be haunted by my secrets anymore." Opening her eyes, she looked at him bravely. "Your voice rings in my ears and head constantly. The sound of it is sweeter than any other music of nature to me. Only to think of your smile, of your laugh warms my heart. Every time you touch me...in even the simplest, most unintended manner...my insides swell so warm and delighted that I wish I could take flight like a startled sparrow does so easily. Even just your looking at me. Just the sensation of those gray stormy eyes of yours on me...it unsettles me beyond your comprehension." She turned her back to him, for she could no longer face his stare as she confessed. "And...and beyond that, you should be able to imagine. Do you know, Ransom Lake...do you know what power you have over me physically? Surely you've noticed how I've melted in your arms each time you've taken me in them. How completely I bask in the heavenly euphoria that envelopes me when you...when you..."

"When we kiss," he finished for her.

Vaden winced at the sound of his voice and brushed the tears from her cheeks only to feel them being flooded once more with the moisture from her eyes.

"There are times when...most of the time, to truly confess...my arms, my body ache to be held by you. To have you confide in me...simply speak to me. And because I know that you're no fool, that you're very intelligent, I will admit to you now that...that I've loved you from the first day I arrived here and you drove your wagon past the mercantile. I suspect that you know that all too well."

"Vaden," he began and she heard him take a step toward her.

Immediately, however, she shook her head and hugged herself tightly, moving away from him.

"Please. Please don't say anything to me just now. Please just walk away from me and let me be."

She couldn't look at him. Couldn't let herself hear his voice. She feared that were he to try to comfort her in any manner she would completely lose control of herself and end up a sobbing, weakened mess, throwing herself into his arms and begging him to become hers to whatever extent he chose.

He did speak, however. Against her innermost wishes he spoke, and Vaden struggled to keep herself from him.

"I'll leave you to yourself if that's what you want, Vaden. But it is perhaps...no. It is definitely a very good thing that you chose to say these things to me here...in the cold, muddied winter of the outdoors...on a road that is well traveled by the people of this town...instead of the night we were sheltering in the old house before a warm fire...alone."

As her brow puckered in a puzzled expression, she heard his footsteps becoming fainter and fainter as he left her. She turned when she sensed he was too far for her to catch up with him, and her hand covered her mouth firmly as she tried to suppress her audible sobbing. Her stomach was wrenching with pain and anguish and she feared for a moment that she collapse in the mud and die from the misery of her heartache. In fact, in the next moment her body did fail her and she fell to her knees, sobbing over the grief and pain of what would never be hers. Several times her stomach began to heave and she feared she would not be able to keep its contents inside herself. Though the sensation of extreme illness did not pass, she was able to gain control of herself enough to stand and stumble the rest of the way to her creek and her tree. But she found no solace there, only further pain, for it reminded her so of Ransom Lake.

Rather aimlessly she wandered for over an hour until she found herself in the grove of elms, the horrid scene of so much anguish for herself and for Ransom. The now charred and branchless, yet still tall trunk of the old dead elm seemed a sentry for the place, an ominous reminder of the pain and terror endured there. Vaden wandered among the trees trying to clear her mind of any thoughts. How blessed it would be to have nothing but a void there. Nothing to torment her further. No memory of Ransom Lake. No knowledge of him would perhaps be better than the pain with which she was stricken. Then she came to the tree where she had been led, by whatever presence, to Ransom Lake. She realized somehow as she stared at the tree, the ropes that had bound Ransom still lying on the ground around its base, that she would rather endure a life of sadness, regret, sorrow and pain. She would rather be miserable for the rest her life than never to have experienced the man. Reaching down, she picked up a length of the rope, studying the now brown stains made by the dried blood from Ransom's injuries. It was true. However horrible the pain of loss, the old cliché rang true to Vaden at that moment. It was far better to have loved the man and not been able to possess him than never to have known and loved him at all.

"Fancy meeting you here."

The sound of Jerome's voice immediately angered Vaden. Turning to face him, drained of defense and having only the strength to hate, she said, "Leave me alone. I have no feelings for you other than distaste at seeing your face. Leave me in the knowledge that you were right. I am in love with Ransom Lake and he returns nothing of it to me. You were right. But you're wrong if you still think I will turn to you to give me what he won't. I despise you, Jerome Clayton. So, stop wasting your time and leave me alone."

So drained of strength and emotion was Vaden that even the fiery red glint that jumped to Jerome's eyes did not intimidate her.

"I did so much for you, Vaden. I tried so hard to prove that I was worthy of you."

"You were very attentive and sweet, Mr. Clayton. Of course, we both know that was a facade." She began to walk away from him, but his next words stopped her.

"I had it all planned out so perfectly. And Ransom Lake had to mess it up for me. That day he was shot in the store. I had that all worked out so cleverly. And Halloween night. It would've been perfect."

"What? What are you talking about?" Vaden asked.

"It wasn't those kids playing with a gun in the street, Vaden. Don't you know that? *I* shot Ransom Lake. I meant to shoot near you to frighten you, then rush to your side to be your comforter, your protector. But, my aim must have been off because, indeed, my bullet would have hit you had Ransom Lake not stepped in front of you. I was grateful to see that he'd taken the bullet. I realized that it was for the best because now you would see how weak he was...how such a small injury could shake him...I knew that you'd turn from him and back to me.

"And Halloween would've confirmed my worthiness to you. I worked it out with Nathaniel and Toby and the others. I was going to ride in there, your hero on a magnificent stallion. I was going to save you from that horrid trick. I had to pay those boys to do that to you...and even then they were hesitant. But when I told them that it would surely win you over for me...they were willing enough. Then I followed the wagon home that night. It wasn't Nathaniel that told me what went on between you and Ransom Lake while he was driving the team home. I followed you. I saw what he did to you. How you let him do it.

"Of course, those friends of mine...they wouldn't help me anymore. They told me I was wrong, Nathaniel even said I was crazy to go after Ransom Lake and his brother. I could see how weak they were, so...I simply went up north and hired some real men to help me out. He would've died out here, too, if you hadn't showed up to save his worthless hide."

Vaden could only stare at him at first with a brief inability to believe what he was telling her. "You shot Ransom when he was in the mercantile that day?

You were the cause of that horrid event on Halloween? You intentionally had me drug out there and nailed into that box?" Vaden began shaking her head, unable to understand what would drive a man to do such things. Surely she could not be the cause of all Jerome's diabolical actions.

"It would've worked out wonderfully, Vaden. But that Ransom Lake...he's like a fly in the ointment at every turn."

Vaden could only stare at Jerome as her mind fought to understand the situation. Jerome hunkered down, picking up one of the lengths of rope that lay at the tree's trunk.

"How did you get him loose from here, anyhow?" he mumbled. Vaden's heart began to increase in its beating and she drew in a worried breath as she saw Jerome pick up something from the ground. "Well, look at that," he muttered as he held Ransom's knife before her face, frowning as he studied it intently. "Hmmm. Did he have this on him?"

Vaden did not answer, but took a tentative step backward. It was only then that she realized the danger she was in. This man was mad. Capable of unimaginable things.

"I stripped him of his shirt, checked his pockets." Jerome frowned as he studied the knife. "He had it in his boot. Is that it, Vaden? And how would you know to look in his boot for a knife?"

"You sit there and puzzle on that for awhile," Vaden said calmly, taking another step back from him and indicating with one hand that he should stay. "You'll figure it out, I'm certain. As smart as you are, it won't take you long."

Before she could turn and run, Jerome jumped to his feet and took hold of her wrist tightly. Vaden's instinct told her that to struggle would only serve to further agitate him, so she stood before him trying to appear calm.

"Where are you going?" he asked.

"I do need to be getting back. Aunt Myra will be furious if I don't finish up my chores before..."

"You don't see yourself as men see you, Vaden," he stated suddenly. "I know that you think everyone in this town is thinking that your sister is the prettiest thing around. The most finished and refined of young ladies. I know that's what you think. But you don't understand men. There's something about you. Something that makes a man start burning inside. Makes him want you above anything else."

Forcibly he pulled on her arm causing her body to bump against his. Then he released her wrist and put his arms about her, holding her firmly against him. Immediately, Vaden began to struggle, to lose control of her sensible plan to not flee from him desperately.

"Now, come on, Vaden. Do you think it was easy for me to stand by and watch Ransom Lake have his liberties with you? That night I followed Nathaniel's wagon home...watching the two of you and the way you...believe me, I wanted to kill him long ago. To slit his throat open and watch him die, knowing that when he did you'd be in my arms."

Vaden ceased her struggling when she heard a click as Jerome then revealed the blade of Ransom's knife and held it to her neck near the jugular vein. The blade was cold as death and Vaden could only close her eyes and swallow the lump in her throat, waiting.

"How do you think Ransom Lake would feel knowing that it was his own knife that bled you dry? Hmm?"

Vaden only tried to breathe evenly and keep her wits about her. She would be patient, waiting until Jerome's defenses dropped somehow. Then she would run. Run for her life!

"This coat of yours," he mumbled. Vaden could feel the heat of his breath on her face and she winced at the sensation. "It's far too bulky. Let's just remove it, shall we?"

"It's cold out," Vaden stated calmly, looking him directly in the eyes. "You...you wouldn't want me to catch my death out here, would you?"

Jerome raised his eyebrows and chuckled. "Take it off. Or you will definitely catch your death."

Vaden paused, however, for the blade of the knife was firm against her flesh. Sighing irritatedly, Jerome, using his free hand, removed her mittens, scarf and coat, letting them drop to the snow covered ground at her feet. She was instantly cold. The breeze among the elms was icy and frost had begun to fall from the sky.

"My, my," Jerome sighed, as he placed a gloved finger in his mouth, letting his teeth tug at his glove until it was removed. Then his fingers began to fiddle with the lace at Vaden's collar. "What a lovely shirtwaist, Vaden. Did you sew it yourself with your dainty little fingers?"

Vaden reached up, shoving his hand from her neck, but she stilled herself again as the blade of the knife bit slightly at her flesh.

"Hold still!" Jerome shouted. Then his voice was low and soft again as he nearly whispered, "You know, not that I'm criticizing the seamstress who made this shirtwaist for you...I'm sure she was talented with a needle, whoever she was. But...it seems to me that this seam here...this one at your shoulder here..." Vaden felt the pressure at her neck from the knife disappear as Jerome moved it to her shoulder then. "It...well, it just seems to me that there's a flaw in the stitching." Vaden gasped and her body began to tremble as in one swift move Jerome inserted the knife into the fabric of her shirtwaist at the shoulder, ripping the seam there from her shoulder to the base of her collar. "This side looks a bit...well let's just..." he mumbled as he repeated the process on the other side of her body. "Hhmmm," he mused, wrinkling his brow and studying Vaden's shoulders a moment. "Well...must be the collar that's wrong."

Vaden held her breath as Jerome then slipped the knife down beneath her collar at her throat. The blade was facing away from her flesh, but one false move could still mean that it would be buried at the hollow of her throat. She felt her stomach wrench as Jerome used his free hand to tug at the torn fabric at her right shoulder and then bent and placed a long, lingering, sickeningly moist kiss on her exposed flesh.

"Yes," he mumbled, "I do believe it's the collar."

With that, he pulled the knife forward, severing the fabric at Vaden's throat. Instinctively, Vaden's hand went to her throat to hold in place the fabric of her shirtwaist. For now the yoke of her shirtwaist threatened to slip down slightly, exposing her shoulders, and clavicle. She felt the chill bite at her upper back, for the torn fabric of her garment gave her little protection, exposing her skin to the elements. Jerome grinned mischievously, produced a striking match from his pocket, struck it on the bottom of his boot and let it fall to her coat, which immediately caught fire. Pulling her forward, his knife once more at her throat, he moved her away from the burning clothing as he chuckled.

"Now then," he whispered, putting his lips against her ear. "What is there to protect you, Vaden? What else is there to warm your body?" He glanced about him as if searching for something. Then, looking back to her, he raised his eyebrows and added, "I guess that leaves me."

The realization had been building, the knowledge trying to make itself known to Vaden all along. But it was at that moment that she was assured, that her mind accepted what horror may be in store for her.

"Jerome," she began, addressing him by his given name in hopes that it would serve to calm him, "please stop this. I…"

The words and her breath were knocked from her lungs as he turned her, slamming her back hard against the trunk of the elm.

"Didn't your mother teach you that you don't say anything unless you can say something nice?" he growled.

His hand went around her throat then, pushing her head painfully against the rough bark of the tree. Out of the corner of her eye Vaden could see that he still held the knife in his other hand, too close to her bosom to make a struggle safe. But at the repulsive feel of his mouth kissing her shoulders, the moist, abrasive sensation of his tongue grazing her flesh now and again, the danger of the knife he held seemed trivial and Vaden began to push against his chest, trying to maneuver her right foot so that she could kick at him. But his hand squeezed her throat all the more violently and he paused in his tasting of her skin long enough to cover each one of her feet with his own, standing on them painfully and rendering her helpless. She felt as if the life was being strangled from her so she ignored the horrid feel of his kiss on her cheeks and forehead and her fingers clawed helplessly at the hand at her throat.

"I can't breathe!" she choked out. And then she thought, *He's killed me.*

She could not draw air into her body. His hand about her throat was suffocating her. She felt her arms and legs begin to tingle with an odd numbing sensation and the strength left her hands as she felt her arms drop to her sides. She winced at the pain of not being able to breathe. As she felt her dying body slipping to the snow covered ground, a heavenly vision of Ransom Lake appeared for one last brief moment in her fading mind.

All was dark. There was no light and no sound. Then suddenly she felt the warmth of life-giving air fill her bosom. Vaden began to feel cold, to sense something tickling her face, to again feel the breath of living being forced into her lungs. Gasping painfully, Vaden drew her own breath and opened her eyes for a brief moment to see Ransom's perfect face near to her own as he wore an expression of grief and deep concern.

"Take in the air, Vaden," his voice echoed in her mind. Then, she saw Ransom turn and look over his shoulder. Saw Jerome struggling to his feet just behind him, wiping blood from the corner of his mouth, his face twisted with fury. As he lunged toward them, Ransom sprang to his feet and shouted, "You're a dead man for this!"

There was an excruciating pain in Vaden's throat and she closed her eyes again, unable to focus properly. She could hear the two men scuffling. She heard one of them fall to the ground, groaning in anguish. Then she knew her body was being lifted, and parts of her were warm again. She could hear the crunching of snow beneath feet that bore a heavy burden and she could hear the panting of a human being whose body was being pushed too hard considering that it was still healing from its own trauma. Opening her eyes only a narrow slit, she could see Ransom's chin and jaw from where her head rested on his shoulder. Still, she was too weakened and disoriented to respond to him.

"Oh, please!" a familiar voice echoed through her mind, "let me make it back! Drop me dead after if you will...but please wait until I've made it back."

She wanted to ease the pain and worry that she heard in Ransom's voice. She wanted to tell him that she was all right, to shout out that he must not push himself to harm for her benefit. But Vaden could not speak the words. She could not even open her mouth without the searing, burning pain increasing in her throat. The rest of her body, limp and nearly lifeless, was as if she had no control over it. She heard Ransom's pleadings with heaven as he carried her toward home. She felt the frost still falling, tickling her nose and lips. She felt her hands, arms, legs, feet, every part of her begin to grow colder and colder. She felt Ransom stumble and fall to his knees once, only to mumble something under his breath, force himself to his feet once more and move on. She heard his heavy boots as he climbed the stairs to the porch and she heard his voice begin shouting as his feet carried him into her uncle's house.

"Vaden's hurt!" he shouted. "Hurry! Help me! She's hurt!"

Vaden was able to open her eyes slightly then. But her throat felt dry and bitterly sore and she still couldn't muster the strength to speak. She realized, indeed, the strength of Ransom's arms, for he'd carried her home from the elm grove.

"What in tarnation?" It was Aunt Myra. Vaden looked through clouded vision to see the woman entering from the kitchen, drying her hands on her apron, only to find such a dreadful sight before her. "Ransom! What...take her to the bedroom." Aunt Myra cried.

Vaden felt herself fall abruptly onto the familiar softness of the quilt that covered her bed. All the time she watched Ransom through narrowed eyes that couldn't focus completely. Ransom dropped to his knees beside the bed and shouted instruction to Myra over his shoulder.

"Go for the doctor, Myra! Now! Where is everyone? Go, Myra! She wasn't breathing when I got to her and...go!"

"Ransom! What happened?" Myra cried hysterically, tears streaming down her face.

"Now, Myra!" he shouted back.

"What's going on?" Uncle Dan entered the room then having heard the commotion, his attention going directly to Vaden, who tried to speak, to reassure them all of her well being. However, she was still unable to utter a word and she closed her eyes again for a moment, feeling completely exhausted.

"Myra!" Ransom shouted once more.

"Go for the doctor, Myra," Uncle Dan instructed calmly then. Vaden watched her aunt flee from the room sobbing hysterically as Uncle Dan reached to the foot of her bed and pulled a warming quilt over her trembling body. "What happened, Ransom?"

"I...I found her in the elms. It was Jerome...I left him there bleeding in the snow, but I don't think I got the job done. I didn't have time...I...she wasn't breathing when I got there."

Panic dominated the intonation of Ransom's voice and Vaden herself couldn't follow what he was trying to say, for his thoughts were spoken so incompletely. The expression on his face stricken with anxiety and distress and he panted dramatically, no doubt from the taxing effort of carrying Vaden all the way home from the elm grove.

"Why don't you lay down for a minute, son," Uncle Dan told Ransom. "Just come on over here and..."

"Don't touch me, Dan," Ransom growled, pushing Uncle Dan's hand from his shoulder.

"Ransom, you're not well yourself. You need to..."

"Leave me be. I'll sit right here until I'm sure that she's..."

"Okay. Okay, son. I'm going for the sheriff. This has gone far enough...too far, and it's time the law did something about it." Vaden watched her uncle hurry from the room, pausing to look back over his shoulder at her for a moment before leaving.

"Vaden," Ransom whispered.

She inhaled the comforting scent of his hair and felt the warmth of his whisker covered cheek against the chilled flesh of her shoulder as he laid his face against her neck. Immediately the bitter cold, the horrid lingering sensation of Jerome's touch began to disappear. She wanted to speak, to tell him how his touch healed her, but again her strength and voice failed her. Her arms felt as if they were weighted down with lead and she could not move. Ransom laid an arm across her body just above her stomach, his hand coming to rest on the opposite shoulder, and she felt him place a tender, but very fervent kiss on the hollow of her throat. She closed her eyes for a moment and when she opened them again he had raised his head from her shoulder and with a frown furrowing his brow deeply, caressed her throat and neck softly with his fingers. His fingers traveled carefully across her shoulder and with an anguished moan escaping his throat she felt his kiss caress her skin just below her collar bone.

"Look at this," he muttered. "Look at the marks he's left here." She coughed quietly, the only sound she could force from her throat, and he looked to her. "Vaden?" he whispered. His eyes were filled with concern and the hint of restrained tears. "Vaden. I'm sorry. I shouldn't have left you. But you were so insistent. Still...I'm sorry for this. I shouldn't have..."

"Stop. Please," she managed to whisper, though her throat ached with pain. "This wasn't your..."

"I went to the elms and there you were. He had you up against that tree and I saw you fall to the ground and when I finally beat him enough that I could get to you...I realized you weren't breathing!" He buried his face against her shoulder again and she felt his kisses on her skin, at her shoulder and her upper arm, his fingers burying themselves in her hair. "My daddy used to blow into the mouths of calves that were born without breath, you see...and I hoped the same thing would work on you. But I wasn't sure and..." He raised his head to look at her again, taking her face between his strong, trembling hands. "I thought you were dead! I should never have left you!" Then, brushing a tear from her cheek, a tear that had managed to escape her exhausted eyes, Ransom Lake's stormy, guilt-ridden gaze searched her eyes for a moment.

"What did he do to you, Vaden?" he asked then. His voice was angry and deep.

"Just...just...he cut my shirtwaist and...his hands...his mouth was on my shoulders...my skin. I...I..." It was still difficult to speak and she couldn't tell him exactly anyway. It was too humiliating. She only wanted to forget it.

"Ssshhh," he breathed quietly. "Don't think on it again."

He brushed the hair from her forehead and forced a smile, but she could plainly see the guilt that consumed him. He wore the same expression of guilt, of feeling responsible, as he had the night he had related the story of his family's extermination to her.

"Don't look like that. Please, don't look like that," she whispered. She wanted to comfort him, help him understand that he was in no way at fault for what had happened to her, but a great exhaustion overtook her and she could no longer hold her eyes open.

It was shouting that woke her next. Vaden opened her eyes in time to see Ransom take hold of Doctor Sullivan's coat lapels and slam him violently up against the wall. "Watch what you say!" Ransom growled into the man's face. "I'm not the one who did this!"

"Ransom. Calm yourself, son," Uncle Dan spoke calmly, placing a hand on Ransom's shoulder. "I'm sure that Doctor Sullivan didn't mean to imply..."

"Of course not! Of course not, Ransom," Doctor Sullivan assured the infuriated man. "I merely asked who had done this to the girl. I only looked to you for an answer because you were the one to bring her home." Doctor Sullivan was obviously very rattled at having been so violently confronted.

"It was Jerome Clayton," Uncle Dan offered bluntly.

Sheriff Howard approached the bed, but Vaden still watched as Ransom hesitantly released the doctor.

"Miss Valmont," the sheriff began, "I know you're not feeling well...that you've been hurt. But I have to ask you...was it really Jerome Clayton that did this to you?"

"Yes," Vaden answered in a whisper.

"You see. One of your properly bred and raised local boys did this," Ransom nearly shouted.

"Calm yourself, Ransom Lake," Sheriff Howard warned, "or you'll find yourself in jail all the same." Then, putting a calming hand to Ransom's shoulder, asked, "Do you know where Jerome is now?"

"I hope he's burning in Hell!" Came his hateful answer. Ransom drew a deep breath, though his eyes were still the color of hurricane clouds. "I left him out at the old elm grove...and I left him out there to die."

"This ain't the first time he's tried to hurt my niece, Sheriff," Uncle Dan stated.

"What do you mean by that?" Ransom shouted angrily, turning to Dan.

"He tried to force his attentions on her a while back and we told him he wasn't welcome..."

Ransom violently clutched Dan's shirt collar in one fist and demanded, "Why didn't you tell me this before?"

Dan took Ransom by the shoulders calmly and answered, "I was afraid of what you'd do, Ransom. I never thought he'd do somethin' like this. I'd a shot him first if I thought he would."

Ransom released his grip on Dan's shirt and closed his eyes for a moment. He inhaled deeply trying to calm himself and mumbled, "I'm sorry, Dan."

Uncle Dan touched his shoulder and reassured, "I understand, son."

"Vay!" Yvonne cried as she entered the room, pushing her way through the others to her sister. "Oh! Vay!" she cried. Quickly she dropped to her knees on the floor beside Vaden's bed and took one of her cold hands, stroking it affectionately. "Denver and I were out looking for you. I was so worried! I...oh, Vaden. What happened?"

Denver entered the room in time to restrain Ransom from assaulting the doctor once more when he said, "It's so hard to take in! That Clayton boy has always been such a fine young man."

Ransom flew at the man, his fists, whose knuckles still bore the remnants of healing scabs that had come about from his own beating, aimed directly at the doctor's skull.

"That Clayton boy isn't anything but a filthy..." Ransom shouted.

Denver took hold of his brother around the shoulders, staying him. "Let it go, Ransom. Let him tend to the girl."

"I can't examine her with the entire township in the room," Doctor Sullivan grumbled. "Sheriff, clear everyone but her aunt out of here please."

"I'm not taking a step out of this room while that idiot is anywhere near her!" Ransom shouted.

Vaden tried to speak, to calm him and reassure him that all would be well. He seemed completely out of his mind.

"Come on, boy," Uncle Dan said calmly. "We'll all wait together in the parlor."

Ransom began to argue the fact again, but when Denver nodded, confirming it to be the wisest choice, Ransom glanced worriedly to Vaden one last time before turning and storming out of the room.

"He's positively a heathen," Vaden heard Doctor Sullivan mumble under his breath as he began to inspect her bruises.

"No," Vaden forced from her hurting throat. "I swear that Jerome Clayton did this to me. He tried to kill Ransom and Denver. I..."

"Don't talk, sweet pea. Don't talk," Aunt Myra whispered in a soothing voice, forcing a smile onto her tear-streaked face, and putting a cool glass of water to Vaden's lips.

Vaden sipped the refreshing, healing liquid for a moment before closing her eyes once more. Then, she drifted again into unconsciousness.

It was not until the bright rays of sunlight drifted in through her window that she woke. It was Yvonne's concerned expression that she saw first as her eyes opened.

"Oh, Vay! I've been beside myself!" her sister exclaimed.

Vaden smiled and swallowed, noticing the incredible difference in the feel of her throat. "That must've been hard to endure, Yvonne, considering that there is only one of you."

"Don't tease, Vay. I'm serious. We've all been so worried these past two days."

"Two days?" Vaden exclaimed, suddenly very alarmed. "Two days?"

"Yes. You've been sleeping for two days, Vay! And so much has happened. Ransom Lake was utterly a madman and went storming out of the house just after he had brought you home and the doctor and everyone arrived. He went out determined to find Jerome and...and I'm sure his intent was to cause a torturous fatality."

"Yvonne!" Vaden gasped, sitting up awkwardly in her bed. Her body was stiff and aching from lying down so long, but otherwise she suddenly felt quite recovered. "What happened? He...Ransom...he's all right, isn't he?"

"He's in jail, Vay! Imprisoned!"

Vaden shook her head, for her first thoughts were that Ransom had succeeded in ridding the world of Jerome Clayton. And now...would he hang for murder?

"Yvonne! He didn't..." Vaden began, fearful of the answer, "you're not trying to tell me that he..."

"No! Oh, no! Jerome...actually, Vay...it seems he wandered into the creek bed after...after Ransom found you. Vaughn Wimber found him there talking to himself and going on and on about how it was some voices or something...voices in his head that told him to do those things to you. Oh, he's quite mad, Vay. They've taken him up to an institution in the Springs. He's quite mad. But Ransom is...well, he's an utter mess, Vay! He's been going on and on about how this was all his fault. How he should've known you were in danger. How he shouldn't have left you on the road that day. Oh, Vay! I fear he may eat away at his own mind and end up as mad as Jerome. We've all been waiting for you to wake up. The doctor says that your body is fine, your injuries were minor, but that you were in a state of shock from the cold and the anguish of it all. It's why you slept so long. Oh, Vay! You've got to go to Ransom at once!"

Vaden threw back the covers and tried to stand. Her head went spinning at first, for it had been so long since she had been fully conscious. Taking Yvonne's arm for support, she went to her wardrobe.

"Of course, there's no way Auntie and Uncle Dan will let you leave the house, considering that you must still be hurting and stunned. So we'll have to go out through the window."

Vaden paused in her dressing to turn and look at her sister inquisitively. "Yvonne? You are encouraging me to sneak out the window...and to the jail of all places...to visit a man...to visit a man unchaperoned, I might add...a man of whom you don't approve?"

"For pity's sake, Vay! Hurry up! We don't have time to think rationally!"

So, determined and knowing that no doubt much more than Yvonne had told her had transpired during her convalescence, Vaden did, indeed, dress hurriedly. She securely buttoned the coat Yvonne handed to her and climbed out through the bedroom window after her sister. The bright morning sun tried in vain to warm the cold winter's day. Vaden noted that it must be only a week until Christmas now. Hurriedly she followed Yvonne toward the jail, thinking how cold it would be for Ransom in the confining building.

"Denver says they're just keeping him there because they think he'll follow the Claytons up to the Springs after Jerome. But I'm sure that once you've talked to him, he'll be fine. Denver says Ransom is still blaming himself for what happened to the family," Yvonne babbled quickly, barely pausing for breath.

"You know about the family?" Vaden asked, stunned that her sister should hold the knowledge.

"Yes. Denver told me all about it. How horrid for poor Ransom. And for dear Denver...to think his entire family was lost all those years. Not knowing that all the time he still had a brother to hold to."

Yvonne sighed heavily and Vaden's brow wrinkled in wonderment. She could not believe the change in her sister. It was obvious that Yvonne and Denver had spent a great deal of time together in order that she would know such intimate details of the story.

When they at long last arrived at the jail, Vaden burst into the building behind Yvonne. Upon seeing Sheriff Howard sitting at his desk casually reading a book, however, her temper flared and Vaden stormed over to him.

"You let Ransom Lake out of here this minute, Sheriff Howard!" she ordered.

Startled, the sheriff looked up, frowning. "Miss Valmont?" he mumbled. Then, clearing his throat, he closed his book and stood up, offering his hand to her. "It's good to see you're recovered from your..."

"You're holding him here, aren't you?" Vaden nearly shouted.

"Ransom Lake? Well, yes...I have him in..."

"You release him now! Do you understand me? He hasn't done anything to deserve being locked up in here!" Vaden felt hot tears of frustration filling her eyes, but she was determined to stand strong. Ransom was not the one who deserved to be confined.

"Now, settle down, Miss Valmont. I've just had him in here for a couple of days until he could settle hisself down. When he left your place he went out looking for Jerome. When he didn't find him in the elms he took out to his family's home. He kicked their front door down, went charging through their house, shouting threats about how he was going to make certain that Jerome didn't live to see the light of another day. He scared the waddin' outta every one of them. And then he come stormin' in here, shoutin' at me to find that Clayton boy and string him up to a tree. I just figured it would be safer for Ransom and everybody else if he spent some time pinned up so he could think things out, and we could find Jerome. Oh, and he was all fired up to go stormin' off to your aunt and uncle's house to make sure Doctor Sullivan did right by you."

Vaden shook her head, astounded that Ransom would react so extremely. "Well then, now that the Claytons are out of town and I'm better...you will release him, won't you?" she asked.

"If you can go in there, Miss Vaden, and talk some sense into that man...get him to swear off revenge of any sort...then I'll let him go. He's calmed down otherwise now...near to despair it seems. But I want his word that he's got his temper under control."

"You just take me to him. I still can't believe this was necessary." Vaden frowned at the man disapprovingly and the sheriff hung his head guiltily for a moment as she followed him to the back of the building. Denver sat on a chair just outside the bars that enclosed the jail cell and he stood up, an expression of profound relief overtaking his face as he looked to Vaden. Vaden was surprised when Yvonne rushed forward from behind her, throwing herself against Denver, he embracing her tightly.

"Miss Vaden," Denver sighed relievedly. "You're a sight for sore eyes, indeed you are."

Immediately Ransom was on his feet, rushing to the bars as Vaden approached him. "Vaden!" he exclaimed, grasping the bars tightly with his hands at either side of his head as he gazed at her. "Are you all right?" he asked anxiously.

Vaden felt a tear trickle down her cheek, for he looked so careworn, so thoroughly exhausted. The room was not comfortably warm even for the fire that burned in the nearby hearth. Still, Ransom stood before her, his shirt unbuttoned and gaping open, his face unshaven, his hair not brushed and the dark circles of fatigue shading the area beneath his eyes.

"I'm...I'm fine," she managed to answer. Everything was so unfamiliar around her. A jail cell, Yvonne and Denver in each other's arms, Ransom looking tired and defeated. Tentatively she reached out and placed a small hand over his cold, roughened one that grasped the iron bar before him.

"You gonna behave if I let you out of here now, Ransom?" Sheriff Howard asked.

Ransom looked up, glaring angrily at the man. "I suppose," he mumbled.

"I suppose ain't good enough," Sheriff Howard reminded him.

Ransom closed his eyes for a moment and drew in a deep, calming breath. "Yes."

"All right then."

Vaden stepped back from the cell as the sheriff unlocked it with a large key. Ransom stepped from the cell in one long stride and instantly Vaden was in his arms, her face pressed firmly against the warm skin of his chest as he hugged her savagely. His hands clutched at the fabric of her coat, squeezed her arms roughly, wound their fingers in her hair. He held her to him so tightly that it was a difficult chore to draw in breath. Vaden, in return, let her arms slide under his gaping shirt and around to his back, returning the fierce embrace. It was wonderful to be in his arms once more! To inhale the scent of his skin, to feel his powerful hands at her waist!

"I'm so sorry," he whispered then, his lips brushing her ear briefly as he spoke. "I'm so sorry that I failed you, Vaden."

Vaden raised her head to meet his gaze which was painfully filled with guilt. "You didn't fail me. As always, you saved me, Ransom Lake," she told him.

He was so strong, so completely capable of overpowering anyone, anything that might try to break him. But it unsettled Vaden that she would cause him such despair. And then, he slowly pushed her away from him. He stood staring down at her, the turbulence in his eyes disturbing Vaden.

Vaden's heart began to pound violently as she saw, as she could actually *see* and read the resolve forming in his mind. His eyes narrowed, his shoulders straightened and his jaw tightened as he looked at her. The expression of concern and guilt left his face and in its place was the look that Vaden at that moment recognized. She'd seen it blatant on his handsome face several times before. The first time he'd kissed her, the day he'd awakened from his unconsciousness in her aunt's spare bedroom, the night in the wagon after they'd shared the intensely passionate kisses, the night they'd spent together in the old house, on Thanksgiving and even the day when Jerome had assaulted her. The day when, she only at that very moment remembered, she had confessed her love to him only to send him away, dooming herself to Jerome's will. Yes, she'd seen the expression many times before, but it was only at that moment as they stood in the cold jail house, the sheriff and Denver and Yvonne looking on. It was then that she recognized that expression as resolve. Resolve to not let himself take her. Resolve to not allow himself to have her. Vaden was sure then, that he did love her. That he did want her. But his past was still haunting him. He was still blaming himself. Now, perhaps, more than ever. It frightened Vaden. Broke her heart once more. Broke her heart violently, and she stepped back from him.

"Don't do it, Ransom. Don't you dare do it," Denver growled, releasing Yvonne and going to stand ominously near to his brother. But Ransom's resolve only seemed to strengthen and, unable to endure it any longer, Vaden turned and fled from him.

"Vaden!" she heard him call out. The tears had already escaped her eyes and were flooding her cheeks, and she clutched at her bosom, hoping to somehow lessen the pain in her heart. "Vaden!" he shouted again and she knew that he was at her heels as she fled. "Vaden," he breathed as he caught hold of her arm, stopping her escape.

"Don't do this to me!" she cried out, turning to face him and wrenching her arm free of his grasp. "Don't give me glimpses of my dreams of you coming true and then snatch them away because you're...because you're..."

"Scared," he finished for her bluntly and admittedly. "You're thinking I'm weak, I know," he mumbled, holding her hand to his chest, clutching it tightly in his own.

"How could I ever think you were weak? It's just..." Vaden began, but Ransom interrupted her.

"I am. I admit it. I didn't have the courage...I didn't have the faith to pursue you. To tell you what I feel for you. I...I didn't think it was conceivable that you could accept me when you knew what I had...what I hadn't done for my family. I had gone cold inside. I thought I was incapable of feeling, of...of loving anyone ever again...any kind of love. And then you conked me on the head with a pair of boots and some remnant of who I was before flickered warm inside of me."

He sighed heavily and his eyes caressed her face as he looked from her mouth to her cheeks to her hair and at last to her eyes once more. A slight grin spread across his face and he chuckled a moment.

"You were so completely unspoiled. So completely in love with nature and ideas of romance. In love with life. And like everyone else you touch...you touched me and I began to see that there could be reasons to smile. I began to appreciate the simple beauties around me." Reaching down, he tucked a strand of hair behind her ear. "The grand beauty before me."

Vaden's soul began to rejoice, for the resolve to resist was gone from his countenance. The throbbing pain of heartache began to leave her body as joy began to fill it. She glanced away shyly for a moment. As much as she had longed to hear him say these types of things, as often as she'd dreamt it, it was still difficult to believe, to accept in her mind that it was true.

"And then...it got to where every time I saw you I wanted your touch, your smile...I wanted you to be mine. Every time I'd come into the mercantile and find you there weaving a tale for those little ones, I'd think how wonderful it would be if they were our children...yours and mine. Children that you'd born of me."

It was as if she had to feel him saying these things to her, so, taking his rugged face in her hands, she let her small, soft thumb caress his flawlessly contoured lips. How enticing his mouth was, how perfect, she thought. He closed his eyes for an instant, causing a tear to trickle down his cheek as he reached up, taking her hand from his cheek and pressing her palm firmly to his lips as he kissed her there.

"I'd think of you...in my arms...of our children...and," he continued as she could feel the guilt and resistance leaving his body, "it would frighten me because I'd remember the pain of losing my family. I'd imagine what my parents must have felt watching their children die and I'd run from you for a while. Then I'd smack my thumb with a hammer while I was putting up a fence or forget to feed the stock...because my mind would be on you all the time."

He took her face firmly in his hands then and his eyes narrowed as he spoke through tightly clenched teeth. "If you only had a shred of a notion what kind of fire you spark in me, girl, you'd run from me like you would the plague! There have been times that I feared for your virtue at my own hand when I had you in my arms because my desire for you fought so furiously with what I knew to be right in my mind that I wasn't sure right could win out."

Vaden tried to look away from him for the depth and meaning of what he was saying was truly exhilarating to hear, but also very intimate. It caused her to blush that he would say such things to her.

"You found me, Vaden," he mumbled in the sultry tone that sent her senses tingling. Releasing her face, obviously not wanting to force her to look at him, he added, "You looked and looked beneath the stone, the hard cold stone until you found me. Your smile melted that solid ice that was around my heart and your kiss heated the flames of desire within me to a point that I am no longer able to bury them."

Vaden gasped and put her hand to his lips to silence his forthright words, but he only kissed her hand. She pulled it away quickly as the feel of his kiss there unsettled her will to resist taking his mouth for her own. She glanced about them quickly to ensure that they were not being watched. Chuckling lowly, he tugged on her arm, leading her into the space between the jailhouse and the barber's shop. Then, gently pushing her back against the wall, he continued, his gray mesmerizing eyes weaving a spell about her, his voice low and alluring.

"Don't you see, Vaden? I can say those things to you now. All the things I've been thinking about you since the moment I laid eyes on you. I can speak them to you now because of the faith...the confidence you give me."

He took her face in his hands as he let his body lean fully against hers. As his thumb caressed her lips softly he said, "I want you in my arms, every night. Every night forever. I want to hold you, feel the warmth of your body in my arms, know that your soul is there with mine. Know that you're there every night for me to hold and love. Know that I can touch you, kiss you and look at you whenever I want to...whenever I need to."

It was too overwhelming to have him saying it all to her. Could she possibly believe that she wasn't dreaming?

"I want my children to grow inside of you," he mumbled. "I want the Lake blood and the name of Lake to go on. I want you to help me ensure that it does not die away." He paused as he struggled to remove the ring that was on the smallest finger of his right hand. "This...was my mother's wedding ring, Vaden. I know you've wondered about it. Her name was Darlina."

As Vaden's mind fought to hold on to reality, to believe that what was happening before her truly was real and not a dream from which she would wake, she watched as Ransom Lake took her left hand in his and placed his mother's ring on her ring finger.

"This was the ring my father placed on her finger when they were married. And I know..." He paused and grimaced painfully before continuing. "I know, Vaden, that even though my father and mother were killed...that perhaps one had to watch the other die, they would not have wanted to be anywhere but together. I want you to know...you need to believe the truth of it...I love you like that." Vaden felt the tears burst from her eyes more readily even than they had before as he finally, after so long, told her that he loved her. "I would do anything for you. Go anywhere for you. I would endure a thousand times the death that my father and mother did...for you. Because you are my life. My love...my heart and my soul. The reason that I love living again. The reason that I am willing now to endure whatever pain life may bring. I love you, Vaden."

His lips kissed hers softly for a moment as if he was unsure that she would accept him. But in a moment she let go the need to resist him, and, taking his face between her hands, she encouraged him to take her mouth passionately, which he did, causing her body to melt against his own. It was then that her mind confirmed once more to her that no verse of poetry, no matter how cleverly written or labored over in pursuit of perfection, could describe the sheer ecstasy of this man's kiss. He was all she wanted in the world. The only touch, the only breath.

He broke their kiss for a moment, though his mouth lingered teasingly over hers as he studied her. Vaden was hypnotized by his gaze. The gray storm in his eyes was warm and inviting and the true feelings in his soul were evident in them. He had forgiven himself at long last. And having done so, could give himself to her, finally. He was so handsome! So flaw-lessly attractive. Her mind still struggled to accept that a man so perfectly formed in body and spirit could truly mean what he had spoken to her.

"How can a man like you...how can you truly want me?" she whis-pered.

Laughing heartily, Ransom pulled her up from her brace against the wall, gathering her securely in his arms. She pushed at him slightly for a moment when one of the townsfolk walked by, raising an astonished eyebrow.

"It's not proper," she mumbled.

"Very little bodily contact between unmarried lovers is, Vaden." His eyes twinkled impishly, the moisture of emotion still evident in them as he con-tinued to smile. "That's why you must marry me, Vaden Valmont." He brushed an independent strand of hair from her cheek again as his eyes gazed lovingly at her. "I can't believe how you've allowed the tables to turn, girl. In the beginning, you didn't care a whit for what you had to do to have me. And now...I'm beginning to think you're a tease. You have me here in your arms, confessing my undying love for you...not to mention my physical desire for you...and you're suddenly shy and unconfident. Where's that girl that dug my old boots out of the trash barrel?" Vaden gasped again, astonished that he would know such a thing. "Where's that girl that shaved my face so that she could see if I was handsome or not beneath that mess of a beard?" Again he took her face firmly between his hands. "Where's that woman that can make me doubt my own self control when she gives me the taste of her kiss?" He kissed her softly once before continuing. "I've watched you closely, Vaden. Watched you go from having an unquenchable curiosity about me to not knowing what direction to take in life because you had fallen in love with me. I've watched you battle with uncertainty because you loved me so desperately and feared I could never be yours. I'm sorry that it took me so long to find my way to forgiving myself and confessing to you. And I have to tell you now my secret, asking your forgiveness and that you not be too angry."

Vaden raised her eyebrows. What secret could he possibly hide that was more traumatic, more important than the one he'd already revealed to her?

"I knew what could be between us before you ever arrived to spend a year with your aunt," he confessed guiltily.

"What do you mean?" she asked, completely unprepared for such a remark.

"I woke up one night just several days before you arrived here," he began. "I woke up because I had seen you in my mind. In a vision I had seen your beauty of soul and body. It's how I knew where you were on Halloween, and that the storm would put you in danger if your Uncle Dan came instead of me on Thanksgiving eve. It's how I know you've hidden my old boots under your bed, that you put the apple seeds on a maple leaf from that tree you like to sit in and sent it down the creek to me. I was a man plagued, or blessed, with visions. Since the day my family was killed, I've had them, but, when you arrived, I began to have them less often and it seemed they only pertained to you. Now, my premonitions...the visions of Ransom Lake, whether horrid or pleasant...come less often. They began to fade the first time I let myself hold you...tasted your lips and the promise of love for me on them. They've been even fewer since the night I told you of the great guilt I bore. And now that you're holding in your arms what you were so diligent and faithful in getting, are you going to tell me that don't want to have it?"

Vaden looked away for a moment trying to control her sniffling, which was fast turning into a sobbing born of bliss. "When you've wanted something so badly...dreamt of it constantly...prayed for it every night...it's sometimes hard to believe that you can simply reach and take it all of a sudden," she whispered her confession.

Ransom kissed her neck lingeringly and then placed a short, but enticing kiss on her mouth. "Reach out and have me. I'm yours, Vaden. Will you take me?"

Standing before her ill dressed for the weather in lacking a coat, his shirt still unbuttoned as it was, Vaden worried not for him, for he was strong, powerful and apparently immune to fatal harm. His expression was alluring, tempting and tantalizing. He was his confident, powerful self again in that moment. He knew what her answer would be before she spoke it aloud and his mind and body were already prepared to act upon her answer. Smiling, she slipped her hands beneath his shirt again, caressing the breadth of his strong shoulders.

"I've always been yours, Ransom Lake. You know how completely I am yours."

Tentatively, she let the fingers of both her trembling hands be lost in the soft black of his hair and when he closed his eyes for a moment, smiling triumphantly, she melted against him once more, letting her head rest tenderly on one shoulder as her hands slid to his neck and down his powerful chest. She finally let her arms rest lovingly about his waist for a moment.

Then she let one hand caress the rugged smoothness of his unshaven face and he kissed her fingertips as they rested on his lips for a moment.

"Will you really...will you really..." she began in an uncertain whisper.

"Marry you?" he finished.

"Yes," she said smiling at his familiar way of finishing her sentences when she was too shy to do so.

"The minute your parents step off the stage and see that you're all right."

"What?" Vaden gasped, raising her head from his shoulder and looking at him.

"These past few days as you've been recovering...I've been so angry! Angry with myself for not having protected you...for not confessing to you, asking you sooner. Angry with myself for my own cowardice...my lack of self-confidence. It's why I sometimes wear that expression you dread so much, and I'm sorry for it. Sorry for my weakness. I...I can feel it control-ling my face as my mind battles with my soul. My soul tells me that you're mine...that all I have to do is reach out and take you for my own. But all those years of guilt, of agony from the loss of my family...the images flash through my brain and I...I...I hesitate. But, you must understand that it's only an old wound that causes the fear in me, Vaden, and it passes. It leaves more quickly each time. And this time...this time it's gone for good. I've been so angry and I actually drew strength, courage and confidence from it somehow. So, day before yesterday, before I could reconsider, I had Denver send a telegram to your daddy telling him what had happened with Jerome and...and...asking him for his permission to take you to my bed."

Vaden gasped. "You're lying!"

Ransom chuckled. "Yes. Actually, I told him that I intended to marry you the minute you were well once more. He replied immediately that they'd be here as soon as they could get here. And even though...back at the jail...I know you thought I was resolving not to take you...not to take your love into my life...but it's just that I realized what I had done and..." His face went solemn for a moment and he asked, "Are you mad at me for planning...for assuming that you'd accept me?"

Vaden smiled, joy bursting like radiant sunshine from her heart. "You know I'm not. I'm only glad that you did not pause to reconsider. I don't know if I can wait even one more day to be..."

"In my bed?" he finished, chuckling and smiling mischievously.

Vaden giggled. "I don't know if I can wait one more day to be yours." Vaden slipped her arms beneath his shirt again and hugged him tightly around the waist. "Oh, how desperately and thoroughly I love you, Ransom Lake."

"I love you," he whispered. "And thank you."

Vaden gazed lovingly at the powerful, astoundingly attractive man as he took her hand and raised it to his lips, kissing it tenderly.

"No," she whispered. "Thank heaven. Thank heaven for giving me you."

And then, Vaden's soul reveled in the feel of Ransom's arms about her as his mouth rendered a kiss to hers so sublime that it raised the vision of heaven on earth to come. That being the vision of Ransom Lake.

Kevin

As ever, my eternal love and endless gratitude to my husband, Kevin...
For being such a good sport...
(Letting me dress him up and take his picture,)
For being so witty...
(Reminding me that the garbage disposal, *"Doesn't take quarters..."*)
And for being the perfect man for me and my world!

Also...A special, 'Thank You,' and my infinite appreciation
To *"He, Whom I Adore,"*...
For making the publication of this book possible,
And to, *"She, Whom I Treasure,"*
For still encouraging me to believe in myself.

ABOUT THE AUTHOR

Marcia Lynn McClure began writing novels as Christmas gifts for her closest friends...friends who long for a breath of the past and miss the romance of bygone eras; friends searching for moments of distraction from the stressful, demanding times we live in.

Knowing that it is the breath of the past and the "take me in your arms and kiss me" kind of moments that so many women long to relive, Marcia spins her tales of love, life and laughter...adventures woven around those compelling romantic instances that most appeal to a woman's loving heart. Marcia feels that if her readers close one of her books with a contented sigh and a delighted smile, feeling rejunvenated, cheerful and edified, then she has achieved what she set out to do...shower refreshment and happiness on anyone having experienced the story.

Currently Marcia lives in Washington State. There she writes her stories, nestled in a creamy butter-colored house, surrounded by her wonderful husband and three adorable children.

Marcia enjoys corresponding with her readers. You can write to her at: P. O. Box 2055, Ferndale, WA 98248, email her at MarciaLMcClure@cs.com or visit her websites, **DistractionsInc.com** and **MarciaLynnMcClure.com.**

Photo by Tina

Marcia Lynn McClure

295

Let yourself be led deep into a new and fantastic labyrinth of mystery and secreted passion! Steeped in the concealment of age-old secrets, of betrothal to a stranger and envious villainy, Marcia Lynn McClure captures our imaginations and our hearts, entwining us in her fascinating new adventure:

SHACKLES OF HONOR
By MARCIA LYNN McCLURE
Available Fall 2002!

ORDER FORM

To save $2.00 off the cover price of additional copies of current titles
order online at **DistractionsInc.com, MarciaLynnMcClure.com**, call
1-877-2README or send this form with a check or money order to:

DISTRACTIONS INCORPORATED
P.O. Box 2055
Ferndale, WA 98248

THE HEAVENLY SURRENDER _____ x 12.95 = $ _____
THE VISIONS OF RANSOM LAKE _____ x 12.95 = $ _____
Sales Tax (WA residents only, add appropriate WA state sales tax) $ _____
Plus Shipping $ _2.00_____
                                                                    TOTAL $ _____

SHIP TO:

Name: _____

Address: _____

City: _____ State: _____ Zip: _____